# SANDSTONE HEART

# BRIAN BLACKWOOD

Tellwell Talent
www.tellwell.ca

ISBN
978-0-2288-1213-5 (Hardcover)
978-0-2288-1214-2 (Paperback)
978-0-2288-1212-8 (eBook)

# VULTURES AND LINOLEUM

There was a sound.

It was enough to stir me, but not enough for me to open my eyes. Not enough to remember what that sound was. But I had heard something. The linoleum on my face was cool and soothing like a summer breeze off the lake. It was enough that its embrace held me in place despite my aching leg and the smell of vomit not far off.

"Dad."

That was the sound then. Such a simple word, but laden with pull and depth. Caryn. I was someone's dad and she needed me. It was enough for me to open one eye. It creaked open like it was its first time doing so. The light burned my world and caused my head to ring in pain. I winced. A small lake of vomit lay several feet beyond me. It was close to the toilet - a near victory...though a near victory is often called something else entirely. There had been wine last night. Three bottles: far too much. They were from our wedding reception, 15 years past. We had planned to save them to drink on our 25th anniversary. Given the situation, I figured this was as close as we were getting. Like most wines, they were bitter.

"Dad."

The word again. Dragging me back from my wallow. Somewhere near was my daughter and she needed me. She needed the pathetic hung-over heap that was hugging the linoleum for comfort. My one bloodshot eye scanned around. A foot. There she was. Caryn. My daughter. The thought of her filled me with so many conflicting emotions. There was shame: a child should never have to see their parent in this state. I knew that but couldn't stop myself from frequently being there. I felt gratitude as well, as without her I think I would have slid further and further into the abyss, until my light vanished entirely. And I felt pride. My daughter was a capable one. No matter how much of a wreck I became, she held on. She cooked when I could not. She cleaned when I didn't care to. She gave me privacy when she likely needed my comfort. All of this gave more weight to her insistence this morning.

"Caryn? What is it?"

My own voice sounded gruff and grainy. My mouth was completely dry and my voice box cracked such that only a crow would have likely understood me.

"We are out of food. I'm hungry."

I peeled my face off of the floor. It felt like a layer of skin was left there in my absence, a memento for the linoleum of our time together. My knee shot out in pain as I struggled to stand up. It was a twin to my head. I stumbled. The wine still had me groggy. I caught a peek of my face in the bathroom mirror and didn't recognize it. The sunken cheeks must belong to another man.

An older man.

"You need to eat too."

She was right. She was right about both things. We were probably out of food. My head had been foggy since I discovered what my ex had been up to. I just plain forgot some things. Essential things. And I did need to eat. Food was problematic for me though. I simply didn't have any desire to eat anything. When I did eat, it all tasted the same. It was like I was eating a cardboard paste. It was tough to summon the will to eat when it all tasted like that.

"I know. I'm sorry Caryn. Let me clean up and we'll get some groceries"

"Can I help?"

"No," I sighed. "A man must clean up the messes he makes"

*"A man must clean up the messes he makes".* I find myself saying out loud these things that my father had said to me as a boy. To be fair, he had said them both to me and my sister. It was understood, even by my sister, that this was a gender neutral thing; that what he meant was *"A person with any honour takes care of the problems they make".* I think he was the only man my sister would forgive for using a gender-specific statement without an out-and-out verbal battle.

But I did not disagree with it. No one enjoys cleaning up vomit. Having children gets you more used to the activity, but no one likes it. However, even in my wine slogged state, there was a certain satisfaction in it. Part of it was the simple creation of order from chaos as the mop sloshed left and right in rhythm to the wine in my head. My higher mind briefly wondered if 'the vomit' and 'the mop' are good metaphors for order and entropy in a bigger universe. The other side of the satisfaction came from my father's antiquated sense of chivalry that he had passed on to me. It was a sense of pride in keeping something unpleasant from others. Metaphorically it was like jumping on a grenade. This particular grenade was of my own making and seemed to have had bits of nachos and ground beef in the explosion.

Grocery stores are cruel and evil places meant to punish those of us with hangovers. They are stupid places anyway, but especially nasty after a night of vinegary old reception wine. The fluorescent lights left mild tracers in my vision and their minor buzzing seemed like an angry wasp in my inner ear. Then there were the cryptic PA announcements that sounded like someone speaking underwater even when you weren't hung over. It is a modern marvel that we have these cell phones that shoot out every breath and grunt through the air for miles with alarming clarity, yet a request for 'Wet cleanup on Aisle 3' still sounds like it was uttered in Klingon. The imbalance of that seemed to match the rest of our society, so perhaps it was right on the money. And the sudden 'clang' of cart on cart collisions was, I am certain, designed in a lab to make every hung over person twitch.

"I'll go get ground beef, ok?"

Caryn bounded up the aisle towards the meat department. In the background, some vaguely recognizable heavy metal song was playing over the intercom, though it had been converted into Muzak. That amused me slightly. Elevator music was like the end of the food chain for a song. And for it to happen to a metal song was like the neutering and lobotomizing of a prize fighting bull.

Every week Caryn made her famous spaghetti sauce. I was not about to tell her that ground beef and mushrooms added to tomato sauce is likely the same famous spaghetti sauce that half of the country makes. I was just grateful she picked a lot of our groceries. I would just eat ice cream and potato chips otherwise. It's unhealthy, yes, but I just didn't care. Dying of ice cream consumption would pale in comparison to the pain I was feeling. I had to prioritize the concerns in my life, and being healthy just didn't win out. But she cared. And it made me happy that she did. Some days I ate only because she pleaded with me to do so.

"Dylan? Dylan...is that you?"

A woman pushed a cart down the aisle towards me at a brisk pace. Her long dark hair and pouty lips seemed familiar. I scanned my memory for her. A name popped into my head...Yvette. No... that wasn't right, though her slight French accent seemed to lend weight to the name. No, it was Annette. I remembered now. She used to be a friend of my wife's. She owned a coffee shop downtown where she had a stage for local bands and comedy acts and so on. When my wife first started her singing career, the two had become close friends. For months Annette had been a fixture in our lives. The memories came flooding back. The friendship had died off at some point but I had never asked why. I had become used to my wife's flash in the pan friendships. She would often find a new friend that was 'amazing' and 'they totally understood each other like sisters'. Then my wife would do something thoughtless to ruin the friendship, or she would find another friend that was more 'amazing' and more like 'sisters' leaving the previous friend in the dust. It just happened and I got used to it, just as I got used to her anger if I did ask questions.

This was one of the other reasons I hated public places since the split. I had discovered a really dark and sexist secret in our society, and it hurt like thorns every time I brushed against it. My first time had been when I was in the hardware store months ago. A mutual acquaintance waddled up to me, recognizing me. We exchanged pleasantries and she then asked where my wife was. I told her we had split. The chivalry in me made me keep this a matter-of-fact statement, rather than shouting "I kicked the cheating whore out!" I knew that saying it would hurt my ex-wife and a chivalrous man protects people from pain even when he hates them. The lady just said "Oh" under her breath and gave me a look that said a lot. It said "You are a man and probably cheated on her"; it said "You are a man and were probably beating her"; it said "You are a man and therefore are in the wrong." It said "You are bad" and "You are scary" and "You are the wolf they warned Little Red Riding Hood about." It hurt. I didn't correct her misconception as I knew I had already been judged and it would not change her opinion. I just lowered my head in shame, used all my man power to keep the tears from welling up in my eyes, and continued shopping. It had happened several times since. It hurt every time. I dreaded seeing 'mutual acquaintances'. However, I knew I should not prejudge Annette based on this. That wouldn't be right. But I would be lying if I said it didn't give me a bit of fear.

"Annette, it's good to see you. How have you been?"

She smiled at me and stepped around her cart.

"Oh, I am not horrible today. And where is the missus?"

I always hated that expression. I tried to steel myself. This was always a very hard thing. To say the words always brought up a flurry of images that were extremely painful: the adultery, the money she had stolen, the hurtful things she had said in the end. It was like reliving the whole mess. It got easier each time, but even that was sad. Such things should not be acceptable for people to get used to.

"We split." I blurted out.

Her smile turned to a frown. Here it comes-just like I suspected. First that hint of pleasantness would end, then "The Look". Then the uncomfortable moment before we each went the other way. The moisture started gathering in my eyes. I could not allow one to leak down into a tear. The shame would be too much.

The look didn't come. Instead she was gesturing me forward with her arms. I didn't understand what she wanted, but I stepped forward anyway. Before I knew it her arms were around me in a hug. With her mouth close to my ear she whispered.

"She was cheating on you, wasn't she?"

I went to answer but a gurgle nearly came out instead. I was too upset to talk without giving away my emotional state. There was shame too. It was a crippling amount of shame. These sorts of things don't happen to real men. It meant you were unattractive or a bad lover or poorly endowed. It was impossible to make those words that made me less a man. So I nodded. She seemed to feel my nod and she hugged me tighter. I put my arms around her in a hug as well. It felt wonderful. The physical connection was something I missed.

"You poor man. I always admired you Dylan...back then. You are such a good man. You deserve better."

Our arms dropped, but we continued to look into each other's eyes. Hers were a dark green that I could have lost myself in.

There was a long moment where we did not say anything at all. A moment of mutual feeling; that we both may have enjoyed the embrace more than we were willing to admit. Her smile broke our impasse.

"It was wonderful running into you. And to tell you the truth I would not have come over to say 'Hi' if I saw Merideth with you."

She took out a notebook and started writing.

"Look, I may have a piece of the story you need to hear. Here is my number. Why don't you give me a call and we can catch up over a drink tonight."

She gave me the slip of paper and patted me on the shoulder as she slipped by with her cart.

I was still holding the paper when Caryn returned with her arms laden with groceries.

"Who was that?"

My mind wanders to the beach. Not just any beach, but the rocky beach in front of the cabin our family used to rent every summer on the shores of Kootenay Lake. It wasn't one of those beaches people think of in when they conjure an image of a lake and a beach. This was not pure white sand and sun. There were rocks and pebbles. There were daisies and hawkweed growing in patches. These things did not detract from the beach being wonderful. In my mind they added to it. The rocks were of all different colours and textures. Some were bright red, like sleeping lava. Some were shiny with flecks of galena mixed in; these would catch the light, and to a young boy (like I was) they were riches greater than gold. Each day at the beach I would assemble a pile of them. They were my treasure. I was a knight that spent the day fighting a lake monster (with a stick for a sword) to save the princess from its vile clutches. In return the princess fell in love with me and the king rewarded me with a pile of galena rocks. My sister Jenn would never join me in my games. She spent her time braiding daisies in her hair and diving down to see if she could pull up seaweed from the bottom. What use was that?

But my mind does not dwell on the galena rocks, as shiny as they were. It keeps coming back to the sandstone chunks, as if there was a magnet pulling me back to their image. I don't even think they were actually sandstone. I just called them that as a boy. I still call them that now, even though I know it's inaccurate. They were clumps of sand-like rock that were so brittle a little boy like me could pull them apart or rip chunks off. I would pretend I was a superhero with great strength - someone as far from the little boy I was as possible. And that is the image that replays in my mind over and over: a piece of 'sandstone' from the beach with my little boy hands pulling off chunks from every side in a fury.

"Why are you dressing nice?"

Often the simplest questions have the most complex answers. Caryn was only 14, so the question was both innocent and not. It implied things. She knew I was talking to a woman in the grocery store. She probably saw us hug. And now I was dressing nicer. And I shaved. She wasn't wrong to notice those things. They were a difference in my behaviour. Why was I dressing nice? I actually had no idea. I don't think I was trying to impress Annette: I barely knew her. Perhaps it was because, as adults in our society, you dressed nicer and shaved when someone invited you over. That was it.

"Sometimes, kid, it's just nice to dress up."

I loathed my answer as soon as it was out of my mouth. It was the type of non-answer that I hated when I was a kid. It didn't explain anything. When my parents answered questions like this, I always thought they were just hiding one of those "when you are older" secrets from me. As an adult, on the flipside of things, I now know they probably just didn't have a good answer. Nothing quite takes the magic out of 'adulthood' like being an adult yourself.

"Oh, wear the green shirt then, it makes your eyes look nice."

Caryn was either more perceptive than I was as a kid, or more naive. Given the look in her eyes, I think it was likely more the former. Perhaps she knew better than I did why I was dressing nice. Girls always seem to know. Either that or they are absolute masters of self-fulfilling prophecy.

Annette's place was as eclectic as she was. It was above her coffee shop in Kensington and seemed like it had been quickly cleaned. Though clean was not the word I would use. Nothing was really in place: the tea kettle sat on top her stereo; a pair of tights lounged on the kitchen counter; her purse sat on one of the burners of the stove. It was haphazard, but one got the impression that it had been more so only an hour previous. There was a pants-shaped clean spot in the carpet whereas the rest of the carpet was just devoid of debris.

She poured red wine into mismatched wine glasses as we sat on the couch. She sat in that side kneeling pose that showed off her legs and left a triangle of shadow at the bottom of her skirt that hinted at more. She lifted her glass.

"To the grapes!"

We clinked glasses. I hated red wine. I have never found one that didn't taste like vinegar and look like beet juice.

"To the grapes…and old friends!" I toasted back.

"Ah yes. Too true. And like grapes, the fuller fruit may be sour, yet the finer fruit is unnoticed, but right under our noses"

I smiled back. She had a way with words. Truly though, I liked hearing her subtle French accent pour the words out. Somehow even foul words were fairer in that accent and her higher-than-normal pitch. We drank.

"Look Dylan..."

She set her drink down and put her hand on my knee. I twitched away instinctually. What if my wife had seen her do this? I felt guilty. The guilt washed over me. I felt horrible and disloyal. Wait, though. I wasn't with Merideth anymore. She has cheated on me and left in a hurricane of emotion. Why did I feel guilt? It was silly. I was single and all Annette had done was put a hand on my knee. People do that all the time. And Annette was a person that liked to touch. Likely she did that with all her friends. Now I felt guilty in a different way. What if I had offended her when I twitched away? I was a guest in her home and I had a duty as such. She shared her wine with me and I repay her by recoiling at her touch. I felt like a caged animal.

I looked up. She was looking at me softly. I could see the question in those deep eyes. No words needed to be spoken. "Have I offended you?" was all they said.

"I'm sorry...about that I mean. I just...well...I don't know how to..."

I fidgeted with my hands and put my wine down. Her eyes never left mine. She didn't even look down as she took one of my hands between hers. I didn't pull back.

"Tell me."

"Ok. It's silly. It's just, when you touched me on the knee. I had this feeling like I was cheating. It was a simple touch I know... and I know that I have been separated for a while, but I have always taken these things very seriously...you know?"

She smiled. Then her tongue licked the wine from her upper lip. It seemed to take longer than it should. But I could not look away and savoured the sight of it.

"Look. Do not, and I mean *not*. Do not feel sorry about that. You are an honourable man and there are so few left. I love that quality. Don't change it."

Were there only a few of us left? The honourable men? It was both easy and hard to believe. It was tough to imagine another man's upbringing and having a different father that didn't teach them about chivalry and honour. It was tough to imagine any little boy who didn't love knights and the code they lived by. Then again, we lived in a culture that taught women to adore the bad boy. We lived in a culture that got you angry looks when you held a door open for a lady as often as not. We lived in a culture that rewarded ruthless and asshole-like behaviour. I'm sure many men caved to that - I had felt that pressure myself. That code was just so ingrained in me that it was never an option to cave. She took her wine and drank deep.

"However, she is gone. Good riddance! And we are friends, right?"

"Yes, of course."

She had a board on the table with some cheese and crackers. I am not the pretentious sort that knows about cheeses and wines. I never taste 'notes' of oak and mango in a wine and I never engage in conversations about which brie is best. In fact, I have my doubts that anyone tastes oak or mango in their wine. I suspect it is much like the emperor's new clothes. Everyone talks about it to sound smart, but underneath it is invisible bullshit. For me wine and cheese were far simpler. Either I liked them or not. She had the kind that was soft and spreadable. She reached to spread some on a cracker for herself.

"So, I have a bit of a story to tell you about Mer, but now that you are here, I am not sure I should. It involves cheating."

The word still stung. It was like being slapped every time I heard it. It was this subtle reminder that the person I had loved most in the world had in fact been a lie. I had loved a fiction. The person I had married was nothing like the woman I thought I knew and loved. The person I had actually married had no problem sleeping with other men on the side. The person I had actually married had no problem secretly getting us into debt to fund her narcissistic music career. The person I had married had no problem callously abandoning her daughter. Children have nightmares about monsters under the bed. I had lived a different reality. The monster had shared my bed. Every time I heard the word 'cheat' or 'adultery' I was reminded of that reality.

"It's no problem. That Band-Aid was ripped off months ago. I know what type of person she was. Besides, I was always curious about why your friendship ended. I'm assuming this had something to do with it."

Annette nodded while chewing on some cheese and a cracker.

"It does. Do you remember Laird?"

"The drummer in Merideth's band? Crooked nose, big mop of ugly hair?"

Annette laughed.

"That's the guy. Well I was dating him, you see. After one of the shows here, I came back into the supply room and found your ex with her top off making out with him."

It didn't surprise me. I recall when Laird was her drummer. Caryn was still young. I would come home from work and she would take off immediately for 'rehearsal'. I was left with a mountain of dishes that had built up in the day, making dinner for Caryn and myself, bath time and storytelling before bed. She would show up back home well past midnight. Once I asked the lead guitarist why they needed to rehearse for so long. She told me that they never did. I had confronted Merideth about it and she had told me I was just paranoid and crazy. She said that of course every band needs lengthy rehearsals and that her guitarist was a coke addict that never remembered things correctly. I don't tell anyone this stuff as they will wonder how I could be so naive. Of course, in hindsight it looks obvious, but at the time I trusted my wife. I feel very stupid now that I believed her for so long. I was wrong to do so.

"That sounds about right."

"There is more. I was upset, you see. She started yelling at me saying that I was trying to *control* Laird. She said he was free to explore his sexuality as he liked and that I was too judgmental. I asked what you would think of her tryst and she told me to stay out of it; that her marriage was her business alone. Then she refused to pay me my cut of the gig."

I nodded.

"That sounds like her. Whenever she was caught doing something wrong she would play the control card. Even to the very end, she claimed that because I was upset about her affairs, I was trying to control her. It's like she didn't understand that it has nothing to do with control. A relationship is a bond between people with the understanding that you will only be with each other. It's a beautiful thing, not a controlling thing. I really wish you had told me what you saw. I think people like Merideth...and Laird...operate on the silent consensus of the masses. People are cowed by the premise of not interfering in someone else's marriage. The reality is that if we adopted a policy where we *always* told when we saw someone cheating - there would be less cheating."

Annette took another cracker, spread some cheese on it, and took a big bite. A piece of cheese stuck to her cheek as she did so.

"I know. I wish I had told you as well. Then we could have been sitting here having this conversation years ago. Hindsight is everything, eh?"

I motioned to her face.

"No worries. You have a piece of cheese there."

She put her tongue to the opposite side of her mouth. Completely the wrong side. I shook my head. She laughed. Then she moved her tongue slowly over the top lip and looked me in the eyes. Good gods, was everything this girl did so sensuous? I shook my head again.

"Can you get it for me? I am such a retard at these things."

I reached out and wiped the cheese of her cheek with my finger. Her skin was like porcelain. I held it up in front of her.

"Thank you!"

Before I knew it she had my finger in her mouth and when it came out the cheese was gone.

"Waste not, want not. Am I right?"

Her action had an effect on me. I glanced briefly to my pants to ensure it wasn't visible. She was just a friend. It would be embarrassing if her innocent actions were marred by my physical response. She noticed me glance down.

"Tell me Dylan, have the vultures been circling the wagons?"

"Um, what?"

"Well, what I mean to say is you are a good man. There are too few of those around. You are handsome and successful. Are there ladies waiting to snatch you up?"

I didn't know what to say. I had not even considered the possibility. Merideth's betrayal had made me feel so ugly, so unwanted, that I didn't think I would be attractive to someone at all. Even thinking such, I knew it was ridiculous. It was a conflict within me. My rational mind knew that I was attractive to women before Merideth and even though I had aged I was still the same man. But the emotional side of me had been pushed down by Merideth for so many years; I was convinced of my ugliness. Annette had called me handsome. That sudden realization caused a surge of warmness in my chest. I mean sure she meant it as a friend, but it still meant something. I found her very attractive as well. Should I say something? I wasn't sure. On one hand, no one ever hates hearing that someone finds them attractive. On the other hand though, it could make our friendship awkward and she was the only friend I had. The rest had abandoned me. I decided not to say it.

"Thank you. No, I don't think anyone is interested."

"Well, I am sure they are. Sometimes you men are absolutely naive about seeing a woman's interest. Am I right?"

I nodded. I caught a look at my watch as I did so. It was 9:30. Caryn needed help with her math before bed. How did it get so late? I only got here at 7 and we had just one glass of wine.

"I have to go. It's late."

She smiled and stood up.

"Well, when you are ready to venture into the dating world

again, let me know and I will hook you up with someone marvelous."

She really was a good person. It was the lifeline I needed. I had seen the black heart of many people; and of society in general because of my ex. It was just reassuring to find someone else out there with a good soul. We walked to the door.

As she hugged me her lips brushed my cheek. It could have been a kiss. It could have been accidental. The prospect excited me.

"Don't ever change."

Her words were soft and slow in my ear. She squeezed tighter. I did the same. She hummed slightly and briefly. Our hug lasted longer than it should have.

"I don't like her"

Caryn's words were simple and direct, but that was Caryn's way. I admired that about her. There was a blunt truth to the way she spoke that I knew that even if I didn't like what she was saying, she would never lie to me. In this case it caused me inner conflict. Caryn and I were a team. It was important to me that we agreed on these things. That and I respected her opinion. But I also liked Annette. She was the first person I could call a friend since the split. I had had other friends before that; male friends even. The problem was that they were 'Couple Friends'. My ex and I were collectively friends with these other couples. Some of them I considered close friends; even best friends. They were the type of guys that tell you "Dude, I will always have your back". It was a complete lie though. If someone ever writes a handbook for males going through separation it would tell you that you will lose all those friends. Their wives will maintain the friendship with your ex and their balls are firmly in their wives' purses. That is just the way of it. It didn't matter one bit that she was an adulterer or that she betrayed me financially. Hell, it would not have mattered if she stabbed me in the eye with a pickle fork. This type of friend will be gone in a separation no matter what. It is a shame those were the only sort of friends I had had. Now that I had a new friendship, I was loath to give up on it.

"But why don't you like her? She's the only friend I have had since your mom and I split."

Caryn scrunched up her face in thought. She got this expression from her mom. It was hard to see traits and features of her mom in her; I loved Caryn to bits and completely hated Merideth, so when those traits emerged I did not know quite what to think.

"I don't know. I think it's because when she smiles, it's only with her mouth. Real smiles happen with the eyes as well. The whole face really."

That didn't make any sense to me at all. I was pretty sure that a smile was, by definition, something done with only the mouth. Regardless, it seemed like a silly thing to dislike someone for. I suspected, instead, that Caryn didn't like her as she thought I was dating Annette. She was not ready for that.

"I'm not dating Annette, she's just a friend. Can you try to give her a chance for me?"

She looked at me dead in the eye for an uncomfortable moment.

"Fine."

I worked downtown as an accountant, on contract to B.R. Pratt, who in turn contracts out accounting services to Oil & Gas companies. I have always been rather gifted with numbers and math and I had a pretty secure job given the money I had made for B.R. Pratt over the years. Since the split I had been doing less than exemplary work though. I knew it. My boss knew it. I think she suspected something was going on in my life but we didn't have a close enough relationship where she would feel comfortable asking about it. I did the bare amount of work to get by. Most days I still felt so shell-shocked by Merideth's actions that I could do little more than answer emails. I was at my desk pondering if I smiled with my whole face or just my mouth when her email came in.

"'Hey. You looked too thin the other day. Come by the coffee shop and I will fatten you up.' - Annette"

I read it three times. It was like having the sun shine through the clouds on an otherwise overcast day. It said two things to me. First, that she cared about my wellbeing, and second, that she must have enjoyed our time together or she would not have emailed.

Kensington was just a short walk away.

I had always appreciated her coffee shop as I could still order a coffee there without learning a new language. The coffee shop was much as I remembered it. Fancy copper hot beverage machines lined the counter on one end. A small cedar stage sat at the far end. Lighting was low and warm and soft music played in the background. The walls were lined with oversized handwritten inspirational quotes. I especially liked the one written nearest the entrance: "Laughter leads Love in all things!"

Annette came out of the kitchen as I entered and made a beeline for the barista.

"Jory, the afternoon order won't be here until..."

As I approached, she looked up.

"..Dylan, Oh my God, you arrived at the perfect time."

She quickly walked over and gave me a hug. I could feel her breasts press up against my chest as she kissed me on the cheek. They were firm and not something I could ignore. The barista looked up from her machine and rolled her eyes.

"Don't mind Jory. She's a perpetual spinster and mistrustful of all men."

She quickly had me at a table with a bowl of thick soup. Her red dress caught the eye, but once we were seated it was her mouth that I found intoxicating. It just had a sensuousness about it. It was as if her lips made love to each word as it escaped them. I was the silly sort of man that envied a word.

"So what ever happened to Laird?"

It was curiosity more than anything - that and keeping the conversation flowing. I had no designs on revenge against Laird for the adultery. There would have been a time when I would have put all the blame on Laird and accused him of seducing away my wife. However, with what I had learned about my ex-wife, I knew what she was. I knew she was no innocent lamb in these matters. She was the wolf. Their affair was likely more her idea than his, not that he was wholly innocent. In fact, I had some pity for Laird as my ex was certainly charming and manipulative. She was generally good at convincing people to give her what she wanted.

"Well, we dated off and on after that. Yes, he had his affairs, and yes he got out of hand with his fists once in a while, but when things were good, they were good, you know?"

"Wait. He beat you?"

She nodded. This enraged me immediately. My opinion of Laird again shifted in an instant. He had broken one of the most sacred rules of being a man: *A man does not start fights; a man only uses his strength to defend those who cannot defend themselves.* It was another mantra that I had learned from my father. It was hardly uncommon though. Every comic book, every action movie, and every heroic story back to the dawn of the written word echoed these same sentiments. Laird had broken this rule. He was not a man. He was a monster. He was the sort that paints all men in a bad light. He did not deserve compassion. He deserved a slice of his own actions. He deserved rage. I felt protective of Annette as well and that added to the fury I felt for Laird at this point.

"That's horrible. I am so sorry to hear that. Real men don't do that."

The words felt hollow as they came out of my mouth. *Real*

*men don't do that.* They don't and I believed it wholeheartedly, but it just ended up feeling like it was one of those things you say as a disclaimer. It felt like it had no weight next to the thought of Annette hiding her bruises under sunglasses and makeup. How could my silly phrase make up for that?

"I know...I know...some men still have a sense of chivalry."

She looked at me then. It wasn't a stare, it lacked that fierceness. But it was a long gaze. In it, I could see her fighting back tears. Her eyes had a slight glaze to them. It made me want to protect her from every small danger in the world.

"Why did you keep dating him?"

She looked down, ashamed. I took her hand and held it between mine as she had done for me the other night.

"You don't have to answer. It was a thoughtless question on my part."

"No. No. It's O.K. It is hard. I mean when it was good, it was good. He was sweet. He would pick daisies for me and write me poetry. We would lie on the banks of the Bow River and look for shapes in the clouds. You tend to gloss over the bad parts. I guess I thought my love could cure the bad parts. And...and...some part of me thought I didn't deserve better..."

A small tear did escape one eye then. The poor woman. Here was a woman that had it all. She was smart, funny, attractive, and caring. That someone would push her so far downward was a crime. I took a napkin and brought it up to her cheek to wipe the tear away. She grabbed my hand as I did so and leaned into it. It felt like her very existence depended on that hand.

"Annette. You deserve so much better. You are a wonderful woman."

Her mouth carved into a slight smile and she sighed.

"Thank you. Sometimes it helps just to hear that someone cares."

"Of course I care. Look, Annette, you are a real light in my life right now..."

"And you are in mine."

I was going to say more, but she had cut me off. I didn't mind. It was forgotten. Her response filled me with warmth. The depth in her eyes drew me in as she leaned against my hand that she still had pressed against her soft cheek. There was a silence then, long, but not uncomfortable. Then she took my hand and placed it on the table.

"What about you? Why did you stay with Merideth so long?"

That was a good question. Our relationship had started out well. Things were easy at the start. It was all laughter and kisses and equally sharing all the burdens and the victories. I was proud to be that modern man who has an equal partner in life. I looked forward to all the moments going forward. I am a romantic I suppose. But it had gone wrong somewhere along the way. I had ended up with more and more of the burdens while she ended up hoarding the victories. I had worked like a devil in both my job and my domestic duties at home to support her career. *"A true man sacrifices for those he loves"* (another saying from my father). But she was using my hard work, in the meantime, just for herself, and putting us in debt to boot. I did not know quite how much debt until we split. And that was not even considering all of her adultery. Why did I stay with her so long?

"Well, I think I was a bit like a frog in a pot of water. You increase the temperature slowly enough that the frog doesn't realize he's in trouble until it's boiling. I just didn't realize I was being abused in the situation. Well, not strictly anyway. I caught her in an online affair about 6 years ago. It was really inappropriate stuff. She never apologized. But you know Merideth; she was always horrible about apologizing. She didn't seem to think it was wrong, but she did agree to stop it. I worked through the pain of that internally for years. But that kind of unraveled when I found out about her affair with the lead guitarist from *Elemental Anguish*…and then I was told about the journalist. There were likely countless others."

"You poor man. I wish I had told you all those years ago. I am sorry. And you never strayed yourself after you found out about her online affair?"

In truth, I was not angry at Annette at all about her not telling me. What was done was done. But what a simple and effective tool an apology is. Whatever misgivings I may have had lingering about not knowing about that affair just melted away with that simple apology.

"No. I wanted to at first. I so wanted her to understand the pain she had created. I thought if she understood how deep the pain was, she would never do something like that again. But I just couldn't bring myself to do it. First, I still loved her and didn't truly want to cause her pain. Second, it would have destroyed my honour to cheat on anyone. How could I look at myself in the mirror every morning if I had betrayed someone like that?"

"You are sweet, you know that? Have you always had these views about honour and cheating?"

"Yes, but it's crazy. I mean, before I was married I would consistently have these steamy dreams. Sex dreams. It was always the same girl. And they were wild. But after I was married, I could not even cheat within the dream. When I had dreams about the girl, I would back away from her advances and tell her 'I can't! I'm married!' Eventually those dreams stopped. Stupid, right? Who shies away from a sex dream?"

I was flooded with memories. I hadn't thought about the dream girl in years. I had ended up just calling her 'Dream' as we had never exchanged names in the countless dreams she was in. I can recall her every feature: her raven hair; her dark, nearly black eyes; her almond-toned skin. What I remember most was her laugh. It wasn't the dainty laugh of demure ladies you see in the movies. It was a hearty laugh that spoke of independence and mischief. It wasn't just sex dreams with her either. Dream had been with me since I was a young boy and she was a young girl. We would play and be pirates or slay dragons together or sometimes simply sit together quietly in a desert on some foreign planet under a rainbow sky. It was only once I was past puberty that my adventures with Dream turned to kissing and eventually to sex. Dream had actually been my first sexual experience. We were on a beach and kissing pretty furiously when she pinned me on my back, laughed her trademark laugh, and simply just took me. It was marvelous and I remember every detail. Thinking of her made my heart ache. It had been years since I had seen her and I felt the loss acutely. It physically made my chest hurt.

"I was going to say that I understand about Merideth and apologies. The best I ever got from her is 'I am sorry you feel that way'. Did you know that not being able to apologize is a marker for narcissism...and I mean not just someone who likes themselves... but the personality disorder? I think it's sweet that you were loyal even in your dreams. It says a lot about your character. What I think is crazy is that your sex dreams were always just with one girl. Most guys have all sorts - dreams with mountains of bikini super models and different girls each time. You never had that?"

"No. It was always just the one. I suppose the Narcissism make sense, right? Music is likely a common field for that."

"Then you are a loyal man even in your dreams. Your dream girl is lucky. What is she like?"

I didn't want to tell her. I am not sure if it was because her tone changed. There was a hint of jealousy in it. I am certain she wanted me to describe a woman that was exactly like her. But I could not do that as Dream was nothing like Annette. It could also have been that Dream was someone I held close to my heart. She was private.

"You have to let a man have some mysteries."

Annette smiled and took a deep drink of her coffee.

I woke up confused. I was on the couch and the T.V. was blaring. I must have fallen asleep while watching T.V., but the last thing I remembered was helping Caryn with her homework. I don't remember coming to the couch. I don't remember turning on the T.V. or what I watched before I fell asleep. I don't even remember if Caryn got to bed alright.

I had come to expect this though. I had blank spots in my memory, not because I had blacked out, but because my whole world was fuzzy. There was this illusion of what our society was. Happy couples, marriages, children, fulfilling work, loyalty, honour, and all the good things that go with it. The problem was that it was all a lie. It was a lie sitting on a thin meniscus and that meniscus had been stripped away from me. It made my head fuzzy to try to live in this society while at the same time knowing that it is false. It feels like when you hit a baseball wrong with an aluminum bat. Once you knew this stuff, it was rather impossible to drink the Kool-Aid again (so to speak).

I turned off the T.V. and headed up to my own bed. If I was going to fall asleep, it might as well be where I am supposed to fall asleep.

I was in a room that had wooden walls and there was a hook where my left hand should be. There were maps scattered all over the table and there was a bowl of slightly unripe fruit holding the maps down as the room swayed back and forth. I lifted my hand to my face and felt a good 1/2 inch of stubble.

"Yar."

Did I say that? It sounded like my voice. There was no one else in the room to say it. Oh right, I forgot. I was a pirate. I have always been a pirate. It is strange that for a moment I thought I was an accountant in some other place with some other worries. I have been first mate on the *Scallywag* for years and I had come down to the captain's quarters to get her jade-handled fish saber. I forget why she needed it but I grabbed it and headed up the stairs.

As soon as I got on deck, I remembered why the captain needed her jade-handled fish saber. The *Scallywag* had been boarded by a platoon of Slobber-Headed Mud Fish. Their orange uniforms and polished black tail boots contrasted with the dangling sucker tentacles and drool that accompanied their brown faces. They were advancing on the captain with their rusty scimitars while she fended them off with her regular blade. Everyone knows that you cannot defeat Slobber-Headed Mud Fish soldiers with a regular blade. You need a jade-handled fish saber for that sort of work.

"Captain!" I yelled.

I threw the fish saber into the air. She looked at me with a glint in her eye and laughed her hearty laugh. She caught the fish saber with her left hand and kicked the neared Mud Fish in the chest. He barreled backwards as she stabbed the Mud Fish approaching her from the rear. I jumped up and grabbed a rope from the sail and swung towards the brawl. My feet flew into a group of Mud Fish as the Captain dispatched two more. She kept fighting as I ran between the barrels on deck with two Mud Fish hot on my heels. I turned and punched one square in the face. He stood shocked and then shook his head violently, getting his dreaded slobber all over me. The second turned to fight the captain as the Mud Fish in front of me slapped me so hard with his fin that I flew across the deck. I hit my head against the anchor and my world went topsy-turvy. Blackness was creeping into my vision while I saw the Mud Fish approaching with his scimitar out. I had no strength to fight back and as I prepared to feel his blade, a jade-handled fish saber suddenly jutted out of his chest. The Mud Fish dropped to the ground revealing the captain behind him.

"Where have you been?"

"I'm sorry captain; I got the fish saber as quick as I could."

Somehow I thought she meant something else. I was only gone a moment. Or was I? It felt like a long time since I had seen her. She grabbed my hand to pull me up. Her long raven hair ruffled in the breeze. It had a small streak of white in it. That was new. Her eyes drew me in. They nearly had tears in them it seemed. What was wrong with my captain?

"You know what I mean. It's been years and I had to fight the Slobber-Headed Mud Fish all by myself, not to mention the eight-legged swamp Knax and the Grollian hill tribes. I needed you."

"I'm sorry. I went away I guess..."

She hugged me tight and quick, and then slapped me. A tear drifted down her cheek.

"Well dammit man, what happened?"

"I got married."

She sat on a barrel and wiped the jade-handled fish saber clean on the uniform of a Slobber-Headed Mud Fish soldier.

"I did too, that's no excuse. I thought we were a team."

"I know. It felt wrong to want your kisses so badly when I was married."

It was such a simple truth and I didn't know it was inside me. It wasn't simply my honor that kept me away from her. I desired her kisses and her touch. I yearned for them and felt guilty and wrong about feeling that way. I had sent her away as a result. I felt badly about that. I brushed the hair away from her face. She looked up at me.

"You always were a chivalrous bastard. And now? What's changed?"

"Well as it turns out, I married a segmented slime eel by mistake. We are split now, though she might roam these waters still."

She sheathed her sword and looked to the sky. Then she started to laugh.

"You're kidding, right? Same thing happened to me. I married a Slobber-Headed Mud Fish soldier by mistake. He was a captain, but still a Mud Fish is a Mud Fish."

She kicked one of the dead soldiers hard.

"These fellows were my in laws."

She turned to look at the rest of the corpses.

"Look at them now."

She was stunning in her captain's outfit. It was giving in all the right places and tight in others. It was definitely the most womanly pirate outfit I had ever seen. Her pants were sheer and white and I could make out a thong underneath them. I could not hold myself back. She was my captain and my love and I had found her again after all these years. I walked up behind her and slid my arms around her. She inhaled in surprise as I did.

"Mmmm...it appears my first mate is back."

Her hair ruffled around my face. I pushed it aside and kissed her neck. She moaned and I held her tighter. She spun in my grip and looked me in the eye. It was one of those looks where you don't know if she is going to throw you overboard or just give you a wink. Her eyes sparkled and as she smiled they seemed to look happier as well. There was something about that I had to remember.

She touched her lips to mine and my world spun. They were like satin. My eyes closed and my mouth opened. Our tongues touched lightly. It caused a stirring below. I didn't worry about it as she knew my body as well as I did myself. It felt less like a kiss and more like we were melding into one being. Our eyes opened and we stepped back from each other still holding hands. Another tear streamed down her cheek.

"I've missed you. I've missed you like there was a hole within me."

I nodded.

"I know. I feel a completeness here and now that I haven't in a long time."

We stood there just looking at each other. They were soft gazes. Grateful gazes. The purple sails of the *Scallywag* rippled above us, but our eyes were still locked.

"Why do you always get to be captain?"

"Because it's my boat, silly!"

I jarred awake due to my alarm clock blaring. There is nothing ruder to sleep and good dreams than the alarm clock. It slams good dreams away and forces you naked into the harsh world of reality. I ought to have sliced that damned machine in two with my fish saber. Wait, what the heck was a fish saber? It was from my dream. I was on a pirate ship and she was there. I hadn't dreamed of her in years. I don't recall much else, but I was happy she was in my dream. I felt I had regained something knowing that Dream had come back into my life. I wished I could just go back to bed and back to wherever she was. But Caryn needed to get to school and I needed to go to work. I pulled myself out of bed and started the trudge towards the shower.

"Yar!" I said to no one in particular.

When I got downstairs, Caryn was already eating her cereal and had her school bag by her feet. I was lucky that she was so organized.

"Good morning, kid."

She mumbled something with her mouth full as I pulled up to the table with my own cereal and juice.

"Any good dreams last night?"

"I had one where I was riding a horse made out of balloons. We were flying in the air until a vengeful seagull came up and started popping them. What about you?"

We always shared our dreams. It was a special morning ritual. I was unsure what to share about my dream, but I felt I could safely share the base information.

"Not much, I was a pirate and I was fighting fish soldiers."

"Fun."

She may not even have heard me. She was a teen and prone to being more interested in what the letters in her cereal spelled than what I had to say.

"Annette, I'm coming over right away. Stay where you are."

"Thank you. I knew you would help…"

I clicked end. Caryn was looking up at me.

"What about our movie?"

It was hard. Since her mom left, I had been sharing my favorite action movies with her. At first, it had been to take her mind off of her mom completely abandoning her. I knew that would be hard to take as a kid, so I arranged more time for just the two of us. Now it was just special time we had together every Friday night.

"I am sorry Caryn. Annette had a break in and needs me. Can we finish tomorrow? We can even watch the third one if you like."

Caryn sighed.

"Fine. Go. Just make sure she doesn't have a break in tomorrow too."

When I got to Annette's apartment, the door was open and the lights were off. There were clothes and things strewn about, but I had no way of knowing if that was due to burglary or just her regular lifestyle. I closed the door behind me. I had brought a baseball bat with me in case I had to deal with a burglar.

"Annette?"

There was no answer. Her dining room window was open as she had said and the curtains were fluttering in the night breeze.

"Annette?"

Again, nothing. I might as well check the apartment head to toe then. If I find a burglar, I stop him. Otherwise I might find Annette. I went through every room finding nothing. I entered her bedroom and it seemed to be in the same disheveled state. I heard a noise coming from the closet. I opened the closet door in one fluid motion and found Annette curled up inside. She screamed briefly and then held her chest breathing hard. I reached down for her hand to pull her up.

"Dylan, thank god. I heard noises out there but I didn't know if it was you or the burglar."

She hugged me and held me so tight I could barely talk.

"Hey. It's ok. I checked the entire apartment. If there was a burglar here, he's gone."

She nodded.

"Thank you for coming. Can you stay a little while?"

"Yes. It's no problem."

It felt fulfilling to help. That chivalry deep down inside me was satisfied to know that I could come to the rescue. Helping a damsel in distress was about the best thing in the world. Even better if there was a burglar and I fought him off. I would have gladly done so for Annette.

We moved into the living room and she scuttled to the kitchen to put on the kettle.

"Tea?"

"Yes, thanks. You think he came in through the window?"

The kettle was on the burner now and Annette had two mismatched cups on the counter. She came over to where I was standing by the window.

"Yes. I don't remember opening it. I always close it...and..."

A car backfired in the street. Annette screamed and grabbed me. She was pressed right up against me. I could feel her heart beating hard through her chest. Her nipples erect and pronounced as she held on to me. My hands reached around to her lower back. She tilted her head up and looked up at me. She let out a small, almost inaudible sigh. I could not take my eyes off her lips. They were so red and inviting. I felt compelled and moved in slightly towards her. She moved towards me as well. Before I even knew what was happening, her mouth was on mine. Mine was on hers as well. I had forgotten how good kissing was. Her lips were soft yet insistent. They were constantly in motion to match my own. Her tongue, darting in to touch mine, to tangle with it, and then back away. It was a subtle game where we both won. My hands moved downwards, grabbing and pulling her closer. I was engorged down below and she could certainly feel it and didn't seem to mind. I was entranced. Here was a beautiful, smart, funny, caring woman and she was making out with me. I never wanted it to end.

The kettle took that moment to whistle and Annette broke away.

"Mmm...wow...that was...let me get the tea."

I was left wondering if that was it. Was this a momentary make out due to a backfire, or was there something more here. I hoped there was something more. I cared about Annette. I found her extremely attractive. I admired how she was independent and ran her own business. I loved the way her mind worked. I used the word love. It's a scary word.

She brought the two mugs over and sat on the couch. She motioned for me to sit down.

"Dylan, look. That was lovely. I am just not sure you want me..."

"Can I just say something?"

She stopped. She put her mug down. Did she somehow get closer to me on the couch? Did she move closer or did I? Or both?

"Those may have been the very best kisses I have had in my life."

She looked at me. I swear she was closer still. It was true too. Merideth had been a horrible kisser. I loved to kiss. The feeling of it, the intimacy, was nearly better than sex when done right.

And then we collapsed together again. Our lips and tongues were a tornado of action. We angled onto the couch. My hand slipped downwards and then up her shirt. She gasped as I caressed a breast and then kissed more furiously. Both her hands were up my back, scratching as we made out. It was painful, but I did not mind at all. It was a counterpoint to the moment.

She grabbed my shirt and pulled it over my head, frantic. She threw it on the floor and jumped on top of me. She bent down and kissed me quickly twice before kissing my neck and biting me lightly on the shoulder. It was wild. I had never experienced it like this with anyone else. There was something both gentle and animalistic about her. She got off me and stood up. She grabbed my hand and led me toward the bedroom. I was filled with conflicting thoughts. Foremost, I was filled with excitement and anticipation. It had been months and months since I had been intimate with someone - since my split. I have always been a very sexual person. I missed that. I was excited to be with someone new. But I was also a bit worried. This was very sudden. Would it ruin our friendship? Would we become a couple? Where were we going here?

Before I could think, she had tackled me onto her bed. She was all over me. Her hands were everywhere. She kissed my chest and then bit me again slightly below my left nipple. It was both strange and arousing. She made her way down to my pants and I shuddered slightly.

"Can I just...?"

It was gallant of her to ask permission, but I figured the bulge was enough to signal that. I nodded. She unzipped me and pulled my pants down. My underwear was no barrier to her hands. She pulled me out.

"You are a big boy!"

In her French accent, somehow it made it all the more enticing. Her mouth was like silk on me. I could barely contain myself. I thought of as many unarousing things as I could to take my mind off the pure pleasure she was giving me. She got up and kissed me deeply before standing to remove the remainder of her clothes. I kneeled as she got back on the bed and kissed her passionately. She pulled me down on top of her. Again, the thoughts crept back in my head. Were we a couple now? Did she care about me like I did about her? There was no doubting that I cared about her. I think I was beginning to love her. But shouldn't we talk about that before going any further? We really should talk about it. I pulled back into a kneeling position again.

"Annette, I..."

She gritted her teeth and looked at me.

"Get inside me right now!" she insisted.

There was a primal annoyance in her voice I could not ignore.

All of my conflicting thoughts melted away. This woman wanted me and wanted me now. And I wanted her. She moaned as I entered her and her arms were on me pulling me down. We were a jumble of arms and ecstasy. She was kissing and then not, gentle and then feral. She was biting and grabbing. Her arms were everywhere. It was like wrestling an octopus.

And when we finished, we had soft kisses and the cold tea we had forgotten about. We sat on the couch drinking it, naked, under a hand woven blanket.

When I had to go, she walked me to the door. She hugged me tight and looked into my eyes.

"I love you Dylan. I want us to see each other."

Her words warmed me more than anything else this evening. Just to hear that, if we had done nothing but drink tea tonight, would have made this the very best of days. My heart felt like a tree stretching towards the sun of her affection. I felt strong. I felt happy. I felt wonderful.

"I love you too, Annette. You are wonderful."

She looked sad for a moment and then hugged me tight.

"No matter what, please don't change."

The next day I felt better than I had in a long time. I whistled to myself as I made bacon and eggs for Caryn and myself. I hadn't made a big breakfast like this in a while. I enjoyed cooking though and it made me feel good as I slid the eggs from their pan onto our plates.

"What has you in such a good mood today?"

I added hash browns and bacon for each of us.

"I just feel happier."

I have never tasted such good bacon. Food had been like eating dry wall paste since the split, and now it suddenly jumped with flavour. It was like watching a bright rainbow-hued cartoon after months of watching black and white movies. I ate until I felt full.

I phoned Annette. She did not pick up, but perhaps she was a late sleeper. It went to her voice mail.

"Hey Annette. It's Dylan. I just thought I would phone to see if you wanted to drop by tonight for a movie. Give me a call back."

"Dad, no. We were watching that movie together. You said we could finish the one from last night."

This was going to be a problem. Annette and I were seeing each other and Caryn didn't like her.

"We will. I just thought it would be nice if Annette joined us. Please try to like her for me."

"I don't trust her"

Annette did not phone back. Caryn and I watched the movies ourselves and she was perfectly happy with that. It worried me that she didn't call back though. She was a very caring and thoughtful person. It would be unlike her to not call back. I thought of the burglar too. I hoped she was O.K.

I called her on Sunday as well.

"Hi Annette. I didn't hear back from you yesterday. I was thinking of going for a hike today. I would love it if you came. Give me a call before 10 AM to let me know. Or...umm...just call me back. Ok?"

I did not hear back from her. It confused and worried me. What if she was hurt? What if she had been in a car accident or something? I wish I knew how to contact her. If she was hurt, I wanted to help.

Monday rolled around and I found myself at work and I still

had not heard back from her. I sent her an email in the morning knowing that she checks that regularly at the coffee shop. I heard nothing back from her. Something must be very wrong. I decided to skip out and walk to the coffee shop: if Annette was hurt or in trouble, her barista would know. Then I could figure out how to help her. Whatever she needed, I would help. *A man sacrifices for those that he loves* - another kernel of wisdom from my father.

I entered the coffee chop. Again I was greeted with the over-sized philosophy. "Laughter leads Love in all things!" How like Annette that was. I could see the subtle touches of her in this coffee shop everywhere.

Jory was working the big copper coffee machines as usual. I scanned around looking for Annette. I was about to go ask Jory when I spotted her. I nearly didn't see her as she was almost hidden behind another customer she was talking to with a mop of dark frazzled hair. Why did he seem familiar? Annette caught my gaze.

"Oh God" I heard her whisper.

Laird. That's who this was. All of a sudden it made sense. Laird that had cheated on her. Laird that had beaten her. Laird had caused her trouble and she was talking to him now. Laird must have done something this weekend to cause Annette some problems. I was so stupid. I should have gone to see her on Saturday instead of assuming she was O.K. I was a horrible boyfriend. I could have helped if she was having problems. I walked towards the table.

I was hit with mental images of Laird making out with my ex-wife topless in the supply room as Annette had told me. I saw images of Annette behind sunglasses to hide bruises. I saw images of Laird yelling and shoving Annette. My hands balled into fists. This was no man. *A man does not start fights.* It was the gravest of atrocities to hit a woman. I wanted to hit him with everything in me. But *a man does not start fights.* My father's words echo in my ears. And yet…and yet it is chivalrous to fight a monster. Laird was a monster. *A man only uses his strength to defend those who cannot defend themselves.* Was there ever a better example than this?

I walked up and tapped Laird on the shoulder. As he turned, I slammed my fist into his face with all the force I had. His head toppled back, blood flying from his nose and spaying on the cream topped table. His hand went immediately to his nose.

"Are you fucking out of your mind, man?"

I hit him again. Then once more.

"Dylan, stop!"

Annette stood up and looked at me furiously. Then she grabbed me by the arm and escorted me to the back room.

"Stay here."

I sat down. I was confused. This was the man she said had cheated on her numerous times. This was the man that had beaten her many times. He was a horrible person. He had caused her some kind of problem this weekend. But I didn't know that for sure. I had assumed. Why else would Annette not have returned my calls and my email?

She came back in the room.

"He is not going to press charges. But it's only because I told him that you knew about your ex and him."

"I'm sorry...I just saw him there and I hadn't heard from you... and I thought he had done something to you this weekend..."

She sat down and crossed her arms.

"Dylan. Laird and I are a couple."

I was baffled. This didn't make any sense.

"What? After him cheating? After the physical abuse? How are you a couple? Why didn't you tell me? What about last night?"

She let out a long sigh.

"Look. We have rough patches, but he is always there for me regardless. And last night was last night. It was fun, right?"

"Yes, but I don't understand."

"Hey, it wasn't about you. Merideth had taken something that was mine and now I took something that was hers. It's all about balance. Besides, men separate emotion from sex, right? It was just a roll in the hay for you, right?"

That was the stereotype. All men have heard it. That we do not get emotionally attached with sex: that we can have sex without a close connection to someone. It was both true and not. I could certainly have sex just for fun without emotional attachment. Purely recreation. Or so the theory went. I had never technically been able to, but I could understand that on a base level it was possible. In fact, in talking to men in our more honest moments I have not heard of one man that had been able to separate sex from emotion completely. That was the stereotype though. I suppose it could be done. However, for that to work, it would have to be agreed upon beforehand. I had been emotionally invested in Annette before that first kiss. I was certainly tied up with her emotionally by the time we slept together. But she had me in a logical quandary. By her wording, if I admitted I had feelings for her then I was not a man. If I admitted that my heart ached for her, I was not a man. This was not a 'roll in the hay' for me.

"But...but you said you loved me. What about us?"

She sighed and looked at me like I was an annoyance. The look crushed me.

"I do love you Dylan...but as a friend. Ok? There is no 'us'."

I nodded. I tried my best to hold back my tears. *Men don't cry.* I was unsuccessful. One leaked out of my right eye followed quickly by a second. I turned my head to hide my shame. *Men don't cry.* I walked away. She spoke as I got to the door.

"Dylan. You don't want me anyway. I am a wreck."

I didn't say a thing. A tear escaped my left eye and hit the floor. Even if she didn't see it, I am sure she heard the dull smacking sound it made as it hit the concrete.

I didn't go back to work. I couldn't. I went home. I don't even remember how I got home, but I was there. I felt ill. I had been used. She had orchestrated this from the start. She had played the damsel in distress perfectly and I had fallen for it. I bet there wasn't even really a burglar. And if there was, she would have called Laird, right? That is all she wanted from the start. I felt like my heart was ripped open once again. Merideth had broken my heart most completely, but it was healing slowly. Annette had ripped the scab right off and it was as if all of my pain had happened just today instead of months ago. It was like a searing bright light of pain in my chest. It would have been better if Annette had just come up to me in the grocery store that day and said "Look, your ex cheated with my boyfriend years ago, so I would like to take you somewhere and fuck the bejesus out of you in vengeance." I may not have agreed to that (or I may have) but at least it would have been honest. Who knows if he even beat her either? Perhaps that was just a ploy to play the damsel. It had worked.

I threw up. My stomach was just so upset I felt sick. This time I hit the toilet. There were bits of bacon in it. That surprised me as I had not eaten bacon since Saturday. It is a cruel thing to be lucid when you throw up and recognize bits of previous meals you had eaten, but even more cruel to recognize the smells. They smell vaguely like what you ate, but as if the food had turned to the dark side.

I made it to the kitchen before I collapsed on the floor. Then the tears came again. I cried so hard I was shaking. I cried so hard that I had no hope of controlling it. I had no hope of getting up off the floor. I was happy I was home alone. I was happy Caryn was still at school. Then no one had to see me like this. I didn't have to feel ashamed. Because...

*Men don't cry.*

What bullshit. I couldn't count how many times I had cried in my life. I was a man. I had seen my own father cry several times no matter how hard he tried to hide it. It was fucking hypocrisy. I should have repeated that phrase to him in those moments. "Real men don't cry dad! How does that feel?" I had seen other men cry as well. I had read stories like the *Iliad* and the *Odyssey;* ancient stories of manly heroes and guess what? They cried.

*Men don't cry.*

I lay there on the floor sobbing, contemplating how much I wasn't a 'real man'. It was such a lie. That saying was crap. Men cried. Period. I needed to stop saying it in my head. I needed to abandon that bit of false chivalry. But if that one was wrong, then perhaps all the others were as well. There were plenty of Lairds out there going through life stealing, cheating, and generally being assholes and they seemed to get whatever they wanted. It seemed to work for my ex-wife as well. Those of us who stick to a chivalrous code just seem to get screwed over. Maybe I should stop being the good guy. The good guy is a fucking doormat. *Real men are not fucking doormats.* There is my bit of wisdom to add.

I managed to get up to a cross-legged position. The floor was wet with my tears. I needed a drink. Badly. I had drunk the last of the wine in the house though and I had nothing else. Except that wasn't true. I had 'remnants'. I had nearly full bottles of stuff that I mix with other drinks here and there and then left in the cupboard. I went to check. Yes! There was a half a bottle of banana liqueur, a nearly full bottle of melon liqueur and some black spiced rum. I hated banana flavoured anything. It never really tasted like banana. This is what I had to work with though. I mixed up a couple of liters of lemonade and mixed in my poison. It was the best I could do. No one wants to drink banana liqueur straight.

I drank it and I cried. It's not the sort of happy drinking they show you on television ads. It's the medicated drinking of "If I get drunk enough, I won't care about this shit". But still I thought about it.

I thought about how I worked like a dog only to come home to do laundry and dishes and take care of Caryn all so that she could have her singing career.

*A real man sacrifices for those he loves.*

I thought about how Merideth let this happen. I thought about how she would tell me "We will work on your dreams later."

"DAMN YOU MERIDETH!! I loved you so much I sacrificed everything for you. You loved me so little that you let me!"

*A real man sacrifices for those he loves.*

I threw the empty bottle of melon liqueur at the stove. It shattered. I didn't give a fuck. I thought about how even though I gave everything, she didn't want me. She cast me aside. She used me for money and slept with others. Worst of all, she didn't see it as wrong to do so. Then she just left. She left me behind. She left Caryn behind all without a care in the world.

"WHY!!"

I tried to stand when I shouted, but I was too drunk. I slipped. Then blackness.

There was a sound.

"Dad."

Ah, Caryn again. This seemed familiar. The feeling of linoleum on my face. So cool. My skin was stuck to it. I knew it would sting to pull off. I opened my eyes. Caryn's feet were near me.

"Dad, you're bleeding."

I peeled myself up. There was no pile of vomit this time. There was a small pool of blood and some splattering of it nearby. I had cut my arm on the broken glass when I fell.

*A real man cleans up his own messes*

"I'll get the mop."

# THE BROKEN PEOPLE

"So, Mom said you tried to kill yourself again."

Jenn. I wondered what I had done to deserve her call. Someone must have told Mom about my recent accident. I think the word 'again' stung the most. I had never tried to kill myself even once. The first time Jenn was alluding to was just a day or two after I had found out about Merideth's affairs. I was raw. I was in shock. I recall it feeling like I was perpetually being bitten by a rattlesnake. Merideth had gone out to perform a gig. Even though I was in a rough state, her 'career' was more important to her than my wellbeing. I thought I would work on a project I had put off for a while. I thought that working with wood would calm my mind - it often had in the past. While it calmed my mind, it was not enough. My tears blurred my vision and my jig saw slipped and cut my arm. Merideth came home to find me sitting in a dining room chair, watching the birds outside, as I bled out onto the floor. It was true that I made no attempt to bandage myself. However, not caring if one dies is very different than trying to kill oneself.

"I wasn't trying to kill myself, Jenn. I slipped and there was some glass. That's all. Who told Mom? Was it Caryn?"

"Caring? Yes. I am calling because I care. A slip, eh? What was it this time?"

She had misunderstood Caryn's name, but she had never been

that invested in her niece's life. I found that strange, for someone with a raging case of feminism like my sister. I proceeded to tell her the whole story with Annette. I left out the details where I was an emotional sobbing mess as it was unmanly to admit these things. It was a sacred duty of all men to keep these secrets.

"Good for her. It sounds like she saw what she needed and took it."

I could not believe what I was hearing. My sister had phoned me for one of two reasons. Either she was concerned for me or my parents had told her to phone. This was not caring at all, though. She didn't see how much this hurt.

"But she told me she loved me....that she wanted...I mean she acted like..."

"Just stop, Dylan. What you have to understand is that men do this all the time. We live in a patriarchy that allows men to say whatever they want to get into women's pants. She, like all of us, was likely pushed down by this patriarchy. Rayne Kale says that *what suppresses, impresses.* She just took back the power. You shouldn't take it personally."

It was personal, though. I had opened my heart to Annette and been duped. I had been used. It wasn't just that though. I had thought I had gotten better at reading people since my split. I had thought I could recognize the dishonest ones. Merideth had pulled the wool over my eyes to absolutely betray me. And in my first foray into romance since that time, I was duped as well. I was disappointed and angry with myself, really. It was more that than being upset with Annette's actions. Worse than this, I think I was worried that I would make the same mistake over and over again. I could have thanked my sister for this revelation. I could have, but the rabid form of feminism she followed left me with a sense of nausea.

Rayne Kale. The very name made me shudder. I had heard it uttered from my sister's lips more times than I cared to count. Ever since Jenn moved to Vancouver, and especially after her divorce, she had been an avid follower of Kale's. Rayne was one of those motivational speakers/self-help authors/feminist activists that painted feminism in a negative light. To me there were always two types of feminism. The first type I call 'Equality' feminism that seeks to have equal rights and equal opportunities and equal everything for each gender. I can really get behind this type as it is logical and fair and just. In fact, I have never met any man who would bristle against this sort of feminism. How could they? It just made sense. We lived in a modern (and hopefully enlightened) world and of course women and men should be equals. The second type I called 'Pendulum' feminists. This type saw atrocities committed by men (and the 'patriarchy') against women through history and sought balance by way of swinging the pendulum the other way. It came off as very 'man hating', especially to men like me who were behind equality between the genders. It alienated men like me. It was certainly true that men had behaved poorly towards women at times in the past - but that wasn't me. The very strange thing was that neither faction believed that the other existed. The Equality feminists, when told about someone espousing Pendulum views, would claim they were either expressing their personal opinions or were not truly feminists. Similarly, Pendulum feminists would claim that someone showing Equality views were either lying about what they believed or were not true feminists. It was generally only men who saw both factions. No wonder it was such a confusing topic for us. Rayne Kale was a Pendulum feminist. I disliked her philosophies that led to women being equally big assholes to men as men were to women in the 16th century. This is very much like Jenn telling me here that Annette was right to tell me what ever she needed to in order to sleep with me. It's horrible behaviour, in my opinion, for either gender. I hated her catchy slogans with coincidental rhymes. Slogans like *"What suppresses, impresses"* which is meant to excuse bad behaviour because one had experienced similar suppression previously. Others like

*"Once allowed, forever cowed"* and *"A man in need, a felon in deed"*, I had heard voiced by my sister many times.

"I take it by your silence that you are off in deep thought as usual. I have perplexed you. What you need to understand Dylan is that it is not her fault. You cannot blame her."

"Of course I can blame her. They were her actions. Just because men have been thoughtless jerks in the past and said whatever they needed to to get into a woman's pants, it doesn't mean it is acceptable for her to do the same. That is unjust. Besides, I have never behaved like that towards a woman...how did I deserve this?"

I would never have treated a woman the way I was treated here. It seemed colossally unfair that my sister thought it was completely O.K. for me to be treated this way. It seemed especially so since if I had ever treated a woman in the same way, I would be condemned by her for being a misogynistic asshole. This sort of hypocritical double standard would seem to undermine that message of equality. I could never have treated a woman so poorly anyway. It would go against how I was brought up: *A man always treats a woman with respect and honour* - and - *A real man never lies.* Though I was sorely tempted to wish such treatment on Rayne Kale, but I know this would only lead to more pain, more inequality, and more annoying and coincidentally rhyming faux-motivational slogans.

Jenn let out a long sigh.

"You don't understand. You aren't a woman."

She was right. I did not understand, though I didn't think it had much to do with my gender. As divisive and damaging as Rayne Kale was, I could understand how my sister got there. My father taught her to stand up for herself and that she was equal and that she could do anything a boy could do. He was right to do so. I hoped I was teaching Caryn the same. If I was born a girl, I may have ended up following Rayne Kale as well. Instead, being born with a penis, Rayne Kale made me feel like a target.

"Thanks for calling, Jenn. I'm fine. I have to get back to work though."

I was at work. I could have told her that I had to run to a meeting or that I had another call coming in but *Real men never lie*. It would have been easier though. My split had been tough with respect to family. My sister had these unhelpful feminist views and my parents were of a strong religious background that gave them the opinion that you don't "Throw marriage away." While they were horrified by Merideth's actions, they were of the mind that I should have stuck it out with her and worked things out. I believe they thought it was we "of the younger generation" who were more prone to throwing things away than fixing them. It is one of those things that every generation likely thinks of the generation after them and is likely false each time. Either way, other than "Keep your chin up" and "This too shall pass", I did not get a lot of support from my family. When Jenn had found out about Merideth's infidelity, she gave me the following advice:

*"When a man cheats it is his fault as he was a faithless dog. When a woman cheats, it is also the man's fault as women only cheat because their partner was emotionally unavailable to them. You need to figure out where you failed her and fix that."*

I found this very unsupportive and illogical. It basically says men cheat because they are evil and women cheat because men are evil. I tend to think cheating has nothing to do with gender. Cheating happens because one partner is selfish and lacks empathy. I would think that a true feminist would own up to this fact and acknowledge that women are sometimes assholes too. To blame men for everything is not in the spirit of equality.

"Look, Dyl. It's not that I think it was right that this was done to you, just that she was not wrong to do so."

I could not even begin to understand the logic behind that. How could something be both right and wrong at the same time? At one time I would have argued this point with her, but I was simply too tired to get into a debate that would lead us nowhere but angry with each other.

"Ok. I should go."

As I reflect on my life, I cannot pinpoint an exact moment where gender differences became an issue. Let's face it, in our society, if gender issues were not an issue in the adult world, then there would be no need for movements like feminism. People would just be people and equality would be rampant like the Plague.

Yet I know this is not the case, so I know gender issues must creep up sometimes in life. They must be sneaky as a hunting cat though as I cannot remember their start.

I can recall as a young boy playing games of hide and seek or tag in large groups of children in my neighborhood. The nostalgia of it reminds me of that amber of twilight. We would just play. No one cared about skin colour or gender. The game would go on. Everyone seemed to have an equal weighted opinion. The game evolved with new rules and new ideas, but everyone just played.

And I can remember sun scorched days on Kootenay Lake. We had no boat, but our rental always had a dock. Kids would drift to our beach from beaches down the way. Some were locals and some were summer renters like us. We would race down the dock at breakneck speed to see who could get the first and finest cannonball of the day. Again, gender never came into play.

In a way, I wonder if my experiences with Dream just wired me differently in this regard. Our adventures were always equal. She was always the pirate captain, but I was always the lead jungle explorer. When we were super spies, we were always just 'partners'. It is worth some thought to explore whether these experiences made me less likely to see gender differences than the regular male. My gut says they didn't; my gut tells me that it is the adults that raise us that start to instill the ideas of 'us' and 'them'.

I recall one such moment. I have always had both female friends and male friends, but when I was 6 or 7 I had a good female friend. I don't even remember her name at this point as she only lived in our neighborhood for a few months. I think her name started with a 'J'. We got along marvelously and played non-stop during the time she lived there. I recall asking my mom if she could have a sleepover at my house and was met with a blank stare and a firm "No." When I asked further I was told that it wasn't appropriate. This was very confusing to me at the time. It just didn't make sense. Why were sleepovers with my male friends appropriate, but not with girls? This was my first experience with gender division.

I continued to have friendships with girls as I grew up. My uncle used to call me 'Little Casanova' as a result. When I was little I considered it a compliment, but as an adult it frightens me a little that my uncle didn't seem to understand that a boy could have a relationship with a girl without it being romantic in the slightest. I can see how these types of experiences can lead to boys having "No girls allowed" clubs, or girls doing something similar due to my gender's proliferation of "cooties". If you were not sanctioned free play with the opposite gender, it might be just easier to exclude them.

Caryn sat at the kitchen table as I ate my dinner. She had an array of books in front of her. It was some end-of-year science project she was working on. I was extremely thankful that she was an independent kid. I just didn't have the energy to help her completely with her school life. My meal was not all that inspired - frozen perogies and fries. It was likely not good for me, but health was not even close to being my priority. It is hard to be concerned with what is healthy when your life is emotionally unstable. The world seemed off kilter - it was hard to conjure up worry for cholesterol or omega 3 fatty whatevers or which foods dieticians had villainized this month. I just didn't give a shit. It was enough to try to muster my interest in eating when everything tasted like drywall mud. I ate only for Caryn. If she wasn't around to care for me I may have wasted away. After I discovered the adultery I lost 25 pounds in two weeks. Betrayal is the best diet ever.

My hand throbbed in pain. They had given me stitches for my cut, starting at my palm, spiraling over to my wrist and bandaged it up. I didn't mind the pain. The physical sharpness of the pain took the edge off the emotional pain I still had as an undercurrent in my daily life. It hurt when I used my fork, so I did so vigorously. And sometimes through my day, I would make my hand into a fist as it would cause a searing pain that would block out all my other worries like an eclipse. It was an exquisite reprieve from my torment and likely worse for me than the perogies and fries.

"Caryn, have you had friends who were boys?"

She dropped her pen and looked at me quite perplexed.

"Where is this coming from? You mean like boyfriends?"

"No, not like that. I mean a good friend that was coincidentally a boy. I'm just curious and I don't remember if you had."

I could tell she was concentrating.

"No…not really. I mean we all played together when we were in kindergarten but I don't remember having any specific friends who were boys. Is this about Annette?"

"Yes and no. I just remember having female friends growing up. It's not really about her, I was just thinking about friends in general…and gender."

She nodded and went right back to her books. She pulled out a highlighter and ran it across a line in one of her textbooks. I wasn't really thinking of Annette with this, but perhaps I should have been. It appears she was on Caryn's mind. It clearly upset Caryn that I had had a romantic interest in someone new. Even though her mom had hurt her terribly by simply abandoning her, obviously it upset her for me to move on. I was suddenly a little disgusted with myself. It was very selfish of me to carry on with Annette when it upset Caryn. *A man protects those that he cares about. A man sacrifices for those he cares about.*

"With respect to Annette, I should have listened to you. I am sorry. I won't date anyone until you are comfortable with the idea."

Caryn sighed and slammed one of her books closed.

"It looks like my project will have to wait. Dad, I don't have a problem with you dating at all. I'm happy you're moving on. I just didn't like her. I didn't trust her and I was right."

She was right on the money with Annette. Her eyes didn't smile. I understood that a little better now. I was quite surprised that Caryn was ready for me to date. The matter-of-fact way she said it made me think she had actually been waiting for me to date.

"Ok, well what do I do then? I mean obviously you get the final sniff test on whoever I date."

"Well, there is loads you can do. You could meet up with other people in your situation, you could try speed dating, or online dating..."

She opened her laptop and started typing furiously.

"Let me make you a profile."

The thought of this whole thing both horrified and excited me. The prospect of finding someone new to fall in love with; to share the little moments of life; was intoxicating. It was all those things I had hoped for in a partner growing up. I had hoped to find someone to adventure with and someone who could finish my sentences and thoughts as I could hers. I had hoped to find someone, that even though we were distinct people, our essences also melted into one. In essence I was looking for someone like Dream. On the other hand, how would I know if the person I was interested in was a good one or not? How was it even possible to find someone amazing who had not been scooped up yet? What if they were another Merideth - just interested in the money while betraying me on the side? What if they were another Annette? What if they weren't even single but just playing the game to get some action on the side? I had Caryn to weed these out a bit, but even still, I was terrified I would get hurt again. I was terrified that I was just a sucker who would get played over and over again. And I was scared that if I let someone new into my life (and into Caryn's) that she might get hurt as well. How do you know when your heart is healed enough to date? Then again, how do you heal your heart without exercising it?

I moved around behind Caryn to see what she was writing about me. She was using a picture from our vacation to Fiji six or seven years ago. It was not a bad picture of me. It was certainly more exciting than an accountant usually looks.

"So what are you saying about me? Are you making me sound gruff and manly? Or is it more sensitive modern man? What are women looking for these days?"

"Dad! You have to be honest. I am writing *exactly* who you are while emphasizing the interesting parts."

*A Real Man never lies;* though apparently a real man can emphasize.

My mind drifts back to the beach. I sit in the shade of a Douglas fir with my big chunk of sandstone. Beside me lays a bucket full of water and clams. I used to track them all day, with my snorkel and mask. You could follow the dotted lines in the sand underwater. When the dots stopped, I would dive down and find a clam every time. It always felt like some sort of bank robbery. I only had so much time before my air ran out. I had to be quick and efficient. But often, despite the time limits, I would look up from the bottom of the lake to marvel at how the sun's rays played and drifted under the surface. It was a whole new sun under there. I would never keep the clams or eat them. I just liked catching them. At the end of the day I would skip them like rocks back into the lake.

I sit with my sandstone chunk, the size of my head. My boyish hand reaches down and pulls off a large clump. I can feel the grittiness of it on my fingers and palm. I squeeze with all my might, but this chunk is a tough one. I rest the sandstone in my lap and use two hands on the chunk. Then 'pop', it breaks apart and offers no more resistance. There are smaller chunks that have broken off from the main chunk. They are easy and satisfying to squish into sand. It amazes me that it could hold such resistance to start with. I mean, it must have been sand all along; just sand sticking together. My dominance of it broke its will power I suppose.

I don't know why I keep digging up this memory. It feels both random and purposeful at once. The feeling of the sun on my face, the smell of coconut from my sunscreen, and the tactile roughness of the stone makes me feel comforted and safe though. Perhaps that is the only reason a memory needs to come back into your mind.

I tossed and turned in my bed. My blankets looked twisted and gnarled like an old tree. I looked at my alarm clock and it glared 2:03 back at me with crimson eyes. I had tried sleeping on my side at least 50 times it seemed. And my back. And my stomach. I had tried beating my pillow like a boxer on a bag to fluff it up a bit. Nothing worked. It is like this many nights. In general, since the split, sleep has been elusive. Before that, I slept like a log for at least 8 hours every night. Most nights I try to exhaust myself by watching TV until I fall asleep in front of it. On the best days I get 5 hours of sleep, but in general it is 4 or less. I flip onto my side again. '2:05' my clock gloats. I hate my alarm clock. It mocks me all night with its glowing red numbers and then when I finally manage to get to sleep, it slaps me awake with its screams.

Most times it was like my mind could not shut off. I had these pieces of sharp emotional pain floating around in there. During the day, when I was working or when I was busy or when I was talking with Caryn, I could mostly ignore them. But when the world got quiet, my brain would start picking at them. It was much like having a sore in your mouth where your tongue repeatedly wants to explore it despite the pain or lack of common sense.

Some nights the bit of pain was me wondering how any mother could just walk out and abandon her own child. Some nights it was how Merideth could have racked up nearly one hundred grand in debt in my name for her music career right under my nose without me knowing and then leave me to deal with that debt. Some nights it was her utter lack of remorse for her adultery. She would say to me "Why would I feel bad about my dalliances, they were beautiful, positive, and meaningful." Those words haunted me like angry poltergeists. She would also say that remorse was a useless emotion that she would have no part of. I may have tried to work it out with her if I thought she was remorseful in the slightest. I can still hear the sobbing words of the other man's wife on the phone that September day.

"Is this Merideth's husband? I have something you need to hear...something horrible...your wife...and Trent...I mean...they... oh God..."

The pain in her voice had been raw and crisp. She could barely make a sentence. My mind dwelled often on what sort of monster can create that sort of pain for many people and not feel any remorse or shame. Instead such actions were seen as beautiful, positive, and meaningful. The words echo in my mind often. Strangely, the actual adultery was not something I dwelled upon. It had happened and it was done and gone. In the early days of the split, I would often conjure flashes of it in my mind, but that had long since passed. My mind could put that to rest. But I could not seem to let go of her lack of empathy and remorse. Neither could I shake the disappointment in myself that she had duped me so completely.

Yet tonight, none of these were the problem. I had this deep yearning, almost like an ache. I had experienced this before. When Merideth left, all of a sudden, my bed was lonely. I missed having someone next to me when I slept. I missed the intimacy and the sex. I missed the closeness. I would get restless with a yearning for that. Or perhaps it was my body grieving for the absence of another body. It was so powerful of an aching of the soul that I felt like screaming in anguish. It wasn't even arousal either. If I was simply aroused, I could have dealt with that. Instead, I tossed and turned and cried into my pillow. These feelings had diminished over time. I had come to get used to my solitude and unintentional celibacy. However, now Annette had awoken that again. It is something that I only think people who are separated or divorced can understand. We should have a term for it so we can discuss it amongst ourselves. We could say something like "Have you experienced 'Empty Bed Anguish' yet?"

It was frustrating me even more since reconnecting with Dream. I was craving more of her. I wanted to sleep deeply and find her. Even if we had no adventures or kisses or more, I still wanted to find her. Even if we just sat in silence, there was just something about her. Her soul was a balm to my own broken soul. I felt like it was healing me just to connect with her. I needed to sleep for that connection, but the more I worried about not sleeping, the more it kept me from sleeping.

I looked at my clock again. 2:14. Fuck.

As I walked into the high school, I was overwhelmed by the smell. It was not a bad smell. It was the smell of a high school. No matter how many I had been in, whether as a student or an adult, they all had the same smell. I could not describe what it smelled like if I tried, but it was unique to high schools. Perhaps it was a combination of the smells of 'Textbook' and 'Angst'. I was here as it was Wednesday night and Caryn had signed me up for a separation and divorce support group. Her idea was that this might be a good place to meet someone new. It was not a horrible idea. My initial worry with dating is that all the really good partners had likely already been scooped up by the time they got to my age. But, thinking about my own situation, Merideth left not because I was deficient or she was unhappy, she left as a consequence of her own selfishness and lack of empathy. It only made sense that there would be others in a similar situation. This is where those people would be.

It had been raining outside and when I walked down the hall my shoe made a loud and echoing squeak. I immediately stopped and looked around for a teacher. No matter how old you get, these sorts of reflexes never leave it seems. If my shoe had squeaked when I was in high school I would have been in trouble. When I think of it though, even as an adult, I can only remember my shoe squeaking like this on a high school floor. Perhaps their floors were simply designed for trouble. I was looking for room A103, which was the regular meeting place for 'Separation and Divorce - Alberta South' Society. Their acronym spelled 'Sad Ass', which I hoped would not be prophetic. I knew I was approaching the right room when I heard a murmur of voices. After a brief check of the number on the door, I dove right in.

"Hey, did you bring any fucking donuts? Cause Pam here only brought muffins."

The man in the red flannel shirt and ball cap made no bones about his feelings for muffins, judging by his air quotes as he said the word. His demeanor was rough and his belly a bit more pronounced than it likely actually was as he sat there stuffed in a desk. There was a circle of desks all facing each other all filled with people. At the back table there was a tray of muffins and coffee.

"Sue me for trying to bring a healthy alternative, Mike."

"Do I look like I give a fuck about healthy? I just want something with flavor."

He was being a bit hostile, but I understood his point.

Everything tasted like ash to me as well. However, donuts, candy, and pop all still had mild amounts of flavour. I can understand the need for that. If I had gone that way with my change in appetite, I may have ended up with a gut like Mike as well. Pam sat down. Her blonde ponytail waved left and right as she wiggled into her desk. Her eyes glossed up with tears.

"Do you always have to be such an ass?"

"Oh here we go..."

The room was tense for a second. Pam's eyes looked ready to spill into tears while Mike's glare showed he wasn't going to back down. I quietly moved a desk into the circle and eased myself into it, hoping not to get caught in the crossfire. Across from me, a lady with strawberry blonde hair noticed my attempts at stealth.

"We have a newcomer. Introduce yourself."

It diffused the tension in the room immediately. She smiled. Her smile was one of those ones you wish didn't happen. It made her face erupt into more wrinkles than you were expecting.

"Hi. I'm Dylan and I have no opinion on the muffin vs. donut debate, as long as the muffins have icing and are 'O' shaped."

There was mild laughter in the room. It was not enough to consider a career change into standup comedy, but enough to know I had eased my way into the group.

"Dylan, it is customary with new people for them to share their story."

So I did just that. I left nothing out. I told them about my discovery of her affairs. I told them about her secret line of credit opened against our mortgage. I told them about her leaving Caryn completely. I told them about her lack of remorse about her 'beautiful, positive, and meaningful' experiences. I told them about the sleeplessness and the shakes I randomly had in the months following. I told them about food being tasteless and how the world seemed completely different and bare - stripped of its meniscus of civility. All along they nodded. All along I could see the sympathy in their faces. Many times it sparked their own stories of "that happened to me too..." or "If you think that is bad, my ex..." It was refreshing to know that others had been through similar experiences and were still here to tell the tale. Through these side stories, I came to understand a lot about these people. Amber, the strawberry blonde, was the resident expert as she had two divorces under her belt. Her latest marriage ended because of physical abuse. Mike's wife left him for their dentist who had apparently been "filling her cavity" for years. Pam's ex had simply been gone one morning with a note that said "I don't love you and I never did". Sarah, the short brunette, had an ex who mounted a huge gambling debt and had been sleeping around. She only found out when her annual STD test turned up positive.

It seemed to me that they all had a similar kernel to their stories. They were all married to someone who seemed selfish and lacked empathy. It made me wonder where those people were now. They were also separated or divorced. I can see why they would not come to a meeting like this. They would likely be lynched. I pondered briefly if they had their own meetings: Pam's ex and Mike's ex and Sarah's ex and all those that were similar. It would be some dimly lit room with a pentagram on the wall. The men would all have oiled bent up moustaches while the women would have drawn in eyebrows that made them look sinister. One would say "And then I mounted her sister at the same time as I was stealing money from her nightstand" and everyone at the meeting would laugh maniacally. It could be called the 'Coalition of Uber Narcissistic Turds'. I don't need to elaborate on the acronym.

As I finished my story, it was met with quiet all around. Mike broke that silence after he finished swallowing his mouthful of coffee.

"Fuck man! I thought my wife was the biggest queen bitch, but I think yours may have stolen her tiara."

Sarah looked a little disturbed by Mike's response.

"You don't have to use the 'B' word Mike. You don't know her story."

"Actually, he is right on the money. I think that is probably too kind of a way to describe her."

I just couldn't stay quiet on the subject. There was nothing more to know. She was a serial cheater. She secretly saddled me with debt. She abandoned her daughter. She caused pain to nearly everyone she interacted with in life. I am not sure if anyone deserves the 'B' word more. This kind of talk always bothers me. It's the naive and 'head in the sand' way of our modern society to not place judgment on people. It's crap really. With actions like those, there is no story that could excuse them. Society should judge actions like hers every time - and judge them harshly. How else would they learn not to behave in such horrible ways? All our modern 'non-judgment' did was teach them that what they did was O.K. and that no matter how horribly they treated others, the cookie jar of apathy and forgiveness would remain open.

Mike nodded. Sarah shot me a dark glare, but Amber piped up before Sarah could open her mouth.

"Regardless, we try not to descend into slagging our exes here. Otherwise that is all we do. This group is about healing and moving on. And we try not to use words like 'bitch' and 'cunt' as some in the group are offended by them."

Her lips lingered on the words *Bitch* and *Cunt*. I got the feeling that she enjoyed saying them to make Sarah squirm. It was an intelligent mind that could craft a statement aimed at both telling people not to say something and to mock those who don't want it said in the first place. Intelligent - with a streak of cruelty. Sarah didn't seem bright enough to catch the slight though, smiling while Amber spoke as if she had an ally there.

"Onwards and upwards then. Does anyone have anything new this week? Is anyone dating?"

There was mainly silence and uncomfortable looks in the room. Pam shifted slightly in her seat.

"I updated my online profile this week. I didn't get any bites though other than this bald guy."

Amber smiled again. It was a genuine smile I could see, but again, those laugh lines were like tectonic ripples on her face.

"Oooh. Did you meet him yet?"

"No, I didn't even respond. Bald guys are gross."

"Fuck Pam, did you ever think that maybe he might be a great guy? It's just like you women. It's fucking hypocritical. You can say bald guys are gross and that's fine, but if we do something similar and say we don't like fat chicks, you jump all over us."

I would have wondered if Mike was bald as he was so passionate about it. His scraggy brown mullet could not have been faked though. And even if it could, who would wear a scraggy brown mullet wig?

Sarah leaned forward, wagging her finger as she talked.

"It's completely different. When Pam talks about not liking bald guys, it is just her talking about her preferences. If you say you don't like plus sized women, you are just being mean."

"Why? It's just my preference, Sarah. And say the word. It's 'Fat', not 'Plus-Sized'. It's a stupid fucking phrase. It's like calling bald 'Minus-Follicled'. Granted, fat chicks might be upset knowing that I am not attracted to them...but don't you think bald guys would feel the same hearing something similar?"

"No. It's different. Women are emotional creatures. We feel very deeply when we are attacked like that. When Pam shows discernment over baldness being attractive, even if someone bald hears that, men don't even care; it just rolls off their back. They are built differently."

"Sure Sarah. I once heard a story of a man that kicked puppies because he claimed they didn't feel pain like humans did. I can't imagine why that story now springs to mind right now."

Mike's comment was laden with sarcasm and caused instant tears to well in Sarah's eyes. She looked away while digging in her purse for a tissue. Mike just continued to look at her, nearly challenging her to keep talking. Sarah continued to fumble in her purse. I noticed a box of tissues on the table next to me so I grabbed the box and handed it to her. She turned and gave me a small smile. It was a small kindness, but one that was built into me. It was another one of my dad's maxims: *No matter the size of distress, if it is in your power to save the Damsel - do it.* I looked back to find the other women smiling as well.

"Look, you both have points. Pam is not wrong to not be attracted to bald guys. It's not like she told him that to his face. But also, Mike is right. Bald guys can be extremely sexy. Would you want to miss out on a wonderful guy because of his hair?"

Pam sighed after Amber finished.

"I know. I get it. It's just that I have certain criteria. He needs to be tall, like over 6 feet. He needs to have dark hair and olive skin. He needs to be rugged, yet also tender. He needs to be active but also intelligent. He needs to have his own business and a vacation house of some sort."

"Oh, I think I know a guy like that."

All eyes turned to Mike.

"Yeah. I think I last saw him in 'Sleeping Beauty'. That's how real he is, Pam."

"Jerk."

Such a simple word from Sarah. For someone who hated words like *bitch, jerk* was a strong sentiment. Mike just nodded and shrugged his shoulders.

"And what about you, Sarah? Any dating."

She was silent for a moment. She looked down and then back at Mike. Her eyes echoed all the pain she had gone through with her ex. Everyone could see than plain as day.

"No...I mean...I just don't think I could. Maybe eventually. I could see someday maybe having someone I went to a movie with once every week or two. But I could never live with him or marry him. There is just too much risk there. But companionship might be ok. Not yet though."

It had been four years since Sarah split with her ex. If it was

"Not yet" this far in, it probably meant "Not ever." I noticed Mike's eyes welling up a bit too.

"Yeah, I get that."

It was amazing to me that people who had been heatedly arguing just moments before could now be sympathetic with each other. Where earlier I had seen them as bitter rivals, now I could see that, while sometimes antagonistic, they were on the same path. Amber broke up my moment of introspection.

"Well, I dated this week. Twice. First was this guy named Paul. He had these huge arms and a birthmark on his neck that looks like Ireland. He was a real sweetie. He took me to this place with a waterfall in the restaurant..."

I kind of lost focus as Amber droned on about her date. I got the feeling this was a weekly thing for her. I was not sure how I felt about this group. On one hand, it felt really nice to find a group of people who had been through similar experiences and truly understood the pain of it. It was nice to be able to share my feelings openly. That felt good. However, no matter how similar our paths were in life so far, I could not help feeling that there was some key difference between them and myself. I am not sure what that difference was, but it was there. It felt like when you have a word just on the tip of your tongue. I felt like I could 'nearly' identify that difference, but kept falling short. Perhaps it was just my own vanity trying to make me feel special and separate.

Mike leaned over and tapped me on the shoulder.

"Hey buddy, you wanna grab a beer later?"

Amber kept talking

"...and his lips were so soft. He was a great kisser. And then the other guy, Erik, he was smaller, but had a really cute moustache..."

"Sure, where?"

"There's a place near here on Northmount."

"With the black awning?"

"Yup."

"Sure."

Sometimes I was in awe of male communication. We had rules about our conversations. They should be short and have the fewest words possible. We said what was needed and no more. We didn't talk about different locations. We didn't talk about who we knew that frequented each place or what they ate. None of that was relevant. We had arranged a meeting in twenty three words, which for guys may have been nearly a soliloquy.

The pub on Northmount Drive was called the 'Sunken Chest'. With the name I figured it either had some sort of pirate theme or was a topless bar. It was neither and that left me a bit perplexed. What I also noted was that Mike was late. I was used to this. I was the sort that was always on time. We didn't really specify a time to meet but I figured "After" meant immediately after, not hours later. After all *Being late is stealing someone else's time*. I was used to being on time and waiting for others.

I was using my time to scroll through profiles of possible matches on the dating site Caryn set me up on. It was an amazing thing to me. I could sit here in a pub and use my phone to scroll through potential dating partners. I could slice and dice them however I wanted to find exactly who would match me. I could search on age, hair colour, interests, religion, and pretty much anything else I could think of. I found myself looking through the pictures and trying to find pieces of Dream. Did one have her smile or her hair or her eyes? That as the sort of question I was posing to myself. It was ludicrous as these were real women and Dream was a figment of my imagination. Reading through the profiles, I was struck by their similarities. Inevitably, they all said they were down to earth, liked to laugh a lot, loved sports and snowboarding especially, and were looking for a partner in crime. The profiles were so similar that I could almost imagine a computer algorithm spitting them out. It was either amazing that all these incredible women were single, or they were just writing profiles they thought would attract a man. They could have taken it one step further and said they loved to give blow jobs and had well stocked beer fridges in their living rooms.

I suppose I should not have been surprised. There was a reason they called it the dating 'Game'. People showed you the face they thought you wanted to see until they were comfortable showing you their true selves. Really what I wanted to read in the profiles was the things that made people unique or even weird. I wanted to know if someone had a full Star Trek uniform in their closet or collected Roman coins or snort laughed during funny movies or had an irrational fear of frogs. Those are the things that would have made it real for me. At the end of the day, I think it is not the face and eyes and body that we yearn for, but a matching of our weird spots. I could be deeply attracted to the curve of the hips or breasts or to a beautiful face, but it is the hearty snort laugh that I would fall in love with. If only there was a dating site that catered to this thinking.

I pushed through these thoughts and found five profiles that I thought sounded interesting enough. Of course they were all down to earth and loved to laugh and liked to snowboard, but they also showed a hint of personality as well. I sent all five an email introducing myself.

I took a sip of my cider as Mike strolled up.

"Hey, sorry I'm late. I had to make sure my kids were still ok with the sitter"

"You have kids?"

"Well yeah, two of them. One is mine and one is from my ex's last marriage."

Mike snapped his fingers as the waitress walked by.

"Beer."

"Wait, she was married before you?"

"Yup. She was married out of high school. She had a kid with the guy. He was a bit of a deadbeat, but I only have her info for that. She started seeing me while she was still married to him."

"What?"

Mike had just admitted that he had been sleeping with a married woman. It was shocking.

"I know, I know. I can see the look on your face. In my defense, I didn't know she was married. She left that part out. And once I found out we were a year into our relationship and she fed me all sorts of stuff about him. She said he was emotionally abusive and cruel. And she told me she was leaving the marriage. She did leave it and got married to me. I felt like the knight in shining armor sweeping in to save her."

I understood that well. I think all boys are raised to be knights. We are all raised to want to protect the damsel in distress. I thought about my own recent experiences with Annette and understood all too well how we can be used because of that. It seemed his ex had done the same thing. The waitress brought his beer and slid it over. As he lifted it to take a drink, a circle of water was left on the table.

"Anyway, her ex killed himself months later. I can never have his side of the story. But you know the rule about damsels in distress, right? You can only remain a damsel in distress if you create a new villain. I'm sure he was that 'new villain', and now I have likely inherited that title. Did you know that divorced males have the highest rate of suicide?"

"No, I didn't."

It was not exactly a shock. Separation was a truly gut wrenching emotional ordeal. That went for both genders. However, it seems that females retain a system of support through their separation - friends, family, etc. Males lose all their friends. Most males only have couple friends before a separation as their single friends are often squeezed out. Single male friends often don't mesh well with a couple. After a separation, all the 'couple' male friends stick by the woman in the relationship and not the man. The male is left with no support. Add to this that there is a stereotype in modern society that in a split it must be somehow the man's fault. I had believed this at one point as well. I had assumed that since relationships failed because of something wrong that the man did, and since I was a good guy that always honoured his relationship and his partner, that my relationship would never fail. I never dreamed that it would be my wife who could do something to break us up. It put pressure on men even when we were the victims. Add to that being cast as the 'new villain' when you had been nothing but chivalrous, and the pressure could be unbearable. In essence society fails separated and divorced men and leaves them with no hope. It is no wonder many kill themselves. I have wandered around not really caring if I died since the split, but I never went as far as to try to kill myself. However, it did leave me wondering if I was the 'new villain' to my ex's new boyfriend and my old friends. I likely was. I was curious what fictions were being spun to cast me as such.

"Well, welcome to the club. I pretty much raised her daughter from that guy and had a son with her as well. She technically has full custody of her daughter and shared custody half time of Jason, but they both end up at my place quite often as she has a bit of a cocaine addiction and can't handle the stress of kids."

"So you take care of your step daughter as well?"

I was getting a different picture of Mike here. He seemed so gruff and abrasive in the group, but it really showed a lot of compassion to not just father your own kid, but take in your ex's kid from a previous marriage because she can't handle it.

"Yeah, life is fucked up eh? I take care of them nearly full time, while also paying her child support and spousal support every month. I can barely afford my two bedroom apartment and Kraft dinner while she lives with the dentist like a princess. And I still have to pretend to these kids that their mom is a wonderful person and not a monster. What a fucking crock, eh? I wish they would just get married so I could at least stop paying spousal support. I should have known since she cheated on her ex with me. Once a cheater, always a cheater."

These are the stories you just didn't hear in our society. You always heard about the deadbeat dad, the dad that refused to pay anything to support his kids. You heard about the saintly single mom working three jobs to pay for her kids. It is not that I didn't think that those existed. I believe they do, however, it seems that it goes the other way as well. Mike was an example of that. It seemed so unfair that his ex could cheat on him, hardly take care of his kids, live in luxury, while he busted his ass to take care of everyone and barely scrape by.

"Tell me, Dylan, what made you join the group?"

"Well, to be honest, I was hoping to jump back into the dating pool and thought it might be a good place to look. That and I wanted to talk to people who had been through something similar. And you?"

"Fuck, I just like a good place to vent my pain. Why would you want to date? I will tell you that the only thing out there are other women looking for a free ride in life. Either that or they are looking to upgrade to a better free ride in life."

I didn't agree. I had been screwed over by Merideth and more recently I had been taken advantage of by Annette, but that was hardly representative of everyone out there. There were lots of people in happy relationships and I am sure there were lots of women out there who still valued things like honour and trust and honesty like I did. Wasn't there?

"I don't know man...I still think there are women out there who aren't like that."

"Let me put it to you another way. I read an article about adultery and primates a couple of years ago. It was on chimps or something. This lady went out and lived among them for a while and looked for patterns in how and when they would cheat. You won't find this article out there anymore as her research was treated with scorn. Anyway, she proposed that relationships were like a contract. Since primates, us included, have a long period where the young need to be protected, the mother needs extra protection and help. The contract is basically the female saying to the male 'If you help protect and provide, then I will allow you to have abundant sex with me'."

Mike took a giant swig of his beer. I saw his other hand shaking as he did. I could only assume that this was tough for him to talk about as adultery talk would only bring up pain points for him. I didn't mention his hand shaking and I didn't look him in the eyes as I am sure I would have found them glazing up with tears and it would have shamed him to know that I knew this was affecting him emotionally. I felt honoured that he would talk about something that hurt him so much, likely to save me pain in my life. He barely knew me.

"What she found is that the males cheated when the contract was broken. When they were refused sex, they went elsewhere to find it. It is crappy of them, but I can understand the base logic of it. The more disturbing thing that she found was that the females cheated only when the contract was *solid*. When she had a stable partner who would protect her and provide for her, she would then use that stability to gallivant around and sleep with partners she found more worthy. If the more worthy male worked out, then she might make a new contract with him. But often it was just adulterous sex that didn't go into a new contract."

I downed a big gulp of my cider. What he was saying to me disturbed me on a deep level. I did not want to think that these behaviours were something that happened on a basic animalistic level. Was adultery instinctual and ingrained in us then? I could not believe that. Even the primates in this study were acting on more than instinct. It seemed, based on the description, that they were putting calculated thought into their actions. I guess all it proved to me was that animals could be assholes too.

"That is chimps though. We are a bit more evolved, right?"

"Are we Dylan? Ask yourself this - have you had any experiences that were different than this? I know I didn't. My ex did that to her first husband. When it was stable, she sought out something better. And when it was stable with me, she upgraded again to the dentist. And it is more than just an upgrade, she gets the dentist and she also gets all sorts of money from me as well. It's a super deal for her. Your ex did exactly the same."

He was right. I could not think of one example in my relationships either with Merideth or before where I could contradict him. I felt like my world was sinking beneath me. How could that even make sense? Though how could there be so much practical experience that verified it without it making sense?

"I mean, come on. Haven't you always wondered why guys who are complete assholes to their women always seem to have women who stick by them? It's simple. To the women, the contract is not stable, so they stay faithful and loyal. Haven't you always wondered why women stay with these assholes and don't leave? Doesn't it make sense now? I bet you were like me. I bet you were the good guy and did all the right things and treated her like a queen. And she fucked you over anyway. Am I right?"

I nodded. He was right. He was right about all of it. I had always wondered why women would stay with men who treated them horribly and cheated on them and generally made them lesser. Now it made sense. The contract was unstable, so they stayed. I had countless crushes on women (and girls when I was a boy) in these situations. I had naively thought that if they hung out with me and saw what a good guy I was; if they saw what an honourable man really was; they would leave their asshole boyfriend and want to date me. That never happened even once. Now I know why. Hell, it even explained Annette. She stayed with Laird as their contract wasn't stable. It truly bothered me that there was a kernel of belief growing inside me. This primate adultery theory had tied it up neatly and given me explanations for many things which seemed illogical to me in the world. I didn't want to believe it, but it was tough to defy belief in something that had so much empirical evidence. The world was exactly opposite to how I thought it worked. I thought that if you were honourable and good that you would get good things in life and a good relationship. Instead, it appeared that the slime balls of the world got the good things. The honourable folks got taken advantage of. There was absolutely no benefit to being a good guy. Perhaps I was just a late bloomer. Perhaps other guys had figured this out earlier and traded in their honour for a life of success and happiness. Perhaps I was a fool - a fool who believed in some antiquated sense of honour. I was like that last kid in a class to believe in Santa Claus. Maybe it was time I grew up. Fuck honour. All of my dad's wisdom and mantras and rules did absolute shit for me in the real world. Maybe it was time to abandon them.

Mike looked at me. I am sure I looked like I had been hit by a truck. Sometimes truth is like that. Truth is like a cement truck with no brakes.

"Look man. These are just my thoughts. Perhaps the 'good woman' is out there, but she is rare - like fucking unicorn rare. Personally, I am not going to risk it. No dating for me. I will take care of my kids and fuck when I can and fill my life with other things that make me happy. For example..."

He downed the rest of his beer.

I was walking in a swamp. Or at least I think it was a swamp. My feet were getting stuck each step I moved forwards, but it was too misty to make anything out completely. I was not sure why I was here or where I was going, but I knew I had to keep doing so. The water and mud between the toes of my bare feet felt odd and disconcerting with every step I took.

A small hand took my own. I looked to my left to see Caryn walking with me.

"Caryn, why are we here?"

She simply put her finger to her lips and kept walking. In front of us in the mist, a wall formed. It was a massive stone wall covered in runes and vines. It was very tall, but only ten feet wide. Caryn let go of my hand.

"I will go around one side and you go around the other"

I nodded and smiled all the while being filled with a sense of horror. Why would we go different ways? That made no sense. But she was already walking around the left side of the wall. The mist swirled around me as I walked around the right. As I got around to the other side, Caryn was nowhere to be found. Where was she? Oh my god, I can't lose her! She is the most important thing in my life. I turned back to the wall to find the runes gone. The wall was now smooth and concrete and dripping with slime.

"Caryn! Where are you? Caryn!"

There was no answer. I sprinted left and right looking for signs of her. Nothing. Where had she gone?

"Caryn!"

I turned to run the other way and ran right into someone. I looked up. Her hair. Her eyes. The smile. It was Dream. Happiness came over me like a sunrise. She would help.

"My daughter, she's missing. Can you help?"

"Are you sure she was here?"

"What? Yes...just a moment ago..."

She chuckled.

"Are you sure I am here?"

Then she faded. She disappeared. She melted into the mist.

"No! Come back!"

Everywhere I turned now, the wall was in front of me. I was in a box made up of those walls and the slime was filling it up fast. I cried out as it rose up to my head.

"NO!!!"

I woke up. The TV was blaring some horror movie. I must have fallen asleep watching it. My dinner plate was on the coffee table still. It was only half eaten. There was no sign of Caryn. She must have eaten hers and cleaned it up. I was relieved it was just a dream. I could not lose her. I would have to talk to her about watching horror movies though. I was not sure it was appropriate for her age.

It was Monday and I was back in the board room at B.R. Pratt. It was our weekly status meeting which I found pretty useless. Everyone on the senior team would talk about their client (or clients) and specific problems they were facing. The problem was that no one really gave a shit about the other people's clients and it was considered a *faux pas* to comment on their strategies. Most people were quick on their status updates, but it was Tim's turn and I absolutely despised Tim. He was the type of person who liked to hear himself talk. He was talking about his client's ongoing 4 way joint venture partnership on some oil wells that turned into an acquisition of two of the joint venture partners and the strategy he was taking to account for that. The problem was that his strategy was absolute crap. It may even get his client in trouble if they were ever audited. Normally I would do one of two things. I would either just keep my mouth shut or I would make subtle hints about the project until Tim 'came up with' the idea himself. I was done with that though. The good guys never get ahead. Time to be bold.

"Tim, that's a dumb idea. I will tell you why and I will tell you what you need to do instead..."

I laid out my reasoning for why Tim had it all backwards and my ideas for how it could be done better. I didn't try to spare any feelings; I just told it like it was. Tim didn't appear impressed by my talk, but the rest of the team was entranced. I was expecting some backlash or something. I expected there to be uproar if I ever behaved like that.

As the meeting let out, my boss tapped me on the shoulder as I was exiting.

"That was bold, Dylan. Very bold. I like it."

My first foray into abandoning being 'the good guy' was so far a success. I had helped B.R. Pratt, my boss was happy with it, and the almighty Tim had been taken down a few notches.

I entered the coffee shop high on my new found work accomplishments. I normally didn't take breaks in my day to stop at a coffee shop, but I had arranged a 'Coffee Date' with one of the women I emailed from the dating site. I had never even heard of a coffee date before, but apparently it was a micro-date to make sure you were normal enough to go on a real date some other time. I guess it was a prudent measure when your first interaction with someone is online. I would have rather just jumped right into a regular date, but I understood the reasoning.

I ordered a coffee and sat down in a comfy couch next to a table. I didn't think my date was here yet. I was looking for a slim blonde who was down to earth, liked hiking and snowboarding, and was very active. There was no one that looked like her picture in the coffee shop. I was used to waiting for people though. People were always late.

"Dylan?"

A woman with shoulder length auburn hair was staring down at me. She was slightly plump but had a pretty smile and hazel eyes. I had no idea how this woman knew me. I quickly rifled through my memories for someone that looked similar. I came up blank.

"...Ummmm..."

"It's Heather...you know....from the site?"

I couldn't believe it. This was not the slim blonde I was looking for. She sat down opposite me.

"Yeah, I know, you were probably looking for a blonde. That's my friend Karen's picture. Men like blondes more so I thought I would have more luck with her picture. So far so good, right?"

"Good to meet you Heather."

It is not that I was disappointed with her looks. I am one gentleman who doesn't always prefer blondes. She was attractive and maybe a bit on the chubby side, but not anything that was a deal breaker. I would have definitely sent her an email if she had put her own picture up. But the deception of it bothered me. I felt tricked. I decided to press on with the coffee date though as that was just one small thing. Who knows, she might turn out to be great. I decided to ask her a question about her profile.

"So, where do you do your hiking?"

"What do you mean?"

This was not the answer I was expecting. Around Calgary people will answer this with Banff, Waterton, Kananaskis, or maybe 'The Ghost'. I figured it would be a good conversation jumping off point.

"Your profile said you liked to hike."

She laughed.

"Oh that. I put that on there as they suggest you have a sport on your profile. I don't really do sports though. I am not sure why people hike with all those bears out there and stuff."

I was not sure what to think here. It's not like I needed someone to be a hiker to date them. I just don't like being lied to. Merideth lied to me for years. I am still uncovering her lies. I think it is only understandable l that I am a little sensitive to someone lying to me.

She smiled at me. I think she took my silence for something other than annoyance.

"This is going well, don't you think? I can't wait to tell Karen!"

"Actually, for me, it's not."

The old me would have just played along. I just saw no need

to let this down easy. How could any relationship make a go of it if it started out with deception?

"What do you mean?"

"Well, look, you seem really nice, but you lied to me twice before we even met. I am just sensitive to that."

She stared at me for a moment.

"Well your profile is getting a frowny face, mister."

I deserved that.

Mike's belly laugh echoed off the walls. It was Wednesday night in the separation and divorce group and we once again got on the topic of dating. I made sure to bring donuts this time. This week I had something to share so I regaled them with my 'Heather' story.

"Frowny face. Hilarious."

"Maybe she was just scared to share herself to start with"

Sarah was always quick to defend the women's side of anything. I could understand that, but it made it frustrating to talk about.

"Come on, Sarah. Would you have started any sort of relationship with someone when the first two things you learned about them were lies?"

She shook her head. She got that. She had been lied to for years by her ex as well. She understood the pain of lies well enough.

"Just the one coffee date?"

Amber was always thirsty for this information. I think it fueled her somehow. She was wearing big hoop earrings tonight that made me wonder how her ears supported them.

"Well, there was another one, but it was even worse. It felt like a job interview. She asked me how much money I made, how big my house was, what kind of car I drove. When I told her where I lived she commented on how much closer that was to where she worked. It felt like she was moving in already. It felt a bit like I was being measured up as a new 'provider'. I guess it made me feel a bit dirty, like I was going to be used, you know?"

"I don't know. Those are important things to know. Maybe she already found you attractive and engaging and just wanted to make sure you fit the other things on her list."

Pam and her list. That is exactly why lists are bad. No one wants to feel measured against an impossible Prince Charming. We want to feel loved for us and not for our paychecks and our 'stuff'.

"Come on Pam, if I was on a coffee date and asked a girl how big her boobs were and if they were natural or not, I would be considered a pig. But those are genuinely on my list."

Sarah and Pam shot Mike an angry look, but Amber just laughed.

"Well, it's true that men initially are attracted to the physical while a lot of women are drawn to that feeling of being able to provide. Either way, it may be a bit rude to size someone up so obviously. Still that is the game. We all size each other up on what is attractive or not. Why should we judge someone for doing so? Why not just try it on like a shoe to see how it fits?"

At the word 'fits', Amber winked while making an 'ok' sign with one hand and sticking the index finger of her other hand in and out of the 'O' in rapid motion. Sarah's eyes went wide.

"Amber!"

"Ah, don't tell me you couldn't use a little *fitting*"

Amber's grin was just as blatant as Sarah's blush.

I carried the clean coffee maker down the hallway of the high school. Amber followed me with what remained of the clean paper cups. It was my turn to help clean up. Amber too, I suppose. I didn't mind it really. There was a certain rhythm people got into cleaning up. We were mainly silent as I swept and she wiped the desks down and cleaned the coffee maker. Once in a while we would talk briefly back and forth. It was amazing to me that the room had an echo once we were down to two people. At what point does an echo start? Echoes are such lonely things. Perhaps they are psychological. Perhaps they start the moment you feel the absence of other people.

As we entered the supply closet, Amber turned and closed the door quickly. I placed the coffee maker on the shelf carefully and turned to see why she had done that.

"What..."

Amber raised an eyebrow.

"Isn't it obvious?"

She dropped the paper cups on the ground purposefully and grinned.

"Oops. Clumsy me!"

She bent over to pick up the cups. It wasn't a gentle bend over. It was like she was folding herself in two and sticking her butt out at the same time. As she did so, her mini skirt lifted up. She was not wearing underwear. Did she not have any underwear on all evening? I am certain I would have noticed if she was going commando when we were all sitting in a circle in those uncomfortable desks. I knew I shouldn't look. A gentleman didn't look. When a lady exposed herself accidentally, a gentleman looked away. But I couldn't. I was somehow ensnared by the whole idea of it. She looked backwards while bent over and caught me looking. This was bad. It would likely embarrass her. She winked with her eye and then with something else. It was shocking and unexpected.

"You like?"

She stood up again and put the paper cups on the shelf next to the coffee machine. She rubbed up against me as she did. There was absolutely no way she did not feel my growing erection as she did so.

"I will take that as your answer."

She lingered as she brought her hands down, her body touching mine. I could smell the wintergreen of the gum she was chewing as she looked me in the eye. I thought back to that moment in Annette's apartment. Oh my god. Amber was hitting on me. I was not sure what to do. I had no kind way to tell her that creviced crow's feet and hoop earrings worked as reverse Viagra for me. But despite that, her stunt bending over had me hard. I wasn't attracted to her in the slightest, but here I was erect. I had to stop this before she got the wrong idea.

"Look Amber, I'm flattered, but..."

I tried to push past her but she was quick as a snake. She blocked the door with her body before I got there and I nearly slammed into her. She looked me right in the eye and didn't drop her gaze.

"Dylan. You aren't my type either. This isn't about attraction."

She took her hand and slid it down the front of my pants. She grabbed me and stroked slowly. It felt wonderful.

"This is about a good old roll in the hay."

She squeeze and twisted just slightly as she stroked while looking me right in the eye. In this light her crow's feet didn't look that bad. She was confusing my mind all around. I knew what she wanted, and I knew that I could. I also didn't think I wanted to. I wasn't sure. I didn't like to be rushed into these things. I really needed to get out of here, but what she was doing felt so good. I felt panicked.

"I just..."

She put her other finger to her lips.

"Shh. You don't seem to understand. I am not letting you go until you fuck me. Ok?"

It seemed too final. There were all sorts of conflicting emotions zipping around in my head. She really wanted something and something I could provide. It would be wrong of me to say no. She would be mad at me if I said no. I wasn't sure I wanted to. If we did it, would she want me to do this every time? I didn't want that.

My mind was against the idea, but my body really wanted to. That and I would have to really force her out of the way to get out and that would be seen as violence, which was not very gentlemanly. Fuck 'gentlemanly' though. Wasn't I through with that shit? Why did I keep thinking like that? What would the stereotypical jerk do? It was easy. He would have sex with no emotional attachment, enjoy it, and get on with his life. This was exactly what she was proposing, so why not?

"O.K."

It was a small word and I was surprised when it came out of my mouth. And soon after our clothes were in a pile on the floor. I was on my back with her on top. She was slow, yet rough, and her hoop earrings swung back and forth in the incandescent light of the supply closet.

It was raining when I got to my car. I had been running to get there as quick as I could. I slammed my door, my jacket and hair were soaked despite my efforts to stay dry. The rain pounded on my windshield so hard that the world looked distorted outside. I was breathing heavy from running. When it slowed to normal, I noticed a smell. It was all over me: wintergreen. Suddenly my mind flashed back to the supply closet. It seemed so small and I wanted to escape. I felt like a caged animal. Why did I agree? Why did I not push my way past her? Why was I weak? I felt really dirty and wrong. I understood what happened, and yet I didn't. I leaned on my steering wheel and cried. *Men don't cry.*

I did cry though. I cried for a good ten minutes while thinking about the whole situation. The rain was my mask. I did just what the jerks of the world would do, and I felt horrible. Sure I just had sex, but it felt so hollow and empty. I felt badly that I agreed to it even though that is what she wanted. I felt badly for being so curt with Heather. I even felt badly about how I behaved to obnoxious

Tim. Outwardly, it seemed like my life was better, but it had pushed me to a place where I felt bad about myself and put me in a situation where I felt very used.

The tears wouldn't stop. *Men don't cry.* Damn you dad. His rules, his honour - they were ingrained in me now. They were too much a part of me. Going against them was like going against myself. It was like putting a mask on and that mask was of every man I despised. It was the mask of every man that went against the code of honour and chivalry. It was the mask of every man that gave men a bad name. How could I wear that?

I was still a mess when I came in the door. I wasn't crying like I had been, but my eyes were bloodshot and still a bit leaky. I came in slowly and tried to me as normal as I could. Caryn came around the corner as I put my jacket away.

"Dad."

I turned away from her and walked down the hallway. That girl had some sort of radar when I was sad.

"Dad? What's wrong?"

"Nothing."

I kept from looking at her as I rushed to my bedroom. The tears flowed again as I closed my door. Caryn pounded on it.

"Dad. It's ok. I know you cry."

*Men don't cry.*

"No. No it isn't."

I ducked down to reload and she covered me while I did. I had stupidly chosen a shotgun as my primary weapon. Sure it looked cool and sure it did a lot of damage, but I only got two good shots off before I needed to reload. She was amazing. I am not quite sure how someone can pull off sexy in that outfit, but she did. Tan cargo pants bulging with survival gear and death dealing devices, a simple grey t-shirt, an eye patch, and a back quiver. I nearly fumbled loading my second shell admiring how awesome she was as she dispatched the walking dead with her longbow one after another.

"There's a clog of them coming!"

I nodded, snapped my shotgun closed, and grabbed a grenade. As I rose again, I saw she was right. There was quite a clump of them coming towards us. It had started about two years ago. No one knew where the virus started. All we knew now is there were hordes of reanimated dead. The only thing they had in common were their glassy stares, their missing ring fingers, and their hunger for the flesh of the living. We were calling them the 'Broken People'.

I pulled the pin and tossed the grenade. She did the same. Then we ducked behind our sandbag bunker. There was a moment of simple moans from the shambling mass, then two bass-filled bangs, then following that, the world erupted in orange. A flaming leg soared above us. She laughed her boisterous laugh as the world came back to normal. My ears were ringing, but I didn't care as she pulled me over and kissed me.

A close sounding moan brought us back to our task. We were up in a flash. Seven or eight broken people were still shambling about. One of them raised his arm as if to point as us, but the gesture was lost without his ring finger. I took out two right away with my shotgun and then dropped it. She had done the same with her bow. I threw one of my throwing knives and hit one the leg. She spun and took him out with her bow. One was crawling over our sandbags behind her. I dived around, pulling out my machete and cut the head off. That was the last of them.

We were breathing heavy and sweating. She lifted her eye patch to reveal a perfectly good eye.

"What? It looks cool. And thanks by the way. I thought that one was going to get me."

I was about to tell her it was no problem, but was interrupted by the heavy drone of a flyer. I am not sure how the living dead figured out how to strap a jet pack to themselves, but they did. A jet pack with flame throwers. The flyers were the most dangerous kind. It tore around the corner, leaving a caterpillar of dark brown smoke behind it. Black goggles covered its face. This one had large golden hoop earrings glinting in the sunlight as well.

My companion didn't even miss a beat. She took her tomahawk out of the sling at her waist and threw it in an impossibly long shot. End over end it went until it sunk into the head of its victim in a meaty thunk. The jet pack then careened the body this way and that until it slammed straight into the side of a building, exploding.

"Wow. That was crazy good."

She shrugged.

"Why hide my awesome, right?"

I grabbed her hand and suddenly the scene shifted. It was twilight on a green hill. A massive gnarled tree stood behind us and fireflies danced everywhere. We each had small nets in our hands. Immediately we were running around the tree trying to catch the fireflies.

"Hey, what was with that bit in the mist and swamp the other day?"

"Oh, I had lost something or someone and I was looking for them."

What had I lost? I had forgotten. It was something important.

"It looked to me like you were losing yourself. You looked like you were transforming into a Slobber-Headed Mud Fish. You had the gills and face protrusions and everything"

Was I turning into a Slobber-Headed Mud Fish? That didn't seem right, but I didn't see what she saw. That and it seemed somehow right. I could remember there being a change in me lately. A dark change. I remember that somehow I was doing this change intentionally and that I thought it would make my life better.

"I nearly did become one I think. It seemed like the Slobber-Headed Mud Fish were the winning team."

"Honestly man! What were you thinking? A thousand lifetimes losing as me is still way better than one lifetime winning as a Slobber-Headed Mud Fish."

She was right of course. What point was there on being on a winning team if you hated yourself for it? Did you really win if you had to compromise your own values and self? To do so I would have to be someone I wasn't. Any time you have to act like someone you are not, you lose automatically. So, I suppose, it was only logical to conclude that when you act with honour and are true to yourself, even if the battle is lost, you can never lose personally. Authenticity is its own victory.

"No worries. It was not something I could ever really do. The transformation would never take anyway. I am filled with too much amazing for that."

She tackled me and we ended up on our backs looking up at the sky and the branches of the tree. It was daytime again. We held hands there and watched the clouds go by.

"And don't ever forget that."

It was a whisper she uttered and it was soft as a newborn wish. I wanted to stay under this tree with her forever. It made the heart beating in my chest fill with warmth. It made contentment within me bubble with effervescence.

"I wish you were real."

She let go of my hand at once and propped herself up on her elbow. There was anger in her eyes. I regretted saying the words even though they were true. The sky turned to dark clouds and lighting struck a nearby hill.

"You don't think I'm real? How dare you! Even when my life got extremely rocky, I always knew you were real. I am real and I am closer than you think."

"I'm sorry. I just yearn for you. I want to know you not just in this world. I want you in the other world too - the one we forget when we are here."

She sat up into a cross legged position. Her face changed. It wasn't mad anymore. It seemed sad. I sat up as well. We looked into each other's eyes for a long time.

"Why have you never found me there, then?"

That was a good question. This was the one person that I felt completely connected to. She was here in front of me as real as any woman I have ever met. Why did I not think she was real before? There are always lots of characters in this world, but some seem more concrete than others, and she did most of all. Of course she was real. Why did I never look for her? I think I was scared to. I think that maybe I thought that if I looked for her and failed, it would crush me. The truth is that there is no one else I would want to be with. What was stopping me now?

"I was scared but I don't think I am anymore. I want to find you."

A bumble bee buzzed around her as she looked at me. She smiled and tilted her head to the left. I found myself mirroring her position. The bee continued to circle her. It landed on her outstretched palm and walked around calmly as if her hand was a flower.

"Where do I look?"

"If you want to find me, follow the bees."

Her eyes drew me in. I could look into them forever. I did not even realize she had transferred the bee to my own hand. I felt it tingle so I turned my gaze to watch it. She became a blur in my periphery.

"Just follow the bees."

I said it to myself. The words came slowly but they rang of truth. Of course. I should have thought of that before. Just follow the bees. It walked up my arm and tickled me as it walked across my chest. Then as it reached the left hand side of my chest, it wiggled its butt in a little dance. Then it jammed its stinger into my flesh. Sting!

OUCH.

He wiggled again. Sting!

OUCH.

Ring!

What was that ringing and why did my chest hurt?

Ring!

It was my phone. Who calls at this time in the morning? I picked it up.

"Hello?"

"Dylan, it's me."

Merideth. It woke me up immediately, like someone dumped a bucket of ice on my bed. It scared me and made me angry at the same time. Why was she calling here? What did she want? Why couldn't she just stay away?

"What do you want?"

"Look, there is a man coming to your house with papers this week. I just need to know you will not be crazy with this."

There is only one reason that she would think I would be crazy about this is if there was something crazy in the papers. I was being 'served' papers. That is what this is about.

"What is this about?"

"Dylan, I need some spousal support. I am entitled to it."

Of course. It always came back to money. She used money like it was candy for her music career. I would bust my ass at work to help fuel her dreams and the money would just flow. Apparently it had more flow than I had thought - nearly $100,000 more. It made sense. She was with Trent now and he likely wasn't giving her money for her music.

"Why?"

"Oh, it's horrible Dylan. Trent's ex is sucking him dry for child support and spousal support. We have no money. You have money from your job and it is my legal right to have part of that."

"So, let me get this straight. It is horrible for Trent's ex to do this, but your legal right for you to do it? Why don't you just get a job?"

"I don't understand. That's a completely different situation. Besides, I have a job. I work part time at the flower shop."

This was classic Merideth. She could never see a situation from any viewpoint outside her own. I had not truly understood this about her until I discovered her adultery and I had tried to work it out with her. She saw nothing wrong with her affairs. I had asked her how she would feel if I had cheated on her. She said she would be devastated and that I would have been a complete asshole if I did that. I then asked her if she understood how I felt then. She looked at me perplexed and then told me that it was completely different. It was hypocrisy. Once I saw this in her, though, I could remember examples of this in all of her failed friendships over the years. She was 100% selfish and 0% empathy; a complete narcissist.

"I mean a real job. A nine to five job. That way you can pay for things yourself. You do have that fancy university degree."

"Dylan, jobs are unfair. They are the yoke of our capitalistic society. They stifle artistic spirits like mine. You cannot expect me to work one. It would kill me inside."

This was not a new view of hers. She had had this view for years. In a way, I could agree. However, starvation was also unfair. One needed money not to starve, so a job was necessary. It was hypocritical again though. It was unfair of her to have a job, but perfectly ok for me to have one and for her to request half my money from it. Besides, she was perfectly happy spending all the unfair job money on her music.

"Look, perhaps we can consider this, but after you pay off the music debt you left me with."

"I knew you would be like this about it. Why do you always have to be so greedy, Dylan? Why does it always have to be about money with you? My music is like my children. You cannot put a price on art like that. It is timeless and should not be shackled with the tyranny of coin."

The tyranny of coin. I used to love the poetic way she thought and talked. Now it made me nauseous. Of course, it was greed when I talked about the debt she should be paying off, but it wasn't greed for her to ask for spousal support. It was only about the money as she had phoned me at six in the morning to ask for money. I could argue more about it, but she never saw the logic of things, unless it affected her directly. It was useless and it made me angry. What made me angrier was her talking about her music as her children. What about her actual child? What about Caryn, who she had abandoned?

"Why didn't you...I mean...why....not Caryn..."

I tried to talk, but the words just didn't come out right. I was too upset.

"That is unfair."

Her words felt like arrows. They shocked me. She was so unfeeling when it came to Caryn. She was a monster. I hung up.

I could never tell Caryn the things her mom said. It was enough that Caryn was abandoned. It would make it worse for her to know her mom was so cold and uncaring.

I thought back to Dream and her words to me last night. Could I really find her? Could she be real? Why not? If I was going to look for someone, why not look for my dream girl. I thought about the 'Broken People' we were fighting. They were zombies, but they reminded me of the people I had met. They reminded me of Pam and Mike and Sarah and Amber and Heather. There were so many broken people out there. They were broken by their exes and how they were treated. They were exposed to the true nature of society and it broke them. Each of them, in their own way, was using a strategy to keep themselves from meeting someone new and exposing themselves to hurt. Mike took on a gruff and asshole-ish persona in order to keep people at bay. Pam put impossible standards out there so that no one would ever meet them. Amber treated relationships as trivial and fleeting so that none would ever be serious again. Sarah was perhaps the most honest. At first she seemed bitchy, but in reality she was just so broken that she honestly said she didn't think she could do it again. She was withdrawing into becoming 'the cat lady'. That's how crazy cat ladies are made. I am sure if I put in the time for years and years, I could bring her out of this state and she would be ready for dating. However, was it worth it? I would rather invest my time in seeing someone that was not broken-someone like Dream.

But was I broken myself? This question lingered in my mind. If I was one of the 'Broken People', then perhaps I did not deserve to be with someone like Dream. The more I thought about it, the more I began to think that I was not broken. I still held out hope for that partner who would love me and whom I would love. I still thought people existed who were honourable and compassionate and loving. I thought they were the minority, to be sure, but I believed they existed. That and I am not sure the 'Broken People' are introspective enough to ask themselves if they were broken. 'Broken People' didn't know they were broken. They thought they were strong in a world where everyone was selfish and evil.

They served a purpose though. I am glad I met them because they showed me what I did not want to become. I didn't want to still be in the divorce and separation group years from now, complaining about my coffee dates and occasionally boinking someone in the supply closet. I didn't want to turn into a gruff asshole to keep people at bay. I wanted to live again. I wanted to love again. I wanted to trust again.

I could continue down the road I was going, or I could chase some bees. It was that simple. The choice was easy.

# THE BEES AND THE ZEE

I woke up early. The sun was just peeking over the horizon and sending spears of gold into my room. The light was refreshing right down to my soul. My eyes were open and I felt rested and for once I woke and didn't feel like I was hung over. I seemed to wake feeling hung over all the time these days whether I had been drinking or not. You start to think you might as well drink. But today I didn't wake like the living dead. Today I felt nearly like a normal person.

I stepped into the shower and the spray felt warm and comforting. Sometimes I would just stand under it without even doing shampoo or soap. Sometimes I just liked that warm and liquid embrace to think under. I closed my eyes and let it pour over me. In ways, I felt like my decision to 'Chase Bees' was completely insane. It made no sense in the civilized and logical world. It was completely absurd. However, deep down inside me, it made complete sense. Dream was the most real and complete person I had met anywhere. Why should she not exist? To me now, it was simply a matter of finding her. The surface absurdity of it didn't seem to bother me, or perhaps since the logical and civilized world had utterly failed me I felt no obligation to play by its rules. In fact, to embark on this journey felt like a bit of a "Fuck you" to the civilized and sane world and that felt good.

When the last of the soap and lather was gone, I turned off

the water with my left hand. Often I called my left hand 'The Betrayer' as its sudden actions turning off the water left only cold surrounding me. I could never stay mad at it though as it was also the hand that grabbed the towel.

I was just flipping my seventh crepe when Caryn came into the kitchen. She was wearing her blue pajamas with spirals on them and rubbing the sleep from her eyes. I was making crepes partly because they were her favorite and partly because it just felt good to make them. There was a satisfaction in forming a meal from base components instead of having frozen waffles or a sugary boxed cereal. I had also always believed there was a certain alchemy to making food from scratch; as if my good mood could be transmuted into a tasty breakfast.

"Mmm. It's been ages since you made these."

I nodded. I guess I just didn't have the energy or motivation to make them lately. I loved them though. My mom always made them when I was a kid. She would pour them, rotate the pan to make them round (or to make shapes she claimed were animals) then flip them. I remember how they sounded as though they were screaming as she pressed the flipper into them after they were flipped. It seemed like some alien language. I didn't know what these flat creatures were saying with their dying gasps, but I knew they were tasty. I mimicked my mother's actions as I made the eighth and final crepe. As I brought the stack of crepes over, Caryn carried over the brown sugar and syrup.

"Caryn, do you believe dreams can be real?"

"What do you mean?"

In a way, I didn't know why I was asking her. I didn't want her to think that her dad was completely insane. That made it tough to bring up the subject, but I needed her to be on my side. If I was going to go chasing a dream, I needed her to understand.

"Well, do you believe that someone in your dreams could be an actual person in real life?"

I was prepared for her to look at me like I had grown a third nostril, but she didn't. She, instead, furrowed her brow as she often does when she is deep in thought. I loved this about her. Instead of a quick response, her mind would attack the question from different angles to truly understand it. It was a sign of a refined mind.

"I suppose it could be. There are lots of unknown things in the world and we learned in science that the electromagnetic activity from our thoughts extends beyond our bodies. There is no reason that those electromagnetic things couldn't interact in a dream. I don't think every character in your dreams is a real person, but certainly some of them could be. Is this about the person you have dreamed about all your life?"

To be honest, I had forgotten I had told her that. Now that she had asked the question, though, I had better answer honestly.

"Well, yes. She has been in my dreams all my life. I dreamed of her again last night and she asked me to find her in real life... and....and I want to."

I had said it. I was now officially a crazy person.

"Do you care about her? Does she make you happy?"

"She does. I can't think of anyone else I would rather be with."

She cut up a piece of her rolled up crepe and ate it. She chewed and chewed until it seemed like an eternity had gone by. I just needed to know she was ok with this. It was a crazy idea, but I needed Caryn and I to be a team. She finished chewing and I thought she was about to respond to me when she took a big drink of her milk. She looked up while she was drinking. There was a mischievous glint in her eye. She put down her milk and wiped her mouth with her sleeve.

"I am torturing you, right?"

"Yeah, a little bit sweetie. I am really out on a limb here; a limb of the crazy tree."

She laughed while rolling up another crepe.

"Oh dad, I think it's great. Really I do. I mean what better example could you give me than to follow your dreams; literally in this case. Maybe you look for her and she isn't real. But perhaps she is just as real as I am, right? Did your mystery woman give you any tips on how to find her?"

It would be cliché to say I breathed a sigh of relief, but I felt noticeably more relaxed. Caryn didn't think I was crazy. Indeed, it seemed like she thought it was cool.

"Umm, she said I need to follow the bees."

Caryn stuffed another section of crepe in her mouth and proceeded to talk with her mouth full.

"Bees eh..."

She pulled out her laptop and started typing with syrupy fingers.

The place Caryn came up with on her internet search was the exact same as the one I thought of when I thought of following the bees in Calgary: The *Honey Comb*. The *Honey Comb* was a little shop in Kensington that sold all manner of bee related products. They had beeswax candles, local organic honey, honey scented shampoo and bath products, and pretty much any product that could be associated with bees or honey.

Caryn and I walked up 10th street on our way to the *Honey Comb*. You could not help but walk when you went to Kensington as there was no parking to be had. I have never found a parking spot on the street there. It is my suspicion that the people who find a spot there are so grateful that they leave their cars there for life. Either side of Kensington is flanked by residential areas where some places are ok to park and others are not and you could be towed for parking in those spots. It was always a bit of a hunt to park there, so I went to Kensington infrequently.

I felt sick to my stomach as I passed Annette's coffee shop. I grabbed Caryn's hand and walked faster. I don't think I actually breathed for two or three stores past that. As we got in range of the *Honey Comb*, I could actually smell the odor of beeswax coming from the shop.

The bell on the door jingled as we entered. The shopkeeper looked up. He was a portly fellow wearing a yellow and black striped sweater. It definitely did give him that bee appearance; enough so that I feared his stinger. The shop had New-Age-y music playing in the background. I couldn't identify the base song, but it had pan flute and ocean noises mixed in. All these sorts of shops played this music, as if it lulled you into buying stuff. I always found it strange. I mean, if I had a dire need for beeswax candles, he could be playing heavy metal or country music in his store and it would not stop me from buying them.

I walked around the store and didn't see anything that screamed "Follow the Bees". The candles and other products were nice enough, but they didn't seem right. I had lost track of Caryn for a moment, and before I could find her, I felt a toque being slipped on my head.

"She would find you in a crowd if you wore this."

I pulled it off. It was a hat that made you look like a bee, including antennae. I put it back on the rack it came from.

"And she would likely run the other way having successfully identified me as a bee-tard."

I felt a sense of urgency. Dream was out there and she wanted me to find her. Groping candles was getting me no closer to that goal. I needed to take a bigger leap. I needed actual bees to follow. Where could I find that though? Thinking on it for a moment, it occurred to me that the giant bumblebee running the shop might know. I approached him at the cash register.

"Hey, where would you go right now if you wanted to see actual bees?"

"Well, there is a great amateur beekeeping society in Calgary."

"No, I mean in the wild."

"Hmm, Louise Riley park. It's just a few blocks that way and all of the flowers are in bloom there right now."

The walk to Louise Riley Park was a short one and the bumblebee man was proven correct. The flowers were everywhere and they were humming with the activity of bees. Caryn wandered down the row of flowers while I stood enthralled by a bumblebee walking over a large showy purple flower. I could not tell you what sort of flower it was. I don't know much about plants and flowers. However, I have always found their reproductive cycle odd. It's like having a sex partner that you never actually meet. You need a third party to transfer your reproductive material. They entice this third party with a lavish marketing campaign (the flower) and bribe it with some perks (nectar) so that it can reproduce. If humans were like that, it would be like Vegas. We would set up lavish casinos and offer you free drinks, and hey, if some of my sperm gets on you and ends up on some lady in at totally different casino, well that would be pretty good. Come to think of it, that is exactly like Vegas. Vegas is like flowers.

As I watched the bee, he suddenly took off and flew right towards me. I was up in a flash and flailing my hands in front of my face like an idiot. I was flush with embarrassment and felt lucky I didn't squeal like a child as well. Insects flying at one's face turns everyone back into a frightened seven year old. I turned and saw the last glimpse of the bumblebee flying out of sight. Some follower of bees I turned out to be.

"Dad, look at this one I found. She is friendly."

She held out her hand to me. In her palm, a bee walked around placidly. Caryn had always been like this; a tamer of animals. Perhaps it was her kind heart and caring nature that put them at ease. She never seemed to have the same adverse reaction the rest of the human species had towards insects.

"Here, take her."

Before I could say anything, she had transferred the bee to my hand. It wiggled its butt a little bit and tested its wings. I was certain it would immediately fly away, but it settled its wings and started to walk across my hand. I restrained myself from trying to fling the bee away. I had to suppress that feeling of wrongness that came with an insect crawling on you. It tickled as it walked up my arm, which was a whole other problem. Once you got used to it, it was kind of fun to interact with such a small creature. When it reached my shirt sleeve, I had a momentary fear that it would crawl underneath. I wasn't sure I could contain those feelings of wrongness anymore and I would be flailing like a moron once again. But the bee continued on the outside of my shirt. It turned 90 degrees at my shoulder and continued on. The world slowed down. This was exactly like my dream. The sounds and smells and colours seemed amplified around me. It felt almost like I was in a dream. It felt so very right to be in this moment except for the fact that, in a moment, this little bugger would wiggle her butt and sting me. Here it came. The bee walked over to the left side of my chest, just like in the dream. It wiggled its butt. Here it came. I was going to get stung. I winced in anticipation. It didn't sting me though. Instead, it flew off. I stood dumbfounded.

"Dad! Chase it!"

I was so caught up in the moment I nearly forgot. In a flash, I took off after the bee with Caryn following close behind. I tore through the park without a care about how I looked. I had always figured that bees took a relatively straight path to and from where they were going. Nothing could be further from the truth. At least for this bee. She seemed to zigzag and meander. Perhaps that was appropriate. I was on a quest of sorts and no hero's quest is ever a straight line. There are always twists and turns. I ran across 4th avenue following the bee without a care for my own safety. It stopped briefly to wander on the face of a dandelion in the cracks of the sidewalk on Gladstone Road. Caryn reached me, panting, just as it took to the air again. And again, I was running after it. This time I had to cut through someone's garden.

"Hey, what are you..."

I didn't even have time to respond as the lady pruned her tomatoes while I ran through her garden. What choice did I have? It was either that or lose the bee and to me the bee seemed the most real and important thing in the world. To be honest, I didn't even care that I had trespassed on this woman's property. I would have before, but these sorts of things didn't seem to matter to me anymore. All the same, I hoped Caryn went around. I hopped the fence in a sprint as the bee continued to head east. It was hard to believe that this little gal could beat those paper thin wings so fast that I had trouble keeping up with her. I was keeping up with her though. It was as if I had blinders on. There was nothing in the world except for me and this bee. Following it was important.

That is when my toe caught a bit of sidewalk that was sticking up. I lurched forward in my run and for a moment I thought I had corrected the slip. I had corrected too far though. My world went wobbly as my eyes stayed on the bee. I felt extremely grateful for the patch of grass running alongside the sidewalk as even though I could not control that I was about to wipe out, I could control where I wiped out. I slid inelegantly on my face into the grass. I could feel bruises starting to form on my legs and arms. I really hoped no one saw me careening to the ground.

I was afraid to open my eyes. Opening my eyes would mean that the bee was gone. It would mean failure. It would mean that the shot I currently had at finding my way to Dream would be gone. I could start again, but this felt so right and real, I am not sure I would find that another time. Perhaps if I opened just one eye it would be a half of a failure instead of a complete one. I opened one eye. Grass. More grass. Wait! My bee! I am not even sure how I knew it was my bee; I just knew. As quick as I saw her, she was in the air again. I scrambled to my feet again and took off down the street, ignoring the searing pain from my left leg. I followed my bee across 10th Street. Ignoring the honking of the car that swerved around me, I followed it past the grocery store to where it landed on a poster amongst many that were stapled to the same electrical pole. The poster it landed on had some graphic art that resembled a honey comb. As I moved closer to investigate, I could no longer find the bee. I did not see it move or fly off, it was just gone. I had a moment of panic until I remembered the honeycomb on the poster. I was meant to find this exact poster. I ripped it off the pole and looked at it closely.

> "Come to the Cheshire Kitten
> And see our newly renovated 'Honey Lounge'
> Free wings and half price drinks on Sundays
> for 'Sunny with a Hunny!'"

It was mainly purple with golden hourglass shapes made of honeycomb. It clearly had a stage, a pole, and a lipstick print on the poster. Wonderful. My quest led me to a poster for a strip club. It filled me with conflicting thoughts. On one hand, the whole idea of a strip club being part of my journey to finding Dream seemed to cheapen my whole quest. Yet on the other hand 'Following the bees' had led me here. Even the poster had bee and honey motifs. It just felt right, but I felt wrong inside because it felt right.

Caryn walked up as I was examining the poster.

"Did you catch her?"

I handed her the poster.

I remember back to when I was a teen. It was a hot summer day and my dad needed something at the hardware store for the garden. He had let me drive there as I had my learners permit and I needed all the practice I could get. After we were done at the hardware store, he asked me if I wanted to get some ice cream. I was at that awkward age where I was old enough to drive, yet still young enough to think that going for ice cream with my Dad was awesome.

The ice cream place was down by the river. It was my favorite as it had nearly every flavour you could imagine. The day was perfect too. There was not a cloud in the sky and the sun was reflecting off the river making it look like a mighty golden scaled serpent. As we walked along towards the ice cream place, a girl was walking the other way. She had shoulder length wavy brown hair and was only wearing a skimpy red bikini. I remember her like she was walking in slow motion. The sun glinted off her sunglasses. Her hips had just the right curve to them and swayed when she walked. What really caught my eye were her breasts. They were large and with each step they bounced ever so slightly. The bits of her red bikini could have been painted on as they did not move with any of the bounces. I could not look away. It reached something primal inside me that said 'This is good. You want to see more of this'. The girl smiled at me as she passed and my dad pulled me aside.

"Dylan, really?"

"What?"

"You were staring. Your jaw was practically on the floor."

"Dad, didn't you see that girl?"

My dad sighed and put his hand on my shoulder.

"Dylan, I am not blind. I saw her. I enjoyed the view. But I did not stare. *A gentleman sees but does not look*. Do you understand?"

I remember how at first I was annoyed that it seemed that he didn't notice the girl and her flamboyant boobs, but then hearing the words '*I enjoyed it*' disturbed me further. What would mom think? It made my Dad both fallible and human in that moment and I am not sure he was either in my mind previously.

"But Dad, she smiled at me. She didn't mind me looking."

"You cannot assume what she was thinking. It is irrelevant though. This is not about her at all. This is about you. What if that was your sister or mother? What if some guy was looking at them how you looked at this girl?"

"But...but...look at what she was wearing!"

"Again Dylan, this is not about her. She should be able to wear whatever she wants. She should be able to walk down the street naked and not have you look at her like that. This is about you. *A man protects those who cannot protect themselves.* If you do not know if your leering would hurt her or not, you should not do it. *A man cannot control what he sees or what he feels, but he can control how he acts.* Do you understand?"

I nodded. I had been angry at him for the public berating, as any teen would have been. But I knew the rightness of what he was saying. I was a man, not an animal, and I could control how I behaved. I could control my actions. Still, my memory is not just of my dad's lecture, but of the glorious creature in the bikini as well. Perhaps I am both primal and civilized then. Perhaps I am both animal and man. Perhaps it is just a thin layer of 'civilized man' on top of the primal animal, but it is an important thin layer that I strive to keep.

I sat in the parking lot of the Cheshire Kitten with my head against my steering wheel. Even though my quest to 'follow the bees' had led me to this point, there was just so much wrong with the situation. The first thing being that it was a strip club. It seemed very dissonant to be looking for clues to the love of my life in a strip club. What if all the signs pointed to the Cheshire Kitten because Dream worked in there? No, that was silly. It was not her style to work in a strip club. Even if she did, I would want to meet her in person regardless. No matter where she worked, our connection transcended that.

My second problem was that Caryn was sitting in the car with me. I am not even sure how we got to this state. She is old enough to stay home alone by herself, but she insisted that she come. She wanted to be involved in my quest because she cared about me. We had argued about it. I don't even recall agreeing to her coming with me. But here she was. The very thought of me going to watch some strippers while my daughter waited in the car was simply horrible. It's the sort of white trash story that would make me the worst father in the world.

"I can't do it. It isn't right."

"Dad, we went over this. I will be fine. I have my laptop and I can get their Wi-Fi from here."

The sizzling sound of the neon lights of the Cheshire Kitten and its red glow were nearly overwhelming as I considered what Caryn said. It dawned on me that the enticing red glow to attract patrons was not much different that the showy flowers that plants produce to attract insects. It was the sort of 'insects' that are attracted to these types of establishments that I did not want walking by my teenage daughter alone in the car.

"Look I trust you on your own. It's just that the people that go to these places..."

"Dad, you have your cell phone and I have mine. If there is an issue, I have you on speed dial. Besides, this is a mystery; an investigation. What you find in there might just be another clue and you might need me and my laptop to help."

She made a lot of sense. It was not like I was going in there to watch the strippers and leave her alone. I was looking for a clue. I might only be five minutes, in which case why was I over thinking this? I still didn't like it, but if my aim was to get in, find the clue, and get back out quickly, I think I could manage my unease.

"O.K., but text me every 10 minutes."

I have always been a bit unsettled in strip clubs. It's not that I haven't been to them and it's not that I didn't enjoy myself per se. I truly didn't disapprove of stripping really. It was my dad's advice: *A gentleman sees but doesn't look.* This was always contrasted with how arousing I found it. In reality, the fact that I was aroused by the spectacle of it made me feel like I was betraying my dad's imparted wisdom. In short, it made me feel ashamed. The problem was it was so damned titillating. When people use the word 'titillating' to describe a strip club, the often add 'for lack of a better word'. Those people are idiots. There is no better word. Titillating describes a strip club well on at least two different levels.

As I entered the club, I was hit by a barrage of strobe lights, glossy paints, and bass filled music. The brightness of the lights and music was barely enough to cover the smell of cigarette smoke and stale beer wafting off the carpet. Everything seemed fringed with pink feathery rope everywhere I looked. On the main stage, a girl was writhing topless on the pole. The place was mainly empty. Three patrons sat in chairs right next to the main stage. Two of them looked well past sixty. The third was very young and had a very slimy look about him. I did not really want to sit near any of them. I didn't really know where to start looking.

I caught sight of a sign with a honey comb on it, so I moved to check it out. It was an entrance to another area with a smaller stage. There was a velvet rope blocking the entrance with a sign on it saying 'Closed for the evening'. Above, the title on the honey-comb was 'The Honey Lounge'. Inside, a blonde was practicing on the stage. I figured whatever bee related clue I was to find must be in the Honey Lounge so I waited until the bar staff was otherwise occupied and I stepped over the velvet rope. Immediately I saw why this room was so named. It was hexagonal with a stage of the same shape right in the middle. Each wall jutted out with hexagonal maple shelving. On each shelf, a candle was burning. It was the only light in the room and it gave it an amber glow. The wax melting off of each shelf only added to the ambiance.

The blonde dancer waved at me and motioned for me to sit down. She was naked except for a length of sheer fabric which snaked around her body. She slowly bent over, put her hands on the stage and put one leg up in the air, then the other, and then planted them back down over the other side of her body. When she moved, the candles cast shadows on the walls opposite them making the whole room seem to shimmer. While the girl out front had a dance that was vulgar and fast, the blonde had a slower and more seductive motion. I sat down in front of her.

"I would say you were lost, but I don't believe you are. Still, you aren't exactly where you should be either."

"I'm here looking for something"

She raised an eyebrow as she danced. Her motions were entrancing. I could nearly be hypnotized simply by watching her fluidity. I figured it was no time to be shy about my reasons for being there. My phone buzzed with a text from Caryn. I quickly typed a response back. I was glad to see she had listened to me. I could not believe it had been ten minutes already.

"And do you see what you are looking for?"

"No. No, it's not like that. I am on a bit of a quest."

She was upside down with her back resting on the pole. She looked at me as her legs came down to either side of her until she made a perfect T. That must take amazing muscle control, but she didn't even break a sweat.

"Intriguing, what sort of quest?"

"Well, if I said 'follow the bees', would that mean anything to you?"

Her legs and body quickly spun around until she was sitting spread eagle in front of me. She was completely exposed and yet I felt none of the discomfort I have previously felt in strip clubs. A broad shouldered man entered the honey lounge and crossed his arms looking at me.

"Sir, I am going to have to ask you to leave."

"It's ok Troy, he's a friend."

"Alright, whatever you say, Venus."

He turned and left the room, leaving us alone once again. I

turned back to Venus and found myself staring directly between her legs. I looked up and she was laughing as I blushed.

"It's all right. It's O.K. to look."

I looked her in the eyes instead.

"So you followed the bees and they led you to me? How interesting. Will you have a drink with me?"

I nodded. She spun around and sat in the chair next to me. Every motion this girl did was smooth and seductive. It was like it was part of her being.

"Troy! Bring us two '*Bumble DownUnders*'!"

She turned back to me and smiled. The way she pursed her lips after the smile made me feel warm all over.

"What's in a *Bumble Down Under*?"

"Umm, Honey Brown Lager, with a shot of warm liquid honey and a shot of Southern Comfort"

I used to never drink even a drop of alcohol and drive afterwards. It was against the 'rules' and I was one of the good guys. So no drinking ever if I was driving. However, recently I found I didn't give a shit about the rules. One drink would be fine. Lots of people drove after one drink.

"So tell me about the girl?"

"Why do you say it's a girl?"

"Well, I find when someone in your state, it always involves a girl."

I trusted her. I don't know why, but she just seemed so open and free. I told her all about Dream and how I had known her in my dreams all my life. I told her how she told me to follow the bees. Somewhere during my story, Troy had delivered the drinks though I don't actually remember seeing him do so. The drink was dark and smooth and lined my throat as it went down. Caryn had pinged me again so I sent her another message back. Venus lapped the story up as I spoke. She seemed to glow more and more as I talked. She almost looked as though she was giving off light the more we talked. It was likely just the candlelight reflecting off of her.

"And then it landed right on my poster?"

"Yup. And then it was gone."

She put her hand on my shoulder. As she did, the room blurred a little. My drink must be kicking in sooner than I expected. But Venus remained in focus. The walls were all angles and hexagons and it made her curves pop right out. I found myself staring at the curve where her neck meets her shoulder. My gaze was desperate to hang lower to her chest, but I snapped back to look into her eyes. I was here for a purpose. I needed to find out where to go next. I could not let myself be distracted. She pursed her red lips and looked at me curiously.

"You have an iron will, Dylan. I should tell you that you have come to the right place."

"I have? Do you know where to find her?"

My heart leaped in my chest. It was all good to chase bees in the park hoping it would lead me somewhere positive, but it was a whole other thing to have a solid lead like this. Dream had told me to follow the bees, I had had faith in that and it led me here, and it was about to lead me to her.

"Let's just say I know how you can find her, not where you can find her. The 'how' is more important anyway as that stays constant, while the 'where' might change."

"So how..."

She laughed.

"Well I am not going to tell you yet, silly. You are too much fun to let that go right away. Have another drink with me. Troy! Two more!"

"O.K."

I am not even sure why I agreed. I found myself nodding and very pliant to her suggestions. Troy slid two more *Bumble DownUnder*s in front of us and I took a big drink. Caryn and I could take a cab home tonight and I could take transit back tomorrow to get my car. That would work. Besides getting the information from Venus on how to find Dream was of utmost importance.

"Tell me about your ex-wife. Tell me how you met. Tell me what you loved about her. Tell me how it went wrong."

So that is what I did. I told her I loved how she looked at the world differently than anyone else and how she smiled every time the wind was in her hair. I told her how she wore mismatched clothes and loved to paint but did it horribly. I told her how I made sure to tell her everyday how beautiful she was and how much I appreciated her. I told her how I worked extra hard so we could put money into her dreams. I found myself pouring out all the things that I used to love about a woman I now loathed. With each thing I mentioned, Venus seemed to get more luminescent. It may have been the drinks or the lighting or both, but she sat there with her eyes closed and a blissful smile on her face with a golden light seemingly emanating from her.

I then told her how I discovered she had been cheating. I told her how I had found out about the multiple other affairs. I told her how she had amassed a debt in my name to further her career and saddled me with it when she left. I told her how she had abandoned Caryn. I told her how Merideth didn't seem to care about any of the pain she caused and had no remorse or regret. Venus's eyes were wide open while I talked about this stuff. With each new item I spoke about the room got darker and darker. The candles flickered and some went out. Things felt colder in the room. Venus's lips were pursed too tight; I think they could have forged a diamond under that pressure.

"That is an abuse of love! That will not do. No! No! No! That will be dealt with."

I didn't know what to say. Caryn texted me again, so I wrote her a message as best my drunk fingers could handle saying I was ok. I was not sure I wanted to look up from my phone as Venus seemed quite angry. Her emotions swayed like a ship in a rough sea. I felt a hand on my leg. Warmth radiated from it through the rest of me. The light within the room brightened again. I looked up and placed my phone on the stage. There was a third fresh drink in front of me and two empty glasses next to it. The room had once again blurred but she was as crisp as ever. Venus looked at me with a simple sympathetic smile and a tear on her cheek.

"Hey, Dylan, it's O.K. I know I can be a bit much, but I'm enjoying your company."

Her hand slid up my leg with the lightest of touches. I breathed in sharply. I looked at her. She had a few wavy blonde hairs that were crossing her face. I wanted desperately to brush them away so she could see her better. She smiled like she knew a secret. I raised my hand to brush the hairs out of her face, then hesitated and lowered it again. This was silly. I was not here to flirt with a dancer. I was here for Dream.

"Why don't you tell me more about her? About Dream, that is."

Talking about Dream was easy. I talked about her raven hair, her boisterous laugh, our adventures together, our simple times just being on a beach together or a desert or a jungle. I talked about how she made me feel and how I felt whole being with her. It was a topic I could have gone on about for hours. Venus was back to glowing and with every sentence I uttered, she glowed more and a pulse of warmth shot up from where her hand rested on my leg. Somehow the 'pulse' made me feel content and happy. So when a 'pulse' hit after I spoke about Dream, I would feel the urge to share more. It was self-sustaining and addicting. That was the problem. With each hit I had an urge to look at her body, to touch her skin, to kiss her. The urge got more powerful and powerful, but I fought harder and harder to retain focus as I was here to find out about Dream, not fool around, as much as I might want to.

"You have a pure heart, Dylan, but you should realize the way to Dream is through me, not around me. Why resist the bliss?"

Why was I resisting? I could not remember. She was beautiful and sexy and was right here and desired me. And I desired her. That was obvious. But there was something. There was some reason.

"I just..."

"There is no reason."

Her voice was soft and pierced right through my guard like sunshine through the clouds. Her hand came up and touched my face. Warmth spread through me. Perhaps it was my drink, I don't know. It was confusing, but wonderful. There was no reason. None at all. My face gravitated towards hers. I don't recall willing it to be so, it just was. I had no control, but I was happy not to have any. Our lips pressed together into a kiss. It was not a frenzied kiss of tongues and lust, but a simple and smooth kiss that was slow and smoldering. The room spun as we kissed and had gone completely fuzzy by the time we stopped.

"That was lovely. Another."

I was overcome with a powerful need to obey. I was in the hive, she was the queen, and I was beginning to suspect I was the nectar. We kissed again. Once more it was slow and profound. The room tilted. I felt my hand on her breast. I looked down to find my pants undone. When did that happen? There were three extra empty glasses next to my old empties. I don't even recall drinking them, but I must have. Venus was texting on my phone. My phone! How had I forgotten about my daughter?

"Caryn? Yes. That's inventive. A man after my own heart."

Was she talking to Caryn? Did she know I was ok? Venus saw me looking at her and laughed. Her laugh echoed off the honeycomb and the room spun again. I heard another noise and was surprised when I figured out it was my own laughter answering back.

I don't know how I got to my car, but I was in the back seat. Venus was back here with me as well. She must have changed in the meantime as she was wearing jeans and a black sweater. Caryn was in the seat in front of me and Troy was driving. What the heck was going on? They must be driving me home. Too many *Bumble DownUnder*s for me I guess. I was too drunk so the bouncer was driving me home. That didn't explain why Venus was in the car. Did they know how to get to my house?

"Caryn...tell him....with the....living spot..."

Fuck. This is part of drunkenness I hated. My mind was still pretty sharp when I was inebriated, but when I went to say a word like 'House', instead my mouth fumbled and came up with 'living spot'. My tongue was dry. I could really use a drink. Everyone turned to look at me.

"Hey, there's the sleepyhead. You passed out on us."

Her blonde hair tumbled down over her shoulders. Her red lips were all I could look at. They were saying something but I couldn't make it out. I was too interested in watching them. Wasn't I in a strip club? How did I get here? Didn't Caryn have school tomorrow? Fuck.

"Wha..."

"I said we aren't going to your place."

Where were we going then? Troy's place? Venus'? Where would Caryn sleep? And more importantly why were we going there? Did Troy know not to rev my engine in third too much?

Venus put her hand on my leg again. Warmth radiated from it. Everything was O.K.

"Dylan. Let it go."

What was I even worried about? I remembered her tender lips and how the room would spin. I briefly wondered if the car would spinout if I kissed her in the car. I must not have cared as my lips were soon on hers. I had no seatbelt on, but that hardly bothered me. She put her hands around my head and gently pulled me deeper into the kiss. As it ended, she bit my lower lip lightly and looked me in the eyes. She was breathing heavily and giving off a golden glow.

"That's more like it."

Her hands moved to my chest.

"Dad, did you know Troy does Kung Fu? Dad!"

I didn't even turn to see Caryn. I was immobilized by Venus and her golden glow. I just wanted to dive in again and kiss and kiss and kiss. Venus smiled. What a horrible dad I was though! I needed to answer her question. How rude of me. Troy turned the car sharply to the left. The tires squealed. I turned to look at Caryn. Her seat was empty. Where was she? She probably slunk down in her chair, mad at me.

"Caryn..."

Venus's hand went to my cheek and turned my head back to her.

"She's O.K. She will be taken care of. Let your worries flow away."

That was all I needed. Her touch seemed to take away every concern. We fell into another kiss. Tongues touched. Hands explored. The car was awash in golden light as Troy drove into the blackness.

I didn't remember how I got here. I was in some sort of bedroom. The walls were sky blue and the bedspread was a cream colour. I tried to move my hand and found I couldn't. I turned my head to look and saw that my hands were tied to the bed posts with white fabric. I tried my legs and found them similarly tied. I was tied in some giant man sized 'X' on the bed. Candles flickered to either side of the bed casting shadows where they hit the canopy.

Every time I tried to move my head, the world blurred and felt askew. It was all that alcohol. I should not have had so much. More disconcerting, every time my eyes blinked, time seemed to jump.

-blink-

There was an amazing feeling down below. It felt the world would melt away and leave me only this bliss. It was wonderful. I strained to look down and saw a head of blonde hair moving up and down rhythmically. Venus. It was like warm satin. My head fell back and hit the pillow.

-blink-

She sat beside me wearing a very see through diaphanous robe. Her hand was on my chest.

"....still with me, Dylan? Your poor heart. The only way..."

-blink-

I did not see much. Skin. I was straining with my tongue. Her skin trembled above me. I could hear her moans somewhere down the bed. Warm satin again. I was confused about what was going on, but I knew that the more I moved and strained my tongue, the more euphoria followed below. So I strained. Oh, I strained.

-blink-

Venus sat beside me looking at me. I was completely erect while she sat relaxed and naked beside me. Some people are self-conscious naked, but Venus looked so completely comfortable in her skin.

"It's the only way I can heal you."

I nodded.

-blink-

She was on top of me. Her hips undulated slowly on top of me. The fluidity I had noticed earlier was nothing. Her motions were smooth and slow and the grip of her felt exquisite. She looked to the ceiling as she rocked on top of me with her eyes closed and a smile of pure joy on her face. I thought I might explode it felt so good.

-blink-

She was a creature of pure light. She writhed on top of me, moving her pelvis with a torrent of fury. I could barely contain myself. Why was I holding back? The walls shimmered in and out of existence. Behind them were clouds of lavender forming into funnels. Her form was still female, but a glowing golden body with hair like a streaming sunrise. She bucked her hips back and forth and stared at me with an animalistic glare.

"Release your pain!"

She bent down quickly and bit me hard on the shoulder all the while keeping up pace down below. Her right hand scratched her fingernails down my side so hard I was sure it must be bleeding. It was too much. I cannot explain it. Her bite hurt so badly, but however much I was holding back, that was gone now. I released. I gave in to the euphoria and became one with it. There was nothing in existence but love and I was melded with it.

"Yes!"

As she screamed, white light emanated from Venus and enveloped the room. Everything went white.

-blink-

It was dark. Mostly dark. I had awoken as Venus was asleep and drooling on my chest. She snored slightly as she slept. My hands and legs were free and we were both under the covers. I didn't mind a little drool. It was unexpected, but hardly the strangest part of the evening.

I snuggled in.

-blink-

I soared over the jungle canopy in my hang glider. Twenty feet away Dream matched my flight in hers. We had purchased the hang gliders in a small shop outside of St. Sebastian. They were not modern in the least. They were canvas and wood with leather straps that held us in. We were headed up a tributary that fed into the Amazon. We took to the air as the Malorri tribe watched the river like hawks and could shoot their poison tipped arrows through the eye of a needle.

We were in search of the fabled 'Jaguar Heart' ruby that the Malorri fiercely guarded. In truth I didn't care for rubies at all, but the chance to explore the Amazon again was one I couldn't pass up. It was peaceful up here in the sky. Just the sound of wind in my ears and my very best friend for company. Suddenly a shadow crossed my aviator goggles. I looked over just in time to see a Pterodactyl saddled by that monocled menace, the evil Professor Rothschilde. His Pterodactyl was in a steep dive towards my companion.

"Watch out!"

She veered to the left, but too late. Rothschilde's monster tore through the left wing of her glider completely. She spiraled down out of control as Rothschilde cackled maniacally. I had no time to go after the evil professor, and I needed to lose altitude quickly to save Dream, so I took out my sawed off shotgun and blew two big holes in my own wings. Immediately I turned into a dive. Dream was spiraling towards her doom, but she was doing it slower than I was. I had to time it just right. My glider came up on hers quickly. As I reached it I snaked my arm around one of her gliders struts. It seemed like a good idea but it felt like my shoulder was nearly torn out of the socket. Linking us together slowed us down, but we were still too fast. The wind rushing by sounded like a freight train.

"Hang On!"

As we breached the canopy I cracked my whip towards the upper branches. I had no way of knowing if it caught on a branch. I could only hope. The ground was coming up quick in 5...4...3...2. And suddenly the whip went taught and our mishmash of gliders came to a rest just 2 feet from the ground. We both breathed heavily for a moment and then broke into laughter. We had a moment of hysteria before the branch we were attached to broke and the whole works came crashing down that last two feet.

We stood up and dusted each other off. I coughed and a cloud of dust came out of my mouth. We checked our equipment and found it was mostly intact. The grettomometer was completely destroyed, but I could make due with a rock and a bowl of llama's milk, so that was ok.

"What's that humming?"

She was right. There was an increasingly deep humming noise. Oh no. I hoped my suspicions were not correct. I jumped up and down on the ground. It was spongy. This was not a good sign. I immediately started digging tuftfuls of grass up. Dream looked at me like I was crazy. Suddenly realization dawned in her eyes.

"You don't think....the Egglington Bees?"

I nodded and pulled up a chuck of bee hive paper. This wasn't ground we had landed on, but a hive. Doctor Egglington had returned from the Amazon fifteen years ago talking of giant, friendly, telepathic bees. Everyone thought he was crazy, but here we were. The buzzing was growing louder. They definitely did not sound friendly. A column of giant bees shot out of the earth near us in a geyser.

"Run!"

Dream took off like a shot, her pith helmet bouncing as she ran; her brown leather backpack jostling with each step. I was right behind her, branches slapping me in the face as I followed her. I briefly looked back to see the mass of hippo sized bumblebees bearing down on us.

"Faster!"

No sooner had I said this than my body was wrapped with bee legs and I found myself rising into the air. I was going to yell for Dream to save herself, but I could see her being grabbed by a bee as well. At first I struggled and tried to resist, but there was something about the hum of the bee that was carrying me. It was so warming and soothing. This bee was happy. I relaxed and found that his legs were carrying me gently where he could have easily crushed me.

"Relax. They're friendly."

I saw Dream visibly relax and ease into her new transportation.

"Where did the other bees go?"

She was right. There were only two bees carrying us forward. I craned my neck to see the rest of the bees distant in the sky, attacking Professor Rothschilde and his Pterodactyl. I looked forward again and could see a massive stone temple rising out of the jungle canopy. The bee's undulating flight was bringing us closer and closer to the temple. This must be the Jaguar Temple. Of course! These were telepathic bees, how could I forget. They knew we wanted to go to the temple, so they took us there. From Rothschilde, they must have sensed only evil and they drove him off. The bees let us down gently on top of the temple and flew away. I tried to think "Thank you" very strongly as they left. The two bees hummed in bliss as they flew off.

In the center of the top of the pyramid was a stone obelisk with many inscriptions on it. Resting on top of it was a big chunk of sandstone. The sandstone seemed oddly familiar. It was strange as I had never been here before. Why would it seem so familiar?

"Can you read the inscriptions? You know the basic Malorri language, right?"

Dream pulled a book out of her backpack, along with some paper and a pen. She began to write furiously and flip through the book. It always amazed me how quick her mind was. No matter what jungle expedition we were on, and no matter how exhausted we were, when there was a puzzle to be figured out, no brain was quicker than hers. The sun glinted off her olive skin as she worked and several strands of hair had escaped her ponytail to frame her face. I could have watched her like this for hours. She was absolutely gorgeous. She looked up at me and grinned.

"Stop burning me with those lusty gazes. I have work to do."

I blushed and set my pack down on the ground. The problem was that I was not sure I could control myself. Here we were in the most peaceful place I could remember, alone, and washed in golden light above what had been the temple of the love goddess of the Malorri. There was just something in the air.

"Fine, just one lusty gaze then. But make it a good one."

I looked at her and then crossed my eyes and put my tongue out. She laughed and stood up, closing her book.

"That was about as far from lusty as I could imagine. Besides, I have translated the inscriptions. It says 'Here sits the Heart of the Jaguar'."

"Excellent."

I dug through my pack to find my rock pick. The Jaguar's Heart ruby must be at the center of this chunk of sandstone. My pick could make short work of that. I pulled it out and started towards the sandstone chunk.

"Are you sure that's a good idea?"

"Why not? We have to break that heart free."

Dream looked panicked. A tear leaked from one of her eyes as I chipped a piece of sandstone away. She rushed over to me and held my arm so I couldn't use my pick anymore.

"You mustn't! It isn't ready!"

I was confused. Wasn't this what we had come here for? All of our recent adventures had led us here. Why would she not want me to get to the core of this? She was upset and frantic, though. Tears were streaming down her face. I didn't want to upset her. I dropped the pick.

"I don't understand..."

When I woke, light was streaming through the windows. The white sheets and canopy reflected this light and created a searing pain in my head. The alcohol last night may have helped that along a little. The pale blue walls were a minor soothing counterpoint. The windows were open and the air that filtered through was cold and sweet.

"Are you a medium or a large when it comes to coveralls?"

The deep voice made me jump. I turned to see a man in dirty, grey coveralls. His large grey beard dominated the front of his outfit and his salt and pepper black hair was pulled back into a pony tail. His skin was tanned and leathery and a lightning bolt tattoo was prominent on his left arm. Who was this guy? Why was he waking me up? A smile creased his face showing several gold teeth.

"Large, I think."

My voice crackled as I spoke. My mouth was like the Sahara desert. He tossed some blue coveralls at me. They smelled like motor oil and a million years of dust.

"Good, I only have large. Just put 'em on. No need to get dressed first."

I did as he said, though I figured underwear was in order at the very least. I didn't want my junk keeping company with the crypt keeper's coveralls. He must be related to Venus in some way. Where was Venus for that matter? Where was Caryn?

"This way. I need someone to hold the light for me."

He led me out of the room and down a narrow hall. It was wood paneled and shabby looking, in contrast to Venus's bedroom. It was lined with family photos though. A lady in a field a wheat. A man riding a jet ski. A young woman with a bow and arrow. She made me think of my own daughter.

"Where...?"

"Venus is making breakfast with her. Gummi Bear pancakes I think. Through here."

He led me into a carport that must have had more than ten motorcycles in it. All sorts of them. In the center was a metallic blue Harley with the phrase 'Ride the Lightning!' painted on the tank. There were other cruisers as well as sport bikes, off road bikes, and miscellaneous tanks, seats and handle bars hanging from the ceiling. Several tool cabinets sat on opposing walls, but from what I could see wrenches, pliers, and sockets lay strewn about the floor. Beyond the carport was grassland as far as the eye could see. We were not in town anymore. He took off his glove and stretched out his hand to shake. His shake was firm and fast.

"Dylan right? Venus filled me in. I have lots of names, but just call me Zed. That's what my friends call me."

"And Venus is your daughter?"

He led me over to a black dual sport bike with a small engine. A work light was on and hanging from the handlebars, and tools lay all around it like shrapnel. Zed leaned down to pick up a wrench.

"More or less, I suppose. I have taken care of her for a long, long time."

"And you don't mind her...umm...line of work?"

He dropped the wrench in disgust.

"Where is my 10 mill? Fucking metric. See Dylan, that is where your society is messed up, they don't know how to judge properly. They have forgotten where proper blame goes."

"What do you mean?"

He dug through the wrenches on the floor, examining each one. I did the same and found the 10mm wrench and handed it to him.

"Thanks. Well, see, they judge some things way too harshly that they should not, and other things they place no blame or judgment on at all where they really should. Take your ex-wife for example. I bet your old friends didn't blame her at all. I bet they didn't give one fuck what she did to you. Am I right?"

"Yup. I think that judging would have made them feel they needed to act on that. It would disrupt their lives, so it was easier just to toss me aside than judge her."

He started cranking on the bolts holding the battery in.

"Exactly. It's why they have all this New Age bullshit about 'Don't judge others'. They only say that because it makes their life easier. The reality is that things like adultery, murder, and theft have always been things that need to be judged. But contrast that with Venus."

The metal holding the battery clanged to the floor.

"Screwdriver."

He held out his hand. I scrambled to find a Phillips screwdriver and passed it to him. He started working on loosening the wire connections to the battery terminal.

"Fucking Chinese batteries are just shit. I am putting in something with some better juice, you know? Anyway, look at Venus. She pulls in a six figure salary. Is she harming anyone with what she does? No. Is she harming herself? No. She likes to dance and she is good at it and she makes money all while bringing a little brightness into people's lives. It's her choice and I couldn't be prouder of her. But she is judged like mad because of it. It's silly really, they get worked up over naked bodies, and yet adultery is 'nothing to be judged'."

He was completely right. When I thought about it in that light, I had no idea why anyone would judge Venus on her career choice. And, aside from murder, adultery is something that should be judged harshly but is not. People who habitually betray the trust of those closest to them should be pushed out of the tribe (so to speak). He pulled out the battery and handed it to me.

"Throw this away. The cans over there. Sometimes these little beasties need a new heart. You know a little about that right?"

I tossed it into the garbage can and it made a satisfying 'thunk'. Zed was already putting in a new battery.

"I do. Just so you know, I didn't judge her."

"Yeah, you did. Why else ask me if I was O.K. with it? It's O.K. though, I think you're beginning to understand. I also think you might assume that this happens a lot."

He motioned with the wrench in the direction of the house.

"What do you mean?"

"I mean that she brings guys back here, like you. Let me tell you, it's rare. Venus is picky. She has to see something special in you. I can see it too, otherwise I would have kicked you out straight away this morning. Where the hell is that Phillips?"

I sprinted back to the bike and grabbed the Philips off the floor to give to him.

"You are looking for a woman from your dreams, am I right? That is why Venus brought you here, I think. It's because I can help you find her."

He cranked on the battery terminals as I sat in shocked silence. Zed could help me find Dream? Suddenly I was all ears. The hangover and all the strange things that had happened so far were worth it in order to get just one step closer to her.

"So you know where she is?"

"I sure do. I could tell you where to find her at any given moment. But, Dylan, I am not going to do that."

"What? Why?"

"Look, did you ever consider that the reason you haven't found her yet is that you were not ready? She is a special person and deserves a partner worthy of her. Did you ever consider that all the troubles you have gone through are part of what you needed to go through in order to be ready to meet her in person? A sword isn't forged with flowers, as they say."

A sword isn't forged in flowers. I liked that. Dream certainly was a very unique and strong person. Perhaps I did need to travel through the fire in order to temper me into the man that was worthy of her. It didn't make the pain of it disappear, but I liked that there was a reason for it. It made Merideth just an unfortunate stepping stone on the way to Dream. Zed started bolting on the bracket that held in the battery.

"I have gone through the pain though. I have gone through the troubles. Am I not ready to meet her?"

He stood up and looked me up and down. He passed me the 10 mm wrench and the Phillips screwdriver.

"Not even close. You have gone through the pain, but it stripped you raw. You need to rebuild yourself as a man first. Only then will I tell you where she is."

"Is this one of those 'a good time to reinvent yourself' speeches? Because I am kind of sick of those."

Honestly I hated that phrase. I am not sure why people gave that advice to newly separated people. I liked myself before my split so why would I want to reinvent myself? They treated it like some sort of silver lining to the whole thing. Like I had always wanted to take up ball room dancing or bowling and now that I had the gut wrenching pain of betrayal and separation, I would finally be able to do that. Yay. If this was what Zed was peddling, perhaps I was at a dead end.

"No, that's more New Age bullshit. It's a lot like 'This is your new normal' or 'You will have to move past it'. These are just phrases that allow those that say them to avoid having to pass any judgment. They don't help the victim at all. What would help is if they instead said 'Your ex is an evil cunt and I will have nothing more to do with someone who treats their loved ones like that'."

I nodded. I was glad he was blunt about this. I liked the truth straight up.

"Well, get over it, because that never fucking happens. What I mean is that you don't want to meet this girl in your current state. You are a wreck. You want to build yourself up before you meet her, right?"

I had not thought of it from that angle. I was a mess. Sure, I wasn't one of the Broken People, but I was broken. Recognizing that was the only way I could heal. Why would I want to meet the love of my life and immediately burden her with my past? That might doom our relationship before it even started.

"What do I need to do? I will do anything."

"Dylan, I think I can help you. I want to help you. But I need to know you are strong enough for what you need to go through."

"Ok, how can I prove that?"

Zed stepped towards me.

"Will you stand your ground while I punch you in the face as hard as I can?"

"What? What will that prove?"

"It will prove you can take a lick or two and still keep going. So what do you say?"

I didn't really want to be punched in the head. I can count on one hand how many times I have been punched really hard and none of them were pleasant. On the other hand, if this was the path to Dream, it was a small price to pay. What did I care about pain? It would only be momentary. Besides, the hang over already felt like my head was splitting.

"Ok. Do it."

He took off his gloves and handed them to me.

"Hold these."

I grabbed his gloves. He winked at me. Before I could even think, his fist had slammed into my face. I didn't think an older guy could move that fast or with such power. I felt my back hit the tool chest as I flew backwards. My head hit something metal. The right side of my face, above my cheek, screamed in pain. The screwdriver, wrench, and gloves flew out of my hands and hit the back wall. My vision was getting dimmer and dimmer, approaching blackness. No! I had to prove I was worthy of Dream! I had to fight it! Despite my tunnel vision and dizziness I put my hand down to help me get up. I teetered this way and that once standing again. My head was ringing but my vision was slowly coming back. I shook my head. I could see Zed lying down with his head near the motor on the bike.

"Can you shine the light down here? Oh, and bring me my gloves"

I was unsure if I passed the test or not. I supposed I would be kicked out of his carport garage if I had failed. I rubbed my face where I'd been hit. It felt like it would swell. I found his gloves by the wall behind me and scooped them up, bringing them to him.

"Perfect, thanks. Shine the light right here."

I had to lie down to shine it under the bike where he had indicated. He moved a big black pan under a small bolt under the bike.

"These Chinese bikes can be tricky. Don't get me wrong, they are all very pretty, but most have motors that will betray you and leave you stranded. There are some out there, though very few, with great motors like this one, that purr like a kitten. Still, it is quirky."

He unscrewed the bolt and reached upwards on the bike to

untwist something and black ooze started to drain out of the bolt hole. It was slow in draining, but steady, like a dark tentacle feeling the pan below it.

"Ah, you see that? This oil is no good. It's a good bike, but sometimes it gets gummed up. It shouldn't be black like this. It should be more like the colour of honey. Let me ask you a question Dylan. Do you understand why you are afraid of me?"

I was afraid of him. I could not quite put my finger on it. I have always had some fear around people who look like they are part of a biker gang. But why was that? I have never had trouble with people like that and I have never known anyone who had, so why was there fear there?

"Do you mean other than the fact that you just punched me in the head?"

He looked at my face and winced.

"Ooh, ya, you should put something on that before your eye swells too much. You take a hit well, by the way. I could feel you nearly grasping the truth of it. You fear me because I exist outside the conventions and rules of your society."

"What do you mean?"

"Well, every society is a fairy tale. You might think everything is solid and logical, but it is not. Society is a fairy tale and it requires people within it to buy into the fairy tale. In essence, a society is a contract between itself as a collective and its citizens that says 'You agree to believe in the fairy tale, and I promise you that your life will turn out according to the fairy tale'. Collectively, those within the fairy tale are frightened of those who are not bound by its rules and expectations."

This was very similar to what I had felt since discovering my ex's affairs. It felt like there was a base way that people were and it was ugly. I felt that most people would lie, cheat, steal and hurt others for their own gain. I felt like there was a meniscus of civilization on top of this that was how we thought society worked. For me, I felt like the meniscus had been stripped away. It was no longer there. I saw people for what they were without these barriers, and it was dark.

"I get it. It's like the pack of wolves who shun the one wolf because he is different. They kick him out because the lone wolf doesn't conform. But also, the lone wolf is dangerous."

"Exactly. I am telling you this because while I chose to operate outside the fairy tale, you have had it thrust upon you. People fear you now. You are a lone wolf, just as I am. The contract of the fairy tale was broken for you. You played along by its rules and when things got difficult, the contract was broken. Society didn't provide you with a life that matched the fairy tale. Society fucked you over. This is why people tell you this is a 'good time to reinvent yourself' or 'this is your new norm'. They want you to, in essence, shut the fuck up about how you got screwed over and buy into the fairy tale again. They desperately need you to either believe in the fairy tale again or go away. Otherwise their belief in the fairy tale might also be compromised. You are a leper. But once you have seen the fairy tale for the lie it is, there is no unseeing that. So you are outside of the fairy tale. They fear you just as you fear me. Can you hold the light there again?"

This was blowing my mind. This was exactly how it felt. I felt like the rest of the world didn't give a shit about what sort of wrongs had been done to me. No one truly seemed to care except for those that had been through something similar. That is why we banded together into groups like 'Separation and Divorce, Alberta South Society'. We were all outside the fairy tale.

Zed tightened the bolt up again and started to pour in a new container of oil in the motor from the top. Amber liquid flowed into the engine like ambrosia.

"Ok, I can buy that, but why are they so accepting of my ex? She broke the rules of the fairy tale and they still accept her."

"That's an easy one. They want her to be quiet about her transgressions so the fairy tale stays intact and she wants to hide her transgressions. It is a perfect match. Basically they both put their fingers in their ears and say 'lalalalala' until the feeling of danger to the fairy tale ends. You haven't asked me the obvious question though. Why would I choose to purposefully exclude myself from the fairy tale of our society?"

I had no idea. It was a painful process, one that had shaken me to my very core, so why would a person choose to do that willingly?

"Ok, I'll bite. Why?"

"Well, you see, I cannot in good conscience buy into a fairy tale that is, at it's very core, ill."

"What makes a society ill?"

"Well, do you know the Golden Rule?"

I did. My dad had grilled it into me. *Treat others as you want to be treated.* It was the basis for all forms of honour and chivalry, so it was part of his philosophy. It was also part of our society, though, so I was not sure where he was going with this. The oil was finished, so Zed put the cap back on and fired the empty container towards the garbage.

"Sure. The Golden Rule is about treating others as you want to be treated."

"10 points. See, pretty much every society is based at one point on the Golden Rule. A healthy society punishes those who break the Golden Rule and rewards those who are shining examples of it. And these activities are often public for all to see. Even when they are not, though, early on in society people adopt these same values and those who break the Golden Rule are often shunned or pushed out of the tribe."

This made sense to me. This is how I thought society worked. This is how my father taught it to me. But it didn't work that way now. This still appeared to be the way we told each other it worked; it was that meniscus of civilization. What happened to us as a society that we were no longer like this?

"But that is not how we are. It seems like it on the surface, like the fairy tale has stayed the same, but the truth seems like the opposite."

"Exactly. Every civilization lasts several hundred years, give or take. It goes through stages of growth and decay, much like a tree. When it starts out it is often very healthy and is aligned with the Golden Rule. Your civilization, however, has passed its peak of decadence and is headed well into decline - though most do not yet recognize that. It is a key marker of that decline that personal entitlement becomes more important as a concept than honour. The Golden Rule takes a back seat to letting everyone have their own path and not judging them. The non-judgment seems enlightened, but for the fact that we use it as an excuse to not care and not act when someone does something counter to the Golden Rule. It is a society that is ill, which is why it furthers its decline and eventually fails."

"Why does it specifically punish those that follow the Golden Rule, though?"

"That part is tricky. They are not really punishing you for following the Golden Rule. You see, at this point in the decline, the fairy tale is still the fairy tale, but underneath is a current of entitlement and selfishness. If a person lives his life with honour in this society, they are inevitably going to be screwed over as they do not understand the game that is played on the decline. When they are screwed over, they notice the fairy tale is only skin deep, and they are vocal about it as it goes against their sense of honour. It threatens the very fabric of the fairy tale for everyone around them. It makes these people frightening to the rest of society. So they shun the honourable and push them out. Like lone wolves, as you say. In essence they behave exactly the opposite of what one would expect in the fairy tale, but they are not conscious of it."

This was very hard for my mind to comprehend completely, but it did make a lot of sense. What I had a hard time swallowing was that this made the actions of my former friends not their fault. They were just drones protecting the hive, so to speak. It took away their accountability in the horrible way they had treated me. I didn't like that, but then again, as Zed said, our society was ill. That they were well adjusted to an ill society made them ill and nothing more.

"So the way people treat others in these situations is not their fault then? They are simply just going with the script?"

"Not at all. They have brains and they are making a choice. They don't have to be dicks to people in your situation. But they are. The crazy thing is that they will justify it to themselves later. They will conjure all sorts of reasons why you were a bad person. That is the way the mind works. If they didn't do this, their mind would be awash in internal strife. You will be vilified. You will be slandered. The trick is to accept this and not give a fuck. These people are your past, not your present or future. So cut them loose and devote no more time or energy to thinking about them. They made their choice out of ignorance. I made mine out of knowledge. I choose to stand separate from society. A 'lone wolf' as you say."

He stood apart from society not because he lacked character or honour, but *because* he had those qualities. I was forced to this spot, but Zed had chosen it purposefully. That must have taken enormous mental strength and will power.

"It must be a bit lonely."

"Hell, it's not as bad as you think. If you get enough lone wolves, they form a pack of sorts. You end up looking for the other people in your predicament and you get good at spotting them. Besides, there are other advantages as well."

"Like what?"

"Well, wolves care not for the rules of sheep. There are subtle rules that go along with the fairy tale of society that are only there to support the fairy tale. Since you have been pushed out of that, you no longer need to adhere to these. If you want to drive in the parking lot entrance marked as 'Exit', go ahead. If you want to walk right up to a teller in a bank instead of walking through their maze of ropes, go ahead. You want to wear a hat at a formal dinner, feel free to. If you want to punch someone in the face in your own garage...well we know how that goes. These are all societal rules, not logical ones. You need to give yourself permission to completely ignore any rule you don't find logical. Society fucked you over, so why bother catering to its needs? Why prop up a fairy tale that ejected you? Mostly it is not even illegal to break them either, and even when it is, barring the major crimes, you will likely only get a fine. Fuck convention. Fuck tradition. You are now free as a bird to live your life however you want. It will make the sheep even more frightened, but fuck them."

I had experienced this just last night. The velvet rope at the *Cheshire Kitten*; I just walked over it. And where generally I would not drink at all and get behind the wheel, I found myself thinking it was O.K. to have a drink. Zed was right. Why would I waste my time on following rules that were set up to propagate the fairy tale and nothing else? Like jaywalking; what a stupid law that was. It made no logical sense. If the street was clear, you should be able to cross. It was an illogical law made under the guise of safety. And think about bylaws like cutting your lawn or weeding out dandelions. Those sorts of rules help no one at all. I would rather pay a fine every year than conform to that silliness. This freedom felt very right to me. I had often found societal laws or conventions to be very illogical. Now I had the freedom to ignore those bits. It previously felt like I would have to abandon honour to disobey the rules, but in fact, I could do so while retaining my honour. In fact it felt very right to disobey illogical rules. Society had broken its contract with me. I was no longer part of the pack.

"I feel like I should howl or something."

He handed me a long Phillips screwdriver.

"Well don't. Start taking off those tank wings."

"Why?"

"Because tank wings are for pussies. Some things in life serve no purpose other than to be pretty. Tank wings are like that."

I crouched down and started unscrewing where the tank wings attached to the bike.

"So, do you feel up to what you have to go through to be ready to meet your girl?"

"I don't even know what I need to do."

One tank wing dropped to the ground. I collected the screws and put them on the rack next to me. Then I moved to the other side of the bike.

"I will give you three tasks to do. They will be difficult and they will be grueling, but they will rebuild you as a man. So, is she worth it? Is she worth a little more pain?"

The other tank wing dropped to the ground. There was no question. Dream was worth it. Besides, I was already living life in pain. Pushing through a bit more pain to gain happiness seemed like a fair trade. I put the wing and its screws on the rack and turned to Zed.

"Yes. Definitely."

"Great. I will have my associate, Mark Curry, get in contact with you this week. By the way, this bike is yours."

I sat in silence looking at it. I could not believe he would just give me something like this. Without the tank wings it looked more primal and bad ass. It was a small displacement bike, but it had attitude.

"Thank you. But why?"

"Look, a man needs a motorcycle. You traded some of your wildness in when you opted for the domestication of marriage. Time to reclaim that."

"I don't even have a motorcycle license."

"That would be one of those fairy tale rules we talked about."

I was overcome with emotion. It was such a big thing to give. And he was right about the wildness. I needed that again. Zed was helping me find Dream and had given me a motorcycle. It took all of my man powers not to cry. He noticed my silence.

"Hey, it's not worth much anyway. It's no big deal. Let's not get crazy and hug or anything."

I nodded.

Then he hugged me.

I came into Zeds dining room dressed in my clothes from last night. Caryn and Venus were busy munching on pancakes with rainbow coloured blobs sticking out of them. Zed was reading the paper.

"Dad, we made gummi bear pancakes. Do you want some? What happened to your eye?"

I reached up and felt my eye. It was definitely swollen from where Zed had punched me.

"Venus, can you get him a steak for his eye? He needs to look good at the end of his journey."

"Really, Zed? Do you have to hit them every time?"

I sat down and took a big bite of the syrupy gummi bear mess in front of me. It was really quite tasty. A stream of syrup escaped down my chin. Caryn watched me eat expectantly. I nodded to show her I thought they were good.

I followed the bees to find the path. I was on the path to rebuild myself. It would all lead to Dream. I was a lone wolf. I truly felt like howling.

# TWO WHEELS AT NOON

here was really no sensation in the world like it. It was freedom. It must be how birds felt when they soared upon the breeze. I leaned the little black motorcycle right over in the corner. It didn't have the speed of a bigger street bike, but it was light and nimble and I was exhilarated with the wind stalking all around me and the world askew. I could feel the tires dig into the corner as I rounded it. I downshifted and the engine roared.

I came out of the corner and shifted up into fifth. I cranked the throttle and let the black beast go as fast as she could. It was probably only doing 110, but it felt like I was arrow fast, like a falcon diving on its prey. I was pushing the bike and it was dangerous. I knew that. It was also liberating. It felt like the one activity in this world that matched my 'I don't give a fuck' attitude. It was always a possibility that my bike could career off the road, out of control, into a fireball of death, but I just didn't care. The world was too messed up for me to care. Besides, this thing was motorized therapy. I could feel the machine literally sucking away my pain and transferring it to the road via screaming motor and rubberized empathy. It was my internal combustion succubus. There was something about that symbiosis of man and machine that freed my mind up to process thoughts that had been kept at bay; thoughts like shadow tigers in my mind. You dared not think of them alone, yet riding the machine opened them up.

I pulled onto Crowchild Trail from an on ramp and cranked on the throttle. Zed was right about this. Every man needs a motorcycle. I know what everyone says. They say they are death machines. When I got married I was told I had to be more responsible and careful. I needed to be safe. I had traded in my wild soul for a yoke of responsibility. It was a fine trade except for the betrayal and pain at the end. Driving this made my heart lighter and brought back the smile I had long since thought lost. Zed could not have given me a better gift. I weaved in and out of the slower traffic on my iron steed like a knife through butter. They were the sheep and I was the wolf; a lone wolf if Zed were to be believed. I growled as I rode. The engine drowned out the noise. How wonderful. I could say whatever I wanted and no one would hear it. The drone of the motor quieted the constant ringing of my ears that hadn't left me since the split. It was a blessed non-silence. I threw back my head and howled.

As my howl stopped, the howling sound persisted. Was someone else howling? No, it was a bit more like a whistle. A siren. I looked in my mirrors to find red and blue lights flashing. Fuck. It was all good to listen to Zed's advice about not caring about fairy tale laws, but here I was racing through town without a motorcycle license, a license plate, or insurance. The license and insurance was a problem, but the speeding I always thought was a bit of hypocrisy. It always seemed to me that speeding tickets were less about the law and more about the money. If caught though, it would be more about the license and insurance. Fairy tale law or not, that would be serious trouble. My heart raced in my chest. What was I going to do? What could I do? It was simple really. I could pull over and likely face jail time or I could outrun the police car. Surely the second option was insane. It didn't matter. When I came back to reality, my body had already made the choice. I found my hand had cranked the throttle, which I definitely would not have done if I was going to pull over.

I could hear the low growl of the police car as he accelerated to follow me. He definitely had more speed than I did, but I was way more maneuverable. I was nimble and quick and could go places he could not. I pulled into the fast lane and passed a van on my right. The police car mimicked my move and pulled alongside the van at the same time. An off ramp was quickly approaching. I shot over two lanes and applied the brakes so that the van was on my left now and the police car was to the left of it. Quickly, I leaned my bike over to the right and drove up through the grass towards where the off ramp led. I could hear the screech of tires as the police car realized my move. My bike flew through the air as it jumped the curb onto the off ramp. I could still hear the police car in pursuit, but I had gained some distance on him. I quickly darted into the first residential street I could find and sped through the neighborhood. I could hear the police car closing. I hopped the curb and drove down a walkway that led to a bike path. Beside the bike path was a golf course. Dotting the side of the golf course were clumps of forest. I sped my bike towards one of those and did not slow as it approached. I could hear the chirp of the police car tires as it came to a stop near the walk way. Branches battered against me as I entered the forest, but a little pain was acceptable given the alternative of jail. I leaned over and slid the bike down on its side. I turned the key off and the motor silenced.

My breath was heavy in my helmet. I could feel the pulsing of my heart. I could hear the radio of the police officer patrolling down the walkway. This was a stupid idea. Who rides without a license? Of course that was always going to lead to trouble. The officer walked slowly down the bike path looking left and right. I tried to slow my panting. I was sure he could hear me breathing like an asthmatic, but he didn't. He gazed into the woods where I lay for a second or two, but just kept on walking. I was sure he would see the broken branches that led to my position, but perhaps the woods was a place even the police felt at odds with. They were a force for civilization and currently I was of the wilds. Those two worlds didn't mix. He prowled the city, but here I sat in the forest shadows, wild like a jaguar. My instinct was to get on my bike and speed away. I suppressed that though as it would just lead to another chase. What would the jaguar do? He would wait. So I waited. I lay in my spot for a good hour before the police officer walked the other direction. His boots clopped loudly on the pavement of the bike path like a goat. The squawk of his radio pierced the silence of my oasis. He walked on up the walkway and entered his car. I heard it pull away.

I waited another hour before leaving myself. I made sure to take a different way home than the path I had taken here so that I didn't run into the police again. It was one thing to ignore the 'fairy tale' rules, but what I did was stupid. I didn't need to play by the rules, but I could be smart about it. At the very least, I needed to fabricate a license plate so that I didn't attract attention. The one good thing about being without one was that this police officer had no visible identification from my bike that could tie it back to me. He had nothing. I had outrun the police. I could not believe it. It was exhilarating. It was also stupid.

The fabric of the couch was pressed firmly against my skin. Sunlight streamed through the window and soaked into me as I lay there like a lump. I had no energy. I often had moments like this since the split. I would go from being up and able to being an unmoving sloth in a heartbeat. It may not even have been that I needed sleep. Sometimes, like today, I would just lie there. My body just didn't want to move. Even the sunlight didn't help. It used to. When I was younger there was not much that sunlight didn't cure. As I lay here, it seemed the reverse. It seemed the sunbeams were force fields pasting me to my fabric jail.

It had been the better part of a week. It had seemed like I had gained momentum following the bees and Zed had said he would send his associate, Mark Curry, my way to help me on my quest, but so far there was nothing. I felt a sense of urgency about the whole thing. I knew there was pain and trials to come, but I was going through pain and trials anyway, so why not do so with the goal of meeting Dream? I think the waiting was the problem. When I was chasing bees or even when I was talking to Zed, I felt the situation was in my control. Now, though, I was waiting. I was waiting passively for someone else to come and help me out. That lack of control over something so important in my life was hard to take. The lack of action on it was even harder. To be fair, Zed didn't tell me exactly when Mark would be in contact, but that didn't make it any easier.

-Ding Dong-

The doorbell shocked me with its intrusion into my introspection and couch surfing. I sat up. Wait, could it be Mark Curry? I hadn't give Zed my home address, but I could hardly see that keeping him from knowing it. I really wanted it to be him, but something felt wrong about that. It just didn't seem like an associate of Zed's would be the 'knock on your front door' type.

It was possible it was one of the Jehovah's Witnesses or Mormons or other door to door God salesmen. I didn't understand those guys at all. I mean, they go door to door assuming that the person's door they are knocking on has a different religion and that the religion (or lack of religion) that they have is very wrong, and then want to talk to them about it. It was the spiritual equivalent of going door to door saying 'By the way, you look fat in those pants'. It is completely rude behavior sold in the guise of 'caring'.

I remembered my ex on the phone saying that a guy would be by with papers to sign. That was likely it. Suddenly my stomach was feeling very queasy and the tinnitus in my ears got very loud.

"There is someone at the door, Dad. Do you want me to get it?"

"Can you take a peek to see what they look like?"

I felt a bit guilty and cowardly letting Caryn check out our potential house guest. After all: *A man fights his own battles.* But I needed to know who it was before I answered and if I peeked out there was a chance they would see me. Then the jig would be up. I needed to know, but safely and anonymously.

-Ding Dong -

"He is wearing a suit and tie, Dad. He has one of those man-purse things to hold documents"

"O.K. Come sit on the couch with me"

She hurried around the corner and jumped onto the couch.

"Why aren't we getting the door?"

"It's a lawyer from your mom. He has papers for me."

She nodded as if it was the most normal reaction in the world. It was logical, but it was far from normal. *A man has courage to face his own calamities.* I just needed a strategy to deal with this particular calamity before I responded to official legal documents.

-Ding Dong -

That aside, it was extremely difficult to simply ignore a door bell. I felt rude sitting here in my living room and not answering my door when someone was out there. I always feel the same when a phone was ringing. To not answer it goes against all societal convention. Then again, I was one of those societal outcasts, so why should I care? Why should I feel obligated to answer the door for this person at all? If it was a guest I was expecting, that was one thing, but this was someone who was here uninvited. Fuck them. Let them ring the damned door bell.

There was a flurry of knocks on my door. Caryn looked at me with a twinkle in her eye. I could tell she was suppressing a laugh. I found that I was as well. Why not? The whole situation was silly. Here I was a grown adult hiding in my living room from some weasel in a suit. I leaned in to whisper to Caryn, but I found a laugh escape as I did. She could not hold back anymore either.

I used to take great pleasure in email and social media. Before the split, my online life was quite active. I posted witty and topical statuses which were often 'liked' and commented on by my friends. I would frequently email my close friends back and forth throughout my days as a way of keeping in contact and conversing. The split had dried up my friends, however, so my social media had dulled to a torrent of kitten pictures and inspirational quotes from mere acquaintances and my email traffic had all but ceased. I would get the occasional email from my parents to 'keep my chin up', but that was about it. The strange thing about it is that I would still frequently check my email out of habit. Sometimes I would press the 'Refresh' button four or five times in succession hoping it would conjure up an email; some sign that the outside world cared.

Today, there was no reason to do this. There was a fresh email in my inbox. It was a curious thing though as it was not from a person I knew: Bradley Channing. My stomach was instantly in knots. It is possible that this could have been spam, like the Nigerian money scam or something, but I didn't think so. My gut told me that 'Bradley Channing' sounded much like a lawyer's name. It is strange that some names sound more like some professions, but it is very true. 'Mike Smith' sounded more like a mechanic, 'Blake Swoon' sounded like an actor, 'Tyler Skank' sounded like a rock star, and 'Barry Trask' sounded like a lawyer. Most people would agree with this even though it seems crazy. If it was a lawyer, it must have to do with my ex. I didn't want to open it. It was silly not to, but I knew it would hurt. It was like pulling off a band aid though; best do it quick. I opened it. It had a 'confirm read' request. I closed it without confirming. I hated those.

Attn: Dylan Gunn

I have been retained by your spouse, Merideth Gunn, as her counsel with respect to her rights and concerns as they pertain to your marital breakdown leading to separation, to help guide her to a peaceful and equitable resolution with respect to spousal support and property settlement.

With respect to spousal support, the Divorce Act decrees that a judge must consider whether spousal support meets one or more of the following purposes:

1. to compensate the spouse with the lower income for sacrificing their own possible career opportunities to instead support their partner.

2. to compensate the spouse with the lower income for ongoing child care; or

3. to help a spouse who is in financial need if the other spouse has the ability to pay.

On a cursory review of your finances, it would appear that there would be some entitlement to spousal support as 1) Ms. Gunn stayed home to support your career advancement during your marriage and 2) Ms. Gunn has incurred undue hardship during her separation due to negligence on your part to provide adequate support.

Therefore, I am hence with requesting that you take this correspondence to a lawyer of your choosing, and have them contact me within 10 days of receipt of this letter. Failure to comply will result in immediate litigation using the full power of the courts to obtain any and all relevant financial documents in order to determine adequate support payments currently and retroactively.

I had hoped to serve this missive in person, but my courier was met with a non-response at your residence. You should be aware that in our current day and age, documents can be 'served' via email. Consider this your notice.

Sincerely

Bradley Channing
Barrister and Lawyer

I sat staring at my computer monitor in confusion. What the hell was this? I didn't even understand what I was reading really. I was angry about it though. It seemed to paint Merideth as some sort of innocent lamb who was wronged and myself as a 'negligent' tyrant withholding money from her. I wasn't the one who couldn't keep my legs closed. I wasn't the one who had abandoned my child. It made it seem like she was entitled to spousal support as she supported my career. Nothing could be further from the truth. Sure, she stayed at home, but she did nothing to support my career. It was me that looked after Caryn and did the dishes and cleaned the house. It was me that worked my ass off to have enough money to fuel her music career. If anything, I was the one supporting *her* career. The 10 day window seemed very threatening as well with its 'immediate litigation'. It did not put me in a good frame of mind. And why would I need to take this to another lawyer? Did I need my own weasel to speak to a weasel?

I felt like replying and asking if he knew his client was full of shit. I wanted to reply telling him to cram his 10 day window and moronic double speak up his weasely ass. I knew that wouldn't help me though, even though it would feel very good. What I did know is that I didn't want to deal with this now, and I didn't have the energy to deal with this in the next 10 days. It was much easier to deal with when I could just ignore the guy knocking on my door. If only there was some way to do that with email as well. But wait, there was! I could use the vacation auto responder. Well, not quite use it - I could fake it. It would be a bit of a lie, but it would keep the weasel at bay for a bit anyway. Except that *Real men don't lie.* I don't generally like to lie, but in this case it was likely ok. His email was sent containing a bunch of falsehoods, why should he expect anything different back. I composed an email.

> Vacation Auto-response: Hi and thank you for what I can only assume was a wonderful and well intentioned email. Unfortunately, I am away on a much needed vacation and I am not able to answer your email at this time. I will get to it when I return, I promise. Until that time I will be sure to have a margarita on the beach in your name
>
> Sincerely,
>
> Dylan

There, it was done. That should stop him from trying to insist on a 10 day window. How could he, when he had no way of knowing if I had even received his email. This should stop him from dropping by in person or phoning as well. If I just stopped answering my phone and door for the next while, I could keep up the charade. It was brilliant.

Creating a fake license plate was easy. I got everything I needed at one of those big box hardware stores. I got a sheet of aluminum, paints, and paintbrushes. I had tin snips and a drill at home already. I cut out a shape the size of a motorcycle license plate and drilled holes in the top where it gets bolted to the bike. I have always found the sound of a drill going through metal satisfying.

I spray painted the aluminum white and was planning on hand painting the frame and letters red, which is the colour scheme in Alberta, but Caryn found me a stencil online that I could paint through. She even fabricated registration stickers that we super glued to the license plate. It was maybe not the best parenting to teach my daughter how to counterfeit a license plate, but she seemed to know all corners of the internet to do this and the whole licensing system was a joke anyway. It deserved some bent rules.

I got out my paint brushes and a can of red paint. I figured I may as well paint the gas tank. That way if the police were looking for a black bike, this would throw them off. I could have spray painted it, but I had bought these paint brushes, so I wanted to use them. Plus the feeling of the paint brush felt nice in my hand. It had been years since I had painted anything. I was only average at painting. My Mom was really good at it though. She had a little studio in our basement where she would paint once in a while. I tried my hand at it here and there, not so much because I had a talent, but because I wanted to spend time with my Mom. I could still hear her advice in my head as I painted the gas tank.

"Long and even brush strokes, Dylan."

It was silly advice, really, as no one does short and jagged brush strokes on purpose. The smell of the paints brought me back though. I could picture my Mom's little studio in my head. It was always neat and tidy, which is not really what you would expect from an artist. You expected paint splotches everywhere and a bottle of bourbon on the counter. I guess my mom was different as she really wasn't an artist per se - she just liked to paint. She would often just sit and stare at a blank canvas. It was her way of starting out. I liked to cut something out of a magazine and try to recreate it on a canvas, to varying degrees of success. My mom liked to stare at her canvas for a while first. When I would ask why, her responses just served to confuse me more.

"See, that is your problem, Dylan. You are trying to force the painting to be what you want. You have to listen to the paints and canvas and help unleash what they truly want to be."

With my Mom, apparently the paint and canvas inevitably wanted to be a picture of a stream with trees on either side of it, as that is what every painting she ever did looked like. So either all paints and canvases everywhere desire to be trees and a stream, or the 'unleashing' was what my Mom wanted to paint herself.

I can see myself beside her in her studio, with a blank canvas in front of me and my chunk of sandstone beside me to paint. I am confused. This never happened in my memory. It is purely a fabrication of my mind. Also, I only have the colour red to paint with. I look from my blank canvas and back to my sandstone chunk. I desperately want to break more pieces off of it. That feels right. I am not here to break chunks of sandstone off though. I am here to paint, but how can I paint this if I only have red. I look at my palette. There are lots of different colours there, but they are all red. My Mom stands behind me and sighs.

"You are thinking too literally, Dyl. You picked that palette for a reason. Paint what it wants to be, not what it is."

My brush touches the canvas. Long and even strokes.

I take the train to work every day. I have generally done this for environmental reasons more than social ones. It is cramped and uncomfortable and smelly. In the past I generally found my spot, opened a book and tried my best to ignore everyone else on the train. Recently, this had changed for me. I enjoyed looking at the different people on the train and discerning things from their looks and behaviour. The woman's brightly coloured scarf was a shout of her need to be noticed. The man's repeated looks to his watch said something about his lateness and what he thought about it. More so, though, I was interested in figuring out if each person was the honourable sort, or someone who would lie and cheat their way through the world, like my ex. Was their makeup used to accentuate their inner beauty or as a mask covering the monster below? I was unsure how accurate I ever was with this, but I think it is likely part of the process of retraining one's intuition about which people are 'good' or not after being utterly betrayed.

Today, something else that caught my attention. It was what I like to call 'being quite aware of my gender'. I was lucky enough to get a seat this morning, but it was an edge seat, not a window one. Others were crammed in standing everywhere they could. I was struck by a drifting cloud of perfume coming from the woman beside me. It was not a scent I had smelled ever before but as it washed over my senses I felt both aroused and calmed. I turned to look at the source of it. She was about my age, brunette, but with the most perfect lips I had ever seen. I could have admired the subtle curves of her red lips for hours, but *a gentleman sees but doesn't look*. I turned away, but the image was still in my mind. I didn't stare, but the lingering thought of her lips and the smell of her perfume made me very aware of my gender and sexuality. *A gentleman sees but doesn't look* is certainly true, but it is amplified once you are married or even dating someone. Sure you might notice a pretty woman, or a beautiful curve of a hip or breast, but you downplayed it in your mind. You told yourself she had an odd nose or legs that were too skinny. You told yourself all sorts of falsehoods to make her un-alluring. At the same time you made positive comparisons to your own wife or girlfriend. You told yourself that your wife had a prettier smile or sexier shape. One had to go down in value and the other up. It was like seeing a juicy steak and telling yourself it was made of soy. For me though, recently, this inner downplaying of other women had stopped. I could have steak again, so to speak, and it made me quite aware of my gender and sexuality.

The urge to turn and look at her lips again was almost too much to overcome. Lucky for me my imagination was very good. I could hold that image in my mind and not succumb to temptation. The train stopped outside the 6<sup>th</sup> Street West station, so I rose to get off. I found the woman with the lips also working her way to the door. She walked down the street in front of me. She was wearing a skin tight grey cotton dress and her bum swayed left and right as her high heels hit the ground one after the other. I was mesmerized by the sight of it. She turned and crossed the street to the north while I waited for the walk light. The pure enjoyment of seeing her walk was such that I felt like grieving when our paths parted.

I crossed 6<sup>th</sup> Street and was still basking in the images of her lips and swagger when I entered the coffee shop. The place was humming with conversation and easy listening music. I got into line for coffee. It was long, but amazingly efficient. It was incredible how swift we could be as a species when an addiction was on the line. I ordered my usual and the cashier told me it would be $2.50. I took a quick drink of my coffee and fumbled in my pocket for my change. A song started playing in the background that seemed familiar. Where had I heard that beat before? It was a slow and addictive beat and was building in intensity. I stood transfixed and curious. The singing started:

*Autumn winds, they whisper away*
*Your name is etched in grey dawn days*

Oh my god. It was one of Merideth's, *Autumn Winds,* from her second album. There was a searing pain in my chest. The world felt tilty. I lost grip on my coffee and it started to fall in slow motion. I was falling as well and it seemed it was happening just as slowly.

Suddenly I was back to when I first discovered her affair. I had opened her email to confirm what the other man's wife had told me. What I had found had hurt like liquid fire. The entire second album was apparently written about this guy. I recall one note that he had sent her in perfect clarity:

*"Your husband is a fool not to realize Autumn Winds is about another man."*

And her response was even worse.

*"Haha, I know. He has no idea. And the icing on the cake? He paid for that album. Loser. Lol."*

Lol. Three little letters showed just how cruel Merideth was on the inside. My chest was burning in pain. I saw the coffee from my cup spill into the air as I continued my descent.

"I think he's having a heart attack!"

It wasn't a heart attack. It felt like one, but it wasn't. I have felt this searing pain before. I used to think people were overly sentimental when they said things like "heartache." Surely, I thought, they knew that emotions were from the mind and all the heart did was pump blood. Logically people must realize that. However, when your love is betrayed like this, it hurts right in your heart. I have no rational explanation for it, but it is a truth.

I hit the ground hard and felt coffee splash onto my shirt and face.

"Someone help him!"

"Call 911!"

Caryn was there, holding my head. How did she get here? Why was she downtown and not in school? She was crying.

"It's ok, Dad. You will be ok."

Why was she here? I shook my head and sat up.

"Caryn?"

I turned and she was gone. I must have hit my head hard. That explained it. I reached back and could feel a goose egg forming. I stood up.

"Sir, are you ok?"

Everyone in the entire place was staring at me. I nodded.

"I must be low in iron or something."

Merideth's song continued on the speakers as I put my change on the counter and left.

I was still rubbing my head when I reached to my desk at B.R. Pratt. I was embarrassed about my tumble in the coffee shop, but I was more ashamed that I was still affected by something like this. I should be able to hear one of Merideth's songs without fainting and hitting my head. It seemed colossally unfair that the victim of such cruelty and selfishness has to deal with consistent and persistent pain while the person who caused it likely sails through life with little to no consequences for their evil actions.

My phone rang.

"There is a man in the lobby who says he is here to see you."

Oh crap. It must be the lawyer or one of his couriers. He must be checking to see if I really was on vacation. I could avoid it, but what if it wasn't the lawyer?

"What does he look like?"

"Sir?"

"Just describe him to me."

"Black suit, dark hair, briefcase."

That certainly sounded like a lawyer, but it was tough to say. I could not put off an actual client just because I feared it might be my ex's lawyer.

"Can you ask him his name and what business we have together?"

"Sure. Hold on..."

I could hear the clop of her shoes across the tile floor over the phone and then muffled voices. Then the clopping noises again. What would I do if it were the lawyer? I could tell her to tell him I wasn't in, but all the back and forth on the phone would seem to indicate otherwise. Still, it was probably my best course of action. Sometimes even a poor choice is the best choice you have.

"He says his name is Mark Curry and that he is here as a representative of the Zed Corporation."

"I'll be right down."

He was not what I expected. Zed had looked like a biker from a gang, so I expected Mark Curry to look much the same. He was about as far from Zed as I could imagine. He wore a three piece suit with a shiny purple tie. His hair was cut short. It was dark with wings of grey above his ears betraying his age. The oddest thing, though, were his sneakers. I usually do not notice these things, but he wore a three piece suit with sneakers. I would have figured dress shoes, but when I thought about it dress shoes were mainly uncomfortable. They were something from the 'fairy tale' as Zed would have put it. The fairy tale dictated that dress shoes be worn with a suit, but why not wear what you wanted? He, like Zed and I, likely owed nothing to the fairy tale. However, why wear a tie, then? Ties were a symbol of servitude. They were like trendy silken career nooses. It was bizarre.

I led him down the hallway to one of B.R. Pratt's smaller meeting rooms. He sat down in a chair in the far corner and threw a duffle bag down on the table. I closed the door behind me.

"Firstly, I want to say how excited I am to work with you, Dylan. Zed filled me in on your situation and told me a bit about you and I think this is going to be a wild ride"

He talked a million miles an hour. I did not expect it from someone in a suit. I expected a slower and more measured speech.

"Can I ask you a question?"

"Sure man, whatever you like."

"It's cool you wear sneakers, but why the tie?"

"See, that's what I mean! I think you have a chance to get through this alive. It's a test, my man! I wear the sneakers because they aren't societal bullshit. They are comfortable and functional.

I wear the suit and tie because it *is* societal bullshit. I can move about anywhere I want with this and no one questions it. It's 'bullshit camouflage' as it were. Only the really perceptive see both."

I glanced at the duffle bag on the table. That didn't match either. I expected a briefcase with what Mark was wearing. Something about that didn't seem right.

"Oh that? That is a few things I gathered that will help you. Don't open it right now. What did Zed tell you about the process?"

"Not much. He said he had some tasks for me to do and that it would help rebuild me. He said he would put you in contact with me."

Mark twisted his mouth to the side in thought. Then he paced the floor. He was very expressive with his hands.

"See now, that isn't quite right. You should see it more as a quest. Every man seeks to be a knight, but you get a chance here to become one. Exciting, no? We don't give this chance to just anyone. You have to have that spark you know?"

"What do you mean?"

"Well, it's because of the high mortality rate. Not just anyone can handle it."

I had liked what he said about being a knight. In his heart, that is what every man wants to be from the time he is a little boy. Knights are paragons of truth and honour and go out of their way to save people. It's that last bit which tied together with Mark's comment about mortality rates. Knights were heroes and it was partly due to with the fact that they risked life and limb on a quest or to save someone. A true hero had a goal. A true hero had hardship and danger. The modern concept of hero had been much watered down and I hated it. The modern 'hero' simply meant someone you admired. A modern 'hero' could be an actor or an athlete or a singer. These were people who might be admired for sure, but to me they could never be considered heroes. They were not on a quest. They were not facing hardships and danger. They were mere mortals. The fact that the tasks I was going to be performing were dangerous gave me a pang of fear initially, but I found I didn't care. Any fear was from my life before the split when I gave a shit if I lived or died. That and the romance of calling it a quest overrode any lingering fear I may have had. I nodded to him to show I understood.

"So are you still in?"

"You bet, what is my first task?"

I was more than 'in', I was anxious to get going. This whole thing was a bright beacon in my life. I needed this path and I needed to be walking it.

"Fucking outstanding! Your first task will be to talk with the Sphinx."

"You mean like the lion statue in Egypt?"

I was starting to think this may be not something I would be able to do. I mean, Egypt was so far away. How could I just travel there? Who would take care of Caryn?

"No, no, man. That is just a statue. You must have heard of Sphinxes in mythology. They would test people with riddles and kill them if they failed. I hate to say mythology though as they are pretty fucking real."

The air quotes he made when he said mythology reminded me of a hummingbird as they were very fast. Everything Mark Curry did was fast. A Sphinx though? That seemed hard to believe. I seemed to remember something about a Sphinx from my classical mythology class in university, but I didn't quite remember what it was. I didn't quite believe it really, but this was their show, so who was I to question it? I would go see this 'Sphinx' for myself.

"Ok. I believe you. So where do I find the Sphinx?"

"No man, you don't believe me. But gods, you will! You will believe me very soon. And the Sphinx? The one in Calgary hangs out in Century Gardens. Do you know the statue of the chess player?"

"I do."

I knew the chess player statue well. Century Gardens was just off the C-Train line I took to work every day. It was a small city park that was pretty but prone to illicit drug transactions. Locals simply called it 'The Pharmacy'. At the south end of the Pharmacy was a table with a statue sitting on a chair who was playing chess on a statue chess board. He looked perpetually in thought.

"Well, that's Hershel. He is one of the nicer Sphinxes. Whoa man, you are lucky with that. If you lived in Vancouver, well, that Sphinx is a real asshole. Anyway, drop by and see him this week. He will be expecting you. Oh, and bring him a latte, it will soften him up. That's one tip for you. And don't forget the bag."

Mark motioned to the duffle bag.

This was all coming at me way too fast, but I was anxious to start. I just had to remember all the things he said. Sphinx, Century Park, Latte, Bag. It hit me like a boxer on a speed bag.

"You O.K.? You look a little dazed."

"Yup, fine. I am just processing it all. Any other tips?"

He scratched his chin and looked around the room.

"Hmmm. Well, in general, for these tasks you should do 100 crunches a day. Oh, and fruit smoothies. You can't have enough of those."

"Got it."

"Cool. Well I have a fifty riding on you getting past the Sphinx. Speaking of that, is there anything occupying your mind lately; anything bugging you? I mean you need a free and clear mind to handle the Sphinx."

"Well, there is this lawyer bugging me about spousal support..."

I told him all about it. He smiled as I spoke; like he was amused.

"Uck! Lawyers are the worst. Send me his email. I will deal with it. Done like dinner."

I felt like my words to Mark must have been prophetic. I heard the email notification sound go 'bing' on my computer as I was doing my crunches the next day in my dining room. I checked it when I finished and it was as I had expected.

Attn: Dylan Gunn Re: Vacation Auto-response

Mr. Gunn, pertaining to my earlier email I had noted your email auto-response. While it is acceptable to be on vacation at this time, your email did not actually indicate your return time. As one can assume that a standard vacation is 7-10 days in duration and that you had likely been on the vacation at the time of the auto response (I will presume it to be halfway through), I will extend the olive branch and let your response time be extended 5 days.

Henceforth, I am requesting that within 15 days, you take this missive to a legal representative of your choosing and have them build a response in your name. I will need all bank statements, visa statements, investment portfolios, T4s, and any other relevant financial information for the last 3 years as well at that time. Otherwise, litigation against you will proceed immediately after.

Enjoy your vacation,

Bradley Channing.
Barrister and Lawyer

This guy just didn't give up. He had some nerve trying to presume when my pretend vacation would end. Also, it seemed slightly hypocritical to use phrases like 'Extend the olive branch' while at the same time threatening litigation. I forwarded the whole works to Mark Curry to see what he could do with it. Within half an hour a response came back.

Attn: Bradley Channing wrt Gunn vs. Gunn

Bradley,

It is with great luck that my client, Dylan Gunn, checked his email between his volcano hike and his afternoon MMA bout. He has sent me your missive and it must be mentioned that presumption of termination of an open ended vacation is shaky ground legally.

I am Mr. Gunn's tertiary adjunct advocate for this case and I am a practitioner of Purlieu Collaboration, mainly as it is reflected by the Montreal Amendments with which you are likely familiar. In which case, I must advise you that your insistence of litigation in a primary email is contrary to section 33(a) of the Montreal Amendments to Purlieu Collaboration.

> *33(a) Antagonizing speech/emails/body language/body odor in an initial set of contacts by either advocate or primary client, without prior analysis of secondary client's willingness to engage in the collaborative process, will be considered hostile and aggressive and may be held against the primary client in the proceedings.*

I am certain you are familiar with the Montreal Amendments, but I thought it would be prudent to include this here in case your legal career was more long in the tooth (better than calling you old, right?) or you graduated from a less informed law school. At any rate, if you are familiar with Purlieu Collaboration, I look forward to working with you. If not, I know a few outstanding practitioners in town: Adam Achaen and Serene Cowalski come to mind. Your client may want to retain their services with respect to this, if you prove to be deficient.

As is standard in Purlieu, I will expect a Kensington Dossier on your client. I am preparing one currently for Mr. Gunn. There is plenty of time though as my client is on open ended vacation and there will be no threat of litigation from our side as this is a collaboration after all. However, within the first three hours after he lands back in the country, I will expect that Kensington Dossier couriered to me and on my desk or I will initiate Mirepoix Proceedings as is the international standard.

Warm regards,

Marc Curry
Tertiary Adjunct Advocate, Purlieu Collaboration

    I was speechless. Mark sounded exactly like a lawyer in his letter to Merideth's lawyer. It was incredible. Perhaps he was a lawyer? I didn't exactly ask him his profession, but he didn't seem like a lawyer really. It made me smile though. I didn't know exactly what he was saying, but I could certainly recognize a subtle slight in there (or two). I had to email him to ask him about the parts I didn't understand though.

Hey Mark,

Thanks for sending that to the lawyer. I have to ask though, what does all of that mean? Purlieu Collaboration? Mirepoix?

Dylan

His response came quickly.

LMAO. It's all bullshit, man! I mean they are real words and stuff. Mirepoix simply means 'Stir Fry' in French. Lol. There is no such thing as Purlieu Collaboration or the Montreal Amendments, etc. I figured the dude dropped a grenade of legal-ese in your lap that you didn't understand and told you that you had 10 days to deal with it or else. He needed a taste of his own medicine. I sent him something he didn't understand and told him when you got back that he would have three hours to respond or else. Take that, asshole! It's all bullshit though. We will see if he pretends that he knows it or not. Besides, the more this guy has to read emails from me and look things up, the more he will charge your ex. :)

P.S. Get back to those crunches, I have money riding on you.

Mark

I had to laugh. The lawyer had seemed threatening and scary to me previously. It had not occurred to me to use the vileness of the whole process against itself or to use it as a bit of a weapon against my ex for initiating this crap. There was a sweet sort of karma about it.

I walked through Century Gardens with some nervousness. First, it was littered with the grubbies and drug weasels that I had come to expect. There was an odorously ripe homeless lady sleeping under a tree next to her shopping cart full of rags and cans. There was a sallow eyed fellow with a torn grubby jacket, yet a pristinely new backpack. Obviously that one was a drug dealer. More than the company, I was a bit nervous about the meeting itself. I was going to meet a Sphinx. This was something from mythology. I had to wonder if I was insane. It was logical to assume that somewhere after all the betrayal and hurt and stress that Merideth had saddled me with, my mind just snapped. Was it possible that I lay in a mental ward somewhere right now, heavily sedated and dreaming of Sphinxes and quests? It was possible, I suppose, but I think if I was actually insane, I would likely enjoy it more and ponder it not at all.

I approached the statue at the chess table and sat down opposite him. I placed his latte down in front of him and my fruit smoothie in front of me. I was not sure how this was supposed to work. Surely he did not come alive just by sitting at the same table as if that was the case, it would happen multiple times every day. He was supposed to be expecting me, so perhaps I should just start talking.

"Hello."

Nothing. It would have been helpful for Mark to give me some instructions on how to actually converse with the Sphinx. On the other hand, I could sit here for a few hours and talk to the statue and call my task complete. Something told me there was more to it than that. He did give me the duffel bag. I quickly rifled through it: A plastic sword, a vial of liquid, a pirate hat, and a timer with two buttons. How was this stuff supposed to help me? I took out the plastic sword. This seemed like the most likely thing considering how fearful the Sphinx was supposed to be. I swung it at the statue, but stopped an inch before hitting it. Wait, wasn't the Sphinx all about testing the mind? Why would I need a plastic sword then? I looked at the other items in the bag. Perhaps the timer. I put the sword back in the bag and took out the timer, placing it beside the chess board. Looking at it, it seemed right. I seemed to recall movies where people playing chess hit a button on a timer when they were done their turn.

I cautiously outstretched my hand and pressed one of the timer's buttons. The statue shimmered and came to life. It changed from its statue form to that of a grumpy old man. His face had dark wrinkled skin and black eyes set above a wide nose. His head was surrounded by a large lion's mane. The rest of his body appeared quite feline except for his hands, which were human, and his legs and tail, which were that of a scorpion. He rolled his eyes and sighed as he looked at me.

"I swear to you boy, if you had hit me with that sword, that would have been it for you."

He emphasized his point by thrusting his scorpion tail forward a bit.

"Hershel?"

He wore a dusty green vest with a pocket watch hanging out of one pocket. He dusted it off quickly with his hands.

"You know other Sphinxes in town, I take it? Of course I am Hershel. And you are Dylan. Do you know why you are here Dylan?"

"I am not sure. I was told I was here to talk with you."

He took a deep drink of his latte.

"That much is true, though a bit simple. I am to test your mind to see if it is worthy."

"And if I fail?"

He waved his scorpion tale back and forth. It made a rattling sound.

"Well, then I kill you. O.K.?"

He seemed pretty straightforward about it. I admired that. I had come this far, I was not about to back down. Sure, Hershel could kill me if I ended up being stupid, but I wasn't stupid. And you could die many ways during your day. You could get hit by a bus or choke on a chicken bone. Getting impaled by a giant scorpion tail was just one, albeit bizarre, way to go.

"Fair enough."

"Outstanding. You know this is what we Sphinxes are charged with, right? We get rid of the lowest rung on the human intellectual ladder. It's much like wolves culling weak and infirm deer. It strengthens the herd. That is our function."

It was tough to imagine. I encountered extremely stupid people in nearly every hour of my day. Either the Sphinxes were supremely lax in their jobs or something was wrong with this picture. The drug dealer with the nice backpack walked towards our table. I must have looked awfully strange chatting with a statue.

"I don't know Hershel. I see a lot of stupid around."

"Yeah, I get that comment a lot. What you have got to understand is that it is a matter of breeding. We Sphinxes are an antisocial lot. We mate once every hundred years or so, while you humans procreate like bunnies. There are simply too many of you for us to do the type of job we used to. Do you doubt I can kill?"

I tried to shake my head to indicate that I did not doubt him, but he was already rubbing his hands together and smiling. This would not be good. The drug dealer walked closer to our table. As he got near, Hershel's tail shot out and impaled him through the heart. The drug dealer immediately dropped to the ground, twitching and foaming at the mouth. I was shocked. There was no blood or tear in his clothing or anything else to indicate he was impaled, but there he lay twitching. Then he was still.

"Is he...?"

"Dead? Quite certainly. No one misses a drug dealer though. If anyone checks, he simply had a heart attack. An overdose perhaps."

I was panicked. What should I do? Should I call the police? That wouldn't work as no one would believe my story about the Sphinx and without that there were too many questions. What about the hospital? That would be of no use either as he was already dead. There was absolutely nothing I could do here.

"Well Dylan, shall we play?"

I sighed and nodded.

"Excellent."

-Click-

His hand touched the timer and instantly he was turned into the statue again. The chess board did not re-statueize though. It was still quite playable. I tried to remember all I knew about chess. It had been years since I last played. My dad taught me some growing up, but I had forgotten most of the good moves. I remembered that it was good to take control of the center though as the pieces had the most moves from that location. I took one of my central pawns and moved it forward two spaces.

-Click-

Hershel came to life again.

"Hmm. A smart opening move. It's not very inspired, but it is safe and smart. We used to be famous for our riddles. It was a quick and easy way to establish intelligence. But I find chess better. It's more enjoyable and less chance you get someone on a bad riddle day. Take our classic riddle: What has four legs in the morning, two legs at noon, and three legs at night? Do you know the answer? No pressure if you do not, that is not the test."

That was a tough one. I had never been wonderful at riddles. I knew enough about riddles to know that there was always a trick to them. Things were often metaphorical, so you had to think of things sideways. From the wording, either the legs or the sun was key, or both. There was an emphasis on the times of day, so perhaps that was the metaphor. What if it was a metaphor for a lifetime? Morning could be childhood, Noon could be adulthood, and nighttime could be the end stretch of life. What about the legs though? They could be clock hands, or actual legs, or something else entirely. Clock hands didn't make sense if I was using the metaphor of a 'lifetime'. I could revisit it later if I needed to. If it were actual legs, there are not many animals that have two legs. Mainly it was primates, birds, and kangaroos. All of those had the same number of legs their entire life. But wait though, when humans are young, they crawl. That could be considered 'four legs'. But what about the elderly? Did they have three legs? A cane. That was it.

"Mankind."

"Excellent. You puzzled that out well. If it were the old times that would be it and you would be on your way. We still have more though. Answer me this Dylan; do you believe that it 'Takes two to tango?"

Hershel moved one of his end pawns forward.

-Click-

He reverted back to a statue. That was a good question. I had heard that all my life. Whenever my sister and I had argued as children, my parents would use that phrase. The problem was that it seemed to be used to say "we don't know who was in the wrong, so we will just judge you equally at fault." My sister used to take advantage of this. She was smart. I remember a few days after Halloween when our candy would start to dwindle, my sister used to steal some of mine. I would get upset and we would argue. The argument would heat up and either mom or dad would get involved. They would say it "takes two to tango" and the candy had a 50/50 chance of being awarded to either me or my sister. When I thought of it, it did not take "two to tango" there. She initiated each conflict arbitrarily as she knew without fail that by doing so, she would get candy at least half of the time for her trouble. Essentially, "It takes two to tango" rewarded her for poor behavior. I thought about Merideth too. I treated her like a queen and did everything in my power to buy her what she wanted, to show her I loved her, and to make her life the very best it could be. She betrayed me for it. I know people always think that "It takes two to tango" in marital troubles too, but that isn't the case. I know that clearly from experience.

I realized I need to move a piece. I seemed to remember that it was good to get your knights out early as well. They were the most flexible and unique of the pieces as it was concerned with movement, so they were good to get out as early players. I moved one out.

-Click-

"Honestly, I think 'It takes two to tango' is bullshit. It is meant to exonerate a person from judging fault and rewards the actual instigator for their actions."

"Right on the nose, Mr. G. That relates highly to your situation as I think you have puzzled through. I know all the nuances of what you are going through. Mark Curry and I go to the same spin class on Tuesdays so he told me all about it. Divorces used to be concerned with fault. They were concerned with who cheated on whom or who was beating who and so on. At one point they switched to what they call 'No Fault Divorce'. Can you tell me why they would have done so? Any ideas?"

He moved one of his bishops forward so it threatened one of my knights.

-Click-

That was a hard question. I remember them talking about this in school at one point. I remember them saying that sometimes marriages break down without any fault. In essence, sometimes people just fall out of love and should be allowed to separate without having to justify 'fault'. I could understand that, but in other cases, there was certainly fault, so why abandon that? This was the justice system after all, should they not be concerned with justice when one person has been wronged? I know the original system was meant to protect a house wife from a cheating husband who skipped town with his much younger secretary and left her all the kids and none of the money. It seemed to work well for that, so why was it changed? There must be a clear reason or the Sphinx would not have asked me. The only thing that I could come up with is that perhaps it was difficult to prove fault. Perhaps it was just easier to split things without trying to prove it.

I could not see how his bishop move should worry me as even if it took my knight it was a sacrifice play. The pawn behind my knight could simply take the bishop if he took my knight. I moved my other central pawn instead.

-Click-

"It was likely because proof was difficult to obtain in many cases?"

He hissed through his teeth and rattled his tail.

"Damn Dylan, I may have to kill you yet. And you started out so promising. This was an easy one too. Fault is generally easy to determine. Someone cheated or someone abused their partner. Those are easy to figure out. Or they both did something horrible. Again, not hard to figure out. I will give you another try. This has to do with lawyers, and what motivates lawyers to do anything. Think carefully."

He moved one of his central pawns up two spaces to butt up against one of mine.

-Click-

What motivates lawyers? Money, of course, but how did that relate to this? I suppose if fault was relatively easy to determine, then things would be cut and dried. There would not be a lot of work for lawyers. However, if you moved to No Fault divorce, things were fuzzier. Even though it seemed pretty easy on splitting it 50/50, there could be questions on how much each person truly made and which things each person should own. In essence, there would be a lot of back and forth and the lawyers would make more money under No Fault divorce.

I could see that his move with his pawn had opened up a spot for him to bring his bishop out to put me in check. I moved my far end pawn out to set up a trap for that bishop instead.

-Click-

"It was because of money."

"Bingo. Nice trap you have set up there, by the way. What you have to understand is that family law is not about justice anymore, it is about money. In fact, most of the law these days is about money. You are playing a rigged game, my friend. This is a system designed by lawyers for the benefit of lawyers. This is a system where there is no judgment and no justice. If you expect to get any of that, you are very wrong. It's a system that allows people to behave in any way they want and not even feel shame. Even though it is technically a 'No Fault' system, can you identify where it still has vestiges of the fault system?"

Hershel moved his one knight forward so it threatened one of my center pawns.

-Click-

I had to think carefully here. That giant scorpion tail felt threatening each time I clicked the button. If there was no fault deemed in the breakup of a marriage, then where was the holdover of the old fault system? Perhaps the part of the old fault system was in how it was settled. Of course, things like alimony and child support were definitely punitive. I mean, I could understand supporting your children. Every father would want to make sure that his children were provided for, but some of the child support payments I had heard about were insane. Kids needed money to provide food and shelter, but they didn't need that kind of excess. Anything over and above basic needs was simply punishment. Kids needed love, not money.

I moved my pawn forward to protect my central pawn. If he attacked it with his knight he was going to get a surprise.

-Click-

"It's the support payments. If it was truly no fault, they would just split up the property and go their separate ways. This gives the lawyers more meat to fight over."

"Very astute. Spousal Support worked for the June Cleavers of the world and it worked well. They had been happy homemakers for years when their husbands left them for someone younger and with no way of supporting themselves. That was the scenario in the 40's, but it is rare today. Most women have their own careers, and those who stay at home are often university educated and quite capable of working their own jobs. Now they can divorce and work a job *and* get spousal support."

"That allows them to actually profit from splitting up their marriage."

"Exactly. Divorce nets lawyers billions every year. Now you can add child support onto that as well. It used to be that child support payments were considered part of the taxes of the recipient, but that was changed a few years ago to stay as the part of the payers' income tax. Mothers groups and feminist organizations everywhere fought for this saying that they wanted the most money possible to go to the children. That is a hogwash reason, of course, as the money could just as easily go to the kids if it stayed with the payer. Governments agreed to it. Do you know why?"

I was an accountant; this one was easy for me.

"Of course. If the taxing of that money stayed with the payer, it is at a higher tax bracket and the government makes more money. If the taxing of it was with the recipient, then the government makes less."

"See, now you are catching on. This is all about money. It has nothing to do with justice at all. It has nothing to do with children at all. The government can enact changes like this to get more money for themselves all while saying they are doing it for the children. The government doesn't give a rip about children. They just want their money. If they cared about children, they would mandate that every penny of that child support be accountable and traceable to something that benefits the child. They don't. In fact, the parents who receive child support could use it for lavish vacations and spa treatments and the payer is not allowed to complain. Child support is really just an additional spousal support. You would think this imbalance is a problem for men and women equally, but you would be wrong. Men end up being screwed in this deal more than women. Do you know why?"

-Click-

This made a lot of sense. I should have guessed the entirety of it. It was about the money. It was money for the government and money for the lawyers. The marriages and relationships that broke up and the children who were in the crossfire were of no consequence to the big business of divorce. I knew all too well why this affected men more than women: Honour. It was not that men had honour and women did not. It was that honour was different for us.

> *A man sacrifices for those that he loves.*
> *A man provides for those he loves.*
> *A man knows no dishonour like taking handouts*
> *from another.*

Even though we had feminism and equal rights and were moving towards equality in the genders, we still felt honourable having jobs that could provide for our entire family and allow our wives to stay home and work on their dreams. That is what happened to me. Merideth could have worked. She had a degree. I took satisfaction that I was being honourable in paying for everything. And when my sister Jenn got divorced, I saw the shoe on the other foot. Jenn made way more than her husband Shane. Shane would have been entitled to some support, surely, as he supported her all the way through university and after so she could build her career. When he had asked about support when they split, she told him to "be a man". That was all it took. Shane signed a waiver just days after saying he wouldn't seek support. *A man knows no dishonour like taking handouts from another.* Honour makes victims of men on both sides of the coin.

-Click-

"Honour"

"Just so! Men are not likely to ask for or get granted support. Men are likely to have tried to do the honourable thing and support their wives being at home: wives who were educated and capable of working all along. And they get screwed for it. A woman can cheat, divorce, and move on to another husband and profit from it. Some make a career of it. In essence, a man can be completely honourable and get punished for it. The innocent and the just get punished. Does that seem right to you? The imbalance gets worse though. Custody is often one sided with it defaulting to the mother. In today's no fault, gender equal world, how is 50/50 custody not the norm? And take the child tax benefit. The amount this is based on does not consider spousal support or child support additives to the income. So the person with the lower income gets the lion's share of the child tax benefit, even though after the child support and spousal support, they are likely earning more after tax. This just furthers the imbalance. Given this, what do you think of 'Deadbeat Dads'?"

-Click-

I had always loathed deadbeat dads. I would occasionally hear about one at work, or from a friend, or even in the news. They seemed to be the lowest, most vile sort of men that didn't want to pay for their kid's upbringing and hid all their money away. I did some quick calculations in my head and I was coming to a different conclusion altogether. Alberta is the very best place in the country for taxes, and yet I could see that under the burden of taxes, spousal support, and child support they may not even have enough left to live. These weren't deadbeat dads; these were just people trying to live.

-Click-

"They aren't deadbeats, I mean for the most part. I am sure

there are some actual deadbeats out there, but I can see how some are just trying to get by with the crushing weight of it all."

"That is it. See Dylan, you are catching on, and you are playing well too. You may yet live. Let me give you an example. There was this fellow in Toronto. He and his wife split. They had a million dollar home that was mostly paid off and 4 kids. He agreed to give her the house in exchange for her not seeking spousal support. She agreed. He still paid child support to the tune of $2500 a month. He made a salary of about $100,000 while she had one of about $20,000. Also, the house had a rental suite that gave her another $2000 a month. It leaves him about $73,000 after tax and her with $37000. However after the child support payments, she is left with $67,000 and him with $33,000. On top of this, she was receiving child tax benefit to the tune of $450 a month, so that brings her up to $72500. Anyway, a few years go by and she quits her job and decides to renege on the deal and ask for spousal support. The judge sides with her. She gets to keep the million dollar house and she gets an additional $1500 a month; and it's retroactive. That means she is up to $90,500 after tax and he is down to $15,000 after tax. Can you think of anywhere this man could live on $1250 a month in Toronto as well as eat? Can you guess what he did?"

I was following his math in my head. He was right on the money.

"I bet he refused to pay."

"That seems logical to do, but you are not allowed to refuse. They will garnish your wages to get that money. He fled the country. He left his ex-wife a note that said 'So long and thanks for all the fish'. He saves money in an account for the kids, but he doesn't see them at all. If you think you have it bad, he had it worse. His ex-wife should have learned that you can sheer a sheep many times, but you can only skin it once. There is another one about a man in B.C. whose second wife had the same job as he did with the same salary. He was paying support to his first wife at the time. They split and his wife decided to quit and ask for spousal support. The judge sided with her. To both his ex-wives he was ordered to pay an amount equal to twice his monthly salary every month. Do you know what he did?"

"Did he leave the country as well?"

"Nope, he wasn't that bright. He tucked his shotgun under his chin and pushed the trigger with his toe. Here is another one for you. Right here in Calgary. It is similar to your case. Educated wife, stayed at home. They had four kids. Husband made $113,000 a year. He supported his wife staying home to work on her acting career for years. She put them hundreds of thousands in debt for her career; headshots, classes, paying for productions - that sort of thing. She cheated on him and split. After their split she worked a part time job making about $24000. The courts deemed her acting income to be disallowed in the calculations as it was paid under the table. It amounted to about $10000 a year. After all the support payments and child tax benefit, he would have been left with around $20000 after tax and she ended up with about $75000. He didn't shoot himself. He had some creativity. He paid $10000 for a billboard that said 'The system is unjust and Carolyne de Puis is an evil greedy cunt'. Then he hiked into Kananaskis and jumped off a cliff to his death."

"O.K. Enough. The system is a mess. Are you trying to get me to kill myself too?"

"No, not at all. I just want you to know what you are up against, so you can start using your mind. Suicide is a clear and present danger. With respect to suicides due to divorce and separation, 80% are male. The suicide rate for men has steadily increased since 'No Fault' divorce was instituted. No one talks about it, because no one wants to do anything about it. No one gives a shit about these men. They are just vilified and called 'Deadbeat Dads'."

His queen came across the board and took my knight.
-Click-

My mind was buzzing from what Hershel was telling me. I had not imagined it was so bad. I had it pretty good compared to some of these other guys, but still I had to start thinking defensively. Merideth was looking for spousal support and all of that was based on salary. Her salary was insignificant, but she was capable of work. It seemed unfair that she chose not to work to her fullest capacity. Perhaps I should take a lower paying job. If it was based on salary, I could work at a lesser job to sour the milk for her, so to speak.

I moved my rook in to take his queen.

-Click-

"Nice move there. Not many take my queen."

"If it's based on salary, I could take a lesser job. I could live on less."

"That has been tried again and again and it does not work. Good thinking though. If you take a lesser job on purpose or even if you get disabled and cannot work as much, the courts will 'impute' a salary for you. I bet you haven't even heard of that word before"

"No, I haven't."

"It means that if your salary is lesser for any reason, they will deem that you make the same as you did when you made the most. 'Impute' means you are fucked."

"Can't they 'impute' a salary for her? She could be making much more than she does."

"Sadly, no. They give much more leniency to the person who earns lower. See the government wants you, the higher earner, to keep earning and driving the economy. They don't care about the lower earner that way as she is not driving anything. She is only riding your coat tails. Once it starts down this road, it is essentially slavery. Many men just give up and live as a slave. It's learned helplessness."

-Click-

This was filling me with outrage. How were so many people

getting a raw deal and yet it was so secret? Why were people not up in arms about this? How could the system be so wrong and no one was doing anything about it? It was exactly what Zed had mentioned earlier. Our whole society was sick. The greedy and selfish win and the just and honourable get screwed over.

My bishop slid down to take his rook in the end row.

-Click-

"Why don't men fight it?"

"Oh, they do, but it's fairly useless. Any man who tries to fight the child support or spousal support rules is deemed either a deadbeat dad or a misogynist or both. The feminists have a real strangle hold on the situation, and the government will not change anything as it would lose the tax income. It's quite hypocritical actually. The feminists are riding two horses in this horse race. They push for equality and independence, and yet *also* push for woman to be able to collect and be dependant. In my mind, it cannot be both ways. I think true feminists would be pushing for a system of true no fault where there are only payments enough to take care of the children's welfare. Then again, true feminists should be scathing of any woman who cheats her way out of relationship and immediately goes on the 'ex-husband' dole. Call me old fashioned."

"So you are a slave if you don't fight it and an anti-feminist if you do?"

"Pretty much. It can be even worse. For some men, they lose custody of their kids and their home in one fell swoop. All the mother has to do is allege sexual abuse or physical abuse and the kids and house are automatically in her hands without any evidence required at all. Once she has custody and possession of the house, the courts will rarely change that. Once again, the innocent can be punished and the selfish rewarded."

He slid his remaining knight towards my front line.

-Click-

I felt powerless. It felt like Merideth could just come at me and it would be legally condoned by the courts and she would take everything she could and leave Caryn and myself with nothing.

I was sure that this was not just a male problem. I was sure that there were lots of women out there who legitimately got screwed by the system too. I am sure there were plenty of actual deadbeat dads out there. I had heard all sorts of statistics of women under the poverty line with plenty of kids. However, the more my mind thought on that, the more I knew that statistic was mostly bullshit. I thought of Hershel's example of the woman in Toronto with the million dollar home. Technically she was under the poverty line with her kids. For tax purposes, after she quit her job, she made only $24,000 from her rental income. Her child support and her child tax benefit did not count into her taxable income. However her real after tax was over $90,000. On the other hand, her ex-husband was seen as rich with his $100,000 salary even though he only had $15,000 after tax in the real world. Taxes saw him as rich and her as poor, even though the reality was reversed. It was all a shell game to put pity on one segment of society and to pressure the other segment to pay. It was all about money and greed.

I quickly took his knight with my pawn. How did he not see that would happen?

-Click-

"So how do I fight it, if I cannot fight the system?"

"You have to fight it outside the system, or within the systems parameters. If your ex left you with debt, she has to pay half of that. The courts will side with you on that. She is one of those flaky artistic types and made a few CDs. Tell her you want half of those as you have some buddies who want to skeet shoot. They will be precious to her like her own baby wasn't. She will negotiate then. She will call you all sorts of names, but what do you care at this point? Name calling is much better than servitude. You just have to think outside the box a bit. That being said..."

I noticed my mistake then. He had set me up for my knight to take his pawn. He slid his rook forward. I was done. He had won.

"Checkmate."

My jaw dropped. I had walked right into that. Hershel was all smiles. His tail shook this way and that. It would come any minute. I had played and lost and now I would die.

"What, did you think you had to win to stay alive? No one beats me. No, all you had to do is not be stupid. And Dylan, you are not stupid. You have an intricate mind."

I exhaled. I didn't realize until that moment how much I wanted to stay alive. Hershel doubled over in a belly laugh.

"Oh man, you went white. I mean whiter than your usual white self. Ha! Look man, you are in a rough spot right now, but you are smart enough to find ways to navigate it."

"Thanks."

"Can you come back and play me again? I get bored sitting here with killing drug dealers as my only entertainment."

I sat at my desk at B.R. Pratt staring at my monitor. I should have been poring over files for Coru Oil & Gas, one of our smaller clients. It was their yearend coming up and I needed to process a lot of documents in preparation for that. I should have been doing that, but I just couldn't bring myself to do it. I was in a daze over my time with the Sphinx. First off, I had met with an actual Sphinx, played him a game of chess with my own life in the balance, and had come out the other end alive. That should have been enough to daze me. But more than this, I felt like the Sphinx had altered my thinking in some way. I used to love accounting. Perhaps I should not say 'love', but I appreciated the math and balance of it all. I knew all the rules and regulations and was very good at it. However, since meeting with the Sphinx, I could not help but notice all the bullshit built into it. I no longer saw it as math and balance, but as a fount of greed and manipulation. It was the struggle between government and corporations to wrest control of the most money. All accounting did was put a bland paper smile on that. It made corporate piracy and government theft look legit. That was my job. My job was to legitimize greed and evil. It paid the bills I suppose, and I could push myself to do the work, but I felt that since I had matched wits with a Sphinx, my thinking was irreversibly altered. I couldn't think about career problems right now though. I had enough to worry about with my split and this quest. So instead I stared blankly at my computer monitor.

My head felt heavy all of a sudden, as though the energy had been sucked out of me. I was used to this since my split. Sometimes a lack of energy would hit me like a storm and vanish just as quickly. I felt as if at any moment my head might crash down into my desk asleep and I would not even care if it did. I blinked and there was a voice.

"I need you. I need help."

The voice, it was so familiar. It was Dream. The sudden shock of her voice woke me up again. I looked around to see if anyone was near, but I was relatively alone in my section of the office. My head started to feel heavy again. I felt my neck droop down.

"Please come."

The urgency in her voice evaporated my will to stay awake. I felt my head fall forward and heard the crackle of the keys on my face as it hit the keyboard. I didn't care. Sleep took me.

She stood in a partially destroyed office building. The back wall was completely absent and the room was exposed to the elements. Girders near the opening were glowing red and still dripping molten metal. There were several tears in her red and orange spandex costume, but the sunburst on her chest that identified her as 'Captain Solar' remained unblemished. Her olive skin was a perfect complement to the suit. She wore a scowl on her face, but Dream was beautiful even when angry.

"How did you do that?"

"I don't know. I needed you and called, and you came."

I had forgotten where I was before this. It was also an office. Maybe I was here all along. That made sense. I don't remember wearing my costume in the other place I was in though. I had a black and grey helmet on that looked like a Raven's head. I had a tight grey spandex suit on with a cloak of black wings that were mainly for show (other than for firing mist missiles). And she, as Captain Solar, was able to harness the very flames and heat of the sun. We had been a team as long as I can remember, which made sense as the Raven and the Sun had been mythically paired since time began.

"No matter. I am here now, Captain Solar, what seems to be the trouble?"

She hugged me.

"I am just glad you are here Mist Raven, the Iron Barrister is ravaging the city taking everyone's valuables and shooting off his 'Paper Deluge' cannon at anyone who opposes him. I can usually tackle him, but he has a new weapon at his disposal. It is some sort of audio technology he added to his suit that befuddles anyone who can hear it. I am vulnerable to its frequencies. I barely made it away with my life. I was hoping that with your sonic powers, you could be of assistance."

The Iron Barrister was only a minor villain for us usually. He was not on the same calibre as our regular foes like Heartless Hurricane or the Dastardly Dynamo. It only took one of us to deal with him generally, and he was dealt with quickly. He must have really stepped up his game to give Captain Solar any trouble.

"I am glad to help, as always! Shall we give him the 'Fists from the Skies' attack?"

Captain Solar nodded and before I knew it she had picked

me up and we were flying. Most people thought that Mist Raven could fly because of the wings on my costume, but I could not. I could glide pretty well though. So often Captain Solar would fly me up high and I would glide down for an attack. As she flew me over the city, I noticed the change in the Iron Barrister immediately. First, he was three times bigger. He must be 30 feet tall now. Where before he was simply an absurd robot with wearing a tie and sport coat, now he was monstrous. He opened his mouth and it crackled with red lightning.

"...H-E-N-C-E-W-I-T-H..."

His gritty metallic voice echoed off the buildings. People writhed on the ground all around the Iron Barrister, holding their hands to their ears in agony. His left arm was a vacuum appendage and moved over the stunned people sucking up their money and valuables. As we circled around him, he spotted us, and aimed his left arm (with the paper deluge cannon) towards us.

"...S-U-B-P-O-E-N-A..."

His metallic audio blast echoed out towards us. I knew Captain Solar was susceptible to it, so I broke away from her grip and glided towards the incoming sound wave. As it hit me, I switched to mist form and dampened the sound as it entered my body. I effectively shielded Captain Solar from the blast. The Iron Barrister countered by shooting a blast from his paper cannon at her. It streamed out of his robotic arm in a jet. She pointed her hands at the incoming paper deluge and let loose her solar flare power upon it. Papers incinerated in a shower of embers. I opened my wings and shot mist missiles towards his eyes. If my plan were to work, he could not see me coming.

"...H-E-R-E-T-O-F-O-R-E..."

His next vocal blast echoed out just as my missiles hit him. I could hear people screaming as I neared my target and the ground.

"Mist Raven, pull up or you will hit him straight in the face!"

"That's the plan, Cap'n"

I changed to mist form and phased through his outer iron

skull settling inside his head. I had to remain in mist form in here or I would die, but I could not keep it up for long. My hope was to initiate a sonic caw from inside to explode his head.

"CAW! CAW! CAW!"

Nothing. He must have upgraded his iron armor as well. I would need to weaken it somehow.

"Captain, can you super heat his helmet?"

"Copy that."

I could hear the solar flare hitting his helmet while I was on the inside. I had to wait until it was hot enough. If I did it too early, I would have to recharge my power and I needed to escape from his body to do that.

"...I-P-S-O-F-A-C-T-O..."

I heard Captain Solar scream through the communicator as the Iron Barrister belched his legalese. It was now or never.

"CAW! CAW! CAW!"

There was a brief sound of metal twisting and then an explosion. I felt a sensation of falling and then I was looking up at the sky. Embers were dripping down like liquid sunlight. Dream's face appeared in my field of vision with her sun mask covering her eyes.

"There he is. Well, you really hammered him good there. The Iron Barrister doesn't last long without his head."

I sat up and rubbed my head. It had given me a huge headache as well. In the distance I saw his headless robot corpse lying on top of a fountain; lifeless.

"That was the idea. I heard you scream. I was worried."

"Oh, that. He hit me with one of those sonic blasts and it took me out of commission. Not for long though."

"What set him on his rampage this time?"

"Well... about that... the Dastardly Dynamo was trying to steal my house. We purchased it together, but he was trying to say it was all his. He set the Iron Barrister after me as I was set to fight him about it."

I stood up and grabbed both of her hands. I looked into her

eyes. They were always golden when she had her Captain Solar suit on, but they still drew me in like quicksand for the soul.

"See, that is what you get for going halfsies on a house with someone who has 'Dastardly' in their name."

"Yes, I didn't really think that through. Thanks for the help though."

She pulled me close, hugging me tight. I became very aware of her chest as she did so. I looked down. So did she.

"Umm, yes. The girls. You can't blame me for having them prominent. This is one of the only places I can display them in zero-G. So, I might as well, right? They might look a bit different in real life."

"I don't care. It is not your boobs I am in love with."

She smiled fully and laughed that carefree laugh. I cut it short with a kiss. I could not help myself. She leaned into it. I could feel the heat of her face as we kissed. That solar power was just pulsating within her. I was tempted to go to mist form and phase myself so we would be one, but I resisted. The kiss felt too good to do that.

"Speaking of real life, when are we going to meet?"

"Soon. I am working on it. Soon..."

Everything faded away.

"Dylan..."

I woke to someone shaking me.

"Dylan, wake up..."

I sat up. I could still feel the impression of the keys from the keyboard on my face. I knew they would be red. I was at work. This was bad. I wiped the drool from my face and turned to see who had woken me. It was my boss.

"Looks like you fell asleep at the job."

"I know. I'm sorry. I don't understand how it happened."

"Look you do good work for us, so I will let it slide, but don't let it happen again."

I nodded. She turned and left. Why did I fall asleep? It was Dream. She had called me into the dream. What did she need though? I forgot the details when I had recalled them only a moment before. I know it had to do with her house and a lawyer and a fight. It saddened me to know that Dream was having legal woes as well. I knew the pendulum had swung too far and that men regularly got screwed by our family law system, but women like Dream still got screwed too. Perhaps 'male' and 'female' were inaccurate ways to slice this. Perhaps 'Honourable' and 'Asshole' were better categories regardless of gender. The 'honourable' seemed to get routinely screwed over by the 'assholes' and our family law system helped them accomplish that. I immediately had an opinion on which category lawyers fell into.

My computer chimed with its email notification sound. It was from Mark Curry and titled 'Check out this Bullshit Artist'. I opened it. It was a forward from Merideth's lawyer.

Attn: Mark Curry

Mr. Curry,

Thank you for your prompt response. It is good that Mr. Gunn has sought out your counsel in these matters. I am, of course, familiar with Purlieu Collaboration, but the Montreal Amendments are a bit fuzzy as it has been a while since I have run a Purlieu Case. I will take amendment 33(a) under advisement, though when speaking of litigation I trusted this would proceed in standard family law ways and as such my wording is appropriate. Should Purlieu fail, we will be back to that.

I do not believe I will need additional counsel for the Purlieu Collaboration. It has been a while, but I am familiar with the source documentation and process.

Kensington Dossiers are a benefit in cases like this, so I appreciate you putting that forward as a suggestion. Will you be attaching the financial portion to the Kensington Dossiers, or just the standard? Can you also forward me your Kensington template as I think it would be to the benefit to both of us to work off similar documents? Once in my trust, I will create a dossier for Mrs. Gunn post haste.

I think that suggesting Mirepoix in this matter is likely excessive in this case as Mrs. Gunn is amenable to the Purlieu process.

Regards,

Bradley Channing
Barrister and Lawyer

Unbelievable. Mark Curry had the right of it; this guy was a pure bullshit artist. Purlieu Collaboration, Montreal Amendments, and Kensington Dossiers were all complete fabrications, yet he responded as if he were familiar with all of them.

When I came home, Caryn was doing her homework at the dining room table. She was so engrossed that she didn't see me approach with a helmet in my hand. I am not even sure when I got the youth helmet, but I had found it in the garage. She was hard at work, with two text books open in front of her and was writing furiously in a notebook. I had to clear my throat to get her attention.

She looked up.

"You want to go for a ride?"

She didn't need to answer. Slamming her books enthusiastically and stacking them neatly on top of each other told me everything I needed to know.

Soon we were speeding down Crowchild Trail on my bike. Well, it felt like we were speeding anyway. With a bike that small, anything over 70km/h feels like you are going like lightning. I zipped past a police car in a radar trap. He didn't even blink an eye. I had my fake license plate now that read 'ZED 999' on it so there was no reason for them to give me a second glance. It was my fairy tale license plate for the fairy tale world.

We pulled off onto Sarcee Trail and headed north weaving in and out of traffic like a serpent.

"Are you having fun?"

I wasn't sure she heard me, but she let go of me to hold her hands out to the side like a bird.

"Wheeeeee!"

It was a yell of pure enjoyment. It was all the answer I needed as I felt the same.

# SIN, POISON, AND HANGING OUT

I was jarred awake by machine gun fire. Sleep hung over me like a fog. What was this noise? Was I dreaming about warfare? Were their machine guns in my house? Was Caryn in danger? The last was the most important to me. My eyes flashed open. Suddenly I was listening with my parenting ears which were way more acute than my regular ones. I used to sleep like the dead every night. Not even charging rhinos or jackhammers could have woken me. Since becoming a parent, though, even the sounds of mice skittering may have drawn me out of sleep to evaluate the threat to my child. So here I sat, motionless, in my bed to wait for the noise again to evaluate it.

Another burst of machine gun fire. I leapt to the side of the bed, sitting up. This was not a sound I had dreamed. It was real and in my house. I needed to act. But then there was laughter. It was Caryn's laughter. Perhaps this was ok. I had no idea what the sound was, but if Caryn was laughing, it was probably not all that bad. I eased back down to a lying position. Perhaps I could catch another half hour of sleep or so.

More machine gun fire. And then Caryn's laughter and the laughter of another. It was the deep laugh of a man. I was up and standing in a heartbeat. There should be exactly two people in my house: Caryn and myself. If there was a third, by no means should it be an adult male. This was something that should not be. I rushed to throw on a t-shirt and pants. If Caryn was laughing, it was not a huge threat to her, but it was something that was a huge red flag for me. I at least had time to put on pants though. I may look more fearsome chasing someone out of the house in my boxer shorts, but it restricted me in how I might chase him down the street later legally.

I rushed downstairs like an elephant. It was not intentional, but I think my every footfall on the stairs echoed my internal anger that there was an unknown adult male in my house interacting with my teenage daughter. I could feel that fury of the 'protector' building within me. This was something primal within every man that was likely instinctual since humans began. Men protect. Whether she knew it or not, my daughter may be in danger from this strange male. Whoever he was, I did not invite him here and he was breaking societal conventions by being here, so he deserved the full brunt of my fury.

As I rounded the bottom of the staircase, I saw Caryn on the couch. She had a video game controller in her hand. On the screen was one of those violent warfare video games. As I observed, she shot an enemy soldier as he came around a wall of brick strewn rubble. The shot had hit him right in the skull and it burst like a water balloon filled with blood. Again, that adult male laughter erupted to the other side of her. It was Mark Curry. He lounged on my couch in pajama bottoms and a t-shirt with a fake tie on it. My anger and protective fury immediately evaporated and was replaced with a cloud of confusion.

"Mark. What? Why?"

The TV made a squawk as Caryn paused the game. She swivelled to face me.

"Dad, he brought 'Hell Hath 4: The Dogs are Slipping'. Isn't that awesome?"

Mark turned to me as well. He was drinking a large Cola.

Caryn had one on the coffee table in front of her as well. These were not from my fridge, so he must have brought them with him.

"Hey Buddy, sorry to catch you off guard. I came knocking earlier and was graciously allowed in."

I was, of course, more at ease that it was Mark here and not someone I didn't know or trust. I still had many questions, as even though I trusted Mark, he was an anomaly in my Sunday morning. His pajamas only deepened my confusion.

"It's nice that you dropped by. What brought you?"

Caryn un-paused her game and continued to dispatch steampunk soldiers on the TV. Mark hopped off the couch and zipped towards me in his typical high energy approach. He moved fast, but seemed very casual at the same time. Those things should be at odds, but for Mark, they just seemed to fit.

"So polite. You are old school man, in a world that has moved on. You politely ask 'What brought you by?' when what you really wanted to say was 'What the fuck are you doing on my couch in your pajamas on a Sunday morning?' I love it man!"

His zipping around and emphatic hand gestures nearly hypnotized me into forgetting my question. Mark had said a lot of words here but he hadn't really explained.

"So why are you here?"

"To the point, to the point. Right on. Well the short story is I need a place to crash for a few weeks. But I think when I explain the rest you will agree that is O.K."

It seemed that Mark had a real gift for saying things and yet leaving you wanting. He never quite seemed to answer my questions fully. I could have asked for more information, but I figured a blank stare might illustrate that for me. I was a man, after all, and we were known for our economical use of words. Why vocalize when blinking would suffice.

"Oh, right. Well, you see, Zed sent me your second task. It's a doozy. You will be away for, likely, at least a week, so you might need someone back here to watch over things, right?"

I would be away? Why? I couldn't just take off of work and leave for a week or two. Could I? I suppose I could do so, it was just not in my nature. I liked to give notice for the time I would be away. It was just respectful. *Respect is earned, but once earned never waver in the respect you show.* However, I had noticed lots of my coworkers taking off with a day or two's notice. Perhaps that respect was not there to start with. Why should I not do the same as everyone else? I mean they didn't seem to care about the level of respect I showed at my job. I was treated exactly the same as the employee who took time off whenever they liked.

"What is my task? Why do I need to be away? Can I bring Caryn with me?"

As if to emphasize my point, Caryn let loose with a barrage of machine gun fire as she took down a group of soldiers.

"You cannot take her with you but I will look after her while you are gone. I cannot even say how long you will be gone. What is your task? It's a bit odd, but bear with me. There is a women's retreat in the badlands called *Laurel Lodge* run by a woman named Daphne. Your task is to sneak into the lodge and steal a pair of her panties."

He shrugged and rolled his eyes a bit as he could tell this was a controversial thing to say.

"A panty raid? Isn't that a bit too college fraternity for Zed?"

"Well, you have to understand that every task that Zed gives you is more than what it appears on the surface. There is a method to his madness. We both know Daphne and know that this task is both more difficult and more profound than it appears on the surface."

I suppose he was right. Even talking with the Sphinx was not quite as cut and dried as it appeared. On the surface I just needed to talk with him, but it was a probing of my intelligence and, from what I felt, it was a bit of a de-cluttering and re-ordering of my mind. I don't know how it happened, but I found my thinking felt different since talking to him. I felt more ready, mentally, for the challenges that might come up.

"Is that why you don't know how long I will be gone? The complexity I mean."

"Oh yeah, I mean I know Daphne, and I know other people who have tried this. It is not as easy as it sounds."

I don't even remember taking hold of the video game controller, but I was suddenly on the couch playing the game Caryn was playing. Mark was sitting next to me drinking his Cola. I didn't like the thought of leaving Caryn for an unknown period of time, but I was confident I could accomplish this in short order and I did actually trust Mark.

"When do I start?"

"The sooner the better, buddy. Besides, with me here, I can deal with your ex's lawyer if he comes by."

With all this information about my new task, I had forgotten about my legal woes. I was certainly grateful for the service Mark was providing for me there. It was definitely worth allowing him to stay at my house for months, which was way more than the weeks he was asking for.

"How is that going?"

"Oh man, that guy is a piece of work. He is like a lie walking around in a suit. I sent Mr. Bradley Channing an email where I pretended to attach the Kensington Dossier template. I didn't really attach it though. We went back and forth for hours trying to figure out why it wasn't coming through on his email. I had him check his spam folders, his firewall, and all sorts of things. That's all time that he will be charging to your ex. It's likely at least a thousand dollars she will be on the hook for."

Awesome. Purely awesome.

We high fived.

I figured Mark was correct. I should get my task over with as soon as I could. The sooner I could get through all of this, the sooner I could get to Dream. I entered into the elevator at the building that B.R. Pratt was located in. The doors began to close as I heard a voice call out.

"Hold the door."

I jammed my arm in the closing elevator door. It was a significantly brave thing to do as our elevators had poor sensors and the chance of it bruising or breaking an arm was a real possibility. This time it closed on my arm and likely only left a small bruise. A man swiftly entered the elevator.

"Thanks."

He looked familiar. I couldn't quite place it, but his face seemed familiar and I had his name float through my mind.

"Robert, right?"

"Yeah, I was at Pratt two years ago. I am in the building to see Prairie View on 12 for a consult. It was Dylan, if I remember right. How are you doing?"

I nodded. This was a tough question to answer. There was always a choice for someone in my circumstances. I could tell them that I am horrible and wretched and barely afloat emotionally. Or I could lie and just say "fine" as is expected. It is the choice between giving the harsh truth or the beautiful lie. Most people preferred the beautiful lie. Zed would say it was people wanting to take a pulse to see if the fairy tale was still real. They needed to hear a "fine" to know that the fairy tale was still stable. I decided to test this theory.

"Actually, my life has been about as horrible as you could imagine in the last year. I have really struggled to stay hopeful and happy."

He stared at me blankly for a moment.

"Oh, well, it was good to see you Dylan."

Interesting. He completely ignored it. It was as if he heard what I said, but changed it to 'fine' in his head. He had to calculate in his head if what I said would threaten the fairy tale, and chose to ignore it.

We stood in awkward silence for the rest of our elevator ride.

I was only at work for a few hours before I was back home packing for my excursion. My boss was quite understanding given my request. I listed my reasons as taking a sanity break. Greater truth would have been that I was taking a break *from* sanity. It was an insanity break. She had claimed she had done something similar a few years back and that I had done quality work for them so I deserved a vacation. I appreciated it, though I was somewhat baffled as I had felt like I was merely 'phoning it in' since my split.

Caryn sat on my bed as I packed my backpack. I had already packed the items from Mark Curry's duffel bag save for the timer as I didn't think I would be needing that. Now I was down to considerations of how many pairs of underwear I would need and how big of a tube of toothpaste would be required. As a man, I needed to keep up the stereotype of packing light. I was already wearing pants. All I would need is likely 3 days' worth of underwear, socks, and maybe another shirt.

"Do you have to go?"

"I do. This is all part of the quest we started with the bees. I need to follow it through."

I could see in her eyes that she understood but was reluctant. How could I blame her? She had already lived through her mom abandoning her, and now here I was going off on some crazy quest from which I may or may not return. That had to be disconcerting. Kids needed stability and this must feel very unstable to her.

"Why can't I go with you?"

"Well, it is tough to explain, kid. This is a quick in and quick out stealth mission. I have already done Zed's first task and it only took me an afternoon. I figure I should be able to get this one done in a day or two. Then I will be back. Besides you will have Mark here. You like him, right?"

She nodded as I zipped up my bag. I knew she would be fine. So did she. It was more to do with her being an independent and responsible kid than it had to do with Mark. She had only met Mark once and I got the feeling that out of the two of them, she might be the more responsible one.

"Just be careful. If you fail I am not sure what will happen to me."

I dropped my bag on the bed. We needed no words after that; just a giant hug.

I passed through the town of Wayne, Alberta just as sunset was approaching. You could hardly call Wayne a town, though, really. It seemed more like an Old West ghost town where gunslingers would draw and measure out justice in lead. The sun cast a red glow on the badlands. I was nearly hypnotized by the beauty of it. I felt my motorcycle wobble and realized that the sunset was drawing way too much of my attention. As I re-focused on my driving, I took a look at my odometer. I needed to travel 3.3 kilometres past Wayne and then head west into the badlands.

As I reached 3.3 kilometres I noticed a small trail heading up into the hills. I turned my bike off the main road and onto this trail. It was narrow, but my dual sport motorcycle was meant for this sort of riding. I was barely a few hundred feet into the trail when I ran into trouble. The trail got steeper and my bike started to spin. I got off my bike and I was surprised by the terrain. I had been to the badlands before, but I had never actually walked in them, I had just looked at them. I had assumed they were kind of sandy. I was very wrong. The badlands substrate was hard, and it was actually a bit slippery. My bike was just not up to the task of climbing this hill. I pulled the bike off to the side and turned off the engine. This was my route. If I wasn't riding my bike there, I would have to walk. It would have been even easier to just take the road that went to the retreat itself, but Mark was insistent that this surreptitious route was the way to accomplish my deed. I grabbed my pack and headed onward.

As I crested the hill, I began to curse myself for forgetting an essential piece of gear for this task: a flashlight. The light was fading and while it was pretty, I knew I would be in total darkness soon. I knew I needed to head roughly due west from here and I thought there was a faint glow in the distance where the *Laurel Lodge* was located, but I could not be certain. As the light faded further, I stumbled and tripped a few times. It scared me a bit as I thought there were prickly pear cactus in the badlands and I knew landing on one of those would be a little bit of horrible. I found that the darker it got, the slower I went.

I approached what I thought at first was a creek. It was dark and hard to tell. It was clearly in motion and it was making a slight whoosh noise. I stopped and looked at it for a moment. It must be a small creek. What else could it be? I stepped slowly towards it. All of a sudden the river halted and I was greeted with a symphony of rattle noises. I jumped back. This wasn't a creek at all, but a freeway of prairie rattlesnakes. There did not seem to be a way around it. If I tried to jump over, I am pretty sure I would be bitten. Perhaps they were protecting the *Laurel Lodge*. Perhaps they were part of my challenge. I sat down and pulled out my backpack. There was a pirate hat, a plastic sword and a vial of liquid. I couldn't imagine any scenario where a pirate hat would help against snakes, and ditto for the vial of liquid. The sword had promise though. Knights had swords and they went off on quests to fight dragons. I was on a quest of sorts and snakes were sort of like dragons, were they not? This felt right.

I took out the plastic sword and strapped the pack back on. I stepped forward. The snakes had resumed their river-like movement across the path. I might as well get it over with. I lowered the blade slowly. The snakes stopped and started to rattle. It was the same behaviour as before. This time, though, I had a sword. I chopped my sword down swiftly and hit one of the snakes. It stopped and then lashed out to bite me on the leg. The pain was searing. Before I could back up, I was bitten again by another one. Clearly the sword was not the way to go. I was already bitten so I figured that I may as well press forward. I rushed with all my strength to run through and I was bitten once more for my efforts. I could hear the snakes resume their creek behind me. I was through, but I had been bitten three times. The sword was definitely not what I should use. The pain was like white fire. It was starting to tingle there as well. I could feel my heart racing. Was rattlesnake poison deadly or was it just hard on the system? My legs started to feel numb. I fell to the ground. My face caused a small cloud of dust to rear up. I was unsure if a person could survive three rattlesnake bites, but even if it was not fatal, I could not move my legs and I would likely die of exposure. My vision started to blur as well. Lovely, I would die out here blind and unable to move.

I tucked the sword back in my pack and pulled out the vial of liquid. This must have been the stuff. As I squinted at it, I noticed an etching of a snake on the bottle. Sure, now I pay attention to these details. I clutched it as I lay in the dust. I failed because I couldn't bother to read the label. I didn't read the instructions, so to speak. What a decidedly male way to fail at something.

My eyelids were heavy and drooping. A low rumble jostled them open again. It got louder and louder. Something was making its way towards me. I heard a loud hiss and a few seconds later a snake slithered right past my head. I looked up and saw all the snakes escaping to the left or right. The rumbling continued. Then I saw it. It was the biggest snake I had ever seen. It was as high as a horse to its back and perhaps 100 feet long. Did rattlesnake poison cause hallucinations? It was coming directly for me and fast. I opened the vial and dripped some of the liquid on me. I managed to put the stopper back in before it brought its giant head next to mine to sniff me.

It sniffed for a good minute before I felt like I was being lifted. Suddenly the landscape was moving along. I drifted in and out of consciousness, but woke up firmly when I felt like I had been dropped. I hit the ground with a thud. My legs were still completely numb, so I could not stand. I could see someone's sandaled feet though, and above that, a brown skirt.

"Take him to 7c"

I passed out.

My mind was a jumble. I was tumbled back to my childhood. I had a tree fort in our backyard. My dad had built it for Jenn and I when we were smaller. He had always said we built it together, but really he built it while we hit things with plastic hammers. Jenn had outgrown it, but I still loved the solitude of it. I loved the gentle sway of the tree in the strong Calgary winds. I was lying on the floor drawing a picture of a space war. Dream lay next to me colouring her own picture. It was not Dream as an adult, but as a little girl like back when I first encountered her.

I heard the door open at the back of the house.

"What was that?"

I peered through the window of the tree fort. I was kneeling so that I could just peek over the window without being seen. Dream was kneeling next to me. We were quiet, yet I could hear each of us breathing in the night air. Her hand clasped mine. At the back door, my mom was hauling out a bag of garbage. After two or three steps, the bottom broke out of the bag and the garbage emptied onto our back deck.

"FUCK!"

Dream gasped. It was shocking to hear my mom swear as she hardly ever did so. She raised her fists to the sky and screamed.

My dad rushed out the back door. He noticed the mess and dipped back inside. He re-emerged a second later with a new garbage bag. Dream and I were transfixed by the drama below us. My dad tried to give my mom a hug, but she shrugged him off.

"Don't. Just don't. It's been a lousy day."

"O.K."

He knelt down and started placing the garbage in the new bag. He just picked it up with his bare hands. As a kid it made me cringe thinking of it. How could someone pick up garbage like that without flinching? As an adult, after changing diapers and cleaning up kids puke week after week, a little garbage was nothing. After a few minutes, my mom sighed and knelt down joining him in the process. When they were nearly done and there was only a stray banana peel left, Mom picked it up, grinned, and then threw it at dad.

"Ugh! That's it lady!"

He picked it out of his hair and chased her around the yard with it. She screamed as he chased her out of our field of view. And then things were quiet. Dream squeezed my hand. She wanted to see what was happening. I nodded. We moved to the other side of the tree fort to look out the far window. My dad was kissing my mom like they do in the movies. It was deep and passionate. It was rare to see such a kiss between them. I am sure it happened, but it was private. I felt like I was witnessing something secret, and a little gross. I mean, they both had bits of banana smeared on their faces and bits of grime in their hair and clothing. Were you supposed to kiss when you were so grimy? I turned to Dream and she was focused like a laser. Her breath was fogging up the window.

"It's gross right?"

"I think it's sweet."

She turned to me. Her eyes were glassy. Her face zipped in close to mine and kissed me on the cheek. My hand immediately touched the cheek where she had kissed it.

"Why did you…?"

I stumbled backwards and tripped over the small table I kept in the fort. Dream laughed her boisterous laugh and then disappeared into nothingness. There was suddenly a knock at the trap door in the floor.

"Dylan, are you up here?"

It was dad. I righted myself and made my way over to open it. As I opened it, his head popped up.

"I thought I heard you fumbling around up here. Were you watching us down there?"

I nodded.

"Oh, O.K. Are you O.K. with that?"

"I guess, but you kissed her even though there was garbage."

"Ah. You see son, if you cannot love someone when doing the little things in life, like cleaning up garbage or making oatmeal, it's not love; it's infatuation. That's an important difference. If you cannot love them when they are covered in garbage, it is not love at all."

That made sense. The weird thing is I remember this happening when I was a kid. Of course, Dream was not there though, as it was something in reality, not in the dream world. Why was she here this time? And why was my dad holding a snake in each hand?

"Oh, and I brought these for you, slugger."

He threw the snakes in the fort. They grew bigger and bigger and chased me around the tree fort. I screamed as I ran. My dad had a doctor's lab coat on and a syringe in his hand now. This was definitely not what happened in my memory.

"Stop crying. Men don't cry. Stop moving about and let me give you your medicine."

He chased me around keeping pace with the snakes, slashing at me with the syringe.

"Dad, no! Dad, please stop!"

I tripped over the table again and fell on my face.

"Dad, no!"

My eyes shot open. I was lying down in a white room. I tried to sit up but my hands were strapped to the bed.

"Oh, those. Don't worry about that. You were thrashing about so badly that we had to strap you down to give you the injection of anti-venom. You're lucky I had some"

I turned my head to face her. Her auburn hair was tied back in a ponytail. She set to work straight away undoing the restraints. Her green eyes were piercing in their gaze. When the second restraint was off I sat up, rubbing my wrists where they were chafed.

"Most people don't try to get past the rattlers. You must be one of Zed's boys."

I sat and stared. I didn't want to give away my mission, but I didn't want to be rude and not answer her either.

"There was a giant snake at the end too. I thought it would devour me whole."

"Oh that's Harmonia. She's harmless. You are lucky she came when she did or you would have been jerky out there. You don't have to tell me…about Zed I mean. I can just smell it. It's some sort of secret mission; it always is."

I extended my hand. I wondered what she would think if she knew the secret mission was to steal a pair of her underwear.

"Dylan. Thanks for saving me."

"I'm Daphne. No worries. It's less of a hassle to buy anti-venom than to dispose of a body. You would think Harmonia would do it, but she's a vegetarian."

She reached back and grabbed a pile of black clothes and tossed it at me. It landed in a flump in my lap.

"Look, this is nominally a woman's retreat for them to get their strength back after a bad relationship, but I can tell you are a bit broken that way as well. Perhaps that is why Zed sent you to me. I don't mind you staying, but the ladies are a bit jumpy around men as you might understand. Wear this at all times when you are in the common areas. I don't mind that you are here though. The issues that affect the women here also affect you. Issues like this are not gendered, they are human. I just need discretion."

I unfolded the garment.

"A burka?"

"You have to admit that it's a good disguise. No one will even question your rough voice or hairy legs."

I was kind of against the burka as a general rule, but she was right that it was a good disguise. I found the burka a strange phenomenon. You were not allowed to complain about them as they were 'religious' garments. The problem was that it was a load of shit. They were not religious at all, but cultural. The Koran had no mention of burkas anywhere, just a need to be modest. And while I can understand wanting to preserve your culture, this particular cultural artifact did not make sense in North America. It would be a societal faux pas to go out and around town with a mask that concealed my identity. It should be the same with the burka. I suspected that after a few banks were robbed by people wearing burkas as disguises that a call for their ban may be taken seriously.

"Thanks."

She stared at me as if expecting something. Her face was the model of seriousness.

"Well, go on now. Put it on."

"Now?"

"Yup. Strip. You don't have anything I haven't seen before."

People always said that. I knew their purpose was for me not to be shy or bashful, but it just didn't work. It's not like my reason for apprehension was that I believed they had not seen a penis before and that it might scare them. My reason was that I was private.

"Sure, you just want a free show."

Her serious face cracked into a smile.

"Ha!"

I stripped. It turns out I wasn't that private after all.

I spent my time at the *Laurel Lodge* pretty isolated from the other ladies. In part it was the burka I wore that kept me separate, and the rest was my own decision. During the day, there were activities you could engage in: spa treatments, horseback riding, archery, and so on. Not much of that interested me. I used the archery range when no one was there and read in my room the rest of the time. Only during meal times and the evening discussion, which was mandatory, did I socialize. Even then, the ladies gave me a small greeting of 'Dilla', which is the name I gave them, and kept their distance from me. I enjoyed the nightly discussions, not so much for the content, but for the warmth of the fireside. There was something about a bonfire that was mesmerizing. I think it tickled the inner cave man. It was like cave man TV.

"How are we strong?"

Daphne's voice boomed as she walked around the fire with her multi-coloured staff. The orange of the flame was reflected in her face. The rest of us were mere shadows. He eyes gleamed in the firelight and gave off a fierceness that was tough to deny. It seemed to pull people to want to answer her.

"By not being victims."

"Wrong! You are victims. All of you are. You have been abused and betrayed and cheated on. You are victims. Simply saying you are not does not make it so. It does no honour to yourselves to ignore that. Would you tell a rape victim not to be a 'victim'? Would you tell someone that was stabbed in a mugging not to be a 'victim'? Of course not, so why deny the label? You are strong not because you pretend not to be a victim, but because you can pick up and move on with your life after being one."

I had to agree. I hated the phrase "don't be a victim." I had the feeling Zed would agree too and add it to his list of things people say so they can avoid passing judgement on the perpetrator.

"Anyone else?"

"By forgiving."

"Forgiving? Fuck that. Understand that I work on a much

older definition of forgiveness. In modern times forgiveness is akin to 'not letting it affect you'. Let me tell you, ladies, what has been done to you has affected you whether you believe so or not. Otherwise you would not be here. Forgiveness originally meant: to pardon the offence. Unless the other person sincerely apologizes and attempts to make it up to you, why forgive at all? Forgiving doesn't give you strength, but demoting the time you spend thinking of what was done can. What I mean by that is that just because you don't offer forgiveness, it doesn't mean you have to dwell on it much at all. At this point you do, but you can move towards thinking about it not at all. Not dwelling on your ex or their actions is a great strength. They are the past. You don't need to forgive, but file it away and try to open the file infrequently."

I could hear the woman who offered up forgiveness sniffing in derision as Daphne was speaking.

"So forgiveness is not needed?"

"Not in the way you think. Forgiveness of self is key. I guarantee you that everyone here has thoughts that give anger towards themselves. You all have wondered at some point how you chose so badly in a partner. You take some of the guilt of a bad relationship internally. You need to pardon yourselves for that imagined crime. You need to forgive yourself. You made the best choice with the information you had at the time. The fault is not yours if the person you fell in love with was not what he seemed. You need to forgive yourself."

This was something that gnawed at my mind. I wondered often if Merideth was always the monster she showed herself to be and I just didn't notice. Or did she become a monster over time? I felt at fault. I felt that I chose badly. But the reality was that I didn't. Daphne was right. I met Merideth in university and fell in love. She seemed kind and witty and loving and had all the characteristics I wanted in a mate. With that information, I made the best choice possible at the time. If she became a monster after that time, it was not my fault. If she was already a monster and deceived me about it, it was also not my fault. I needed to let that go. I needed to forgive myself.

I could hear the bonfire crackling as the silence of contemplation was upon us.

"What else?"

There was an uncomfortable silence before anyone stepped forward to answer this. They were probably afraid because Daphne had shot down the last two. I was afraid to speak lest I give away my gender.

"By taking what is ours?"

"What do you mean?"

"I mean alimony, child support, and so on."

"Well, I have to disagree with you there as well. You do not scream strength with that; you scream dependency, which is weakness. You should get half the assets, yes, and you should both support the children. I know you have children with this man, Aimee, so it is true he should support their needs. But alimony is not strength. Alimony is a sign that you are too weak to support yourself. It essentially relegates you to the status of an unwanted employee who is resented more and more each time a monthly check is issued."

"But aren't we owed that based on the law? A certain level of living was provided during the marriage so isn't there a duty to continue that?"

"Please don't mistake what the law entitles you to for what is just. You would have your ex, no matter how vile he was to you, give you money every month. You are then tied to him, and keeping you 'in the lifestyle' is likely putting him in the poor house. This is an activity that will increase anger towards you every month. It will make him wish you dead. Do you want that? Does that sound like a strong position? Let me ask you this. There are other things provided in a marriage like emotional support and sex. What would your opinion be if the state mandated that you continue to provide these things after your marriage was over?"

"If they mandated I had to give my ex sex monthly? That would be rape, Daphne. How could you suggest that?"

I agreed that was a very severe analogy. I could see where she was going with it, but I didn't like to equate anything with the 'R' word as it eroded the meaning of that word.

"I am not suggesting it. I am just pointing out that what the state mandates is not exactly just all the time. They don't mandate sex or emotional support, but they do mandate financial support. Does that seem right to you? Rape is not about sex. Rape is about control. For women, control of our bodies taken away from us is the very worst. For men, it is often money. For them, alimony means being held down monthly and told to take it. For them it is akin to dropping the soap monthly in the prison shower. That stripping away of control monthly is an activity that only breeds hatred. No, alimony is not strength. True strength would be to provide for yourself and show the world that you do not need a damned thing from your ex."

That truly was the heart of the fear I felt with Merideth's lawyer. She wanted spousal support; what they called alimony. She felt a right to take money away from me that I worked hard to earn. She felt she was owed this and the state supported her in this. I had no control. If she wanted it, she could take it monthly. It made me feel stripped bare and abused. I had worked like a dog my whole career to further her career, then she betrays me multiple times, and then the government allows her to continue taking from me. It felt very wrong to be locked into giving someone money continually when they caused the issue to start with. It was punishing the victim. It was a horrible thing. Not the 'R' word for sure, but certainly a forcing of control over someone in an aspect of their life. It was damaging to the psyche and self-esteem either way.

"Your silence is deafening. I see anger in your eyes. And you know what? That is good. I like it. It means I have a strong independent batch of women here. Sure, what I am saying runs counter to what modern philosophy says. But let's face it, if that mumbo jumbo worked, you would not be here as it would be working for you, right?"

I could hear a murmur of ascent ripple through the ladies. The firelight danced across Daphne's face.

"I find the truest measure of strength after times of adversity such as the ones you have gone through is it not affecting your future behaviour or relationships. Think about it, if your ex's bad behaviour can make you change or embitter a future relationship, they win. But not having this affect us gives us power and strength. It says to the ex that their actions, no matter how horrible, have no choke hold on us. It says they are weak and we are strong. I would like to tell you of another Daphne; one from classical mythology. Do any of you know this story?"

"It's the one where she is chased by the sun god and turns into a tree, right?"

"That's the one, but I am going to tell you the true story. The official story is that the sun god desired her and she did not return his affections so she ran away. She was a nymph and pleaded to her father so he turned her into a tree. The truth is much different, yet somewhat the same. You see, Daphne loved the sun god very much. She loved his golden hair and his broad shoulders. She loved his sense of honour and truth. She loved his laughter and music. She loved every small bit of his body and soul. She wanted to be in a relationship with him. The sun god, however, felt different. He saw her surface beauty and desired to be with her, but he did not want a relationship. He did not lie to her about this, but it hurt her feelings nonetheless. How could he not love her for all she had to offer? But he desired her and so pursued. And Daphne fled. She did not want to be with someone who did not love her the same way. She desired to never feel this badly again. So she wished as hard as she could to be shielded from this pain. Soon enough her skin turned to the hardened bark of the laurel tree to protect her from the world and her hair into leaves to shield her from the sun. The problem with this is that it was weak. She let the sun god's actions dictate her life. She sat as a tree for millennia. There could have been many wonderful moments in those millennia, but she let herself harden and be closed off to it. Do you understand?"

There were nods all around. I understood as well. It was about not becoming one of the 'Broken People'. It was about not letting past relationships ruin your future ones. It was about not letting sadness eclipse chances for happiness.

I began to look at Daphne in a different light. There was something special about her. I am not sure what it was. She just seemed more real than other people, like she had a booster shot of life injected into her. I also thought about Zed and Mark and Venus and the Sphinx and the giant snake and all the other supernatural things that had been happening to me. I thought about how her name was also Daphne and this place was called the *Laurel Lodge*. The realization hit me fast.

"I think you are that Daphne."

Daphne stared openly at me as the rest of the women laughed at what I had burst out. A few ladies even piped up a response.

"That's absurd, Dilla."

"Yeah, crazy. It was a story from thousands of years ago."

But Daphne kept staring directly at me. Her eyes then shifted to the ground. Her voice became a whisper with the ice of sadness to it.

"Yes. Definitely absurd."

I headed to the archery range after the bonfire discussion. I liked to either hit it late at night or early in the morning. That way I did not have to socialize with the other ladies and I could shoot some arrows in relative peace. Even late at night, the range was well lit by torches and a pit fire behind that shooting area. There was a small satisfaction every time the arrow created a meaty thunk into the target, whether I had a good shot or not. There was something about the stillness it cultivated within you. It was sublime. I could shoot again and again.

As I was shooting, Daphne pulled up into the lane next to me. Within a few heartbeats, she had shot three arrows dead centre. I looked at my target. It looked like I was trying to make polka dots, compared to Daphne who had three on target.

"Have you ever split an arrow?"

"I have been doing this on and off for thousands of years, Dylan. I can split an arrow any time I like. I can hit wherever I want. The problem is that every time I split an arrow, I need to buy a new one."

I shot off an arrow. It hit down and to the left of my intended target.

"Oh, you've sinned."

"Pardon me?"

"'Sin' is originally an archery term, Dylan. It means to go off of target. So what you did there was 'Original Sin'– not the thing with the snake and apple. Do you mind if I adjust you a bit?"

She held out her hands in question. I nodded.

She put her hands on my hips and swivelled them.

"There, better now. You can't shoot facing the target, your feet need to be in one line pointing towards the target. Your body needs to be sideways. Now draw."

I nocked an arrow and pulled back. She touched my shoulder blades.

"No. No. You need to use your back muscles here. Don't use your biceps. Instead try to pull your shoulders together. There. Pull the string back to your cheek."

I could feel her breath warm on my neck.

"Now release."

My arrow flew straighter than usual. It hit just below the centre of the target.

"Not bad. Now tell me your story."

I gave her the Coles notes version; the cheating, the secret debt, the lies, and what she called the beautiful, positive memories. I didn't feel the need to go into minute detail.

"Ah, I can see why Zed sent you to me. The cheating is always hard. It leaves you feeling empty, unwanted and unattractive. What you need to understand is that it none of it is your fault. No one can force a cheater to cheat. They cheat only because there is something wrong inside them. The problem lies within them, not within you. There is never any reason for cheating. There is never any way to excuse it. It is simply wrong. How did it make you feel?"

The feelings were the difficult part. They were hard to face. They were like wounds that didn't close. I would have actually preferred physical wounds to the emotional ones. My man training made me bury the feelings and try to ignore them. I knew this wasn't the healthiest strategy, but it shielded me from breaking the sacred man rule: *Men don't cry.*

"It made me feel worthless. It made me feel ugly and unattractive. It made me feel unwanted. She told me I was undesirable and not charming. What was hardest, though, was that she seemed to think there was nothing wrong with what she did. There was no remorse whatsoever. There were no apologies."

"Take another shot, Dylan."

I nodded and wiped away the tears that had accumulated while I was speaking. I did not even realize I was crying. For once, I had cried and not had it horrify me that I had broken a man rule. It felt liberating. I pulled another arrow from the ground quiver, nocked it, and pulled it back. Daphne's hand was suddenly my arm that was pulling the string back.

"Lower your arm slightly. It needs to be one straight line from arrow tip to elbow. You are grieving for the relationship that was. That is as it should be. Grief is much like gravity; it pulls you down. Even swift and sure arrows get pulled down. And that brings us to the positive side of both grief and gravity; it causes you to aim higher."

I took her meaning and aimed slightly higher to account for gravity. I liked her metaphor. I could see a lot of deeper meaning in it. I wouldn't be satisfied with a relationship like I had. I was aiming higher. Dream was my higher aim. Or perhaps she was always my aim, but I 'sinned' along the way and hit Merideth instead.

"Release."

Her voice was but a whisper. My fingers let loose and the arrow tracked nearly to the bull's eye. I turned to Daphne. I know my face was still full of emotions: gratitude, grief, astonishment. She reached up and roughly wiped away another tear.

"What you need to understand is that this has nothing to do with you. You are a ruggedly handsome man, Dylan. You seem quite attractive and desirable to me. Were you never tempted to cheat, yourself?"

It felt so good to be told I was attractive so earnestly by someone who didn't need to say anything at all. I had felt so ugly after I found out. I had assumed it was a truth as that is the only thing that made sense. I had to be ugly. I mean why else would she have done this to me. But I had had a few people tell me I was attractive now. It made me feel like I was worth something again. The doubt was also partly a male thing. Men just didn't hear that often that they were attractive. Women often told each other that they looked good but such a thing was somewhat taboo between even the best of male friends. And men were conditioned to supply compliments on their partner's attractiveness, but it was just a truth that the same was not true for women. The truth is that men could use a little more of that. Instead we eked by on the breadcrumbs of victory when they laughed at our jokes or when we could provide for them. In ways, it was very unbalanced between the genders. I thought about catcalling and other behaviour like that. It seemed that women got too much attention that way whereas maybe men got too little. This is likely why a lot of men didn't see a problem with catcalling as since they didn't get a lot of attention put on them that way, they would have welcomed it. It was tough for them to understand what an issue it was when they were not immersed in that.

"I couldn't. It would be against my code. A lot of people say that cheating is hard to define, but for me it was always easy. I went through my day as if my partner was standing just a few feet behind me. If any activity was something I thought she would be upset about, I just didn't do it. It was always very simple."

She nodded in agreement. She was unlike anyone I had met before. Her green eyes were deep. She didn't look away when we were talking but always looked me right in the eye. There was a fierceness to her, but she was also gentle. They were traits that should be at odds, but in her they seemed complimentary.

"And it is that simple. When people get it, they get it. I will tell you something, though. If someone is unable to feel remorse over their cheating, the problem goes deeper than mere selfishness. It sounds an awful lot like Narcissistic Personality Disorder. Those people have problems with shame and seem unable to apologize for their actions ever. They are like walking selfishness. You can trust that they will only ever do what is best for themselves, and feeling guilt or remorse is not part of that. Regardless, you deserve better Dylan. I like your thoughts on staying true. Mine are similar, but a bit different. Have you heard of the many moments theory?"

"No, I haven't."

"O.K., well it goes like this. Most people view time as a linear thing where one moment comes after the other. The many moments theory proposes that all moments are happening at the same time and in each moment there is a different you. But even though they are happening at the same time, they are dependent on each other. As Daphne in this moment, I have a solemn duty to the Daphnes in all the other moments that are yet to come, so to speak. To know if I am behaving honourably, all I have to do is think if all the other Daphnes in all the other moments would approve of my actions or not. If I think any of them would wince, I just don't do it."

I kind of liked that. Not only was it interesting to think that this whole process was about a different Dylan in each moment working towards bettering the other Dylans and their moments, but also, it was a bit freeing, as all that pain and all that hurt were mainly in other moments and other Dylans. I could release that pain. I didn't need to hold the pain that the other Dylans experienced. I was thankful for those Dylans and what they had done for me, and I did believe I was doing everything to honour the Dylans in the moments that were dependent on me.

"Wow. That is mind blowing. So, if you live entirely in a moment, what is this moment's Daphne living?"

"I am glad you asked. I am content to talk to you and help you through your suffering. I am filled with gratitude that it has seemed to help. And, to be honest, I am hoping I am laying the groundwork for a different moment where a different Daphne will kiss a different Dylan."

I paused. I had no idea she had that sort of attraction to me. And why should she? In ways, it may lead to a situation where it would be easier to steal her underwear. But that seemed dishonest. However, it may be hypocrisy to talk of dishonesty when stealing. I needed to steal her underwear in the most honest way possible, if that made any sense. And there was Dream to consider as well. I had slept with exactly three people since my split: Annette, Amber, and Venus. Annette and Amber were before I realized that Dream was real. Venus seemed necessary, like an element of my journey towards finding Dream. But Daphne was completely different. If I had sex with Daphne (if it went there), that would be of my own choice and it felt a little like I was betraying Dream.

I backed up a step.

"It's just…well…you don't even really know me."

She put her hands on her hips.

"I know you well enough that you are one of only three people in the last thousand years that has guessed my identity. I know you are smart, intelligent, and funny. I know you are attractive. I am not talking about starting a relationship, just a bit of company while you are here."

I understood. She wanted something casual, like Amber did. Daphne was just more up front and polite about the whole thing.

"I get that. I find you attractive as well. You are very different, in a good way, from every other woman I have met. I am on this quest to find a girl I have known only while dreaming. Zed sent me here as a part of that."

"But you have not yet met her in real life?"

"No."

"Then, Dylan, you are still single. Why is this a problem?"

That had me stumped. It didn't seem like it was logically a problem. She was right. I was technically single and I was attracted to her. It would be nice to have some adult fun. However, the closer I felt I was getting to Dream in reality, the more I felt attached to her. It felt like I was cheating even though I wasn't. What would dream say if she were standing here behind me? That was my test, right? Would she frown at me, or would she say "Hey man, it's not like we are a couple yet" and shrug it off? I could not say which was more likely.

"Think it over, O.K.?"

Daphne picked up her bow and quiver and started walking off. Her jeans showed her muscular legs. I was certain, by the way she moved as she walked away that she was doing so to attract my gaze.

"But don't think for too long."

The ballroom was packed and I was doing the tango. I didn't realize that I knew how to dance the tango, but here I was doing it. Dream was my dance partner, in a long sleek black dress that clung to her curves as though it was painted on. Her red lipstick drew your attention to her face like a magnet. The room was filled with foreign dignitaries, diplomats and heads of state. I twirled

Dream around, dipped her and then brought her straight up into the dance.

"Video Camera. 3 O'clock"

I twisted our dance to look. She was right. When I dipped her she must have spotted it.

"Good catch. I saw another on the south stairs. Any sign of our mark?"

We had been sent on this mission by the Canadian Homeland Association of Intelligence: Terrorist Elimination Agency (or C.H.A.I. T.E.A.) to shadow the terrorist known as Baron Von Krueller to watch where he dropped off some secret briefs. We were then to intercept said briefs and take them back to C.H.A.I. T.E.A. headquarters. We did not know what the briefs contained, just that we needed to grab them, stealthily. We did not need to know the contents. That C.H.A.I. T.E.A. sent their best agents on this mission showed us that the briefs must be important.

"I haven't seen him. I figure the exchange will be on the upper levels though, and with those cameras it will tough for us to make it up there without a diversion."

We continued to dance. As I spun counter clockwise, I noticed a man hurrying up the north staircase. He turned briefly and I noticed the 'X' shaped scar on his cheek. His hair was dyed yellow and he had shaved off his trademark beard, but this was definitely Baron Von Krueller.

"I've got him. North staircase. 7 O-clock."

Dream looked.

"Confirmed. Grab my boob."

"What?"

"We need a diversion. Grab my boob."

I should not have questioned her. Dream always had a plan. I slid my hand up her dress to her chest and gently squeezed.

She broke away from the dance and slapped me. Hard.

"Asshole!"

She turned and ran, fake tears streaming down her face, up the north staircase.

"Natasha, wait!"

Natasha was the cover alias she was using. I ran after her, faking my distress. The other attendees met me with looks of disgust as I passed. I would have to thank Dream for this later. I found her around the corner alcove as I reached the top of the stairs. She had a schematic hologram of the upper floor projecting from her wristwatch. A red dot moved along the schematic.

"It looks like our 'friend' is moving towards the master study. That is likely the place of the drop. We can beat him there if we crawl through the ducting from the ladies washroom."

We hightailed it to the ladies washroom, into a stall and locked the door behind us. It was a tight squeeze, but we were able to prepare our mission gear within that space. Pistols, micro-filament nano-grappler, laser cutter, multi-tool, and night vision contacts.

I had the screws out of the ducting vent quickly and Dream slipped inside. I followed, turning to put the grate back in place. I turned back to see Dream crawling forward towards our goal. My view went straight up her dress to a familiar sight.

"Um. Did you forget a piece of gear?"

"Oh grow up. They leave panty lines in a dress like this and it's not like you haven't seen it before."

After a few turns we quickly arrived at the ducting vent in the master study. The Baron was not yet there. We were squeezed in side by side to get a better view of the office. My breathing was heavy after crawling through the uncomfortable metal ducting.

"Can I ask you a question?"

"Sure. Whisper it, O.K.?"

"O.K. In the other world...I mean in the world where we aren't spies and I don't know you...a girl wanted to kiss me. And maybe more. Does that bother you?"

She bit her lower lip lightly. I knew her well enough to know she did this when she found something funny. She didn't laugh, but I knew that was because her loud laugh would alert security guards throughout the entire complex. I am not sure why she found it funny as it was a serious question.

"Look, if you kissed someone else here, your backside would feel my fury, but in that world, we have not even met yet. Why would I be upset?"

"Really?"

"For sure. I mean I have not exactly been virginal over there either you know. Even since we have talked about meeting in that world, I still had some fun there. Does that bother you?"

I thought about it. I found it didn't bother me at all. I mean we were looking for each other in that world, but we had not even met and it was possible we never would. Why would I expect her to be abstinent until the day we met? If we never met, that would seem unfair. I found I was not jealous at all, other than the mere surface jealousy of wanting to be with her there too.

"No, I guess it doesn't."

"Are we good then?"

"Yes."

"Shhht!"

She cut me off as the Baron entered the room. He looked left and right and pulled a manila envelope out of his tuxedo jacket and laid it on the desk. He turned, grabbed a metal briefcase next to the desk and headed out of the room.

Seconds after the door latched shut, Dream and I were in the room grabbing the file. Dream picked it up and examined it for a moment. We dared not open it as we were ordered not to, but that doesn't mean we were not curious. On the outside of the envelope there were five words handwritten: *"The Fig Leaf of Laurel"*. I had no idea what this meant. It must be code for something.

All of a sudden the doors were rattling with someone trying to enter. I quickly shot the laser cutter at the door lock, melting it.

"Open this door!"

It certainly sounded like the Baron. Dream and I nodded to

each other. She jumped back into the vent and crawled quickly. I followed and turned just as the Baron kicked the door down in a flurry of splinters. I fired off one round of my pistol as he dove behind the giant desk. I scurried backwards down the duct. I heard a gunshot as a bullet whizzed by my head to open up the ducting beside me like a can opener. I fired blindly back at him, for cover more than accuracy. I then turned and scurried out of the duct and into the ladies washroom as quickly as I could. Dream was there to give me a hand down.

We did not even take the time to screw the ducting vent in again. The Baron knew we were here and he would want us dead for our theft. We made our way to the roof as expeditiously as we could. There a helicopter was waiting for us, hovering above, with a rope later dangling before us. I motioned for Dream to climb and followed her after she had climbed a half dozen rungs.

The helicopter started to pull away just as Baron Von Krueller burst onto the roof. He fired off a few shots, but we were well out of accurate range. All the same, I held my breath as I heard the bullets fly by in close vicinity. They sounded like angry supersonic bees. Dream continued to climb. I followed and looked up. I nearly slipped off the rung I was on. I needed to remember to tell her that panty lines do not matter.

The next morning I decided to join the other ladies for yoga. I had never tried yoga and had always put it in the category of 'women's activities' when I thought about it. I knew no other guys who were yoga enthusiasts. It's not that I had anything against yoga, but I thought it mainly an activity that women enjoyed, not men. I was somewhat worried that my burka and boxer shorts combination would reveal my identity to the other ladies. While the burka was fairly loose and flowing, I was afraid that once I got into one of those downward dog or other poses that my junk might get highlighted against the fabric. The women at that point would either guess my gender or ponder if I was smuggling a picnic of summer sausage in my outfit.

The instructor took us through many poses: downward dog, upward dog, proud warrior, child's pose, mountain pose, and so on. I didn't find the poses all that hard to get into, though I did find it made me sweat a bit to hold each one. That was somewhat surprising. They played soft New Age music in the background. It was some sort of pan flute mixed with synthesized ocean noises. I am not sure why this was the music that yoga should be done to. I could think of the possibilities of a speed-metal yoga class. I can picture a more aggressive yoga where the poses are shifted every second and might even be fast like martial arts. That would be bad-ass.

Yoga was supposed to be good for the mind, though I could not figure out how. It was just movement of the body, so how could it clear the mind. In that same philosophy, swimming might be good for solving algebraic equations and football might do wonders for advanced chemistry. It just didn't make sense to me.

I found my mind wandering to when I was a child. I remember the warm glow that surrounded my parents as a couple. You could just feel their love of each other. It lessened somewhat as I grew older. Or perhaps that is the wrong term. It didn't lessen, it matured like fine wine. It is a common misconception that boys and men do not fantasize about love and long term relationships and marriage. We are supposed to think only about one night stands and short flings. The truth is that we all engage in those same relationship fantasies. I can remember as a boy thinking about what it would be like to be married to Sandy Marr (the blonde in pig tails who sat next to me in third grade). I would write her first name next to my last name to see how it looked. I would think about how many kids we would have and what their names would be and where we would live. And Sandy wasn't the only one I fantasized about. It happened frequently any time I had an infatuation.

I think that was part of my problem. My mind had trouble accepting that the marriage I had had was nothing like any of the fantasies I had about marriage. There was not that clear love and equal giving. That seemed mainly one sided from myself. In my fantasy, I was never cheated on or abused or taken advantage of. It seemed sad that my inner desire for a loving relationship had been stripped from me. But when I thought about it, even though it was a marriage, it did not need to be the betrayal of that fantasy. I was still relatively young. I still had lots of chances to realize that loving relationship. Could I simply abandon my anger about the betrayal of my fantasy relationship? I think so. In fact it seemed silly to hold any anger about that. It made it easier to do so knowing I was on a quest to find my one love, the lady that I could trust would always love me back the way I loved her. I felt lighter releasing this. It felt like taking a shower after a long day of manual labour.

By the time I had come back to focusing on the class, we had gone through many more poses and we were almost finished. I am not sure how this stuff would clear your mind, but it apparently made me forgetful as the last five or ten minutes were a blur.

The instructor bowed.

"Namaste."

The class responded in kind.

"That means the light inside me recognizes the light inside you."

It was a nice concept. Though it did make me wonder if evil people had an equivalent for recognizing the evil or dark parts of each other. Something like 'Crapmaste' perhaps.

The next night at the bonfire, Daphne was alight with inspiration. You could hear it in the theatrics of her voice and see it in the fierceness in her eyes as she stomped up and down in front of the blaze.

"Who among you thinks that it is strong and independent to shun relationships altogether and just be by yourselves?"

I saw many hands raise in the crowd. I didn't dare raise my own as I knew this was a trap. Beyond that, I didn't truly think that was a thing of strength or independence. I didn't think that being in a relationship necessarily negated your independence, and I didn't think it was weak to need someone. We all needed someone else. We are beings that crave connection and interaction.

"Well, you would be wrong. That is not strength, it is weakness. You are all here because you have been hurt in a previous relationship. If you shun relationships because of that then you are simply running away. There is no independence in cowering before your fears."

"But Daphne, some of us suffered abuse."

I had too. It was tough for me to admit it to myself, but I was abused. It wasn't the hitting physical sort of abuse. It was more of the mental/emotional abuse. Our relationship started out fine, but by the end, she had me feeling lesser and was actively reinforcing those feelings. I was the one putting all the effort into making her feel loved and special and important while all she did was take that and make me feel undesirable. All she did was take.

"Yes. That is true. But that is where the strength is. The strength is in recognizing that abuse. Don't hide from the fact you were abused by never venturing forth again. Recognize it, admit it, and move forward. That recognition can be one of the hardest parts as sometimes the abuse is so subtly done that you do not even notice it is happening. Especially with emotional abuse, those who do this are masters of shifting the blame on to you. They will tell you that you are wrong. They will tell you that you are imagining things. They will tell you that you are crazy. It's called 'gaslighting' and it is altogether an evil thing to do. They make all the problems your fault and you believe them. So stop it!"

This was true. If I had ever felt slighted by something Merideth had done, she would always turn it around on me. It was always my fault somehow. There was never any responsibility taken by her for the way she had treated me. It disgusted me. I thought about how I had let myself be treated and the person I was now was disgusted by who I was then. The person I was before I met Merideth would have been disgusted by it as well. How pathetic was I that I let someone treat me that way? I was just too blind within the relationship to see it. That and I think the abuse didn't start full blast. I think it was subtly turned up in volume over the years. It was such a slow progression that I did not notice it.

The crowd was quiet after Daphne's last statement.

"There can be gratitude in that place as well though. Just think on it. You know how badly you felt within that abuse. You should be grateful it has stopped. You are no longer being abused, does that not feel good? Do not worry about the rocky road it took to get to this place or the rocky road you still need to travel, just be grateful that it has stopped. You have to think about your bad times in a different way. In life you need to experience sadness to know happiness. You need despair to feel pleasure. If you do not experience the first, the second will be bland and unsatisfying. Yes, you have experienced great pain and sadness. But think! What if the reason for that is that there is even greater happiness and pleasure to come in your life that you needed this sadness to counterpoint and appreciate it? If you shun future relationships, you deny that possible happiness. Right? Would you deny the future sweetness coming to you?"

"How can we trust in that?"

I could hear the woman's pain in her voice. She must have been hurt very badly as her voice wavered when she spoke. I felt lucky in that regard. I was on a quest to find my soul mate. I would either fail in the quest and likely die (in which case my pain would end), or I would end up with the love of my life and all the pain I experienced along the way would be worth it. I could trust in that and it made it easier to go on.

"Well, you can't really, I suppose. It is likely to happen, but may not. What you can trust in is that by avoiding relationships, your life will feel empty. We are creatures who crave intimacy and connection. It is who we are. The silence of being alone is so great it echoes. Sometimes the loneliness is so bad that even after your time here, there are some of you who will go back to your abusers. They will phone or email and tell you they have changed. They will tell you it will be better. And some of you will believe them as there is still that piece of your heart that loves them and wants to believe. And there will be part of you that thinks the possible abuse is better than the silence of being alone. Don't fall into that trap. It is weakness."

I definitely knew that pain of loneliness. Even though I had Caryn to take care of, it was still very present. The intimacy of having a partner is a very unique relationship. I missed that terribly, even though it was an abusive relationship. I missed that connection and intimacy. It was not even the sex I missed so much, but the day to day of having someone to share life's moments with. The quiet of its absence was deadly. There are ghosts in the silence of it. In the quiet moments, my mind would pick at the horrible things that were done. Those were the ghosts that haunted a man. It was tough to imagine people going back to someone who treated them so poorly. There is no scenario where I would ever take Merideth back after what she had done to me. I had sacrificed everything I had in my time with her only to be betrayed. After all *A Man sacrifices for those that he loves.* That was not a mistake I would likely make again. In fact I promised myself I wouldn't. That maxim of my father's was flawed. It is not that I would not sacrifice for someone in the future, but I think it needed to be more balanced. I think a better saying would be *Sacrifice for those you love, but never for those that would not sacrifice for you as well.*

"But Daphne, how will we trust someone new will not do the same to us?"

"Ah, well trust is the key word is it not? Part of it is that you now have ammunition. You know better how to recognize those who would do you harm. You will have an easier time seeing a pure heart, now that you have seen darkened ones. A lot of people think that trust is the key component in a good relationship. They are almost right. I will tell you a secret. I know the killer of all relationships. Does anyone want to guess?"

"Betrayal?"

"Cheating?"

"You are close, but it is a mindset that comes before any of those. What destroys any relationship is selfishness. One who betrays is likely only looking out for their own self-interests while not caring about yours. One that cheats is selfishly indulging in their own pleasures no matter who it hurts. Selfishness is what puts a nail in the coffin of every relationship. Someone who only 'takes' and only thinks of themselves is mentally unfit for a relationship. Selfishness is the opposite of compassion in ways. Trust in relationships is good, but only trust in selflessness and compassion. Trust in other things can wane. You can have no trust that your partner will take the garbage out or have a steady job or be on time, but you can overlook those things. As long as you have trust in selflessness and compassion, you can even love those other bits that you don't trust. You will find love again. You will trust someone new, and it will be easier than you think. You just have to be open to it happening."

The bonfire crackled behind Daphne as we considered her words. I thought they had a lot of wisdom to them. I could tell it was bristling with some of the ladies though as they were shifting uncomfortably.

"You speak of love. Pah! I no longer believe in love. Love is a fairy tale."

It was the same lady who had spoken before. There was anger

in her voice now. I knew she was not alone. I knew there were many who had gone through these experiences who no longer believed in love. I thought of Zed too and how he thought our society was a fairy tale. I agreed with him on that, but I did not include love within that. Love existed outside our society, or in spite of it, I guess.

Daphne turned to the fire for a second. There was nearly a minute of silence before she turned around.

"You know, you are absolutely correct. You all read fairy tales of love when you were younger. They filled you with hope and light and inspiration. They filled you with positivity for that magical future relationship you would have. I would say, love can be just like that. Love is definitely a fairy tale, but it takes both partners to write that fairy tale. If only one person is writing it, it is no longer a fairy tale, but a fantasy. You all had the fantasy. It didn't work out. Now don't you want the fairy tale?"

I found that I did.

Afterwards, I found myself at the archery range again. I found with each arrow I shot, there was a certain calmness to it. I needed a stillness of mind to shoot well and the stillness was rippling through the rest of me. Fuck yoga. Archery had it beat hands down for cultivating stillness of mind. I kept thinking of the many moments theory and how I, in this moment, owed patience and accuracy to the Dylan that stood beside a proud bulls-eye.

Daphne entered the lane next to mine and started shooting. She had three or four shots off before I could even aim the arrow I was shooting. They all hit nearly dead centre.

"How do you shoot so fast?"

She laughed.

"I just have a different philosophy in shooting. Lots of people aim and aim and aim for what seems like eternity. I never hold an arrow for more than half a second. It needs to fly one way or another. And whether it shoots true or the aim is off, I have learned something from that arrow. I just keep shooting and I just keep learning. You learn nothing from a perfect shot. It's much like life, no?"

I let loose my arrow. It gave a satisfying 'thunk' in the target. It wasn't a bulls-eye, but it was in the ring just outside the bulls-eye.

"Not bad."

She fired another volley of arrows on after another. All hit pretty much on the bulls-eye. We walked up to collect our arrows.

"By the way, I liked what you said earlier about love and fairy tales."

"Thanks. I made that up on the spot. There are lots like Jessica – those that are too hurt by their experiences to hope for love again. I want to turn them around, but I won't always be successful. That hurt is hard to overcome."

She fired another volley as I shot my lone arrow. I hit about the same place. What was surprising to me was that one of her arrows was way off of the centre of the target. I pointed to it.

"That's not like you."

"And you don't think I did that on purpose?"

I shook my head.

"Well you should know better. I can hit where I want. It is like love, you see. For those that are unskilled, they have no control of where their arrows fly and where the hurt is caused. Because, you must admit, even in the purest of loves, we sometimes hurt our partners. But if you are skilled, you can control where that hurt goes to minimize it."

I looked at my own arrow and thought about my skill. I had no excuse for mine not being a bulls-eye except for my lack of skill. Was I better when it came to love? She must have seen the perplexed look on my face as she walked over to my lane.

"Can I adjust your stance for you?"

I nodded and drew an arrow. She grabbed my hips and twisted

them so I was perfectly sideways. She adjusted my elbow down. She even moved my shoulders to be in alignment with my hips. She hummed as she did so.

"Now! Loose!"

I felt relief as she said it. My back and shoulders and biceps were on fire holding that arrow for so long. I wanted to not show that I was straining though. *A man never shows weakness.* My fingers released. The arrow left my bow as if it was in slow motion. I saw it wiggle slowly as it travelled through the air to the target. It hit dead centre with a sound that echoed through the archery range. Bulls-eye! I felt a swelling lightness in my chest. My heart soared like an eagle. It felt like that moment on a rollercoaster when you are cresting the first summit before the drop. I had done it. I was now that Dylan who, in this moment, owed his success to the Dylan before who aimed correctly. I owed it to Daphne as well. I laughed out loud. It was not the sort of laugh that came from humour, but more of a sound birthed of pure joy. I turned and hugged her.

"I did it! Thank you!"

She looked up at me with her green eyes. I realized I had not let go of her after hugging her. Her arms had wrapped around my back. We must have looked fairly amusing. In my burka, the hug must have appeared like Daphne was being slowly devoured by a black ghost.

"My pleasure, Dylan. Tell me, have you thought more about what we talked about?"

"I have."

She smirked.

"And?"

"I say yes. I say we are both single attractive adults, right?"

She said nothing, but her eyes blinked slowly, pleading. I tilted my head down and kissed her. Her lips were firm and demanding.

She snaked her hand around my neck and pulled me tighter into the kiss.

Afterwards we were a tangled mess, like a bird's nest made of legs and arms and sheets. She had been very vocal about what she wanted and when and where. I was only happy to oblige. She was aggressive, yet gentle, firm, yet giving. Things built slowly, but build they did, and when that orgasm came it was the rare sort that leaves every cell in your body feeling satisfied. The closeness that manifested led me to know that it was the same for her. Her screams of pleasure only highlighted the point. In fact, it was her moaning, increasing in volume, that put me over the top myself.

But now we laid in silence. It felt as if a glow should be emanating from us as there was such a feeling of satisfaction. We had been silent for nearly ten minutes, save for our heavy breathing and slight movement in the bed. I sat transfixed, watching a bead of sweat slowly make its way down her breast.

"That was incredible."

She turned to me and smiled. Her green eyes twinkled with mischief.

"Mmmhmmm."

Her agreement was so close to her earlier moaning that my penis twitched simply from the similarity. She saw it and laughed. Then she covered her mouth and sat up. The sudden levity had broken our lazy sexual afterglow.

"Dylan, can I ask you something?"

I turned on my side, propping myself up with my arm.

"You bet."

"When your ex cheated, was it the sex that bothered you?"

I frowned. This was tough territory for me. I didn't like to see those memories in my mind. It had been difficult, especially right after I discovered it. She told me a lot of things I likely didn't need to know. She told me about sexual acts she had done that she had never done with me. They were things we had discussed doing, but that she said she didn't want to. That had hurt. I had asked her why she had shared those things with another man, but not me. She had responded saying that I must not have been as charming as him. That had hurt more.

"You don't have to answer if you don't want."

"No it's ok. It wasn't really the sex. Before I knew she was cheating, I always thought it would have been the sex that would have bothered me but it wasn't. It was two other things really. One, it was the betrayal. Two, it was the gifting of something precious to someone else. That closeness and sharing that comes with sex is something sacred. When it is given so freely to someone outside the relationship, it tarnishes every previous time it was given to you."

She nodded.

"So was it sacred here? In my bed?"

She had that mischievous smirk on her face again.

"Oh, most definitely."

"Really, do tell. Because I think it was way more sacred for you than for me. For me it was merely holy."

I was offended for a split second before I understood her double-entendre. We looked at each other and burst into laughter. I descended on her, touching the spot where her hip met her torso where I had discovered she was ticklish. Her legs flailed and she screamed in laughter as she retaliated tickling me. Her phone chimed in the background.

"Wait…"

I continued to tickle for a few moments more.

"No. Stop!"

She twisted away and picked up her phone. She was all business suddenly.

"Hey. What is it?"

There was a muffled voice on the other end.

"Really? Just tell her to use the....no...no...we need those for Saturday. Can't you just....O.K...fine...I'll be right over."

Daphne started dressing. She looked at me and sighed.

"I have to get over to the kitchens. There's always a crisis somewhere."

As she stood up, I noticed her clothes lying haphazard at the end of the bed. On the very top was her underwear. It was orange and lacy. It was everything I was sent here to get. An honourable man would not even think about stealing someone's underwear, but I really needed it to get to Dream. I was damned either way. Perhaps, though, she would understand if I simply asked. Maybe she would appreciate that I asked.

"Daphne, if I asked you for something..."

She saw me staring at her underwear and cut me off.

"Don't even. I know Zed sent you and I know why. Forget about it."

She stormed out of the room while she was tossing a shirt over her head. The door drifted shut behind her. I sighed and laid back. I still felt a bit of that post-coital glow. I could rest and just fall asleep into that ambrosia if I wanted to. I turned my head to the side. Her dresser was in full view. Wait. Her dresser. I could not ignore that there were other pairs of underwear within it. Just looking for the underwear didn't mean I was going to steal it, right?

I walked over to the dresser and opened a few drawers. On the third attempt I found her underwear drawer. It felt like sneaking into a bank to rob it. I was suddenly embarrassed by what I was doing and ashamed. Stealing was wrong. I knew it deep down. It was one of the first moral lessons my father drilled into me. But it was just a pair of underwear. It's not like it was a chest of gold or anything. Underwear or not, I liked Daphne and this felt like a violation of her trust. I had asked her point blank and she had refused so why would I have the right to take a pair? On the other hand, she may not ever notice them missing. I mean, if someone stole one of my pairs of underwear, I would never even know. And it would lead me closer to Dream. I hated the conflict within myself. What I hated more was that feeling I got when I tried to justify something to myself. I knew it was wrong and I could feel my mind glossing over it and trying to justify it. I think I may have been unique in this fashion, but I could always recognize that feeling within myself and it always disgusted me. I could not lie to myself. This was wrong. I was stealing. It was a breach of trust. However, I was going to do it anyway.

I grabbed a random pair of underwear and stuffed it in my pocket. I was horrible for doing this.

I dressed quickly and headed out Daphne's bedroom door. The burka seemed to help me hide my shame. I was only five or six steps down the hallway when I felt a sharp pain on the back of my head and the world went dark.

I woke to find myself sitting in the badlands at mid-day. I was staring at my shadow on the ground. It was so much smaller than I was this time of day.

"Get up."

I looked up to find Daphne pointing her bow at me. She had an arrow drawn back. I put my hands up as I stood. Harmonia slithered around in the background.

"Whoa, Daphne…look…"

She motioned forward with her bow.

"Just shut up. You are just like him. You were only with me because you wanted something, not because you liked me."

"That's not true. I like you Daphne. It's just that Zed…"

"Don't you think I knew why Zed sent you here? He sends them all here for the same reason. It's a longstanding practical joke for Zed. You know what, I don't find it funny. I feel used, Dylan."

I knew it was wrong when I took them. I was the bad guy here. I did like her though. I didn't like that misconception.

"Look. I know I was wrong. I do like you. The sex had nothing to do with…"

"Just get back against the tree."

She motioned her bow forward again, so I quickly backed up until I hit the most enormous and twisted tree I have ever seen. Its barren branches cast shadows like witch fingers on the ground.

"Just remember, Dylan, I shoot where I want."

Her arrow left her bow and I felt a piercing pain in my left shoulder. I looked over to find the arrow had pierced the skin on my shoulder through one side and out the other to tack me to the tree. Blood trickled down my arm. I tried to pull on the arrow, but it causes searing pain to do so. I winced.

"I liked you Dylan. I trusted you. I left you alone in my room because I trusted in your honour."

I could see tears streaming down her cheek. She turned and walked away quickly.

"Daphne."

"Go fuck yourself, Dylan"

I watched her walk away until she was a spec on the horizon.

I hung on the tree for hours. My bare chest was burning. I laughed to myself. There was a certain irony about it. Daphne had fled from the sun god's affections. Daphne felt spurned by my own actions, and here the sun god was punishing me for it. The skin around my arrow wound was still stinging with any minute motion I made or any time the wind kicked up.

The sun was lower on the horizon now. I had no idea how much time had passed. Time had seemed to have lost meaning. I looked out onto the badlands. I was parched. I really could use a glass of water. I was likely going to die out here. Ten feet in front of me my eyes settled on a chunk of sandstone. If I did not know better, I would have assumed that was my chunk of sandstone. It could not be though, but there it was, and it sure looked like my sandstone. I could hear a steady thumping too. Was it just the blood pumping through my ears? It was infuriating being stuck on this tree.

I thought back to what Daphne last said: "I shoot where I want". She could have skewered me right through the skull but she, instead, tagged me in the shoulder where it would be neither fatal nor crippling. It was just painful. It reminded me about what she said about love and archery and how you hurt the ones you love, but if you are skilled you hurt them the least you have to. Was it possible that she didn't send me out here to die? Did she, instead, want me to live? How could I escape this though? I would have to pull the arrow out, though that meant excruciating pain. It all comes down to a choice. It was like what she was preaching all along in the bonfire chats. You had to choose to go forward. Damn the pain. Damn the consequences. Damn the whole situation. I chose to go forward.

I pulled on the arrow with all my might. I screamed as I did so as it felt like the sun god himself was jamming a spear of sun fire into my arm. It wiggled up and down before popping out. A splatter of blood from the wound hit the ground a split second before I followed. I sat up, dust in my wound, and laughed at the sky. I was free!

I found my bag packed behind the tree. That would seem to confirm that Daphne wanted me to live through this experience. I still think I had hurt her feelings and I was genuinely sorry for that. She was right. I had failed my quest anyway. Or had I? I unzipped my bag and right on the top was the pair of underwear I had stolen. She had given them to me anyway. I turned back towards the direction of the retreat.

"Thank you."

The gravelly whisper of my voice let me know the state of my dehydration once again. I spotted the sandstone chunk on the ground. I walked over and picked it up. It felt just like it did in my dreams. The feeling made me think of those amber days on Kootenay Lake as a child. It made me think of the pure bliss of summer. It made me think of Dream. That close feeling to Dream and happiness made me feel taunted by the presence of the sandstone chunk. I looked up at the sun and yelled.

"Fuck you!"

I threw it at the tree as hard as I could. It hit and a rain of sandstone chunks flew off in every direction. The main chunk fell to the base of the tree. I scrambled to pick it up again. Half of it was missing. The other half was an impossibility. What was exposed in the centre of the sandstone was a human heart. I could see just a portion of it exposed, but it throbbed and pumped just as if it were in a human chest. This made absolutely no sense at all. But here it was in my hand.

Thump-Thump, Thump-Thump, Thump-Thump.

What did this mean? Why was there a heart in this chunk of sandstone? I found my mind slid around answering these questions. I just didn't want to process it. I put it in the duffel with the plastic sword and pirate hat and vial of liquid and put it out of my mind. I could still hear the muffled thumping of the exposed heart within.

It took me nearly another hour to find my motorcycle. It would be a long, dusty, dusk ride back home.

I felt lighter as I rode back to Calgary. It was possible that some of that was due to my dehydration. I would have stopped to fix that, but I was too intent on getting back. I think my lightness was more due to the fact that my heart felt better. It seems such a New Age and flakey thing to say, but it was true. I had not realized how damaged my heart was from what Merideth had done to me, but my time at the *Laurel Lodge* had given it some healing. I felt that what was done to me was no longer something that would embitter me in a future relationship. I felt, at least as far as my heart goes, ready to step into a relationship in a healthy way.

I turned my bike off after sliding it into its spot in the garage. I closed the garage and entered my house through the mud room. I could hear sounds of machine gun fire coming from my living room. It was then that I realized how much I missed Caryn. I was not even sure how long I had been away. Had it been a few days? A week? More? My recollection of time seemed a bit fuzzy. As I rounded into the living room, I was hoping to see Caryn, but it was only Mark.

"Hey."

I reached into my bag, grabbed the underwear and tossed them at Mark. They landed in his lap. He paused the game and turned towards me.

"Outstanding man! I knew you had it in you. Did you find anything else out there?"

"Nope."

I am not sure why I didn't tell him. Perhaps it just seemed too crazy to say "Oh yeah, by the way, I found a functional human heart partially trapped in sandstone." He held the panties up to the light for a moment before stuffing them in his pocket. He had a huge grin on his face as he grabbed a can of pop from the coffee table.

"Cola?"

"Sure. Where's Caryn?"

I opened the cola and drank deep. It was like heaven; a sweet rain on my badlands tongue.

"Asleep. Join me."

I jumped over him and grabbed the other controller. Soon the evening was filled with laughter, machine gun fire, popcorn, and victory.

# MONSTERS AND MIRRORS

I had been in the shower too long. I could tell as my bathroom mirror was completely foggy. I wiped away a clear spot with my hand. The squeaky noises my wiping produced were oddly pleasing to my mind, like I was somehow cleaning my mind as well as the mirror. The face that was summoned up in the mirror shocked me even though it had been this way for months and months. It was altogether too gaunt. I remember my healthy and happy self not having such pronounced cheek bones and there were far too many wrinkles or wrinkle-esque structures going on in my face. I am certain that was mainly stress, but it bothered me nonetheless. And finally, when I looked at myself, I could see gray hairs nestled in amongst the dark. I know I was approaching that age where it happens. Hell, some people have plenty of gray way before this age, but this was special. I did not even have one before my split. I could give a name to every one of my gray hairs and that name would be 'Merideth'.

I started my morning shaving routine. I find shaving somewhat meditative. The repetitive motions and concentration just aided in the thought process.

The more I thought about it, while looking at myself in the mirror, the more I was sure that my self-image issues had changed. I think it was worse now than when I had split. Back then, I saw a diminished Dylan in the mirror but I also had a diminished mind and heart. I matched. It was shocking to see myself in the mirror, but not surprising. Now, the bulk of the way through my quest, I felt stronger in mind and heart, so that the diminished Dylan in the mirror was all the more shocking. I would have to do something about that. I would have to start eating better and trying to relax more. I wanted to be a better version of myself for when I eventually connected with Dream. I knew it was likely a longer process back to body normalcy than it was to get into this state, but it was probably good to start now. I also knew that there was no changing the gray hair. It was what it was. Having a few battle scars probably wasn't a bad thing. Scars were sexy, right?

"What the fuck is wrong with you?"

The immediate aggression on the phone felt like a jolt of lightning to my system. If I wasn't awake before I answered the phone, I was now. It took me a second to even understand who the person was behind the voice. It was Jenn.

"Jenn, what are you even talking about? Why are you so angry?"

"On my wall. Why did you post that? My friends are all wondering why my brother is such an asshole."

Her response did not help me at all. I hadn't even looked at any of my social media sites in the last while. I was away at the Laurel Lodge. But I had told Mark to make himself at home. Was it possible that he posted something on Jenn's wall? Or perhaps it was Caryn?

"Whoa, Whoa. Jenn, I have been away for nearly a week. I haven't even been on social media. Can I try to figure out what happened and phone you back?"

"Fuck. Whatever. It will just be another excuse anyway. It's no wonder you can't keep your shit together."

And with a click, our phone call ended on the same jarring note it started with.

"Oh, that."

Mark took another big bite of the waffles in front of him. They were coated with marshmallows with sprinkles on top, and of course slathered in syrup. It was a complete sugar bomb, but perhaps that was what he needed to keep up his high energy ways.

He chewed vigorously and held up his hand to me to indicate that he would respond in a second. I noted that he still had the pair of panties I had taken from Daphne in his shirt pocket. He swallowed and took a big swig of cola. Between the sugar bombed waffles and the cola it was amazing that he didn't float around the room like a hummingbird. He put his drink down and took the panties out of his pocket and wiped his mouth with them.

"Yeah, I perused your social media sites when you were gone. Man, your sister is a piece of work."

His hands moved emphatically as he spoke.

"I mean, I get it. Rabid feminist. That's cool and all. She posts things about the degradation of women, sexism, Rayne Kale quotes, and the supposed patriarchy. I mean that can be entertaining as hell to read, but then she did something I couldn't stomach."

He patted his chest and burped. It was as if Jenn's actions had given him actual indigestion.

"What?"

"Well she had one post about the degradation of women in magazines with them posed sexually. And her very next post was a picture of topless firemen with the caption 'I may just do a little arson if this is what showed up at my door. Enjoy girls!' I just couldn't stand the hypocrisy of it!"

At his last word, he slammed his hand down onto my table.

A sprinkle laden marshmallow rolled off of his plate. He deftly grabbed it up and popped it in his mouth.

"So, what did you do?"

"Mmmmfff."

He mumbled as he chewed. He chewed fast and rolled his eyes as he did so, gulping down the sugary mass.

"Tough to talk and eat, right? What did I do? Well, I wasn't going to do anything as it was your account, but I just couldn't stand it. I posted a pic of girls in flame bikinis and wrote 'Some playmates for your firefighters'".

I couldn't help smiling. I mean, I was a bit annoyed that he posted under my account and that I would have to deal with the aftermath with my sister. But, I had to agree with him. I saw it on social media all the time: feminist friends posting articles on the subjugation of women, or the degradation of women, or simply women being treated like pieces of meat. They cancelled out any of this stuff as soon as they posted something that subjugated men, degraded men, or treated men like pieces of meat (as the firefighter picture had done here). I can recall a lady I knew posting about how women weren't valued as they should be and in the same day posted a comedic post about how dumb men were. Jenn herself once had a long winded post on equality of the genders and then just 10 minutes later posted a picture with the slogan "Men and Women are equal, but women are more equal". It seemed very Rayne Kale. It was all hypocrisy. I mean one could not claim to be fighting for equality while at the same time engaging in the very behaviours they were fighting against. I doubt they even saw it. While I may not have posted what he posted for fear of rustling any feathers, I could see why he did. In a way, I wish I had posted it. I would have been proud to have done so.

I am not sure if it was triggered by Jenn and her hypocrisy, but

I found myself thinking about a time in my childhood when I was bullied. I was in grade 6 and had just started the school year in a new school. My old school was a K-5, so the move was a necessary one. When I was in grade 5, I could walk to school every day from my home, but now I had to take a bus. I found the bus kind of exciting, but it had hidden pitfalls. It meant that the school I was going to was not in my community. It was in someone else's.

That first week of school illustrated this well. The first week is often about shy meetings and figuring out who was who in this new place. It became apparent that while we were all new to the school, the bulk of the kids in my class knew each other from a previous school in the same neighbourhood. They had known each other since kindergarten or before. There was a small minority of us who were bussed in. We were the outsiders. We were foreign.

That was the heart of my problem. You see, in my class there was a girl that I liked: Trish. She was local to the community. And she liked me too. We would share shy glances and smiles as we were taught math or science or reading. We shared those pre-teen displays of affection like trading stickers or sharing a juice box. It was great except for Mathew Fram. Mathew Fram was also a kid from the local community and had apparently liked this girl since they were in kindergarten. It didn't matter to Mathew Fram that Trish didn't like him and never had. In fact, that may have fuelled his fists more. After he found out about us, he found me at lunch when I was alone. I tried to run, but he had friends to corral me in. They dragged me behind the bushes behind the bike racks near the fence, and there Mathew Fram beat me until I could only see out of one eye. I remember his fists falling over and over as he repeated his mantra:

"You're not worth anything! Stay away from Trish. You're not worth anything!"

I could have fought back. I know I could have. I could have sent my fists flying into his face. The problem was my dad and my fear. My dad had taught me not to fight; that it was one of the most dishonourable things you could do as a man. I also feared my own strength. My dad had always made me think of the other side. *Never act in ways that will shame you later.* I could picture myself standing over Mathew Fram's bruised and bloody body, with a twisted smile on my face, as his blood dripped off of my knuckles. That would shame me big time. The pain of that shame would be greater, by far, than the pain of Mathew's fists. So I did nothing but hold my hands up to protect my face as he beat me.

I went to my teacher afterwards, in tears. She cleaned me up and asked me about what happened. I told her everything. She seemed very compassionate and caring until I mentioned that Mathew Fram was the culprit. When his name fled my lips, she frowned and gave a hiss with her sudden intake of air.

"Oh, that isn't good. You see Dylan, I know Mathew's family. I live in the neighbourhood. His father is a bit of a brute. If I phone him and tell him Mathew was bullying you, he will beat Mathew. You understand why I can't do that, right?"

I didn't answer. My head hung low and my tears fell with audible plops on the vinyl tile floor. I didn't understand. I didn't really care if he was beaten at all. In fact, I wished his dad would beat him until he looked like and felt like I did. Shouldn't there be consequences for bad behaviour? Should bullies get a free pass because of their home life? It was too unjust to consider.

"Besides, this wasn't truly bullying. It was fighting. Boys will be boys after all."

If I was older I would have told her that fighting usually involves two combatants, not one combatant and one punching bag. It was 50% wrong. I would certainly never trust any math she taught us. I knew it was her simply justifying her decision, but that did not help.

"If your parents phone I will simply tell them the truth that it was roughhousing."

I hated that 'roughhousing' was a way that male violence to other males was excused. I hated my teacher for making excuses for Mathew's actions. I hated myself because I knew I would not tell my parents as the shame of being thought of as one that starts fights was greater than my need for justice. I hated that my teacher's actions seemed to underline Mathew Fram's mantra: "You're not worth anything". I was certainly not worth enough for her to help me.

So I was quiet about what was happening to me. And it only took 7 more beatings for me to finally shun Trish and become the class loner.

"You're not worth anything!"

I phoned Jenn back as soon as I could to clear up the misunderstanding. I was more optimistic about it than I should have been.

"Yeah, I get it. You have a moronic house guest. Will you take down that post then?"

I was somewhat annoyed with her flippant response. She both insulted Mark and was making demands. I wasn't looking to change anything, merely to offer her an explanation as to what happened.

"Hey, he is not a moron just because he pointed out a bit of hypocrisy. I just wanted to explain why he did it. I am not taking it down. I agree with him, even though I would likely not have posted that myself."

"What hypocrisy? Look either you take it down, or I will delete it myself!"

How could she not see the hypocrisy in this? Was it not blatantly obvious?

"Look, if you post pictures of half-naked men, he can post pictures of half-naked women. It's only fair. I know you don't like that and find it degrading to women, but if you truly feel that way then you shouldn't post similar pictures of men. Hypocrisy, see?"

If you delete the comment I will just repost it on my timeline and tag you in it."

"Arrgh! You are such a fucking child. You are so ignorant of how things are. It is different between men and women. The pictures are not degrading to men as there is no such thing as sexism towards the dominant gender. It doesn't work that way. It's no wonder your marriage fell apart."

That argument never worked for me whether it was sexism, racism, or any other type of 'ism'. These things always worked both ways. If they didn't then the 'ism' just became a vehicle for one side to whine and bully to get their way while shutting out the other side completely. There is a good phrase about having a cake and eating it too that comes to mind.

"Look Jenn, you have always told me that feminism is about equality of the genders and not just women, right? So don't you think that, given that, you should treat men the same as you wish to be treated and not hide behind some sort of victim's privilege?"

-CLICK-

The hang up shocked me. I was not trying to upset my sister, but I didn't feel like I needed to back down on this either. Mark's post was quite over the top and dramatic, but he wasn't wrong and it didn't deserve to be censored.

I think we were three aisles into the weekly grocery run when I realized that something must be amiss. Caryn was her regular self, zipping on ahead to pick out items on our list for the meals we had planned. But there was something wrong with Mark. Where usually he was full of energy like someone drinking a crack latte, he seemed sullen and slow. When I turned to talk to him, he would look like he was about to say something and then turn away quickly. We passed through the entire candy aisle without him even looking at the merchandise where normally he would have observed them like a hummingbird in a field of wildflowers. Something was definitely wrong.

"What gives man? You seem like you have seen a ghost today."

He winced as I said the word ghost.

"I mean really, what is it?"

Caryn bounded down the aisle and threw a pack of steaks in the cart. She looked at my list, turned and zipped off in search of another item.

Mark turned to me and sighed.

"Ok, you want to know what's eating me? I got your last quest from Zed a few days ago."

"A few days ago? And you're just telling me now?"

He nodded.

"Yeah. You see, it's a doozy. Either Zed thinks highly of you and wants to give you a challenge...or...or he wants you dead."

"Why, what is the quest?"

Mark spotted a pack of marshmallows as we went by it. He grabbed it and threw it in the cart. At least that was a return to something normal for him. His sweet tooth seemed at odds with the suit and tie he was wearing.

"It's a straight-up monster slaying. Zed wants you to hike into the Ghost Wilderness, find the monster known as the Malmaerra, and fight it."

"Wait, what's a Malmaerra?"

I picked up a couple of cartons of milk from the freezer and put them in the cart. Mark grabbed one and returned it to the freezer, replacing it with a chocolate milk.

"Do you know the story of Proteus?"

I shook my head as we turned the cart down another aisle. Caryn was back briefly, dumping a bag of French fries into the cart.

"He was called the 'Old Man of the Sea'. He could change into any shape imaginable. The Malmaerra is like that."

"It's a shape changer? That doesn't sound so bad."

"Well, it is. You see, the Malmaerra lives in all slices of the multiverse at once. It can look into your branches of the multiverse and pull out the shapes you find the scariest. It can pull out the very worst possible outcomes of your lives and bring it up in front of you. That's why some call this monster 'The Dark Mirror'. It is very dangerous and very capable of killing you."

"Whoa. Whoa. You're going too fast for me. What is a multiverse?"

"Ok. Hmm. Let's see if I can explain this to you…"

Mark grabbed a package of spaghetti from the shelf, ripped it open and threw it into the air. It landed in a haphazard pile with sticks of spaghetti laying this way and that. An elderly lady looked at us wild eyed as she witnessed what Mark had done. It is the kind of thing that would have bothered me before the split, but like Zed deduced, I now lived outside of societal conventions. I didn't give a shit that he just tossed a package of spaghetti on the floor.

"Ok, picture your life as a line; like a piece of spaghetti, right? One universe."

"Alright."

"Now every life decision, every 'yes' or 'no' you have to answer, splits it into two more universes. Everything exists. The universe where you say 'yes' and the universe where you say 'no'. They are both realities."

I stared at the jumble of dried noodles on the ground. I could see what he was saying. If every decision spawned a new universe, then the collection of my life (or lives) would look much like this pile of spaghetti.

"So there is a universe where I didn't marry Merideth? And there is one where we didn't split?"

"There are likely many of each. Here is what will really bake your noodle, no pun intended. Your consciousness is living in all of these simultaneously but you are only aware of the one you see in your day-to-day life. Which means your consciousness is always split between universes."

That was a very confusing and mind bending thought for sure. My life was not just my life, but a collection of all my lives depending on each decision I made. There was no 'path not taken' in this model. There were no regrets. Everything was explored. Only my limited perception kept me from seeing the other options. Caryn walked up beside the cart as I considered this. She looked down at the spilled spaghetti with a perplexed frown.

"Ok, so what happens if in one universe, one choice, I die?" Mark talked with his hands. He was very animated.

"Ah, see that is a good question. If you die in one universe…" Mark stepped on a pile of spaghetti with a crunch and kicked it to the side.

"…your consciousness flows into the most similar universe available where you do not die. It's called quantum immortality. It's a simple thing to prove to yourself. You have likely had many times in your life where you did something very dangerous, and yet here you are still alive. And anyone who has experiences like this feels 'more alive' afterwards. That 'more alive' feeling is because your consciousness from the other branch of the universe, where you died, flows back into you."

If I followed his logic, it meant that you never truly died. Universes simply collapsed and merged with other universes. Branches of your choices ceased to be, but on a whole, you kept going.

"So, if death is merely a transference, then why should I fear anything the Malmaerra does to me? Perhaps I will just be merged with a universe that is happier for me than this one."

Mark stopped me and put his finger up in front of his face.

"Ah, you say that because of all the bad things that *have* happened to you. But see those are over and done. They are in the past. If you merge with the next most similar universe, you will have those in your past. But this universe is one where you are on the path to finding your true love. That means it may be the happiest of possible universes you could find. It may be the *only* universe where you are on that path. Are you willing to risk that?"

Our cart crunched its way through the spilled spaghetti as we moved down the aisle. He had a point. If I pushed my way through, I could see a life with Dream where it positively glowed with happiness. That was worth preserving. But then again, if I didn't slay the Malmaerra, I would never get there.

"But won't my decisions in the fight with the Malmaerra spawn different universes. If I die in 9 out of 10 of those, won't I still just merge to the tenth anyway and be successful?"

"What if 10 out of 10 end up in your death? You never end up with the love of your life then."

"But Mark, if I don't attempt it, I will certainly not end up with her."

He was silent for a moment. I had stumped him.

"Well, you've got me there."

He picked up the intercom phone at the end of the aisle and brought it to his mouth.

"Dry clean up on Aisle 5."

"I'm coming with you."

Caryn looked at me with defiance as I packed my tent for the journey. I had all my camping supplies strewn about the living room floor as Mark sat drinking cola on the couch. It was like a buffet of gadgets and supplies to live comfortably in the back country. I hadn't been camping in years. I had to quickly think about which items were essential and which were optional. It all came down to weight vs. convenience. Caryn's assertion was similar. I would like to take her with me, but that added extra 'weight'. I would need to provide for her and protect her as well when I was out there.

"Now wait now, I am not sure Zed would be ok with that."

I was about to pipe up myself that Caryn should not go, but Mark's interjection changed my mind. I was already dancing like a marionette for Zed. All these quests and their rules and hoops I had to jump through had me feeling a bit too controlled. My natural urge was to rebel against that.

"Did Zed specifically say she should not go?"

"Well no, but…"

I had stumped him. Caryn cast him a victorious glare. It meant I would need to modify my packing. Twice as many dehydrated meals and a sleeping bag for her. Though it also meant she had a pack she could carry too. It may not be so bad.

"Then she goes."

Mark was up and off the couch in an instant. He shot his hands in the air in exasperation.

"Think man! It's fucking insane! That thing is dangerous. She could get hurt!"

"All the more motivation for me to win. I absolutely cannot lose if I need to protect my daughter. Caryn, get your pack, sleeping bag, and some clothes."

Caryn bounded off with a laugh leaving Mark and I alone. He looked a bit angry that I was not taking his advice. His head was reddening up like a beet. Finally he exhaled.

"Fine! Fine. But I am going to give you some advice. I am really not supposed to, but I care about what happens to that girl."

"Any advice would be appreciated."

He started pacing again. It was his signature move. His hands flailed this way and that as he talked.

"Ok. You will be attacked seven times by the Malmaerra, each time in a different guise. Most people try to fight it physically, but it is next to impossible. That thing is like whirling death. What you need to remember is that it is looking for a certain behaviour or phrase and it will then fade away. Your actions defeat it, not your brawn. Get it?"

"Not really…"

"You will. At least I hope you will."

Suddenly he hugged me tight.

"Good luck, man."

My dad was big into camping and self-reliance. He was always taking Jenn and I out to the wild places to sleep in a tent or under the stars for a night or two. My mom never joined us. She felt inspired by the natural world and loved to paint it, but I suspect sleeping on the ground with a root in her back was likely not the sort of inspiration she was looking for.

I can remember one trip I had taken with my dad. We were somewhere out in the Sheep River Valley. It was one of his favourite spots. I was a teenager and annoyed that I was out camping with him as I had wanted to spend the weekend hanging out with my friends instead. I had punished him for it with grumpiness and biting sarcastic comments to nearly everything he said. I had been quite aware what a wet blanket a moody teen could be on any situation and I was using it to my advantage.

To my dad's credit, he did not get mad at me for this at all. We were sitting on the banks of the river, when he simply gifted me with a few bits of wisdom.

"Son, *Never judge a thing until it is at its end. A convenience can turn out to be a weakness while a hardship may end up a boon.*"

"What the heck does that even mean?"

I turned to him with a frown and a glare. I had been angry as well as we had both been sitting on the same river bank casting the same lines in the water and he had caught two fish already and I had caught none. My teenaged mind could not even grasp that the fish might be repelled by my blackened thoughts.

"Well, take grocery stores. We simply buy our food there when we are hungry. They are convenient. But if we suddenly take them away, people starve. That convenience is also a weakness. You see?"

I was silent. I cast in again.

"That's why I teach you to fish. You know what they say 'Give a man a fish...'"

"Ugh. Dad, I have heard that a thousand times. And how exactly can a hardship be a good thing? It sounds like New-Agey bullshit."

He put down his rod then and looked me in the eye.

"First, watch the language Dylan. Second, have I ever told you about your grandpa working on a farm in Saskatchewan when he was younger?"

"Everyone knows grandpa worked on a stupid farm."

He sighed then. I was being too much a teen. Later I would remember these moments and think *"Never act in ways that will shame you later"*.

"Well, what I didn't tell you is that when he was hired, he was the low man there. None of the other workers liked him. They were mean to him and gave him all the horrible jobs: cleaning out chicken coups, pig slop, and so on. Any job that was gross or demeaning they gave to your grandpa. It was a hardship you could say. But then the great depression hit and the farm had to lay off workers. Lots of those workers who were mean to your grandpa were laid off. They had skills that could be replaced. But your grandpa was one of the only workers that knew how to do the horrible jobs other than the owner. He stayed. And when the depression was over, he was the top man on the farm. You see? Hardships are not always what they seem. Never judge something until its end can be seen."

Even in my teenaged self-centered nature, I found myself nodding along. It was rare for me, at that age, to see things from any perspective other than my own, but I could see my grandpa toiling away on that farm in my mind and see his eventual victory from knowing the low jobs.

My dad picked up the fish and started back to our camping spot.

"Come on, let's cook these."

I look back at our camping trips with new eyes as an adult. We had not camped together since I was a teen. Those times have ended, I suppose. But using my dad's advice on such things, I look back on them now and judge them to be the very best of times. I learned a lot from my dad on those trips and have fond memories even of the trips when I was moody. That one by the Sheep River was our last camping trip together. If I could time travel I would tell myself "Don't be a dick. Your so called friends will drift away but time with your dad is golden."

I wondered how to apply his bit of wisdom to my situation. Was my marriage convenient and a weakness? Was my separation a hardship and a boon?

I had taken highway 1A out through Cochrane and then north on the road to Waiparous. The bike felt different with Caryn and all our gear on the back. It was more sluggish and did not quite feel up to highway speeds. I didn't really care, though: I just wanted this last task done. The road past Waiparous into the south Ghost was likely the worst road I have ever travelled in Alberta. It was riddled with potholes the size of small whales and errant stones jutting up out of the dusty substrate. I felt appreciative of being on a bike as I could weave around the worst of it, though it slowed us down considerably.

The road ended in a steep hill that opened down into the Ghost River Valley. It was not the best of roads and I skidded the bike a few times on the way down. I could feel Caryn hold her breath as I did so, likely assuming a crash was not far off. At the bottom I veered to the right on a trail meant for walking. I didn't care. My bike could fit on the trail and I was going to drive it until I couldn't drive anymore. Unfortunately that was only a half a kilometre up. The trail came to a spot where it led across the Ghost River. It was running swiftly and the banks were very steep. I did not think my bike could make it across. I pulled it to the side and shut off the engine.

"Grab your pack."

Caryn hopped off the back.

"We're just leaving the bike here? Won't someone steal it?"

I started unstrapping our gear and dumping it on the ground for us to assemble.

"Not likely out here. There aren't many people who come out here to start with. Also, I will have the keys. For someone to steal it, they would have to hotwire it and drive it over that horrible road all the way back to civilization."

Caryn nodded as she tossed her bag over her shoulders.

We made our way west along the river bank. I was not sure where to go, but I knew I needed to be across the river. Mark had been vague about the location, other than that we needed to take this road out to the south Ghost. I was instinctively looking for a wider spot in the river. I knew that where it was wider it would also be shallower. I found one such spot with a small island in the middle. I used a stick to probe the water before each step to test its depth. I kept a tight hold of Caryn's hand as I crossed. It would be harder for her than for me. When we got to the island, she zipped on to dry land and danced about moving her feet.

"Gods, my feet are freezing!"

My feet were like popsicles as well, but I had the restraint of an adult that made it appear as though I was unaffected.

"Don't get too comfy, we still need to get the rest of the way across."

"Oh Dad, you are always so 'glass is half empty'."

I looked at the river on the other side of the island and it was deeper than I would have liked. I could not take Caryn that way. I didn't want to back track either. I walked to the top of the island and saw it was shallow if we walked up the river for a bit. I decided to chance that, hoping for a shallower crossing upstream. Caryn squeaked as we entered the water again but followed, holding my hand. About 100 meters up, the crossing became shallower so we headed for the far embankment. It was slow going and cold, but manageable. The embankment was steeper than it looked and we were panting by the time we reached the top. We sat in the sun, catching our breath, as we looked over the Ghost River Valley. It was a fairly wide flood plain dotted with small coniferous scrub trees and boulders.

After our brief rest on top of the embankment we decided to head west towards a large boulder on the flood plain. We were hiking on instinct here and the boulder seemed to be the only thing of any real significance. It was a makeshift muddy trail we were following with only a passing sign of human traffic. Mainly, the tracks in the mud were local animals: Coyote, Wolf, Cougar, Deer, Mountain Goat, etc. Again I was thankful to my dad for teaching me to know these things.

Caryn often pushed past me to see what was up ahead. I should have worried when she reached to the boulder as she stopped, seemingly mesmerized by whatever she saw in front of her.

"Dad, you should see these guys…"

I hurried to the boulder and had just seconds to take in the situation. In front of Caryn were two bear cubs wrestling. I am not sure why they did not see Caryn. Perhaps the wind was going the wrong direction to carry our scent to them. My immediate thought, thanks to my dad, was "Where is the mother?" As I cast my glance farther out, I saw her. What I had originally taken to be the shadow of one of the scrub conifers was actually the mother Grizzly. I grabbed Caryn by the back of her pack to pull her backwards slowly.

"Dad, why are you…"

And that was the moment that the mother saw us. She turned and I saw fury in her eyes. I could not blame her. This was her home and we were the trespassers here. I would never harm her cubs, but she didn't know that. She looked briefly at Caryn, but then settled in on me. I slowly picked up a large stick laying on the ground in front of me while whispering to Caryn.

"Go."

"I'm not leaving you!"

"Go! Run!"

She looked at me and heard the desperation in my plea. She turned and ran. After a grunt from the mother bear, the cubs had scurried up the scrub conifer. It was just her and me now. Generally I would have been running down the road as well, but I needed to protect Caryn. And I knew I should be non-threatening with grizzlies. I should curl up into a ball. All that changed when Caryn entered the mix. I needed to be threatening and if needed, to fight. That would give her the best chance.

The Grizzly charged. I only had my stick, but I held it up like a baseball bat that I was going to swing. There was no way I could win. This would be the end of me, but it would be a good death. Dying to protect my daughter was an honourable way to go. *A man sacrifices for those he loves.* Sometimes he sacrifices ultimately. I prepared to swing my feeble club as she reared up in front of me. I could feel her breath as she "wuffed". This was it. I hoped it would be quick. I hoped Caryn would be able to find her way out of this wilderness and back home.

But then something happened that surprised me. I saw the Grizzly's eyes as she shifted from looking at me in anger, to watching Caryn retreat down the path. I believe I saw sympathy in those eyes. Then she turned her head to look at her own young ones in the conifer. She looked back at me and I saw the anger had left her eyes. Perhaps she saw a kinship that we were both protecting our young. I lowered my stick slowly as she moved back from her reared stance into a regular one. Then, slowly, each of us backed off until we were a good 20 feet apart. At that point I turned and ran towards where Caryn was hiding and watching the scene play out.

"That was incredible. Did you see them? You stayed to save me!"

I nodded. I could not yet respond. My heart was racing with

adrenaline. A man always wonders what sort of courage he has inside. We all talk a good game about protecting our loved ones and fighting the fights that need fighting, but when push comes to shove, many men would turn and run instead of protecting as they said they would. Many would be cowards. Although I didn't believe myself a coward, this showed me definitively what sort of man I was. As scared as I had been, I stood my ground and was willing to lay my life down for my daughter. The imminent death did not seem to have scared me. In those moments I thought were my last, I was happy to know my life had been honourable and that my death would have meaning. That was the type of man I had always wanted to be. That was the type of man I was, apparently. Not many people got the chance to truly know that about themselves and I was oddly thankful for it. I felt a swell of pride as my adrenaline eased up.

We watched them as they walked behind the big boulder. We did not see them come out the other side. I was amazed at their ability to blend in and disappear even though there was hardly any cover to hide behind in this environment.

We ended up picking a camp site in one of the valleys we saw off to the north. We had come to a junction in the trail, with a small game trail moving off to the north. The valley I could see at the end of it just seemed to call to me. There was a small creek running down the valley and it was lush in mosses and a healthy looking spruce forest, which was in contrast to the barren-feeling river valley.

Caryn's mood was electric as we put up the tent. She really seemed to enjoy being in the outdoors and roughing it.

"Why haven't we done this before?"

I had to stop and consider. I really enjoyed camping myself and loved the time that I spent with my own father doing this very thing. Why didn't I take my daughter on our own camping trips? I mean, we did hikes and snowshoeing and those sorts of outdoor activities, but I hadn't ever taken Caryn into the wilds to sleep under the stars. The only reason I could think of was Merideth. She never liked camping. Perhaps it was because the local fauna didn't pander to her ego like sycophantic music fans did.

"I don't know, kiddo. We should do it more often though. I would love to teach you all there is to know about living out here."

"Setting up our own shelter and cooking our own food really makes you think about all the things we take for granted in our modern world."

"Think even deeper. If we didn't bring these nicely packaged meals with us, what would we eat? How would we trap animals? Which plants are good for food? Or medicine?"

She nodded and the fire crackled behind her. That smell of wood smoke was always a comfort to me. Caryn was chewing on a mouthful of beef jerky as she considered my words. It was true. We took everything for granted in our lives. Food was stuff we magically bought at the store. Most had no idea where it came from or where to get it if the magic store stopped bringing it. Even things like indoor plumbing, heat, and light. Most people had no idea how to provide these things if it wasn't handed to them on a platter. We were a dependant society and that made us weak. It would be best to remedy that with my own child and teach her everything I could. There was a certain strength in knowing you could survive on your own skills.

We had our camp set up in no time. I had some nervous apprehension about when the Malmaerra would make itself known. I tried to put that aside though. We cooked a few dehydrated meals and swirled some juice crystals into our water bottles so that we had a good and tasty meal. We cleaned our dishes in the creek and burned the rest of our waste. As the light faded, we lay on the mossy banks near the fire and watched the embers climb to the sky.

"I kind of like it."

"What do you mean?"

"Camping. It's like being alone, but not lonely. It's peaceful down in the soul, you know?"

I knew exactly what she meant. That is what my dad had always tried to instil in me about life in the wilds. There was strength in knowing how to be alone without being lonely. To so many people, alone meant lonely. To them, they were one and the same and that made them dependant. It made them need others because they didn't want to be lonely. I knew what loneliness was. I had experienced that many times and it was horrible. But being out here, I had often been alone and not felt lonely. I felt strong to be alone and content within my own skin and self. I think that strength of being content when being alone makes you ready to be in a healthy relationship as your reasons for entering it were not based on fear of being alone, but genuine love and enjoyment of a new connection.

"You are never truly alone out here as there are thousands of organisms in the area. You can be alone, but not lonely as that sense of connection to these things is palpable."

She sighed. I could tell it was a sigh of contemplation rather than one of exasperation. We lay on the moss nearly silent for the next hour just watching the coming night and the fire's dancing embers. It was bliss. When the first stars started to appear, we headed to the tent and eventual slumber.

"Dylan!"

The sudden sound of my name woke me. Where was I? I opened one eye. I could see light dappling through the orange walls of my tent. Right. I was camping. Somehow those first few moments after waking up can be the most confusing. Did someone call my name, though, or was that the last vestiges of some unremembered dream?

"Dylan Gunn!"

The roar of my name echoed down the canyon. It was primal and angry. That was not a dream. It was actual. I could not ignore it. The Malmaerra was here and there was no escaping my fate. A warmth of dread grew in my chest. There would be a fight and it may not be one I survived. All of a sudden I felt like a complete fool for agreeing to this whole quest business. What man in his right mind agrees to go fight a nearly unslayable monster? I looked over and Caryn had bolted up to a seated position. There was fear in her eyes that mirrored my own.

"Dad? What is that?"

"That…is why I am here. Quick! Find my duffle bag."

I dressed as quickly as I could. I did not put much effort into picking out my clothes as I had no idea what one wears to a battle royale. Caryn dug around for my duffle bag, eventually pulling it out. I only had a few items remaining within it. I left the vial of snake liquid out this time as I did not think I needed it. That left the plastic sword and the pirate hat. I could hear a subtle thumping coming from the duffle bag. Oh, right. Of course. The bizarre sandstone heart was in there too. Thump. Thump. Thump. Caryn stared at it as well. I could not believe I had forgotten that. I suppose when things in your world are so weird and don't fit any reality you understand, your mind tends to make them disappear.

"Dad, what is in the bag?"

How could I answer her? Nothing I said was going to make sense.

"Dylan Gunn! Get your cowardly ass out here or I will destroy your tent and everything in it!"

The Malmaerra screamed out his challenge. He was closer than before. His voice sounded right outside. I had to protect Caryn. The only item I thought would be useful to me was the sword. Perhaps it was more than just a plastic sword. The pirate hat seemed too useless as a tool against a monster, and the heart was something I had found. It was not a tool Zed had given to me. It must be the sword.

"Look, Caryn, I have no time to explain. The thumping you hear is a functioning human heart I found encased in sandstone. Please just hand me the sword that is in the bag."

The look on her face was one of scepticism and bewilderment, but she looked at me and must have seen how much I needed her to just listen. She nodded and reached into the bag. As she handed me the plastic sword, she stopped and grabbed my other hand.

"Be careful Dad. That thing sounds dangerous. I don't know where I will be without you."

"I will be careful."

She let the sword go.

As I emerged from the tent, I felt a sudden weight in my right hand. I looked down and saw the plastic sword giving off a shine whereas before it was a dull gray. I lifted it and it was definitely heavier and bigger. Bringing it closer to my face, I touched the blade with my left hand. It gave my finger a small cut. Blood dripped onto the mossy earth. The sword was now real. I am not sure how it became real all of a sudden, but it was a trick I appreciated. I needed the deadliness of a real blade against this enemy.

As I walked towards our campfire I finally saw it. The Malmaerra. It looked like a thing out of nightmares: its body and face looked like it was puckered with radiation burns. Where it wasn't burned, its skin was a patchwork of reptilian ridges, scales, and matted fur. Its hair was a ragged nest of red and brown dreadlocks. Jagged teeth stuck out like yellowed splinters from an angry-looking face. One of its legs looked canine and was covered in fur while the other was some sort of giant lobster claw. One of its arms was burly and human looking, but covered in hair and ending with some very sharp-looking long claws. The other arm appeared to be an octopus tentacle. I was not sure where to begin fighting this monstrosity. Zed had seriously overestimated my skills. I was starting to rue the day I let him punch me to test my strength and resolve.

"Are you going to come and fight, you coward? Or are you going to stand there like a slack-jawed sissy?"

I walked towards it. I am not sure why the word 'coward' always gets me, but it does. Perhaps because "*a man must fight his own battles*".

"How does this work? What are the rules?"

"There are no rules, little man! We go savage on each other until one of us is dead. And you shine so bright, Gunn, I am going to enjoy gutting you."

As it finished its sentence, the arm with the claws slashed towards me. I stumbled backwards to avoid it and landed on my back.

"Get the fuck back up. Gods, this is disappointing."

I got to my feet and picked up my sword again. The Malmaerra just paced.

"Are you finished? Come at me then!"

His eyes flashed red as he stood his ground. I rushed towards him swinging my sword as I did. He easily blocked it and backhanded me. I was on my back again. I could taste blood. I brought my hand to my mouth and it came away red. Something was bleeding at any rate. The Malmaerra stalked off a few paces.

"You weren't even trying there. I'm here to fight, not just gut you. Why aren't you trying? What are you fucking afraid of?"

I leaned over panting. A drop of blood dripped from my mouth to land in the dust. He was right. I mean I swung my sword at him, but I wasn't really trying to kill him. He was every bit the scary monster one could imagine in their nightmares. Why wasn't I trying my very hardest to simply destroy him? What was stopping me from going all out?

"I don't know."

"Oh, don't you? See, I think you know. I think you fear me."

"Of course I fear you, you're a monster!"

"No, not me. I mean you fear the monster inside you. Everyone has one. You fear letting the monster have the reigns for even a second. How do you think your inner monster feels to always be chained?"

His words stunned me. He was correct. I thought back to Mathew Fram and how I hadn't fought back. I was fearful of being the aggressor; of being the one society deemed a monster. *Never act in ways that will shame you later.* It was enlightening to me that I wasn't truly afraid of losing. I was afraid of winning and what winning looked like. But this was a life or death situation with no one to know if I let my inner monster out. Except I would know. And if I let it out, could I be certain it would be contained afterwards?

"It doesn't matter. I know how to coax it out. I will go over to that tent there and find your little girl. Then I will kill her, but it will be slow. Whether your monster comes to play before her first scream or after her hundredth, I guarantee it will come out to play eventually. Then we will see who you really are."

He walked quickly towards the tent. I could see shadows moving in the tent and hear Caryn humming to herself as she was busying herself in there. I really didn't care if I lost this battle, but for him to torture my child was unthinkable. Something switched within me. Something primal built up in the back of my brain. I didn't think. Or rather I did think, but it didn't matter. By the time my thoughts bubbled to the surface, my feet were already taking me towards the Malmaerra at a sprint with my sword upraised and my mouth releasing a guttural and unintelligible war cry.

As I closed on him, I saw his eyes widen in shock as I brought down my sword in a violent slash to his side. He kicked his lobster claw leg to the side and easily deflected the sword. It fell from my hand, clashing to the ground.

"You won't touch her!"

"Much better. It seems I have hit a sens…"

Before he could finish, my fist slammed up under his jaw in an upper cut. I followed this with a sledge hammer of a right cross. The Malmaerra flew backwards. I stood panting above him making a sound that was a cross between wheezing and growling.

"You can just fuck right off! You don't get to hurt her!"

He smiled then. Yet a second later it turned to a grimace. His octopus arm shot out and wrapped around my neck. He pulled me backwards and held me in place with the pincer on his one leg. I could barely breathe. I gasped for air.

"Good. But not nearly good enough. I see your monster now. You are like a wolf. You are a wolf pacing in the zoo in a cage built of honour and morals. You fear – oh, you fear so much! You fear what happens if one of the walls of your cage fails. Will you still be Dylan when the wolf takes over? Will you howl?"

My hands scrambled on either side of me for something to use as a weapon. I was furious and my vision was dimming with the loss of breath. I could feel the helplessness settling in. This would not be so bad. I could just slip away and die. Easiest thing in the world. No Caryn and no Dream, but also there would be no more pain and no more bad memories.

No! I couldn't! I needed to fight! I could not leave Caryn to be tortured by this beast! My hand grasped the handle of my sword. I brought it up violently in a slash behind my head. I heard a scream as the grip slackened on my neck and the Malmaerra scuttled backwards. As I stood, I realized I had cut off his octopus tentacle. I grabbed it from my neck and threw it at him. As he stood distracted by it, I grabbed my sword and stabbed it into his lobster claw leg.

"Ok, you ugly shit, you listen well! I am not afraid of my own power. My own power is going to end your miserable existence. Do you hear me? Well, do you FUCKING hear me?"

He looked me straight in the eye at that moment and a small smile curled on his lips. He nodded briefly before he disappeared into vapour. My sword fell to the ground and rang out as it bounced off of a rock.

I stood shaking as the adrenaline wore off. Caryn came up and touched my shoulder. I nearly turned and punched her. She saw the rage in my eyes and flinched away. I think that was all it took for that inner monster to walk silently and voluntarily back into its cage.

"I'm sorry, kid. Still recovering from the fight."

"Are you O.K?"

I nodded. It was terrifying, but I was O.K. I just needed to calm down. I had survived this fight. Mark had said the Malmaerra would attack me 7 times. That meant I had to do this whole thing 6 more times. That was crazy. Still, there was some satisfaction from monster slaying. I was pretty certain I still had octopus sucker marks across my neck though.

Caryn was holding the sandstone heart. I could see some more of the sandstone had been chipped away further exposing more of the heart underneath. She saw my gaze.

"Oh, this. Well, I figured I would try to free it from the stone. I am using the file on the nail clippers to chip away at it slowly."

The thought of this terrified me, but I could not even understand why. I felt absolute dread well up in me at the thought of her puncturing that heart.

"Just be very careful."

"Don't worry, Dad. I am always caring."

We sat around the campfire eating beef jerky, dried apricots, and trail mix. It was what I considered a regular camping lunch. We didn't need to cook or clean up; only enjoy. It was the kind of moment that would fill me with peaceful bliss and happiness if I wasn't on a monster slaying expedition.

"Isn't it nice that we are all out here camping as a family?"

The male voice surprised me. I looked over and my dad was sitting there beside Caryn with his arm around her. He was wearing his regular camping vest and his fishing hat with the lures stuck in it.

"Grandpa?"

Caryn turned to look at him. My Dad winked at me.

"Caryn! Go in the tent, right now!"

"But...but..."

"That's not your Grandpa."

Caryn scuttled backwards as Dad began to laugh maniacally. I picked a half burned log out of the fire and threw it at him. He ducked. Embers erupted from it as it landed on the ground behind him.

"Oh do relax, Dyl. You are way too uptight, though I am glad to see there is still some fight in you."

I picked up my sword as Dad examined his fishing rod.

"...And I do like a fighter."

He cast his rod and the lure flew forward through the air and caught me on the cheek. He jerked the rod quickly and the hook pierced my flesh. I screamed.

"Like I always told you Dylan, you have to set the hook."

He started reeling in and I could not help but crawl along with it until I brought my sword up to slice the line free. I raised my hand to my cheek, feeling the lure embedded there.

"Oh, you ruin my fun, son! All the same, I set a hook in you when you were young. It wasn't a hook of steel and pain though. It was a hook of honour and virtue."

I slashed my sword at him and he parried with his fishing rod.

"I filled you with so many rules for living a good and chivalrous life that I absolutely ruined you. You cannot escape it even now."

I slashed wildly again and managed to cut him on the arm.

I knew it was the Malmaerra wearing his likeness, but still, I felt horrible seeing the gash on my father's arm knowing I had caused it. I turned away in shame.

"Ah-ah-ah, son! *A man must fight his own battles!*"

Before I could turn back, he had tackled me to the ground. His fists were flying faster than I could block them. When they hit the lure in my cheek, it was like white lightning.

"*A man never shows weakness. Real men never cry.*"

He laughed as he pounded away.

"I doomed you to a life of pain and misery with all the rules, son. What do you say to that?"

I brought my knee up into his groin as hard as I could. Dad groaned and doubled over to the side.

"I tell you what I say. I can modify your rules. I can live by a better code of honour. Real men cry. Real men show weakness. I am not bound by you or your rules and, yes, I can fight my own fucking battles. So do you want some more?"

I gestured forward with my fists. Dad only smiled.

"*A real man has to live his own life.*"

'Dad' faded into mist as he spoke his wisdom. Two down; five to go.

Caryn took care of me the entire afternoon. She removed the fishing lure from my cheek with the little first aid kit she brought with her. She applied antibacterial cream to the wound and covered it with a band aid. She made me lie down on the embankment near the tent as she put a patchwork of mashed up plant on the areas of my body that were bruised from punching. She told me her book said it was a good plant for helping with bruises and skin conditions. I didn't question her. I was too tired to question. The mushy plants felt cool on my skin and took away, briefly, that feeling of pain. As I lay there, the mosquitoes descended. I didn't have the energy to swat them all away. It is a myth that mosquitoes drink blood. They don't. Mosquitoes drink nectar from flowers. They use the blood to create eggs for the next generation of mosquitoes. So really, it was only the female mosquitoes that were bloodsuckers. I thought of my own situation and wondered if the same was true in my species. I quickly rebuked myself for such thoughts though as I could not think so of Caryn or Dream or my mom. In my species, bloodsucking wasn't gendered; it was the activity of selfish assholes.

As the light started to fade, I got up and made my way to the fire where Caryn was already boiling water to rehydrate our freeze dried dinners. When the water boiled, I helped her portion it into the freeze dried packs. I squished the packs around with my hands to distribute the warm water inside evenly. The warmth of it was comforting and the smell it was giving off made me salivate.

The smell must have drifted father than I thought as soon, some largish birds started to flock to our campsite in ones and twos. They flew up to branches about twenty feet up and watched our dinner making. They murmured amongst each other as we got ready to open our dinner packages.

"D-D-D-D-D" they would whisper to each other. It was distracting, but not horribly.

We portioned the rehydrated dinners into our bowls to eat.

"Dy-Dy-Dy-Dy" the birds said to each other. It was starting to sound agitated.

Caryn looked up. She nearly dropped her bowl as she tapped me on the arm.

"Dad!"

I looked up. At first they looked just like birds. Dark feathers on the wings and bright feathers in their long tails. When I looked closer, I noticed their feet looked like music symbols. Some were Treble Clefs, some were Bass clefs, and some were sharps. That is when I noticed their heads. Where normally a bird would have a bird-like head with a beak and feathers, these birds had a small human head. It was a particular human head. It was Merideth.

Caryn ran off, overturning her bowl of dinner as she did so.

"Dylan-Dylan-Dylan!"

"You shine bright! Shine Bright! Shine Bright!"

The voice of the birds was now questioning and angry. It came from all of them at once and echoed off the hillside.

"I never loved you, Dylan!"

The voice echoed everywhere. I heard a 'swoosh'. I could not tell where it came from. I slashed my sword blindly, but it was too late. Before I could identify a location, the bird had swooped past me and brushed its wing against my arm. It felt like metal. When I squinted to look at the birds, their wings looked like they were made of bronze. I looked down at my arm and found it to be pouring blood out of a razor thin cut. The sight of it was shocking. The birds' wings were razor sharp and so swift I didn't even feel it cutting my skin.

Caryn shoved something into my hand before she dashed back into the tent. It was her slingshot. That is why she ran back to the tent before. I picked up a few rocks and put them in my pockets. I needed to be ready. I could not take many of the cuts that these birds could dole out.

"You were weak. You were a fool."

I heard two 'swooshes' this time. I turned and fired the sling-shot on instinct. One bird exploded into a poof of feathers. I spun again and shot the second bird. As these disappeared, others flew in to take their place. Clearly I was not going to shoot my way out of this one.

"What do you want?"

"I duped you, Dylan. I duped you because I knew you would make money and I could take it. So I did!"

Swoosh. Swoosh. Swoosh. Three birds.

I fired like a maniac, but still only dropped two of them. The third buzzed past my leg. I had no will power to look down to see the damage, but I could feel a droplet or two of blood trickling down my leg. This was no good. I started firing randomly at the birds. Some exploded into feathers on contact, but were immediately replaced by new birds. It was endless.

"I enjoyed cheating on you Dylan. It was easy. It was beautiful, positive, and meaningful. I never once felt any guilt or remorse about it."

Swoosh. Swoosh. Swoosh. Swoosh. Four of them. Fuck. I spun and was able to take two down as they flew towards me. Then I jumped forward and rolled on the ground. I felt the wind of one bird as it passed above me while the last one screeched in anger as it missed completely. I was up quickly and firing. One more bird down. The last one came in for another run at me. I quickly side-stepped and plucked it out of the air by its neck. Its neck feathers were sharp and it resisted my grab with all its might. The neck feathers were not honed enough to break skin, but they scratched my hand up nonetheless.

How was I going to defeat these birds? They were increasing in number with each attack and there was no way I could see to destroy them as they kept replenishing. They were uttering all the things I was afraid that Merideth had felt or thought. Some of them Merideth had told me with her own lips. That didn't mean they were true though. She could have just been saying those words to intentionally hurt me. The problem was that I would have no closure on this ever. I had no way of knowing if any of these things were true. The words cut deeper than the razor sharp feathers. But did they need to? Even if Merideth said and believed all those things, all it did was prove that she was an evil and despicable person. But that part of my life was done with. I was past being hurt by her evil words, true or not. I looked into the small Merideth face in the bird I was holding.

"Look, you might be telling the truth or you might not. But it doesn't matter because I am moving on. I can come to peace with it regardless of whether or not I will ever know the truth."

The bird in my hand turned to mist as the others flew off in a flock.

"Dyl-Dyl-Dyl-Dylan."

They cried it out quieter and quieter as they left.

I stumbled into the tent bleeding. Caryn, once again, patched me up. She used some large gauze bandages and some medical tape to cover the wounds I had taken from the deadly birds that looked like her mother. I would have to replenish the supplies she had in her medical kit if I ever got through this. The aid Caryn and her little kit had given me had been extensive.

I was too exhausted to go back out to the fire. Caryn brought the dinner in instead. It was a camping 'no-no' as our tent now smelled like food to attract any predators in the area. But given the infestation of the Malmaerra in the neighbourhood, I did not think predators would be the problem facing us. I ate each spoonful gratefully as Caryn fed me from the freeze dried meal packet. Rehydrated Satay Beef Noodles had never tasted so good.

When we were done eating, she brought out the sandstone heart. It had far less sandstone on it than I remembered. It was clear she had been working at this.

"I just used the small file and sometimes the clippers themselves. The heart wants to be free. Don't you see that? Sometimes all you have to do is give it a little help."

I smiled as she spoke, but I was just so tired from a day of battle that I soon slipped into slumber.

We had been surviving on this planet for three days. Our small fighter had been shot down by a Skellarian attack squad. We had been aboard the *ISS Vindicator* on an interstellar diplomatic mission to Stimphalia Prime when Skellarian forces ambushed us. My navigator and I were swiftly into our fighter and into the fight. She doubled as a tail gunner so we didn't need to wait for a third crewman. "Sooner to flight, sooner to fight, sooner to glory and valour." That was the thought anyway, but we were soon overwhelmed without the support of our fellow fighters from the *Vindicator*. So down we went. The ship was a wreck but we were relatively unscathed. Dream had a sprained ankle and I had small lacerations on my arm and leg. We survived on freeze dried soldiers' rations and used our pulse rifles to make short work of the reptilian Skellarians that pursued us. Our aim had to be careful as the blood of the Skellarians was a liquid magma that would instantly vaporize any flesh it landed on.

The problem was that we were running short on both rations and pulse bullets. If rescue did not come soon, I feared we would be goners. I scrambled up the hillside and had a peek over with my thermal recording device. Skellarians. Lots of them. I stealthily made my way back down. Dream was resting in the shade of a tree.

"On the ready. There's an entire squad almost on our asses."

She saluted and grabbed her gun.

"Sir!"

I took cover behind a boulder and put my rifle in the ready position. As the first wave came over the crest of the hill I fired two grenades in succession. Skellarians blew apart in shrill screams. Their magma blood instantly vaporized the surrounding foliage.

"On your right!"

I spun to my right and saw a Skellarian creeping up in his bronze armour. I fired two rounds into him and ducked as the splatter of his blood flew above me. I noticed several bearing down on Dream.

"2 O'clock!"

"What?"

"Skellarians at 2 O'clock!"

They were getting closer. I spun to get into position to shoot them myself.

"No."

It was a simple word, but the entire world froze.

"What did you do?"

"Sorry, the alien fighting space adventure has always been your thing. It can be fun sometimes, but I am not really a huge fan of it. Can we do something else?"

I did not realize this scenario was one that Dream did not enjoy. It was odd to sit in this frozen world with fierce Skellarians paralyzed in mid attack.

"Of course. No problem. Is something wrong? You sound stressed."

"I am a bit stressed. I've had to do this series of tasks in the name of meeting you in person. It's worth it, for that, but stressful."

I had no idea that Dream was going through something similar in real life. Zed had made me go through these quests as he said I shouldn't be broken when I finally met Dream. I agreed, but in my mind, Dream was perfect from the start. She didn't need fixing. I had no idea she might be on a similar path.

"Really? Me too. What does Zed have you doing?"

"Who's Zed? I am doing this for June. She's helping me. I stumbled across her in my travels."

I would have to get the entire story from her someday. It seemed there was more than just Zed working as an agent for those who were broken in this world. I wondered if Zed knew June?

Perhaps that was a silly thought.

"O.K., well what dream would make you less stressed?"

"Hmm…how about Jane Austin Afternoon Tea?"

The scene shifted. We were on a blanket in a sunny meadow. A parasol jutted out of the ground giving us shade. Where pockets of Skellarians used to be, there were now other picnicking couples on blankets with parasols of their own. In front of us was a basket stuffed with baked goodies. A teapot sat to one side as each of us sipped a cup of tea. Dream was wearing a poufy dress and her hair was done in that fancy way where it is all up. I found myself in a suit with a fluffy ruffle at my neck and a top hat. I could not possibly have been in an outfit that was less me. But I was happy to do it to de-stress Dream a little.

I pulled a biscuit out of the basket and passed it to Dream as she fanned herself.

"My lady?"

"Oh, thank you. I do declare you are the most dashing gentleman in the meadow today. Would you care for some more tea?"

"No, I shan't. The tea is disagreeing with me, but you would be remiss to not deliver me a kiss."

Dream blushed.

"My word, you are the most forward scoundrel I have met. I shall have to tell Ms. Sainsby about your actions. Mark my word, I shall…"

I found the Jane Austin speak to be tiring. I wondered if she was thinking the same as she stopped mid-sentence. Usually she enjoyed the Jane Austin Afternoon Tea dream. I wondered why she had stopped.

"You aren't enjoying this, are you?"

I could not lie to her.

"It's fine. I want it to be a dream that you can relax in, I just need to blow off some steam as well."

"That's sweet of you. How about we meet in the middle? Let's see now…"

She swept her hand around and our dream changed slightly. It was still Jane Austin Afternoon Tea, but the other couples in the meadow were now Skellarians. They were in petticoats and fancy suits with monocles and top hats, but they were still Skellarians. And I was no longer holding a tea cup. I was holding my plasma rifle again. I had to smile.

Dream winked at me.

"Oh, the Wainwrights have soiled my sister's good name. Do be a good gentleman and aid me in restoring her honour."

I did my best British accent.

"Hmmm. Quite so."

I took aim with my plasma rifle and launched a grenade at the Wainwrights on their blanket. Their magma guts exploded everywhere, as did their basket of goodies. Their parasol shot into the sky. Edgar Corrington got some of the blood on his leg and it melted off. Bad luck, that.

"I say, good shot."

"Rather."

We laughed and laughed and ate spice cake under the afternoon sun.

I got up early in the morning as my bladder was near exploding. I don't even recall drinking that much liquid yesterday, but it could not be ignored. It always seems like that on camping trips. I always have to pee at an ungodly early hour. I unzipped the tent and exited, hoping not to wake Caryn.

I had pants on but that was about it. The moss was chilly on my feet. I leaned against a tree and let loose a stream of urine that caused the moss to steam where it fell. My bladder felt vast relief. I could see the first rays of sunshine peaking over the Rockies.

Everything was wonderful and perfect until I felt the shackles on my skin. They made a clink as they secured around the wrist of the arm I was leaning with, and again when they attached to the tree.

"What are you doing?"

It was a frantic question to someone I had not yet seen as I tried quickly to put everything back in my underwear and pants. Somehow not being exposed was more important than protecting myself against a random malign stranger. Before I finished, he had shackled my legs as well. They were old time thick rusty shackles I had seen on slaves in those movies set in the late 1800's.

"I am merely restraining you. Hold out your arm so I can get that one too."

"Why would I give you my last free arm?"

"Because if you don't I will knock you out and leave you here naked."

I thought about it. Would he? Likely this was the Malmaerra in another guise. He already had one arm and two legs shackled. He could just kill me and there was not much I could do about it. Plus, if I didn't do what he said, he may end up hurting Caryn. It was better that he was focused here. I held out my arm. I heard the last manacle clink.

Then I heard the sound of cutting and felt some tugging on my clothing. There was a ripping sound and suddenly I was naked and shackled to a couple of trees.

"You said you wouldn't leave me naked if I held out my arm."

"No, I said I wouldn't knock you out *and* leave you naked. I kept my word."

My tormentor came around into my view. It was Bradley Channing. Or at least it was what I had pictured Bradley Channing looking like in my mind. He was dressed like a lawyer from the slave-trade era: a dusty suit and one of those bizarre powdered wigs.

"You see, you are always naked to me. There is nothing you can hide from me. I will comb through all of your records and bank statements and history and find every penny and give it to my client."

I railed against my chains.

"Well we will go through her statements as well. We will find the truth!"

He stepped forward and slapped me. Hard. A trickle of blood dripped down from the corner of my mouth. I screamed.

"Dad, are you O.K.?"

It was Caryn in the tent. I had to keep her there.

"Stay in the tent, Caryn!"

Bradley Channing smiled.

"No, you see Mr. Gunn, that is not how it works. In our society, you are the man. You are the big bad wolf and my client is the poor damsel in distress. We have the right to look at everything you have. Why would you get the same right?"

"But that's not true. She is the one who cheated. She is the one who lied and stole."

He punched me in the stomach. I doubled over in pain as far as my restraints would allow me.

"Oh, poor baby. This is the law, Mr. Gunn. The law doesn't give two shits about the truth. No one cares about what is true in this case. No one cares about it and no one cares about you."

He grabbed one of my fingers and bent it backwards.

"I could break this, right now. It's much like that, Mr. Gunn. No one cares. Go ahead. Cry out."

I did. I cried out. I yelled for help. All the while, Bradley Channing stood there laughing.

"This is you, Dylan. You are locked into pain because of someone else's fuck up. You might have a chance if both sides were willing to tell the truth. In fact, it is your weakness that you assume both sides *will* tell the truth. My client is not willing to do that. Since the law doesn't actually give a fuck, it will settle somewhere in the middle between her lies and your precious truth. You will pay! Oh, you will pay! I will ruin you financially. So what are you going to do?"

That was my fear really. I feared that the law was not on my side. I feared that no matter what Merideth had done to me, she would end up being legally allowed to hurt me more. There was no justice in our system of family law. She could lie and cheat and steal and get away with doing more. It was my fear because it was also the truth.

I spit at Bradley Channing. He took off his powdered wig and wiped his face with it.

"I don't give a shit about your fucking law. You get that? I care only for justice, which is sadly lacking in your law. I will always strive for true justice no matter what is said and decided. Do you understand, you arrogant prick?"

He bowed at me briefly before disappearing into mist.

I had lost count how many fights that was.

I woke to someone opening my mouth and pouring in water. I coughed it up. It was too fast. I opened my eyes. I could not believe what I was seeing. It was Dream.

"How?"

It was all I could get out.

"Shh. Don't talk now. Let me get you out of these."

She quickly undid all the shackles. When my arms were unbound, I fell to the ground. I was naked and ungraceful for the first time we met in real life. How embarrassing. She took a blanket and covered me. I was very grateful. She passed me the cup of water again.

"Zed sent me. He thought you had suffered enough here. He thought you were ready to meet me in person."

Suffered enough? I definitely had. I was grateful it was over.

"I think he was right, Dylan. I mean, look at you."

"I'm just glad you are finally here, Dream."

I reached for her hand, but she pulled away.

"Oh, that is not even your name. I'm sorry. What do I call you?"

She frowned at me.

"Well, you know Dylan, now that I see you, I think I have changed my mind about this whole thing."

"What? Why?"

"Well, seeing you in person, I realize I am just so much more than you. You are not really worth anything."

It stung. I could recall Mathew Fram and those same words. They were the words that had stuck in my psyche all these years.

"Why would you say that?"

"There just isn't anything to you. You are not worth anything. You are essentially an unlovable person. No one would love you."

I tried to look at her but couldn't. It stung my eyes to look. I tried to hold it back but was failing. *Real men don't cry.* Yes, they fucking do! I was a real man and I was crying. Deal with it. I let the tears spill down my cheeks freely. I was a sobbing mess.

"I am! I am worth loving. I am worth something!"

"No Dylan, you really aren't. Look at you. You aren't even a real man, sobbing like that. You aren't worthy of me."

Then it dawned on me. My trial here was not over. This wasn't Dream. This was just the Malmaerra in a new shape. And while it wasn't physically hurting me, the emotional pain of this was the worst yet. I was outraged that he would dare take Dream's form to torture me.

"You are NOT Dream! Dream loves me! I am worthy of her love!" Dream smirked at me. Her eyes flashed red and she disappeared.

I tumbled into the tent with just my crumbled up pants to cover my nakedness. The blanket Dream-Malmaerra had given me had disappeared when she, herself, had vanished. Caryn was waiting. From the look she gave me, I must have looked like deep fried death.

"Oh, Dad."

She tried to hug me but I brushed her away. I knew her intent, but somehow it just felt like it would be odd in my naked and bruised state.

"Let me get some clothes on first."

I dressed quickly. Just putting on a layer of clothes seemed to wash away a bit of the pain. Perhaps it was just that psychological pain of being naked and tortured. Clothes were suddenly a suit of armour after an experience like that. When I turned back to Caryn, she was holding out the Sandstone heart. I could barely call it that anymore though; it now looked like a regular heart with just a few bits of sandstone clinging to it.

"Wow, Caryn. That is amazing."

"You think? I am nervous to try getting these last pieces as they are really stuck on there and I don't want to damage it. When a heart has been encased in stone it is likely a damaged heart to start with. I want to take as much care with this as I can."

Where before I was nervous about her removing the bits of sandstone, now it seemed like the most important thing in the world. She needed to finish. I had no idea what purpose the heart would serve, but it now seemed vital that it be free of sandstone and soon.

"You need to clear those bits. It is possible I may need it. You can do it. I trust you."

She smiled.

That is when I heard the distinct sound of a tent zipper. There are lots of zipper sounds in the world, but the sound of a tent zipper is unique. As the zipper on our tent was still closed, I could only assume this was the Malmaerra concocting another torment. I winced at the thought.

"How many more times do you need to do this, Dad?"

"I don't know. I have lost count."

I reached for our own tent zipper and unzipped it. I looked across the little creek valley and it was like looking into a mirror. On the far side of the creek was a tent just like ours. Peering out of it with a tent flap half unzipped was an exact copy of myself. I was dressed the same and was in the exact same pose. I stepped out of my tent, as did my doppelganger. I turned back to Caryn. He turned back to his tent.

"Stay in the tent."

I wondered who my duplicate spoke to. Was there a Caryn copy in his tent as well? I trudged down towards the little creek sword in hand. He did as well. I wondered if he exaggerated my bodily motions or if I actually looked that puffed up and arrogant as I walked. We stood on opposite sides of the creek staring each other down.

"What, you don't think I will be able to fight something that looks like me?"

"No, no, Dylan. I not only look like you. I *am* you. You see, I can pull things from other multiverses. Even though you run bright in the multiverse threads, I was still able to find a version of you that still loves Merideth."

He stepped into the creek. I felt compelled to do the same.

"You still love her? How could you still love her after all she's done?"

"Because a part of you still does. I am just the version of you that stayed with her. I took the abuse and lived in it and stayed married to her."

I stood shell-shocked by what he was saying. How could there be a version of me anywhere that would live with being treated like that? I could not even believe there was a piece of me, even deep inside, that still held love for Merideth. But I feared it. I feared he was right.

"And if I win, good buddy, that is just what I will do. I will take our daughter home and plead with Merideth to come back. And she will. And this version of you, which you will become, will live in the maelstrom of her abuse and adultery for the rest of your days. To death do you part, right?"

Fuck that. Fine. He could be the one that still held love for Merideth. That meant that there was none of that left inside me. I could get behind that. It fueled the rage within me. I must destroy the 'me' that still loved her. It was all too easy.

I swung my sword in an arc towards his side. He parried and sliced at me with his own. We went back and forth trying to cut each other for a good solid minute. It felt like an hour. It made my shoulder sore and tired and I knew his must be as well.

"Ah, I can see you get it, then. One of us must die. Either I win and reconcile with Merideth, or you win and you can chase your pathetic Dream."

The creek rushed by our ankles as we fought. It was cold and numbing, but it kept me awake and on my feet. My shoulder was starting to hurt horribly from the extensive sword work. I could see the same ache in him. It was making him slow in his strikes just as it was making me slow. Perhaps I could use that to my advantage. I faked a cramp in my sword arm and dropped it down to my side. The Malmaerra smiled and pulled his arm up to swing it, but he was so very slow. I slipped forward with my sword arm stabbing. He saw my tactic at the last second and moved his arm in front of him. It probably saved his life. My sword stabbed right through his forearm and stuck there. He stumbled back screaming. I followed him as he fell back, jumping on top of him and punching him in the face.

"That was stupid. Did you think I would lose if there was a chance of Merideth entering my life again? I would never let that happen."

He smiled at me with a vicious grin and followed it with a laugh. I was starting to think I had made a mistake, but I could not figure out what. He wrapped one leg around me and spun. Suddenly, he was on top of me and his sword was at my throat.

"No, my friend, stupid would be giving me your weapon, even if it was to stick it into my arm."

He was right. I had stabbed him, but now he had both swords. I tried to squirm, but all I succeeded in doing was nicking my neck in the process.

"Please don't…I need to be the one that lives."

He sat up on my chest, laughing. I felt helpless. He put the sword point down over my heart.

"You know what I am going to enjoy even more than knowing that I am ruining your life?"

I sat motionless. There was nothing I could do to win. I had lost. Everything I had hoped for in life was ruined. I would never know Dream. I would never see Caryn grow up. I would never even walk out of this valley. This was the end of me and it was not a good one.

"I can see you are not in the mood for talking so I will just tell you. I will enjoy that it will ruin your daughter as well. It will teach her that lying and cheating and abusing have no consequence. It will teach her that those who do that are the strong ones and should be emulated. She will likely lie and cheat and abuse a husband of her own one day. You were too weak to defeat the monster, so she will become one just like her mom."

With the last word, he pushed the sword down slowly into my chest. The pain was excruciating at first and I screamed. But then a numbness washed over me. I could see him digging with the sword, but it no longer hurt as badly. I could see when he reached in and pulled out my beating heart, but I felt nothing but detached curiosity. He stood up, dropped his sword, and walked to his campfire, laughing. I could hear the sizzle as he set my heart in his frying pan.

I could no longer feel my arms and legs. But I was still here, bleeding on the bank of the river. I still had thoughts. Should I not be dead? Why was I still alive? I had little energy left, but I felt disturbed that I was still alive. Though with all the weird stuff in my life lately, why would my lingering life essence strike me as bizarre? I mean, I had played chess with a Sphinx. I stole the undergarments of a nymph who was thousands of years old. I battled a shape shifting monster in many guises. I found a functioning heart covered in sandstone, for goodness' sake!

Wait. The sandstone heart.

That was its purpose. I tried to call out but I had no voice. How could I call to Caryn? All I could do was think. Perhaps if I thought really hard, she could hear me. It was my only shot.

*CARYN! BRING IT! BRING THE HEART!*

It felt foolish to do, but what choice did I have? I thought it was fruitless, but moments later Caryn was bounding towards me with a worried look on her face. She stood over my bloody torso with tears in her eyes. She carried the sandstone heart. It was perfect. There was not a speck of sandstone on it. The Malmaerra continued frying up my heart by his campfire. He had no aware-ness of Caryn.

*PUT IT IN!*

Such a simple statement. She knelt and took extreme care as she placed the heart in the space where my old one had been. I could feel it beat. Blood squirted out of my chest. New heart or not, I still had a hole leaking in my chest.

"I love you, Dad."

Tears streamed down her cheeks as she leaned down to hug me. Her care for me was so pure. I felt nothing but light in its presence. I could feel tingling in my arms and legs again. They twitched. Caryn sat up straight. I looked at my chest. My shirt was stained with blood, but the chest wound was healed. There was not even a puncture wound where the sword had gone in. Caryn was blood stained as well, but there was a smile on her face. I have no idea how her love had healed me, but it had. I moved my arm to test it. It was sluggish but worked. I sat up. The Malmaerra had not moved. Why would he? He would still think I was just a corpse on the creek side.

I stood up quietly, picking up the sword he had dropped. Caryn grabbed my arm. When I turned my head to look at her, she was shaking her head 'no'. I had to whisper.

"I have to. It's the only way."

I walked slowly over to the Malmaerra. I could see my old heart in the pan. He had cut it into pieces. He flipped the pieces over with a stick and as they turned, they sizzled fresh. He hummed while he worked. I must not have been as quiet as I thought as when I reached him he turned quickly, surprised.

"Wha…"

I almost felt sorry for him in that instant. The shock and fear on his face saddened me. I had seen that look in my own mirror many times since the split with Merideth. But then again, this guy; this other me, stuck a sword in my chest and dug out my still beating heart.

"I am the one that lives!"

I yelled it as I swung my sword. His head came off in one swift motion. It was bizarre to look into the lifeless eyes of a decapitated head that bore my likeness. However, the lifelessness in his eyes was contrasted with the feeling of vitality and purpose in my own. I was alive. The head of the Malmaerra was at my feet. There would be no more battles. There would be no more tests. I had won. I had tested my mettle against the beast and come out of it standing tall.

I stood mesmerized by the moment on the banks of that creek while Caryn clung to me in a hug.

I wiped away a clean spot on my mirror. It felt good to shower after coming home. Caryn and I had packed up and left the very hour I slew the Malmaerra. I had taken his head in the duffel bag as proof. Showering was always wonderful after a camping trip as you felt like you were shedding layers of grime to look and smell civilized again. This time was even more so. I felt like I was shedding the dark parts of my life as well.

And I was sore. It felt as though every patch of skin and muscle on my body ached. It was a good kind of ache though. It was the sort that reminded you of victory. Any challenge that doesn't leave you sore in one way or another could not rightly be seen as a challenge. As sore as I was, to me it was a reflection of how big of a challenge I had faced and won. My aches and pains felt like victory.

I looked at myself with a keen eye. Yes, there were some wrinkles and yes, there were some grey hairs. So what? That was aging. That was life. Why look at those things and only see them? Why not look at those as only the frame for the picture instead of the picture itself? The picture of my true self within that was much better. I was strong. I was worthy. I was ready. Zed was right to set me on this path. It had made me whole.

I had the feeling like reading a good book and a chapter ends. You turn the page and there is a certain feeling of closure of what was, and excited anticipation of what would come in the next chapter. That was how my life felt, in that moment, looking in the mirror.

# EVERY NEW DISCOVERY

"Hi."

He didn't hear me. Zed was bent over his workbench. He had thick goggles on and his oxy-acetylene torch was lit and burning in his left hand. A section of angled steel was gripped within the vice on the bench. I walked closer.

"Zed?"

He turned to me, startled.

"Damn it Dylan, you shocked me there!"

He turned off the flow to both the oxygen and acetylene torch. There was an audible 'pop' as he did. He laid the torch back down on the bench and lifted his goggles up. His skin was whiter where the goggles had been than outside of where they were. This told me he had been out here working on this for a while.

"I've got something for you here."

I passed him the bag with the head in it.

After a brief look inside, he squeezed the opening of the bag shut again and looked away.

"Aw shit, Carl's head. Why?"

"Carl?"

"Yes, the Malmaerra. He had a name. Fuck, I am going to have to get this back to him. Why did you cut off his head?"

This was outrageous. I almost died fighting 'Carl'. 'Carl'

would have gutted me like a freshly caught trout. Why should I be reprimanded for doing the same to him?

"I was told it was likely a fight to the death."

"Well, if you got this far, you had won. You could have just left."

"How was I supposed to know that? I will apologize for killing him if that helps."

Zed bent over in a hearty belly laugh.

"Boy, you didn't kill him, you just inconvenienced him. You were literally a pain in his neck. Once I get his head back to him, he will be right as rain."

"Wait, you are going to give him back his head and that monster can just go on his merry way?"

Zed set the bag with the head in it on his work bench and wiped his brow with his sleeve.

"Dylan, I thought you were beyond just looking at things from the fairy tale's point of view. You see monsters as merely things of terror, but Carl serves an important function in the world. Often people wander around in this life wondering who they are inside; if they are courageous or cowardly. Carl sets up in the guise of a Grizzly or Cougar most often and tests people. Through him they get to know their courage and are better for it."

I had wondered about the numbers of battles I was supposed to do, but this now made sense. Mark told me it would battle me seven times but I had only counted six. There was the monster, my father, the birds that looked like Merideth, Bradley Channing, Dream, and the mirror of myself. That was only six. I had assumed I had bested him before we could get to the seventh, but it seemed to me now that the Grizzly and her cubs from were also the Malmaerra. I had felt tested there and felt more courageous for it.

"So you are saying they can work positively by using negative emotions like fear or anger? Do I have that right?"

"Yes, monsters work from fear to show the positive within people. It's a bit of contrast. Light from shadows, that sort of thing.

Most people try to ignore their fears, but if you don't understand your own fears, you are ignoring half of who you are."

This made sense to me. When I thought of each battle with the Malmaerra it did seem to center around a fear of mine, whether it be inadequacy or helplessness or just fear of emotional pain. And through each trial, I felt I knew more about myself, and I grew stronger. People always categorize emotions into positive and negative. Love is good and hate is bad. Compassion is good and fear is bad. This tilted those thoughts on their axis. I mean, perhaps there are no bad emotions. Perhaps emotions are simply emotions, neither bad nor good. If we shed the labels of 'good' or 'bad', it becomes clear that fear can be used to aid in discovery and enlightenment. There simply are no bad emotions.

"I have a question Zed. The Malmaerra, Carl, he mentioned a few times that I shone bright. What does that mean?"

"Oh, you know about the multiverse, right?"

I nodded like it was old knowledge to me and not something I just learned about in the last week or two.

"Well, it's like this. It branches every time someone makes a decision. Think about it like this: let's say a person is a light bulb of a certain wattage. If you divide that wattage up among lots of multiverse threads, the wattage each thread has is lower, or dimmer. But if a person branches less, then their wattage will be higher than the average person. Make sense?"

It actually reminded me of what Mark had said about dying in one multiverse thread and feeling 'more alive' in the other. I supposed that when one branch was snuffed out by death, the rest shone brighter.

"But what makes someone branch less often?"

"Oh, that's easy. If they have a strong code they live by, at some junctures there isn't any decision to make as their code leaves them only one choice. Regular folk will branch at that point, but those with strong codes will not. Have you never met anyone that seemed 'brighter' to you?"

It was a strange question. I had certainly met people like that. I recall seeing a person on the bus one day who seemed to just shine bright, though metaphorically. I remembered a former coworker who did as well, but he was an arrogant, greedy, evil, asshole.

"Yes, I suppose, though I am not sure they lived by a code of honour. The one I am thinking of did some pretty vile things."

"Oh, but I didn't say anything about honour or goodness. I just said they had to live by a strict code. That code could be one of extreme greed and selfishness."

That made sense. It is why I always had a problem with the word integrity. People said so-and-so had 'integrity' as if it implied honour and goodness. Integrity only meant that you were integrated with your own values and lived those values day to day. In reality those values could be good or evil.

"I see I have you got you thinking. That is good, but let me really sizzle your noggin with something. They say that with the multiverse theory, there are actually no stories or songs or anything else. They say that each story or song someone writes is actually a whisper from another thread in the multiverse. So there are no stories; there is only truth."

That was quite a statement to make. The implications of it were staggering: it meant there were multiverse worlds where your favorite superhero lived, or where vampires roamed the earth, or virtually anything you could remember reading or seeing in the theatre. It made every fiction a probable documentary. It made me wonder if the life I was living would simply be a story to someone else. That others might read or hear my story seemed both preposterous and arrogant on my part.

"Whoa."

Zed grinned and clapped me on the back with his welding glove-covered hand.

"I know. But Dylan, I am surprised that you have not asked the one question you came to ask. You ask me all these things, but not the one thing that is driving you. I put you through all these trials and troubles for this one question, and when the time comes to ask it, you don't."

I felt stupid. Of course. Everything led up to this point because I wanted an answer to one question. I wanted to be ready for the answer to that one question. I suppose I just had the confidence now that Zed would tell me. I no longer had the anxiety that I would never know. Still, now was the time for me to ask.

"Where can I find Dream?"

"Ah, that's more like it, my boy! And you are ready for the answer. You are whole and complete, if a little bruised and battered. I am proud that you made it through to this moment."

He left me hanging for an uncomfortable moment as he looked out onto the grasslands by his house.

"Zed?"

"Oh, right. She will be at the Glacier Skywalk at noon this Saturday. That's up Jasper way. Can you make it there?"

I felt free. I felt expansive and light like I had just been given the keys to the universe. I could not speak. It was just not in me to make a noise; I was so filled with joy.

"Alright now, don't have a coronary on me. Just nod if you can make it."

I nodded.

When I got home, Caryn had made dinner. It was simple: a couple of hot dogs and some chips, but it was thoughtful and caring of her. She sat on the couch watching TV. I scooped up my plate, got myself a drink and sat down next to her.

"Thanks for this. Where's Mark?"

"No problem. I was hungry so I made myself something and just made extra for you. Mark? I don't know. All his stuff was gone when I got here, but he did leave this note."

She handed me a sheet of paper from the coffee table.

Dylan,

Thanks again for your hospitality. I had to run to another gig, but I know you will do fine here without me. Just a heads up that Mr. Bradley Channing has figured out my ruse. Apparently he looked up more on Purlieu Collaboration and couldn't find any reference on it. I do not think he will make a big deal about it as doing so requires him to admit he was full of shit as well. But you will need new legal representation (I have attached some suggestions to this note).

I think you will end up O.K. on this one. You split the value of your house with your ex when you left. She wants alimony, but she also needs to pay you back for at least a good chunk of her music debt, etc. Also, there have been some successful cases like this in the States where 'fame' is valued as an asset in a marital split. Since you helped develop her fame, that could also factor in. Once she is legally shown that she needs to pay that back as well, she may decide just to drop everything.

And one final note: don't look for justice in the family law system. That system is fucked. Get your divorce final, forget about the whole thing, and move on. I know you will do well. Good luck with Dream.

Your buddy,

Mark

I appreciated his note. I found that I was not as worried about the legal proceedings as I used to be. I knew the system was fucked and had a severe gender imbalance which mainly villainized penises. Also, it seemed very odd to me that he did not mention that Merideth may owe me some child support as I took care of Caryn 100% of the time. That should help offset any alimony she wanted to claim. However, I knew I had some ammo just as he said and truly I just wanted it done. It seemed more trivial than it did even a few weeks prior. What was paramount in my mind, instead, was finally meeting Dream.

"Hey, you want to take the bike up Jasper way this weekend? Maybe we can see the Glacier and go on that new Skywalk thing?"

"Umm. Sure. Wait, is this another 'task' you need to accomplish? Because the last one was a bit much. Don't get me wrong, I like camping with you, I could just deal with fewer monsters."

"No, no more tasks. I am done with that. This is to meet the woman I told you about; the one from my dreams."

"Ok….hmmm…"

Suddenly she had her laptop up and was typing furiously. I loved how the transition was so swift for her. One second she was worried about the stressful tasks I would possibly have to embark on and the next she had general excitement about what we were doing. Well, it was the passive sort of excitement that teenagers showed. The fact that she was searching up images of the glacier and the Skywalk told me she was excited enough.

Soon she was overwhelming me with a deluge of pictures on her laptop.

"Is this the place?"

"Yup. Though I have not been to the Skywalk, that looks right."

Caryn nodded to herself.

"In that case, I'm in."

The entire week I felt like a caged animal. I had come so far and been through so much to get to a spot where finally meeting Dream would be a reality that it was torture to have to wait for days and days for it to happen. It felt like having a birthday where your presents were still in the mail.

At work I barely got anything done at all. I mainly just looked at my computer and used my Web browser to look up passing flights of fancy. Mostly I looked at pictures of the glacier Skywalk and imagined myself and Dream upon it. Part of my lack of work that week was due to my lack of concentration as I was just filled with anticipation to meet Dream. The other half was simply that the work didn't interest me as it once had. After one had battled a mythical monster and lived to tell the tale, pushing paper just wasn't as glamorous as it used to be. I may have to do something about that eventually. I would have to either settle into my non-'monster slaying' life again, or find a more alluring job.

At home I was not much better. While I did not have the pressure of looking like I was productive, still I was lazy about my regular tasks. Making meals, cleaning up, doing laundry, and taking out the garbage were things I had trouble pushing myself to do. There, I was my own boss, and perhaps that was worse. With Caryn, I had become snippy, and I was angry with myself for doing so. The little things that never used to bother me were suddenly big issues in my mind. When she forgot to clean up her dishes or replace a toilet paper roll, suddenly I was on edge. I knew I should not be, but such was my mood during the week.

I just really needed the week to be done and for my journey to be complete. I could sense the closing of a chapter in my life and a new one beckoning and I wanted to read ahead, so to speak. A wiser course of action would have been to enjoy these last few moments in the life before that chapter changed, but wisdom was not something I always strive for. In fact, I personally believe it is completely wise to *not be wise* on occasion. The statement was a paradox, but that didn't keep it from also being true. How does one learn without being foolish?

The only peace I had the entire week was when my mind wandered into daydreaming. I often thought about the cabin on Kootenay Lake. It was the source of so many fond childhood memories and yet I had not been back there as an adult. Why not? Why did I not want to share that place with Merideth when we were married? Why did I not share it with Caryn? Those were different questions in my mind. With Merideth, it made sense. Perhaps there was a place deep down that saw what she was and held back trust from her as a result. That wooden cabin on the rocky shore was a representation of peace and happiness that I think I could only share with someone I trusted completely. It was a sacred relic that was attached to my heart and I should only share it with those of purity and love. Perhaps that place was my true Sandstone Heart. With Caryn, I think we hadn't been, just the two of us, because I just hadn't had it together enough to arrange it since my marriage fell apart. I needed to arrange the rental, buy enough food, and perhaps rent a boat for a few weeks. It was just too daunting for me before. Only now did I feel whole enough to contemplate it. Guaranteed, I would change this deficiency. I would show my daughter the place that burns like summer gold in my heart.

The person I really longed to share it with was Dream. Sometimes in my memory I recall us playing in the lake or building sandcastles topped with shining galena stones. I know these memories are just from our shared dreams, but they bleed into my memories of the place as well. I have no idea if that place was something she dreamed as well or if it looked much different in the dreams she was having. But I can picture us swimming in the lake as adults and breaking into laugh-filled water fights. I can picture us lounging in the double hammock strung between the two tall Douglas firs out front of the cabin. I can picture us making dinner together in the tiny kitchen with its propane powered stove and 50 year-old fridge. I can picture us sitting quietly on the deck sipping wine and holding hands as the last rays of sunlight dance on the lake's evening ripples like the scales of a fire dragon. They would be days where we eked every measure of goodness out of the golden time we had. They were daydreams that burned bright and made my heart fill with effervescent luminance. I would show her that place someday. I was sure of it.

I think it was possible that the contrast of these bright daydreams made my days that week seem gray and lifeless. I am not sure how I could have felt so very positive and so very gray at the same time, but I did. Humans are complex creatures I suppose.

I had originally planned to take the bike, but after analyzing the situation I decided on my car instead. I don't think I had even driven the car since the night at the Cheshire Kitten. I threw my duffel bag in the back seat as well as a bag filled with drinks and snacks for Caryn and I on our road trip. First it looked to be a bit chilly on the forecast for Saturday and as it was a longer trip, I didn't want Caryn to get cold riding there. Second, the only route to the Glacier Skywalk was on the Trans-Canada and I wasn't sure my bike was up to highway speeds. Once I turned onto Highway 93 heading to the Glacier, I had a third reason for taking the car on this trip: the road wasn't filled with potholes per se, but it was rough. So much so that driving a motorcycle on it would have been akin to taking a jackhammer for a pleasure cruise.

We pulled into the parking lot of the Columbia Icefield Discovery Centre about an hour and a half later. Getting out of the car, the breeze off the glacier made me shiver slightly. It was amazing it could have that effect, as it was all the way across the valley, but it did.

"Wow, that is one huge chunk of ice!"

It was hard not to feel infected by Caryn's enthusiasm for the glacier, but I had been here several times before. I was more impressed by the large array of tour busses. I had to admit that the sight of the glacier was a bit awe-inspiring too. Just thinking that it had been here thousands and thousands of years put things into a bit of perspective.

I was unsure of where to go to get to the Skywalk, but I knew that you had to start at the Discovery Centre. I headed to the ticket office as Caryn checked out the Centre. I soon had two tickets in hand for the bus that would take us to the Skywalk.

"On your left you will see…"

The guide on the bus was attentively trying to point out details for us to notice on our drive, but I just could not rouse myself to listen. Caryn was rapt to the whole thing, but she had always been a sponge when it came to knowledge. I had a growing nervousness and anticipation in me. My chest felt warm and tight. This was it. I was on the bus that would take me to Dream. My lifelong love would be in front of me in the flesh. What does one say to someone in that first meeting? Everything I could come up with in my mind ended up sounding pretty cornball. It was hard as she had been a part of my life always, so I could not use small talk. We were beyond that. But I couldn't use something more familiar since we had never met in real life; it just felt strange. I was deathly afraid that what would end up escaping my mouth would be unintelligible utterings and noises like I used to spout as a nervous teen asking a girl out for the first time. Slightly less embarrassing, yet still stupid, would be if I said something like "Aren't glaciers cool?" to fill an awkward silence. I was nervous. That was all.

As the bus rounded a corner, I could see a bit of the structure of the Skywalk. It seemed built into the mountain. Somewhere up there was Dream. I felt like asking the bus to stop so I could run the rest of the way. At least then my exertion would match the feeling of nerves I had in my chest. And perhaps I could get to her just moments sooner.

"Dad, just relax."

I nodded. She was right. The bus soon pulled to a stop and we filed out. Everyone was heading up the pathway towards the Skywalk. It was like being caught in a current. I was holding Caryn's hand and even that felt strained by the rush of people. Suddenly I was caught in a panic. Here I was going to meet the love of my life. This was the woman I would likely spend the rest of my life with. My single life, such as it was, could well be over. What happened if I met with her and she decided she didn't like me in person? What if I didn't like her? If we didn't end up together, would our dreaming end? I didn't want it to end. Perhaps I should not meet her in person. Perhaps it would be best to leave our relationship as it was. I had to get out of this throng of people. It was just too much. I pulled Caryn out of the stream of tourists to sit at the side, panting.

"What's wrong?"

There was always genuine compassion in her voice. I was proud of that. She truly did care about me and what was going on with me. I realized this was rare for a teenager.

"Nothing, just nerves I guess."

"Well, try not to worry. This is what you were working towards, right? Just do it."

She was right. I thought about Daphne's 'Many Moments' theory. I actually owed this meeting to all the Dylans from the previous moments. They had worked hard, battled monsters and done epic things for me to get to this moment. I owed it to them to go forward. And I owed it to myself. Perhaps it would not be perfect, but there was a chance at true love and happiness here. I needed to take that chance.

I took a deep breath.

"You're right. I'm ready."

I turned to the path and immediately turned back. I hugged Caryn and then grabbed her by the shoulders.

"There is just one thing."

"Sure, anything Dad."

"I need to go by myself. I know you wanted to see the Skywalk, and you still can, but can you wait here until I have met her? Then we can go see it together. Sound good?"

She nodded. I headed up the path.

Most of the walkway was interpretive signs for educational purposes. I ignored them and the groups of people crowded around them and beelined for the Skywalk itself. When I got to the entrance, my heart sank. There was a velvet rope blocking my access with a sign that said 'Closed for Private Function'. Fucking wonderful. Here I am to meet the love of my life and someone was having a wedding or something where I needed to go. But when I listened, I did not hear anyone past the velvet rope. I could just step over it and go anyway, right? This was one of those little societal conventions that Zed would advise I ignore. I tended to agree, but I was second guessing myself. Perhaps I was supposed to not go over the rope and Dream would walk by out here. What if I went over the rope and she walked by and I missed her? My chance would be shot. I stood there perplexed as to what to do when a buzzing noise broke my concentration. A bumble bee flew by me and into the Skywalk. *Follow the bees.* It could not be clearer.

I stepped over the velvet rope and onto the Skywalk. The sensation was immediate and disorienting. The floor was transparent, as were the walls. Everything was. I mean, you could see it was a floor and feel that it was a floor, and you logically knew that you were not going to plummet to your splattery doom, but still there was that instinctual part of your brain that said that this was dangerous and that you shouldn't be doing it. It took a certain amount of willpower to overcome that feeling. Willpower, or a distinct lack of caring for your personal wellbeing. I didn't want to analyze it too much. I continued walking. I found my gait was slower and more methodical due to the transparent floor, but I kept a steady pace.

As I rounded to the middle of the Skywalk, I stopped in my tracks. There sitting on the floor of the giant glass arc with their backs to the outer glass wall was a line of people. They were all looking at me and they were people I knew or had met on my quest. At the far end, I could see Carl, the Malmaerra, but also there was Daphne and Hershel and Mark Curry and Zed and Venus. But what confused me the most was that closest to me was Caryn. I had left her back down at the start of the path and asked her to stay there. I am not even sure how she could have zipped around me to beat me here.

"What are you doing here?"

"I have to tell you something Dad. But you need to promise not to be mad at me, O.K.?"

She had moisture in her eyes and a sad look on her face. I had no idea what could be affecting her this way.

"What is it, sweetie? What are you worried about? Of course I won't be mad at you."

"Dad, I don't exist."

What was she talking about? She was here in front of me. I could see her, smell her, and give her a hug.

"This is nonsense! Of course you are real. You're right here!"

She shook her head back and forth.

"No, not 'real' the way you think. I was here and I was present for you, but I don't exist. When your marriage ended, you desperately needed to believe there was something caring about the relationship you had. You so very much needed to feel that you were cared for that your mind invented me. I am a manifestation of that. Even my name, Caryn, shows you that. 'Caring?' Get it?"

"No! It isn't true! That's crazy!"

"It's not crazy; it's how your mind processed a crazy time you were going through. The situation was crazy, not you. Ask yourself: can you remember my birth? Can you remember my first word? Or my first steps? Can you recall any friends I had or any parent-teacher interviews? Can you remember anything about me before Merideth left?"

The world felt twisty and I felt like I was going to fall. The clear floor did not help that sensation. I felt myself rocking over and slammed a foot forward to stop myself. How could this be true? She was right though. I could not remember any of those things. Could I have made her up? Yes, I think I did. Tears started to well up in my eyes. *Men Don't Cry.* Fuck that. *Real men cry.*

"But I need you Caryn. I love you."

"I know Dad. I love you too. But you cannot move forward to meet Dream if I am still here. You know that."

Tears were streaming down my face. She was right though. I knew Dream loved me, but it would be tough to accept a potential love interest when they consistently talked to an imaginary daughter.

"How can I lose you?"

"You won't. I came from your mind to start with. You can never lose me since I was never here. At least not like this. I am always within you."

I hugged her tight as I felt my mind accept the idea. It felt wrong to do so, but it also felt true.

"I love you, kid. I'll miss you."

"I love you too, Dad. Always and always."

And just like that the tightness of the hug dissipated. She was gone.

"NO!!"

I fell to my knees and banged my fist on the floor like a child. Tears flowed freely and I let out an uncontrollable wail. In looking for love I had lost the most important thing in my life.

"Dylan."

Zed stepped towards me. He held out his hand. I just looked at him. He knew. He knew the whole time.

"Dylan, take my hand, boy."

His words were shakier and filled with more emotion than usual. I slowly reached out my hand and he gripped it and pulled me up. He embraced me in a hug and then let go.

"You have to let her go."

"How was she here? How could she not be real?"

He sighed.

"You have a real problem there, man; you and pretty much every other human. You tend to see 'real' like a light switch. It's either on or off. It's either real or not. You have to stop doing that. Reality is more of a continuum. Caryn was real, she just didn't exist. There are threads in the multiverse where you and Merideth had a daughter and that girl is much like Caryn. You pulled from that unknowingly to create her. She was here. She interacted with you. You have memories of her. Don't let her lack of existence tarnish that."

He was right of course. It seemed strange to mourn something that was my creation, something that was part of me and likely continued to be part of me. But I did. She was gone. Perhaps it was as he said, she was real. She just didn't exist. That was hard to get my mind around. From what I was taught in school, those things should not be at odds. It made me think of the monster and Hershel the Sphinx and all the other strange things I had experienced. What was real? What existed?

"Are you real, Zed? Do you exist?"

He laughed a good belly laugh.

"Yes to both, Dylan. In ways I am more real than most you meet. I exist on all multiverse threads simultaneously."

I didn't even ponder what that meant or even what it implied about who or what Zed was. He shook my hand and stood back.

"I'm proud of you, Dylan."

Mark Curry stepped forward. He raised his hands and started to motion with them swiftly as he spoke.

"Hey buddy. Now you see why I never talked about child support, eh? I know it's fucked up. I suggest not overthinking it. Let it be what it was and let yourself just move on from this moment."

"That makes sense."

"No worries. I will be over to play 'Hell Hath' and drink all your cola sometime soon. So keep a supply of snacks handy, will ya?"

I smiled. I knew he wasn't just saying that either. I was pretty sure I could wake up any random morning to find him on my couch with a cola in hand.

"Hey Mark, what was the pirate hat for? I still have that in the duffel bag in my car, but I never needed to use it."

The whole line of them burst into laughter. When they recovered from that, he spoke again. He winked and put his hand up in the air motioning like he was cocking a gun.

"You will, slugger. You will."

Venus walked forward and embraced me in a warm hug. Then she pulled back and wiped my tears away.

"That's better. You can't go meeting your love looking all puffy and sad, can you?"

I looked around. I was told to meet her here, but I did not see her. Where was she, was this all a ruse of some sort? Some sort of test?

"I don't see her here...when do I get to...?"

She put her finger to her lips.

"Shh. Shh. This part is not about her. I guarantee she is near and you will see her soon. Don't rush to that moment though. Enjoy each moment. Enjoy the view here. I am so happy for you Dylan. You just being here today represents a victory for love itself. Darkness could have dragged you down. Hopelessness could have cut its teeth upon you. But you didn't let that happen. You cut away what was not you at the core and now you are on your brightest path."

I nodded. She smiled at me and continued. When she batted her eyes I could nearly forget about the rest of the world around me and be lulled by her honey voice.

"People often think love is all lightness and fluffy and easy. It can be. They forget that love can be difficult. Love is a mountain. Only sitting on the peak is easy and light. Getting there can be a warrior's path of turmoil. And here you are."

I had to trust in her words. I had to trust that I would meet Dream soon. What other choice did I have? She motioned for me to walk on.

I stood in front of Hershel next. He was in his human guise instead of looking like a Sphinx. As always, his wry grin let me know there was more going on in his mind than he let on. I shook his hand as he outstretched it. He didn't let go. Instead he gripped harder and stared at me.

"I am the beginning of the end, the end of every race. I am the start of eternity and the end of time and space."

Great. Another riddle. Would he kill me this time if I could not answer? That would be a shocking let down to my journey. I beat all manner of monsters and challenges to be defeated by a riddle. The ones with beginning and end were often cheating sorts of riddles that had to do with the actual words, rather than with what the words themselves represented. Let me think. Oh! It was easy!

"Ah, the letter 'E'"

He let my arm go.

"Great job, Mr. Gunn, though it was a simplistic riddle. It's stupid and cute but it reminds me of where you are."

"And where is that?"

"You are at a moment of change. You humans have these words 'beginning' and 'end'. What you fail to realize is that they are the same thing. There are no true beginnings and there are no true ends. There are only 'Markers of Change' which is what a beginning or end truly is. That is where you are. You feel it deep down, like when you are reading a chapter in a book. You are nearly at the chapter's end and nearly at the next chapter's beginning. You are at a marker of change."

I liked that. He was right. I could not think of any ending that was not followed by a beginning. Similarly I could not think of any beginning that didn't come after an ending. Why did we have those words then? Why not some word that just meant 'change marker'? Perhaps we needed a new word like 'Chamark' or something? It would be nice. There could be a whole industry of greeting cards made for the sole purpose of sympathy for people going through 'Chamark'.

"Cute riddle or not, it made me think."

"Well I have another one for you. What happens with every new discovery?"

I thought about this one for a moment or two but came up with nothing.

"I have no idea."

"Think of the phrase: Every New Discovery. The letters spell 'END'. I like this one as it makes you think similarly. With every new discovery in life, what you knew previously is at an end and you are at a new beginning going forward. Every new discovery is an end -or at least a change marker, right? Is that not where you are?"

"It is. There have been too many discoveries. I find out my daughter doesn't exist. It makes me wonder about other things. Are you real, Hershel?"

"Ah, Dylan, just because I don't fit the current fairy tale, it doesn't mean I am not real."

I seemed to recall a drug dealer impaled with the Sphinx tail. I bet he would argue that Hershel was real.

"You have a keen mind, Dylan. Come by and have a game with me again sometime."

"As long as you promise not to kill me if I lose!"

A great white smile split his face.

"Only if you lose badly."

I stepped to the right in front of Daphne. Before she could speak, Mark Curry spoke up.

"Hold up."

He reached in his shirt pocket and grabbed the underwear that he kept there - Daphne's underwear. He threw it over and she caught it. I felt myself blush.

"I'm sorry about that. I usually am not the kind of man that steals."

Daphne laughed.

"You have to understand that it happened as it was supposed to happen. It was supposed to be challenging, Dylan, otherwise it is not a quest. It has happened countless times. Zed has sent countless men my way, but I must admit that you are the very first who actually asked my permission to take them. No hard feelings on the shoulder?"

I reached my hand to feel where she had shot me. It was still tender. I didn't really blame her though. I shook my head. She leaned in to hug me close and whispered in my ear.

"If it doesn't work out, you know where I am."

She released from the hug and raised an eyebrow at me as she tucked the underwear away in her pocket. It was a wonder to me that she could at the same time be seductive and fierce. Somehow it worked for her. I admired that.

I moved down to face the last person in the line; the Malmaerra. It was strange to think of him as 'Carl'. He was in the monster form I had first seen with the octopus arm and lobster claw leg. He looked me up and down for a moment or two then he reached up to his neck feeling where his head had been reattached. He squinted distrustfully.

I shrugged. I had decapitated him, true, but I looked at his octopus arm recalling how he tried to strangle me to death with it. Neither of us was innocent.

"Sorry man. I didn't know I wasn't supposed to."

Then he smiled. I would not say it was a pretty smile. It was the kind of smile dentists could put their children through college with, but it was warm. He reached his octopus arm up in a high five. I could not resist returning it, though when our arms parted, it made sucking noises and left marks on my palms.

I looked at my hand, staring in awe at the damage the brief contact had done. Carl shrugged.

"Now get going!"

Zed spoke up.

"If you don't go now, you might miss her!"

"But where will I find her?"

"Gods Dylan, do I have to do everything for you? Pretend you have a burning urge to buy a postcard from the Discovery Centre. I have said too much even with that."

He grinned as I took off in a run.

The bus ride back down to the Discovery Centre was hard. My mind had made me a parent now for so long that I felt guilty. I felt like I was leaving my daughter up at the Skywalk and abandoning her. I felt like a neglectful parent. It took a lot of self-convincing to keep telling myself that Caryn never existed. The empty bus seat beside me did not help. It felt way too quiet. No more constant chatter and questions. I suppose those were never there to start with. I suppose it was the constant chatter of my own mind talking to itself. It seemed surreal to ponder a thought about my mind conversing with itself while my mind conversed with itself.

I should have been excited about Dream. I mean, Zed heavily hinted she would be in the gift shop at the Discovery Centre. However, he told me that I would meet her after I finished his 'tasks'. He told me to go to the Skywalk to meet her. Neither was exactly true. It was not a fabulous track record of truth he had going on there. I had some hope that I would finally meet her there, but I also recognized it may just be one more step on the road to finally meeting her someday in the future. The future was open before me like an alpine meadow. Strangely, I was O.K. with that. If I met her today that would be wonderful. If it was years from now, so be it. I would live my life and enjoy it either way. It was not dependent on meeting Dream, though I was pretty sure she would amplify the happiness I would have. The bus stopped in front of the Discovery Centre.

I walked in, but took my time. It was as Venus said, why rush? Why not enjoy every moment? I made my way to the gift shop without expectation. I had hope, but not expectation.

I heard her before I saw her. I heard her boisterous devil-may-care laughter coming from the gift shop. I looked in the direction of the laughter and saw the back of a woman's head. Black hair, pulled back into a pony tail. She was in front of a rack of greeting cards. They were the kind with racy humour. I knew as I recognized one on the rack I had purchased at one point of my life. It had a squirrel with an acorn on it and inside it said "I know you think I'm crazy, but I feel you're nuts".

She laughed again. I dove behind a rack of hats that looked like animal heads. Why was I hiding? I had come all this way and done all these crazy things just to get to this moment. Perhaps that was the reason. The moment itself seemed so epic and I had nothing to reflect that. I had no great first opening line. I had no gifts to give her. I only had myself. Or did I? The pirate hat. That was what it was for!

I sprinted back out to my car. I didn't want to miss this opportunity with Dream, but I knew the pirate hat had a purpose and I knew this was it. I recalled a dream we had shared within the last few months: it was the one with the Slobber Headed Mud Fish in it. I remembered our conversation at the end.

*"Why do you always get to be captain?"*

*"Because it's my boat, silly!"*

This is why it was important. Some would see it as a symbol that I was saying she was always in charge, like I was giving up my independence to be her second in command. This could not be further from the truth. I enjoyed our dreams where there was a constant back and forth. Sometimes she was in charge. Sometimes I was. Sometimes we were equals. The pirate hat was a symbol of that partnership. It was a symbol that I considered us equals. It was a symbol that I respected her. It was a symbol that I wanted to continue our adventures in the waking world as well.

As I got to the car, I ripped open the duffel bag and took out the pirate hat. I closed the door and sprinted back to the Discovery Centre. I didn't even take time to lock the car. There was no time. I did not want to miss this opportunity. I ran as fast as my body could take me. As I reached the gift shop panting, my heart sank for a moment as she was not in front of the racy greeting cards anymore. I had missed her.

But then I heard her again. It was not her boisterous laugh; just her regular voice at a murmur.

"You are right, these are really good!"

She was speaking to a sales lady at one of the counters and trying out a sample chocolate. My heart was racing in my chest. My very being felt warm all over. This was the moment. This was all that mattered. This was the end and beginning; the change marker that Hershel was talking about. I felt it, that 'closing of a chapter feeling'. I approached the counter slowly with the pirate hat gripped in my hand. As I neared, she turned. I saw in her face first confusion and then recognition. She knew me. She smiled a smile of pure joy. I know my face was the mirror of that. Everything else just faded away. The world didn't matter. It was hard for me to break the gaze from her deep dark eyes and come back to reality, but I did.

I handed her the pirate hat. She laughed her boisterous laugh as she took it. I think she knew what it meant, just as I did. She didn't put it on, but clutched it to her chest like a precious treasure.

There was a sound. It came from my own lips.

"Hi."

CPSIA information can be obtained
at www.ICGtesting.com
Printed in the USA
LVHW031933260419
615746LV00001B/3/P

9 780228 812142